ON THE CHARGE

A Ryan Kaine novel

Ryan Kaine
Book 13

KERRY J DONOVAN

Edited by Nicole O'Brien
This book uses UK English, grammar, and punctuation.

Chapter 1

Thursday 27th May - Gregory Enderby

Sandbrook Tower, Soho, London, England

"Very good, Sir Ernest," Commander Gregory Enderby, director and second-in-command of the UK's National Counter Terrorism Agency fawned. "I'll deal with the matter right away."

Arsehole.

He laughed and tried to make it appear genuine. If Hartington had told him to go boil his head in oil, he'd have reacted in a similar manner. Sucking up to the old man had worked in his favour so far, but he wouldn't have to suck up for much longer. Not if Enderby had his way.

"See that you do," Hartington said, "and while I think

of it, we need to reconsider GG Cleaning Systems' status on the list of strategic contractors. They haven't exactly covered themselves in glory so far."

"Yes, sir. That sounds like a good idea, sir."

"Why I ever allowed you to talk me into hiring those people, I will never know."

"They came highly recommended, sir. And they did manage to secure the services of Will Stacy. One of the best agents MI6 ever employed, according to their personnel records."

"This Stacy fellow's one of the people who vanished into the ether, isn't he?"

"It would appear that way, sir."

"And we're assuming Ryan Kaine is responsible for the vanishing act?"

"Indeed we are, sir."

"Stacy can't have been all that good at his job then, can he?"

"It would appear not, Sir Ernest. Either that, or Ryan Kaine is even more highly skilled than we gave him credit for."

Hartington snorted. "The fact that Kaine has managed to remain free all this time demonstrates his proficiency rather well. Does it not?"

"I can't argue with that, Sir Ernest."

As usual, Hartington rang off without issuing a salutation, the ignorant arsehole. Manners cost nothing but meant everything, as Enderby's father continually reminded him.

Enderby replaced the handset, leaned back in his chair, and stared through the only window in his office.

What a fucking cockup.

Enderby shook his head. He'd set things up perfectly.

Anyone with a modicum of smarts should have been able to act on it and bloody well end the story. By now, Ryan Kaine should have been pushing up the bloody daisies. He should be stiff and cold, lying in an unmarked grave, never to be seen or heard of again. It should have been an inauspicious end to a thorn in the government's side. A thorn in Enderby's side. But GG Cleaning Systems and Will-fucking-Stacy had ballsed it all up.

Bloody moron.

That was the trouble with private contractors. Fucking people talked a good game with their slick promo literature, their slogans, and their "lightning speed of response". As it turned out, they were no more efficient than the in-house operations used to be back in the days before privatisation. The prime difference between the two was the cost. Far from saving money, the private firms proved to be hideously more expensive than their in-house counterparts. Outsourcing was supposed to make things more cost effective, but they simply added another layer of bureaucracy to the process. Another cost to factor in.

Over the years, budget cuts had left the NCTA completely toothless, without the personnel to act independently. Hence the need to draft in the private sector to carry out work they would once have been able to perform themselves for a fraction of the cost.

Useless bloody politicians. More interested in protecting their arses than defending the country from legitimate terrorist threats.

On the other hand, the arrival of the so-called strategic contractors had created opportunities for enterprising entrepreneurs to make a few pounds in backhanders. Enterprising entrepreneurs the likes of Greg Enderby.

Enderby sighed as he stared through the office window at the ugly view—nothing but the red brick wall of the building across the street and a postage-stamp-sized rectangle of sky. Pug ugly. He hated it with a passion he tried never to exhibit. In general, Enderby preferred to provide a show of unruffled calm and competence to the world. The outward face of a man in control of everything within his sphere of influence. So far in his life, the ploy had worked pretty well.

The sun shone brightly, raising a warm glow on the red bricks of the building opposite. Good weather rarely failed to lift his mood. Good news had a similar effect, but he'd had precious little good news recently. He looked forward to hitting the gym that evening. All he needed was to clear the decks.

"And now, to work," he said to the ugly view through the window that never listened, never replied, and never took offence. If only the same could be said of everything in his life.

He locked the office door behind him and hurried towards the lifts and the staircase. No way could his next phone call take place inside Sandbrook Tower, whose telephony had ears. Ears attached to automatic listening bots who never slept, not even when the building was empty and secured for the night.

Big Brother is watching.

Enderby avoided the lifts, even though one stood open and ready to accept him, and pushed his way through the fire doors. He jogged down the fourteen flights and reached the ground floor without breaking into a sweat, which demonstrated the benefits of his lifelong, high-intensity exercise programme. Enderby prided himself on his physical conditioning. Few people outside of the special forces or professional sportsmen could match him for fitness, speed, and strength. He'd proven it often enough when sparring in the gym's ring—sparring with much bigger men and holding his own.

Enderby only used lifts when he absolutely had to— usually when accompanying the lard-arsed, senior civil servants and self-important politicians who required liberal amounts of his schmoozing.

On the ground floor, he tapped his identity card against the reader on the wall. The doors unlocked and he pushed his way through to the impressive foyer. Italian marble floor tiles in grey, and shot through with veins of white and pink, graced the floors and more marble covered the walls, these tiles a few shades lighter. The reception desk—more polished marble—imposing and solid, faced the entrance with its revolving doors, all buffed glass and ornamented with brass furniture. The stainless-steel box bolted to the ceiling stood out as highly incongruous, but it contained the blast screen that would drop down in three tenths of a second when activated by any member of the security team. Despite its incongruity, no one would argue with its neces- sity in such dangerous times. Government buildings were constantly under threat, and Enderby appreciated all the security on offer. If he needed protection, why not let the UK taxpayer foot the bill? He was worth it.

Behind the front desk stood a security guard, a large and powerful-looking man in a modest suit. A man Enderby didn't recognise.

"Who are you?" he asked, keeping it blunt. Enderby didn't like change, especially when it related to his personal safety. Nor did he see the need to talk nicely to the hired hands.

"My name's Robert, Commander Enderby," the man

answered, his voice deep, the accent indeterminable. "Robert Fuller."

"Fuller?"

"Yes, Commander."

"We've never met, have we?"

"No, Commander. Not to my knowledge."

"So, how do you know who I am?"

Fuller pointed to the computer screen on the desk to his side. "Your ID showed up on my screen when you deactivated the lock, Commander." He spoke quietly. A serious man with a serious clean-shaven face, and a serious bulge under his armpit, barely concealed by the jacket of his cheap suit. As a member of the Metropolitan Police's Protection Command, Fuller would be one of the few people in the UK licenced to carry a concealed weapon. Enderby happened to be another—hence the need for a jacket when going outside. If not, he'd have had to leave his shoulder holster and gun in the office, and there wasn't any chance of that ever happening. Not in this lifetime.

"I've also received a thorough departmental briefing, sir," Fuller added.

Enderby nodded. "Understood. When does your shift end?"

"I've just come on duty, sir. I'll stay until everyone's left the building. Between seven and eight o'clock, I'm told."

"And what will you do then?"

"Lock up and head for home, Commander. After running a thorough walk-through of the entire building and setting the alarm."

"And what would happen if I wanted to return after you've left so I can carry on with my work?" Enderby asked as a test. The last thing he wanted was to be exposed by the man's inept training.

"I'm afraid you wouldn't be able to, sir. Once I've gone, this building is sealed by a time lock until oh-six-hundred-hours tomorrow morning when the cleaners arrive."

Enderby arched an eyebrow. "So, the cleaners have greater access to the building than the agency's director?"

The thin flicker of a smile broke into Fuller's stern expression. "So it would appear, Commander."

"Very good, Fuller. Very good," Enderby said. "Where's my shadow?"

Fuller pressed a hidden button on his desk. The door behind him opened and a security officer emerged. Even for such a short trip outside, Enderby couldn't be without his armed company—his shadow. He might not survive the loneliness.

Loneliness, ha!

The very idea had him in stitches.

ENDERBY PACED the pavement outside the tower, keeping to the bright side of the street, allowing the sun to warm his stiff neck and his back. His shadow, Upton, a stone-faced, stocky man who chewed gum constantly, stood twenty paces away, skulking in the shadows. Enderby had considered heading for the local postage stamp of a park but decided against it. The call wouldn't take long. One shouldn't drag out a termination conversation, even if it meant little.

His reflection in the coffee shop window across the street showed a trim, straight-backed man in a nicely cut suit, smiling in anticipation.

Behave yourself, Greg. This is business, not pleasure.

He stopped pacing, stepped closer to the polished marble walls of Sandbrook Tower, but made sure to keep the sun on his back. Sitting at his desk most of the day had played havoc with the muscles in his neck and shoulders. And as for the stiffness in his lower back ... he couldn't wait to hit the heavy bag that night and blow away the cobwebs. Building up a sweat would do wonders for his mood.

He withdrew the ancillary phone from his jacket pocket, a phone that happened to be the same make and model as his official mobile. Although it looked identical, it had been registered to a friend of a friend, and could not be traced back to him. It acted as a burner phone without looking like one. He entered the passcode and dialled the number of the company slated for removal from the agency's list of certified contractors. He didn't have to wait long for Guy Gordon to accept the call.

"GG Cleaning Systems."

"Gordon?"

"Yes, Commander. It's me."

With those four simple words, Enderby had his answer. Gordon had never sounded so glum. Defeated. As he anticipated, they both had bad news to relay.

Enderby took the lead. "I gave you until three o'clock to report and it's now three twenty. What do you have for me, Gordon?"

"I'm afraid it's bad news, Commander."

Quelle surprise.

"Still no sign of the cripple, I take it?"

"None. I sent Paul McKenna and Jess Barker to Wales yesterday, but they haven't been able to find Bairstow. Not yet."

"And there's still been no contact from Stacy or Reilly?"

"Again, I'm afraid not. It's not like Stacy to break protocol in this manner."

"Which means?"

"I have no idea—"

"Come now, Gordon. We both know it means that the er ... *target* has liquidated your overrated and overpriced assets."

Enderby lowered his voice and hunched closer to the marble to avoid being jostled by the ignorant pedestrians who insisted on going through rather than around an obstacle. Ignorant pricks who paid more attention to their phone screens than to their direction of travel.

Arseholes.

"We can't be certain of that, Commander. Can you give me a little more time? Perhaps another two or three—"

"Not a chance. You've let me down, Gordon. Badly. I really can't tell you how disappointed that makes me feel. I trusted you. Stuck my neck out when I recommended your company to Sir Ernest for approved contractor status."

Enderby straightened, stepped away from the wall, and received a thump in the back for his pains. The blow shunted him forwards, jarring his elbow against the marble. He pushed himself away with his hand and spun towards the street.

"Watch where you're going, moron!" he bellowed, checking the elbow of his rather expensive jacket for damage. Finding none, he dusted it off and smoothed out the creases.

He looked up to find himself face to face with an extremely large individual—an individual with ebony skin and a deep scowl. A curtain of three-foot-long dreadlocks threaded with multi-coloured beads hung from his head. The man's heavy arms and shoulders bulged through a weightlifter's skin-tight, purple vest. Huge thighs and thick legs poked out below equally skin-tight, purple cycling shorts. Colour-matched boxing boots completed the unsubtle ensemble. A heavy gold chain hanging around the man's thick neck glittered in the sunlight. Less than two metres separated him from Enderby.

"What?" Gordon asked down the phone.

"Nothing. A bloody idiot just barged into me without apologising. Hang on a moment, would you. The idiot's looking rather darkly at me."

Naughty, Gregory. Very naughty. Some might call you a racist.

Beaded Dreads' scowl deepened at the "rather darkly" jibe and he took a step closer.

Enderby raised his hand towards his shadow, indicating he should stand down.

I've got this, Upton.

"What you say, bro?" Beaded Dreads asked, his deep voice booming above the traffic noise.

Some passers-by gave them a wide berth and increased their pace. Others slowed to watch the unfolding spectacle of a slim, white man in an expensive suit mixing it with a heavily muscled Rasta dressed like a circus clown. What could be more enjoyable on a sunny spring afternoon in the nation's capital?

Enderby pulled the mobile away from his ear, hit mute, and dropped it into his pocket. He smiled at the black man and raised his hands, palms open, facing forwards.

"Didn't you hear me clearly?" Enderby asked, still smiling, still staring the man in the eye.

"I heard you, bro," Beaded Dreads said. He bunched and popped his huge biceps and bounced his pecs. If he'd had a hip hop beat to ripple the muscles to, it would have been even more hysterical.

Anyone else would have been impressed, or terrified. Enderby simply wanted to laugh at the performance, and maybe offer a sarcastic round of applause.

"Good, good," Enderby said. "I shall repeat it to make sure you heard. I'll also speak a little more slowly for the hard of understanding. What I said was 'Watch where you're going, moron.'" Again, Enderby smiled.

"Who you callin' a moron, bro?"

Beaded Dreads twisted at the waist and flicked a hand away from his side. A fractionally smaller man appeared from behind him, shorter, but just as heavily built. Apart from the height, the only other differences between the two were the colour of his workout gear—lime green rather than purple—and the troy ounce weight of his slightly less impressive gold chain.

Enderby dropped his smile.

Beaded Dreads sucked air through his teeth. "Y'aren't smiling now. Are you, boy?" he said.

"No," Enderby answered, cool and calm, speaking only loud enough for the two colourfully dressed men to hear. "I'm thinking."

"You thinking?"

"Yep. I'm actually trying to decide how much damage I'll be able to inflict on you two clowns before my security officer arrives and pulls me off you."

Beaded Dreads peeled back his upper lip into a snarl, exposed a gold left canine, and turned to his slightly shorter companion. "Y'hear that, Spike? He gonna damage us, bro!"

"I hear him, bro. He a funny little white man, innit."

Spike differed in a third way. His voice, way too high-pitched for a man of his bulk, could have enabled him to sing falsetto.

In unison, they pushed towards Enderby, corralling him closer to the marble wall, fists clenched. Sovereign rings and other gold trinkets caught the bright sunlight.

What is it with young black men and their ostentatious displays of gold? So tacky.

Slowly, Enderby lifted his arm, index finger extended, pointing towards the sky.

"Gentlemen," he said, still not raising his voice. "Before we start to *rumble*, let me draw your attention to the surveillance camera looking down on us."

As one, Beaded Dreads and Spike glanced up. Curiosity gave them no alternative. While the men looked up in search of the non-existent camera, Enderby opened his jacket, drew his Beretta M9 from its pancake holster, and held it close to his chest, muzzle pointing upwards. That way, only Beaded Dreads and Spike would be able to see it.

"Excuse me, gentlemen," he said, speaking loud enough to attract their attention. "You can look at me now."

Beaded Dreads and Spike, paled, lowered their heads, and their walnut-sized brains found something new to focus on. Enderby would have loved to film their bug-eyed, slack-jawed, hands-raised-in-the-air reaction, but in the absence of actual obvious surveillance cameras, he'd have to rely on memory.

"Lower your hands, fools. This isn't a Hollywood *gangsta* movie."

They exchanged a fleeting glance and complied.

"Excellent, well done," Enderby said, smiling again. "Now that I have your undivided attention, let me make something crystal clear. Had I been of a mind to inflict serious damage, I would have driven a stiff-fingered jab to each of your exposed throats when you were looking up just then. However, the difference in force required to incapacitate two heavily built men such as yourselves rather than inflict terminal damage is rather difficult to determine. To be quite frank, I haven't practised that particular drill for ages. Do you feel me, *brothers*?" He paused but neither man responded. "I said, '*Do you feel me, brothers?*'"

Enderby patted the Beretta against his chest. It elicited a response. Both men nodded.

"Okay, Spike. You can piss off. And don't even think of calling the *po-po*. I have a permit for this Beretta, and I *am* the police. Get me?"

Spike nodded.

"Right then," Enderby said. "Go on, off you toddle." He waggled his fingers at Spike.

Both men made to turn and run.

"Not you, big man. I haven't finished with you yet."

Spike raced away without a backwards glance at his mate. Enderby waited until the man in the lime green clothing had ducked around the nearest corner before turning his full attention to Beaded Dreads.

"What's your name, *bro*," Enderby asked, hiding the M9 beneath the side panel of his Brioni jacket.

All but one onlooker had dispersed, but one remaining seemed to be taking an inordinate interest in Enderby and his new friend. Middle-aged and slim, with shaggy, fair hair, he wore a slightly crumpled, grey jacket and black chinos, and held a phone up in his outstretched arm, the camera lens pointing straight at Enderby and the man in the tight, purple clothing.

"Merlin," Beaded Dreads answered, his voice subdued, high pitched, less brooding.

"Marlon?"

"No, Merlin."

"Merlin what?"

"Merlin Handy," he answered, lowering his eyes.

"Are you playing with me, Merlin?"

Merlin dragged his eyes up from his feet to look at

Enderby. He shook his head. The beads clattered around his ears. It had to be so irritating. The clacking would have annoyed the crap out of Enderby if he'd had to suffer it all day long.

"Do you have any ID on you, Merlin Handy?"

Merlin folded his lips into a thin line. He lowered his gaze to take in the gun arm part-hidden by Enderby's expensive jacket.

"Driving licence. In my wallet."

"Where would you hide a wallet in those clothes?"

For the first time, Enderby noticed the black strap around the muscleman's slim waist. A strap that would likely hold a belt bag.

"Take out your wallet and show me your licence. And if you pull anything out of that belt bag that isn't a wallet, say goodbye to your testicles, big man."

Enderby withdrew the gun hand from its hiding place and pointed the Beretta at Merlin's groin. Involuntarily, Merlin pulled his legs together and bent at the waist. Although, what protection closing his legs would offer against the impact of a 9mm bullet was anybody's guess.

Merlin tugged at the belt and dragged a black, leather belt bag around from behind his back. Slowly, fingers trembling, he opened the zip and dug inside.

In one smooth operation, Enderby racked the Beretta's slide and carefully rode it back into position.

"Easy now, Merlin. Take it nice and slow."

"Don't shoot, man."

"I won't have to shoot if you do as you're told. The licence, show it."

The big man in the tight, purple clothing removed a leather wallet from the belt bag, fumbled with the popper, and opened the flap. The licence, held in place behind a clear, plastic sleeve, confirmed the man's name."

"Okay, Merlin Handy. I think you've learned your lesson in manners."

"Huh?" Confusion spread over Merlin's face.

"It's simple enough, *bro*. The next time you jostle someone in the street and cause them discomfort, apologise. It might just save you from pissing your pants. Now bugger off before I lose my temper."

Merlin stuffed his wallet into his belt bag and tried to pull the zip closed but it caught halfway along the leather.

"Oh, and before you go," Enderby said.

Merlin stopped trying to release the zip and looked up.

"Remember this. Now that I know your name, I can find out where you live. One day, when I'm bored, I might come pay you a visit and give you another lesson in etiquette. Think about that for the next few weeks. Go on now, Merlin. Off you trot, *bro*."

Merlin Handy spun and raced off as though the Hounds of Hell were hungry and he smelled like dinner. Enderby chuckled to himself as Merlin retraced Spike's trail and disappeared around the same corner. He half-turned towards the black marble wall and decocked the Beretta. He returned the gun to its holster and smoothed out the line of his jacket. A quick review of his reflection in the shiny marble showed him a return to its streamlined perfection. This time, he judged his smile as justified.

"Oh dear, such japes," he said, turning to face the long-haired man in the grey jacket and the chinos. "What are you looking at?"

"Nothing, mate. I thought you were in trouble, there. I was thinking about calling the police."

Enderby allowed his smile to drop. "No need for that, my friend. Things are fine."

"What did you say to him?"

"Just shooting the breeze," Enderby answered, grinning.

Shooting the breeze? Oh dear. Stop it, Greg. That really is too much.

"Thanks for your interest," Enderby said, "but don't you have somewhere else to be?"

"Oh yeah. Right."

The man shrugged and wandered off, eyes locked on his phone, no doubt reviewing his footage of the incident and wondering whether he'd captured enough to upload it to his social media platform of choice. Not a problem. Enderby could survive any flak he faced from drawing his firearm. If questioned about it, he could easily claim to have been frightened for his life. After all, Merlin Handy and Spike looked the sort to be walking around the streets with bladed articles—a crime that carried a maximum sentence of six months' jail time. For the briefest of moments, Enderby considered the proactive approach. Maybe he should call the police himself and make the accusation? In the end he decided against it. He'd already had more than enough fun at Merlin Handy's expense. Besides, he had other fish to fry.

He glanced towards Upton, the shadow who stood primed and ready. Enderby nodded to him. Upton nodded back and resumed his watch, head rotating slowly, eyes alive for the next point of danger.

Ah, the life of the bodyguard, whose job required him to throw himself in front of a bullet to protect his client.

Another idiot.

Now, what was he doing before being so rudely interrupted?

Ah, yes. Talking about frying fish.

He reached into his pocket for the mobile and checked the status, surprised to find the line still open and active. He released the mute button.

"Hello, Guy? Are you still there?" he asked, still smiling from the buzz of terrorising a pair of hapless musclemen.

"Yes, I'm still here. What happened?"

"Nothing much. So," he said, emphasising the word, "what were we saying?"

"We were discussing the situation *vis-à-vis* my company's relationship with your agency."

"Ah, yes. As to that, I have some rather bad news, I'm afraid."

Enderby stopped talking and left the nugget dangling. He gazed around him. Fewer people lined the pavement, and space spread out wide. Even the traffic noise had quietened to a distant rumble in the slight calm before the rush-hour storm.

Gordon broke the stalemate.

"Well, Greg. What is it?"

"Sir Ernest has instructed me to remove GG Cleaning Systems from the list of strategic contractors ... with immediate effect."

"Fuck."

"Exactly."

"Can you do anything to change his mind?"

"I'll hold off for now and try to bring him back onside, but ... that's going to take some doing." Enderby crowded closer to the dark marble wall. He hunched his shoulders and lowered his voice. "But you might be able to help your cause, if you have a mind to."

"What? What do you mean by that?"

"Think about it in your own time, Guy. We'll discuss it

face to face. Maybe next week. I have other things on my plate right now."

Enderby ended the call in the middle of Gordon's last strident question and allowed him to stew on it. The wait would crank up the pressure. Make him more malleable. More amenable.

He gathered Upton to his side and returned to his office. Work waited for no one.

Chapter 2

Sandbrook Tower, Soho, London, England

Claire Harper sat in the café across the street from Sand-brook Tower, sipping her iced tea. An empty plate sat along-side her saucer. She often took her lunchbreak outside of the office. It gave her room to breathe, time to herself. Today, she'd missed lunch working on last-minute changes to the end-of-month report ahead of delivering it to Worm. He'd demanded the file two days early, for no other reason than to put her under increased pressure.

Evil slimy creature.

She always thought of Commander Enderby as a worm, and had renamed him accordingly, in her head.

Still, she'd met his ridiculous schedule and earned

herself a welcome mid-afternoon break in the sun as a result. Only, she wasn't sitting in the sun, which was a bit of a pain.

Usually, on a warm day, she'd sit outside, but today, all the pavement tables and chairs had been occupied by a group of Chinese tourists. Instead, she sat inside, staring through the sparkling-clean café windows, watching the passers-by wend their way to who knew where.

Claire enjoyed people-watching. It helped pass the time and enabled her to subdue her troubled thoughts.

In the middle distance, a young couple climbed out of the underground station, raising their hands to their eyes to shade them from the blinding sun. Wearing shorts, T-shirts, and hiking boots, they carried their belongings in backpacks so heavy they had to lean forwards under the load.

Closer to her, an overweight man in a business suit carried an attaché case in one hand and a mobile in the other. He spoke loud enough to be heard through the glass as he passed the café's window, complaining to someone on the other end of the phone about how long it had taken a "bally useless" waiter to serve him lunch, which had made him late for his afternoon meeting.

Claire smiled and sipped her drink. The middle-aged woman in the next chair turned the page on her newspaper, tutted, and shook her head at a headline.

Outside, moving left to right, a crocodile of kids in bright red school blazers each carrying rolled-up towels followed a pair of harried-looking adults, no doubt heading to the local swimming pool. An equally harassed-looking man in a light grey tracksuit brought up the rear, shepherding the tardy kids with open arms, and cajoling them with a sharp tongue.

Hand-in-hand, a family of parents with two young children—one of each—slalomed their way through a gaggle of selfie-stick-wielding tourists who'd stopped in the middle of the pavement. They stood still, pointing their cameras up at something Claire couldn't see.

In the far distance, two huge and brightly dressed black men—one decked out in purple, the other in a garish shade of green—swaggered towards the tower. Clearly, neither felt the need to keep a low profile. They chatted, arms swinging, heads rolling, beaded dreadlocks fluttering in the breeze.

Claire finished the last of her lemon tea, lowered the glass cup to its saucer, and sighed.

Back to the grind.

She scooped her bag from the table in preparation to stand when something caught her eye and she stopped. Diagonally opposite the café, a glass panel in Sandbrook Tower's revolving door flashed in the sun. It rotated and belched a creature out onto the pavement. An evil creature who wore an expensive business suit and a pair of Italian loafers—Commander Gregory Enderby.

Worm.

She recognised the suited black man behind him as one of the personal protection officers who took turns guarding the Top Team. Although how Enderby rated a position on the Top Team and the subsequent bodyguard was beyond her.

The evil man stopped in the sunshine, pulled a mobile phone from his jacket pocket, dialled, and pressed it to his ear.

Claire returned her handbag to the tabletop, leaned forwards in her chair, and waited. She wasn't about to head out and risk bumping into the hideous slime bag. She'd wait for him to pass by.

Only he didn't pass by. No. He stopped walking and

stood close to the tower's marble wall. Frowning, his head on a swivel, Enderby kept talking into the mobile, looking ... what? Furtive?

If not for the fact that the odious man had his back to her, Claire would have been able to lipread his half of the conversation. He was certainly close enough for her to see his mouth moving.

The tall, attractive, long-haired waiter—Marco— appeared at her side, hovering over her.

"You finished, love?"

"Another lemon tea, please," she ordered without peeling her eyes away from the view outside.

"Be right with you, love," Marco said and left with her used cup, saucer, and plate.

Across the street, Enderby jerked away from the wall and stepped directly into the path of the huge man dressed in purple. They collided. Forewarned, the black man threw out his arms, smashed Enderby into the wall, and kept on walking. The man in the lime green leotard sidestepped the clash and carried on in the first man's wake.

Claire grinned.

Nice one, big guy.

Enderby pushed himself off the wall, spun around and screamed something that ended with, "—you're going, moron!" She missed the first part due to the turn.

The black men stopped and spun around, one behind the other. The larger of the two, the one in purple, took a step towards Enderby and said something Claire couldn't make out due to the swinging dreadlocks.

Excellent. This'll be good.

Claire nearly bounced up and down in her chair at the prospect of watching Worm on the receiving end of a first-class thumping. God, how he deserved it. Not that the body-guard would stand back and let it happen. Pity though.

Hello? What's this?

Rather than back away from the confrontation in abject terror, Worm smiled and lifted the mobile phone to his ear. He mumbled something Claire couldn't quite catch, slid the phone into his jacket pocket, and raised his hands in apparent surrender. Smiling, he spoke to the first man, goading him, spoiling for a fight. The one in the lime green workout gear stepped around his friend and they both edged forwards.

"Bloody hell," Claire said aloud.

The woman at her side lowered her paper and frowned at her.

"Sorry," Claire said, "but I know that man."

"Which man?" she asked, her accent American and strong.

Claire pointed towards the confrontation across the street. "The one in the suit who's antagonising the men with the muscles."

"Why's he doing that?"

"No idea. Perhaps it's because he's an arrogant twit, full of his own self-importance."

"Should we call the police? Your friend might be in trouble."

"Don't bother, and he's no friend of mine. He's my boss, and he's a sexual predator."

"He is?"

"Yes. He is. I call him Worm." Claire nodded. "And he has backup. See the man in the dark suit standing in the shadow close to the revolving door?" She pointed to Ender-by's left.

"Yes."

"He's Worm's bodyguard."

"Why is he standing off?" the woman asked. "Shouldn't he be rushing to help?"

"Worm has warned him off. The idiot must think he can handle the situation."

The American scrunched her chair closer to Claire, improving her view.

"Oh dear, oh dear," Claire said, smiling.

"What's that?"

"He's just called the one in the purple vest a moron. Honestly, the man's a total arsehole. Deserves anything he gets."

"Hmm. And a sexual predator, you say?"

"Yes."

"You know this first hand?"

Claire nodded.

"Have you spoken to anyone about him? Complained to your HR people?"

"Not yet. I don't have any proof," Claire said.

Not yet, I don't.

"Your word against his, huh?" the woman asked.

Again, Claire nodded.

"That's the way those sons of bitches operate."

Agreed.

Claire kept studying the scene across the road, trying to read the men's lips. The distance didn't make it easy.

"In that case, I hope they beat the guy to a pulp," the woman said.

"Me too, sister."

The woman folded the paper neatly and placed it on the table in front of her.

"He's still goading them. Calling them 'clowns' and saying how much damage he plans to inflict on them."

"You can lipread?"

Again, Claire nodded. "A little." She narrowed her eyes to follow the words and the body language.

Enderby said something about cameras and pointed to the roofline. The black men followed his lead and looked up. The next part happened so fast that Claire struggled to catch it. Enderby's arm moved. He pulled out something black from under his armpit, hid it behind the flap of his jacket, and started talking. His words didn't make much sense, something about a blow to the throats. The black men raised their arms and lowered them again on Enderby's command.

A few moments later, the man in green—Spit, Spike, or Spin—raced away, leaving his mate alone to face his tormentor.

"Did you see that?" the woman at Claire's side asked. "Your guy, Worm, has a gun. I thought you Brits weren't allowed to carry firearms. I'm definitely calling the police." She reached down by her side and collected a handbag from the floor.

"I told you. He's not 'my guy', and he has a permit for the weapon. The creep's a member of the security services."

"The hell you say? Even so, I don't think he should be allowed to wave it around in public like that. I mean, he's pointing it at the other man's privates. My name's Belinda, by the way."

"Hi, Belinda. I'm Claire."

"Pleased to meet you, Claire."

"And you're right, he isn't allowed to point it at anything. Shouldn't really be taking it out of its holster unless he's in grave personal danger, which is what it'll look like to the police."

"In that case, I'm gonna leave well alone."

Belinda placed her handbag, unopened, on the table next to Claire's.

"Tell you what though," Belinda said, leaning a little closer, and lowering her voice conspiratorially, "this is exciting. Like watching a cop show on the TV."

"Only the wrong man has the upper hand. By the way, the black man's name is either Marlon or Merlin. The way Worm's scoffing, I'm plumping for Merlin."

Belinda edged closer to the table, momentarily drawing Claire's attention. The American pushed her glasses further up her nose and narrowed her eyes. Claire returned her focus to the scene across the street.

"Merlin's taking something from his fanny pack," Belinda said.

"Worm wants to see his driving licence."

"Ah, I see."

A few moments later, Merlin raced off in the same direction as Spit, Spike, or Spin. Worm, chuckling to himself, re-holstered his gun and spoke to a scruffy-looking man who had been filming the action on his mobile. Worm shooed the man away and pulled out his phone again.

"Ah well," Belinda said, reaching for her handbag again. "Fun's over, and I really must be going. Can't wait to tell the girls in my book club back home all about this." She stood and held out her hand. "Great meeting you, Claire. You take care of yourself, now. And watch your back, y'hear? That man's clearly bad news. If you ask me, he's one Grade A psycho."

"I couldn't agree more, sister."

They shook hands and Claire waited for her to leave. She stood, preparing to do the same, when Marco returned with her second lemon tea.

"You don't want this now?" he asked, frowning. "I can put it in a takeaway cup if you like."

"No, no. that's okay. I'll drink it here, thanks."

She sat back down and glanced across the street. Enderby was still engrossed in his phone conversation. Claire sat up straighter and stared through the window, concentrating hard.

She could only understand fleeting parts of Enderby's side of the conversation, but the fragments were intriguing.

"Sir Ernest ... remove GG Cleaning Systems ... strategic contractors ..."

He repeated the names "Guy" and "Gordon" more than once and arranged to contact him again "next week". Shortly afterwards, the creep ended the call and ducked back into Sandbrook Tower, taking his bodyguard with him.

"Well now," she mumbled, "that *was* interesting."

Claire raised the glass cup to her lips and sipped the fragrant infusion. The fragmented conversation rolled around in her head. She ran through questions and searched for the answers.

Why did Worm step outside to make the work-related call when he had a private office? To stretch his legs and take in the sun? Hardly. The answer couldn't have been any more obvious. Worm didn't want to fall foul of the tower's surveillance systems.

Why? Because he was doing something underhand. Something he didn't want anyone knowing about.

Clearly, Sir Ernest Hartington was threatening to remove GG Cleaning Systems from the list of government contractors, which would hurt them financially.

Claire knew who GG Cleaning Systems were. The private contractor had been tasked with following Abdul Hosseini, one of the many asylum seekers on the agency's books. They'd followed the poor man for a total of ten days and had charged the agency an extortionate fee for doing so. Tens of thousands of pounds to tail one clearly innocent man. An absolute fortune.

What would GG Cleaning Systems do to protect their lucrative strategic contractor status? More to the point, why was Worm discussing it in secret with the company's owner, Guy Gordon?

That line of thought threw up another question. What would Worm have to say in the face-to-face with Guy Gordon? How she would love to be a fly on the wall during that particular conversation.

If only.

She felt herself frowning, creating wrinkles.

Stop it, Claire.

Why was she expending so much emotional energy on a creep like Worm? If she had any sense, she'd apply for a transfer and try to put the whole sorry mess behind her. But she didn't have it in her to run away. Claire Harper wasn't one to turn tail and flee from anything. If Worm had preyed on Claire, he'd done the same to others before her, and Claire wasn't about to let it happen again.

Claire had vowed to get even. If it took her years, she'd make Worm pay.

Years.

She sighed, drained the last of her cooling tea, and paid her bill, leaving a decent tip for the attractive and efficient Marco, who smiled his gratitude. Marco had a lovely, warm smile.

Outside in the equally warm sun, Claire looked both ways before crossing the busy road. The traffic crawled along, giving her plenty of time to dodge between the vehicles.

In the distance, to her left, a slim, middle-aged man caught her eye. Long haired and slightly dishevelled, he melted into the deep shadow so well, she almost missed him. Interesting. Why would the man taking photos of Worm and the two brightly dressed men hang around for so long after the main event? She shook her head at yet another question she couldn't answer.

Claire hurried towards Sandbrook Tower.

One day, Worm would pay for the way he'd treated her. One day she would ruin *his* life.

Chapter 3

Tuesday 1st June - Bridget Fraser

**Belham Castle, Tumblethorpe Lake,
Northumberland, England**

Bridget "Bridey" Fraser, always the first to arrive in the
morning, parked her little, rattle-trap Mini in her favourite
spot—around the back of the castle, beside the rear door.
The tradesman's entrance. Her position in life. A position
she accepted as her lot.

Bridey glanced around her. Something struck her as
strange, but darned if she could tell what it was. Her brain
didn't function that well so early in the morning. She
frowned, trying to concentrate.

The castle seemed darker than usual. No lights shone

through any of the rear-facing windows. That was it. It was too dark.

Cold seeped into her bones. Again, she shivered.

"In you go, Bridey," she muttered. "Can't keep 'the great man' waiting." She waggled her head while saying it.

The arrogant bastard, Sir Malcolm Somebody-or-other —he with the roving eyes, the wandering hands, the foul mouth, and the fouler breath—would expect her to set his fire and have it roaring by the time he deigned to rise from his four-poster bed. The fat bag of slime stood out as by far the worst guest she'd ever had the misfortune to serve.

Bridey had made up her mind. If the man shouted at her one more time, she'd scream back at the top of her voice. Might even take a swing at the miserable ingrate, bodyguards or not. They wouldn't stop her. Oh no. They'd probably cheer her on—but they'd do it quietly. The guards knew what side their bread was buttered. No doubt about that.

Some of the guards, no, *most* of the guards, hated Sir Malcolm as much as she did, not that they would ever say so out loud. But she'd overheard some of them muttering to each other when they thought no one could overhear. Bradley Colman, the gentlest and most softly spoken of the lot, had been the most vocal in his hatred of the mean-spirited creature. Bradley once told her that he'd been close to punching the man in the nose during one of his malicious outbursts—a rant that had caused one of the young housekeepers to burst into tears and run from his presence. But he'd done nothing that would risk his fee.

All the bodyguards were in it for the money, the lot of them, even Bradley. Still, truth be told, so was Bridey.

In that part of Northumberland, well-paid jobs were hard to find, and paying the bills was the only thing that would force Bridey from her nice, warm bed at five o'clock on such a damp and chilly morning. She'd considered swapping shifts with Sheilagh, who had two young kids and could do with the extra cash, but Sheilagh was slim and attractive, and an obvious target for the evil slug. Bridey would never let him near the likes of Sheilagh so early in the morning and alone. Not without a bodyguard of her own.

Slim and attractive?

Not something anyone could accuse Bridey Fraser of being. Not these days. In fact, her ballooning waistline, massive hips, and matronly boobs acted as a deterrent for Sir Malcolm's advances, making Bridey the obvious candidate for the role of early-morning fire starter and housekeeper.

Bridey sighed as the Mini's dashboard clock ticked over to three minutes to six o'clock.

Okay, wee girl. Pull your finger out of your big backside. Less of the dithering.

She unlatched the door of her ancient, rust-bucket Mini, leaned her shoulder against the panel, and pushed. The door popped away from its frame and creaked open.

The heap of rust should have seen the inside of a scrap-yard crusher a decade ago, but Jim, Bridey's penny-pinching hubby, kept breathing new life into the old crock. Over the years, he'd spent more keeping the thing on the road than it was worth. They could have had a new car for the cost of the rust-bucket's upkeep.

Every time the knackered, old thing miraculously passed its annual inspection, Jim would say, "We'll get another year out of the old girl." Okay for Jim. He didn't have to drive the rattling pile of nuts and bolts. The bloody heater hadn't worked since the turn of the millennium, and the brakes had grown more and more spongey over the past few weeks.

How could it possibly have passed so recently? Sometimes, she wondered whether Jim kept bunging the mechanic a few quid to turn a blind eye to the Mini's failings. She wouldn't have put it past him.

If only.

Bridey climbed out of the car, slammed the door closed, and left it unlocked. No chance of anyone nicking the bloody thing, more's the pity.

Bridey trudged up the three worn stone steps to the rear entrance and punched the passcode of the week into the keypad. The lock turned and the heavy back door swung inwards, allowing her access to the large and empty scullery. She shivered. Bloody place always felt like the inside of a fridge—or a tomb. But it seemed even worse that morning.

She touched the back of her hand to the cast-iron radiator on the outer wall. Stone cold.

Typical.

The central heating had powered down overnight. Maybe the generator had packed it in again. Run out of fuel most likely. Well, tough. After an accident with the fire in his room, when an ember had fallen out and scorched the hearthrug, Sir Malcolm had screamed like a banshee. Accused the staff of trying to burn him alive. As a result, he'd insisted the hotel be emptied of staff overnight— emptied of all apart from him and his bodyguards. As a result, no one in the castle overnight knew how to fire up the boiler when it tripped out and now the huge, old mausoleum would stay cold for hours.

Sod them. Sod him. Serves him right.

It wasn't Bridey's job to restart the boiler even though she knew how to do it. What's more, she didn't need it. Heavy work would keep her warm enough. The nasty man could freeze to death as far as she was concerned. Apart from the castle being cold, the only real downside would be the beggar's foul mood, which would be off-the-scale horrible when he finally decided to climb out of his four-poster.

Bridey had half a mind to turn on her heel and skedaddle back to her nice, warm home and cuddle up to Jim, who'd still be in bed. She could always phone in and tell the day manager that her car had refused to start —again.

Not a chance. Bridey didn't work that way. She'd honour her commitment to the boss. She'd do what they paid her to do.

Rather than freeze, she left her overcoat on and entered the kitchen proper, where she expected to find at least some of the security guards kicking back and slurping their way through mug after mug of coffee. But no, the kitchen turned out to be as deserted as the scullery. Dark, too. The windows, being too small for the size of the room and facing north, never let enough natural light into the place. Typical of the Victorian architects. They didn't give a hoot about working conditions or about cooks having to scrabble around in the dark all day and night.

She threw a switch. After a slight delay, the LED strip lights powered on in all their brilliant, white glory. At least the castle still had power. It saved someone a trip to the shed. Wouldn't be her though. She drew the line at traipsing all the way over to the outbuildings and playing with the generator. Not her job. No, sir.

At least the kitchen was warm, heated twenty-four-seven by the oil-fired range. Another reason she expected to see some of the security guards in place, the ones who'd be half-frozen after patrolling the grounds and the castle throughout the cold, northern night.

With the power on, at least she'd have use of the service lift, and she wouldn't have to lug half a tonne of cleaning equipment up six flights of stairs. Real log fires looked beautiful enough, romantic even, but no one took feeding them or cleaning up after them into consideration. Bloody nightmare they were. Hopefully, Parker had instructed one of the lads to fill the wood hopper in the Presidential Suite. If not, Bridey would have to ferry the logs into the suite from the top-floor storage room.

Another total nightmare that stressed her aching back.

Bridey hurried through the kitchen and out into the rear corridor. She snaffled a cleaner's trolley from the storeroom and trundled it towards the service lift.

The place seemed deserted. She usually bumped into someone of a morning.

Where is everybody?

What was the point of hiring a dozen security guards if anyone could wander along the halls uninterrupted? Someone wasn't doing their job properly.

She entered the lift, slipped her pass card into the slot, waited for the red light to turn green, and hit the button for the top floor. The cage doors slid horizontally closed, bumped together, and the lift started its rattling ascent. The doors opened again on the third floor, and Bridey reversed out with the trolley. She placed a fire extinguisher in the middle of the opening to stop anyone calling the lift and making her wait ages to descend. Once she'd finished prepping and cleaning the Presidential Suite she wouldn't want to hang around on the top floor in case the old bastard tried it on with her. No telling what the old pervert was into. He might fancy the occasional romp with a well-rounded, older woman.

Bridey shuddered at the thought and pushed the trolley

along the corridor, forcing it through the deep-pile carpet all the way to the double doors at the far end. Once again, the lack of a "Do not disturb" sign hanging from the door led to disappointment. Forever, she lived in hope.

She knocked, opened the door a crack, and announced in a firm voice, "Housekeeping!"

Ready or not, here I come.

She pushed the door all the way open and rolled the trolley into the drawing room and her heart sank. The place looked as though it had hosted an all-night rave. Empty whisky bottles, dirty glasses, their sticky rings fouling the side tables, cushions thrown to the carpet. The library shelves emptied, with leather-bound books strewn all over the place. She nearly burst into tears. The clean-up would take her hours.

And the smell. What on earth? Like someone had defecated on the floor. Where did it come from? She sniffed. Following her nose led her to the left, the suite's bedroom. The door stood half open. It didn't feel right. Sir Malcolm never slept with the door open. The closed door probably added an extra element of security.

God. The smell.

Bridey edged closer to the bedroom.

"Sir Malcolm?" she called. "It's the housekeeper. Is everything okay ... sir?"

No response.

No angry retort. No swearing. No snoring. Nothing.

Three more paces brought her to the open doorway where the stench was even more overpowering. The stench of death. She recognised it from when she discovered her neighbour's body after old Mavis Scarborough had lain dead in her front room for over a week.

Bridey's heart skipped along at race speed.

She pushed the bedroom door fully open and stepped inside.

The lights were on. No one she knew ever slept with their lights on, but Sir Malcolm wasn't asleep. Oh, dear Lord no.

The old man lay on the four-poster, his arms and legs spread wide, wrists and ankles tied to each of the posts with purple ropes. Totally naked, the grey-skinned monster didn't have a stitch on. A small pillow covered his privates, thankfully, and a ball gag—the plastic ball bright red—peeled back his blue lips and partially hid his face. Filmy eyes stared up at the drooping canopy.

Bridey made the sign of the cross and tried to decide how the ghastly display made her feel. Not shocked, not horrified, not disgusted, but … relieved. Delighted. How wrong was that? She crossed herself again.

Dear Lord, forgive me.

Surprised at how calm she felt, no screaming in terror, no tears, Bridey backed out of the bedroom and rushed to the telephone on the desk in the reception room. She picked up the handset and dialled 9-9-9.

Chapter 4

Sandbrook Tower, Soho, London, England

Enderby seethed. He'd been chained to his desk all day, awaiting the long-overdue call.

What the hell was taking so long?

Enderby had been fighting fires for days. He'd had to deal with the fallout from the fiasco in Wales where GG Cleaning Systems had lost two contractors—one of them the valuable asset, Will Stacy—and with them, the chance of taking down Ryan Kaine. That was bad enough, but Enderby had been forced to save face with Jay Wyndham by shifting the blame square onto Guy Gordon's shoulders. After all, GG Cleaning Systems' screwup had nothing to do with Greg Enderby. No. Nothing at all.

As a result of the balls-up, Enderby had come very close to fast-tracking Sir Ernest's instruction to terminate GG Cleaning Systems' status as an authorised government contractor, and he would have done so if Gordon hadn't agreed to increase Enderby's "commission" from fifteen to twenty percent of the contract fee. A lucrative side-line that Enderby didn't want to relinquish.

Furthermore, he'd been able to draw Jay's attention away from the disaster of Wales, and towards the destruction of Ryan Kaine's support infrastructure, which would leave the fugitive vulnerable and alone. Isolated. A sitting duck.

At least, that had been the plan. And a great plan it was, too. Complicated and expensive, but its success would have been worth the effort and the cost.

Malcolm Sampson and his sidekick, Adam Akers, had set up an auction on the Dark Web and offered seven contracts in total. Contracts that sent seven strike teams out across Europe to kill Ryan Kaine's men. And what a bloody disaster that had turned out to be. As far as Enderby knew, each strike team had either been wiped out or had missed their targets through bad timing, bad luck, or bad planning.

For fuck's sake, every single contract had blown up in the strike teams' faces.

How the hell could it have happened? How?

Kaine and his people must have had the luck of the devil.

The primary contractors, T5S, run by John Abbott, had been assigned four of the contracts, while GG Cleaning Systems won at least one of the other three, probably more. Guy Gordon had been reluctant to provide specific details, but Enderby would find out from Akers—assuming the mad bugger ever decided to honour his promise and call him with an update.

Bloody arse-bandit!

Abbott had paid the price for his company's total failure, though. In a fit of pique, Akers had sent a team of his own to Cambridge and had terminated Abbott's contract, personally and permanently. Even now, the Cambridgeshire Constabulary were sifting through the bullet-riddled remnants of Abbott's country home, searching for evidence at a crime scene that wouldn't have been out of place in a Hollywood action movie.

The media had been all over it. Outside broadcast teams from all the major players had swarmed to the area, reporting vague rubbish and offering nothing but wild speculation. The police, on the other hand, had remained pretty tight-lipped about the "serious and unprecedented incident". In a press release, the police had revealed that the body of the homeowner, John Abbott, had been found in his garage. The statement revealed that he'd been shot multiple times. Furthermore, a number of other unidentified bodies had been discovered in the grounds. One survivor, an unnamed female, had been rushed to hospitable suffering a serious, but not life-threatening or life-altering, injury. The survivor was currently receiving medical care and would be interviewed as soon as the doctors allowed. No more information was made available.

So, John Abbott lay rotting in a morgue somewhere. Killed in his own home. Shocking.

Jay Wyndham hadn't taken the news at all well. He and Abbott had known each other for years. Apparently, the two had been long-term friends. Jay had gone apeshit and tried to blame Enderby for his mate's death. How unfair was that?

All he'd done was provide information on the targets—
their names and locations. The operational details had been
left to the contractors' strike teams. Nothing to do with
Enderby. Not his fault.

He'd stood his ground, argued his case, but had lost face
over it. And Enderby hated the idea of losing face to a man
as important as Jay Wyndham. A man who wielded so much
power. A man so close to the movers and shakers.

Enderby had received Jay's urgent call on his burner
phone during his weekend break—a break spent in a hotel
on the south coast to generate distance between himself and
any blowback from the strike teams' expected success. How
wrong that expectation had proven to be.

"What are you going to do now?" Jay had demanded
over the phone, his tone strident, the closest Enderby had
ever come to hearing genuine rage in his voice.

"Me?" Enderby had said, struggling to provide an
answer on the fly. "I'll ... er, I'll contact Adam Akers. He
and Malcolm Sampson won't let this setback put them off.
They want Kaine dead as much as we do. More even. Akers
especially. Knowing those two, they'll be setting up a new
auction as we speak. There won't be a shortage of bidders
for the revised contracts. And Sampson isn't exactly short of
money, is he?"

At the time, Enderby didn't add the obvious. He didn't
add anything about the new contractors having lost the
element of surprise—not that surprise had helped T5S or
GG Cleaning Systems.

God alive. What a bloody mess.

"Okay," Jay had said, apparently mollified. "Let me
know the moment you hear from Akers."

"Yes, Jay. Certainly, Jay."

Jay ended the call without mentioning Guy Gordon or

GG Cleaning Systems, thank fuck. Enderby didn't need any more questions he couldn't answer. Guy Gordon had been conspicuous by his recent absence. Whereas the creep usually contacted him regularly, sniffing for work, Enderby hadn't heard one peep from the man in days. Bloody strange and hugely annoying.

Enderby concluded his sojourn by the sea a few hours earlier than planned, raced home, and called Belham Castle along the way. Throughout a short but acrimonious phone call Akers had been barely lucid. He ranted, raved, and cursed the whole time. In the end, though, he agreed to call Enderby with a sitrep by two o'clock the following afternoon, which was the call Enderby had been waiting for all day long. It occupied so much of his mind that he'd been unable to concentrate on anything else.

Come on, Akers. This is insufferable.

If it took much longer, he'd initiate the call himself. Enderby hated waiting for others. Why on earth couldn't people fulfil their commitments? That wasn't too much to ask, was it?

Akers had promised an update by two o'clock, but Enderby had heard nothing, and the clock on his computer screen had already clicked beyond two thirty.

Totally unacceptable.

Enderby stretched his arms out in front of his chest, keeping them horizontal to the desk. Breathing in deep and holding it in, he interlaced his fingers and rotated the wrists until his palms faced the uninspiring view through his narrow and grimy office window.

God's sake, man. Call, damn you.

He released the breath slowly through his mouth and stretched his palms even closer towards the window. The tension between his shoulder blades eased. Groaning, he pushed even harder, straining his elbows and popping his shoulders with the effort. Another breath, another stretch. Twisting at the waist and tensing his abs, he rotated his body slowly to the right and back to the left, turning through as full an arc as he could manage while keeping his hips locked against the back of the chair.

And relax.

He repeated the rotation three more times. Five long reps.

Not much of an exercise routine, but all he could manage at his desk without building up a sweat and ruining the creases in his trousers and his expensive, silk shirt. The full exercise programme would have to wait until after work when he could make it to the gym. Assuming there would be an "after work" that day. So much to do. So little time and too little help to do it with. The lament of the high-powered and overworked civil servant.

Enderby sighed.

It wouldn't be long before he ran the agency, though. He allowed himself a sly smile and then scowled again at the pug-ugly view through the dirty window.

Sir Ernest Hartington, the NCTA's permanent secretary, Enderby's boss, would soon be gone, and Enderby would inherit the role as his natural successor. He'd finally take charge of the agency. An agency whose sole *raison d'être* was to collect sensitive information and distribute it as the permanent secretary deemed suitable. Sensitive and valuable information.

As the new agency head, Enderby would have unfettered access to a whole heap of resources and a whole database of secrets. State secrets. Corporate secrets. Personal secrets. Skeletons in cupboards that certain people would pay big money to access, and the subjects involved in the

same secrets would pay just as much to keep hidden.
Enderby couldn't wait. So many opportunities beckoned for
a man who had the balls to grasp them.

Once again, he stared through the office window to his
restricted eye on the world. The view from Sir Ernest's
office, one floor higher and facing the river, was different. It
took in the sweep of the city. Enderby would own that view
before long. He smiled at the thought.

The desk phone burst into life, making him jump.

About bloody time.

He snatched up the handset.

"Yes?" Enderby said, curt and efficient. A busy man who
had no time for wasted words.

"Is that Commander Enderby?"

He didn't recognise the deep, male voice on the other
end of the line. They certainly weren't Adam Akers'
cultured tones.

"It is," Enderby answered. "Who are you and how did
you get my number?"

"Ah, Commander," the man said. "My name is
Slocombe. Chief Superintendent Slocombe of the
Northumbria Police."

Enderby had to concentrate hard to cut through the
man's thick, Geordie accent.

Northumbria? Shit.

Enderby sat up a little straighter. Malcolm Sampson
had taken up temporary residence in the frozen north. This
couldn't be good news. What had the miserable, old
pervert done now? No wonder Akers hadn't reported in on
time.

"...head of the Anti-terrorism Unit," Slocombe
continued.

"Sorry," Enderby interrupted. "Repeat that, please."

Slocombe cleared his throat with the grumbling, rumbling cough of a man fighting a heavy cold.

"I'm head of the Northumbria Police's Anti-terrorism Unit, Commander Enderby," Slocombe said, speaking more slowly. "I have standing instructions from the Home Office to contact you with any information relating to Malcolm Sampson, who were released from prison on Friday the 9th of May. On compassionate grounds, apparently." Slocombe sniffed and didn't sound the least bit impressed, or happy, with his lot.

"Okay. What's he done now? Complained about the accommodation? I'd have thought Belham Castle—"

"No, Commander. It's nothing like that. Mr Sampson's body were discovered at a little after six o'clock this morning."

His body? Jesus wept.

Enderby sat up even straighter. The stiffness in his neck returned with greater force than earlier. It spawned a nagging headache.

"His body?" Enderby said through an instantly dry throat. "He's dead?"

"Yes, sir. According to the medical examiner, Mr Sampson died in the early hours of this morning."

"Natural causes?" Enderby asked, daring to hope, but not believing it for one moment.

"Well, Commander ... we're still awaiting the preliminary results of the post-mortem."

"No need to be coy with me, Chief Superintendent. Did you see the body?"

"Yes, Commander."

"Describe it, please."

Slocombe failed to respond.

"Well, Chief Superintendent?"

"Might I ask why the NCTA is interested in the disgraced former chairman of Sampson Armaments and Munitions Services?"

Enderby hesitated before deciding to play nice with the chief superintendent. It didn't pay to antagonise senior members of the police. One never knew when they might come in useful.

"Our interest is entirely related to counter terrorism, Chief Superintendent," Enderby said, smoothly. "The terrorist, Ryan Kaine, used a SAMS weapon to shoot down Flight BE1555. There's your link, and you have your standing orders. Please tell me what you saw."

Another raking cough rumbled down the phone line.

"Do you have access to the Police National Computer, Commander?" Slocombe asked, his tone official.

"I do," Enderby answered. He leaned forwards, nudged his desktop computer awake, and accessed the PNC. "I'm logging into the system right now."

"In that case, you'll be able to see the crime scene photos and the walk-through videos for yourself. And you'll realise why I'm reluctant to speculate as to the cause of death."

"What's the case number?"

Slocombe told him.

"Thank you, Superintendent. One moment, please."

Enderby entered the case number and navigated to the relevant folders. The first few pictures answered a number of his questions.

"Is foul play suspected?" Enderby asked the most obvious one.

"Given that Sampson couldn't have tied himself to the bed in that manner, and his security team fled the scene before the body were discovered, all I'm prepared to say is there are a number of unanswered questions."

"That pillow," Enderby said, quoting the evidence number. "Is it the murder weapon?"

"In all likelihood. But nobody said anything about murder. At the moment, we're simply treating his death as suspicious."

"Really?" Enderby snorted.

"Aye, really. We don't want to get ahead of ourselves, Commander. Looking at the ball gag, it might've been a role-playing game that got out of hand. You did notice the bright red ball gag?"

"How could I not. Is there any sign of the individual who used the pillow?"

"No, Commander. Apart from the person who discovered the body, the castle was completely deserted."

"Deserted?"

"Yes, Commander."

"Malcolm Sampson employed a large security team. They were *all* gone?"

"Aye, Commander. All fifteen who were booked into the castle. As I said, they seem to have left the scene overnight. We're trying to locate them, but ..." He dragged out another long pause.

"But?" Enderby prompted, growing more anxious with each new revelation.

"But," Slocombe answered, clear reluctance in his hoarse voice, "we don't have any idea who they might be."

"What? Belham Castle's a hotel, isn't it? Weren't their names and IDs registered on the castle's booking system?"

"No, Commander. The entire castle were reserved for two months. A block booking with only Malcolm Sampson's name on the contract."

Excellent.

As far as Enderby was concerned, the fewer people the police could identify and interview, the better it would be for everyone involved. Especially for Greg Enderby.

"Apart from those found on Malcolm Sampson, were there any signs of violence?"

"Violence, Commander Enderby?"

"Any gunplay perhaps?"

"Gunplay? You were expecting a gunfight?"

"As I understand it," Enderby said, considering his words carefully, "some of Sampson's security staff might have been considered mercenaries. I don't know about you, Chief Superintendent, but I've heard that mercenaries often like to be armed. And given Sampson's history as chairman of a major weapons manufacturer, it would be logical to assume that his ... employees would have access to firearms."

"That would be illegal, Commander. Bodyguards aren't allowed to carry weapons in the UK."

"I know that, Chief Superintendent," Enderby snapped, fast losing his temper with the slow-speaking and slower-witted yokel. "But some of those people aren't the most law-abiding of individuals. We've had our eye on Malcolm Sampson and his employees for quite some time. Now, please answer me, Chief Superintendent. Were there any signs of a gunfight?"

"None. It would appear that the security guards simply deserted their posts in the middle of the night without warning."

"That is interesting."

"Bloody strange if you ask me."

I'm not asking.

"So, no gunplay?"

"None. The castle turned into the *Marie Celeste.*"

"Hmm."

"If you don't mind my saying, you seem to know an awful lot about the setup here, Commander," Slocombe said, his curt tone displaying a simmering anger. "If you had any idea that Malcolm Sampson billeted a private army on my patch, you should've—"

"Chief Superintendent Slocombe," Enderby said, cutting across the cop's angry words, "I had no idea of the sort. I'm simply making a supposition. Malcolm Sampson was a disgraced former member of the establishment. So disgraced in fact, that he had his knighthood stripped from him. There's no telling what the man was capable of doing."

"Nonetheless," Slocombe said, his anger building, "given Sampson's early release from prison, we really should've been notified of his presence in our jurisdiction *before* his death dropped a pile of extra paperwork on my desk."

"You weren't notified?" Enderby asked, feigning surprise.

"No, Commander. We most definitely were not." Another sharp response. Slocombe didn't sound impressed.

"That seems rather remiss of someone. You'll have to take that up with HMPPS, or the Home Office."

"Oh, you can be certain that my chief constable will be bending the ear of the relevant ministers."

Good luck with that, mate.

Enderby relented and decided to offer Slocombe a bone.

"Tell me, Chief Superintendent, I don't suppose you've heard from Adam Akers, have you?"

Slocombe's murder team were bound to look into Sampson's prison record, and Enderby saw no reason to hinder the police investigation unduly. It would go some way to making Slocombe think of him as being onside. It would also give Enderby an official reason for having contact with Adam Akers, should the brown stuff ever hit the fan.

"Who?"

"Adam Akers," Enderby said. "Before Malcolm Sampson's fall from grace, Akers was SAMS' Vice President of Internal Security. He also visited Sampson in prison every fortnight, and his name appeared on Sampson's list of approved telephone callers. In actual fact, it wouldn't surprise me to learn that theirs was more than a 'business relationship', if you understand my meaning."

Inwardly, Enderby chuckled.

Nice way to muddy the waters, Greg.

"And given the circumstances in which you found the body ..." Enderby added and let the insinuation dangle.

Slocombe could interpret the information as he damn well chose.

"Ah," Slocombe said. "I see. I see indeed. And in answer to your question, no. We've not heard from anyone called Akers. I must thank you for the steer, though. I'll let the murder team know to look for him. If not actually a person of interest in Sampson's demise, he might prove invaluable as a witness."

"Good idea, Chief Superintendent," Enderby said, unable to avoid sounding supercilious. "And I'll ask around at my end. I'll see what I can do to locate Mr Akers for you."

"Thank you, Commander."

"Okay, Chief Superintendent Slocombe, you will keep me informed as to the progress of the investigation?"

"Of course," Slocombe said, sounding as though that was the last thing he intended.

"And if you need any assistance from my agency, please don't hesitate to contact me."

Enderby hung up before Slocombe could respond. He sat back and stared at the handset, taking stock.

Sampson's death threw up a whole heap of questions, none of which Enderby could answer. Who killed him? How would Sampson's death affect Enderby and his future plans? What would happen to the rest of Sampson's hidden money? Finally, and most importantly, with or without Adam Akers' help, could Enderby lay his hands on any of it?

The first and obvious one, who killed the evil shit? Ryan Kaine would be the bookie's favourite, but how did that help? If Kaine *had* worked his way inside the castle and killed Sampson—and Enderby wouldn't put such a feat beyond a man with Kaine's obvious skillset—it would explain why Sampson's goons had cut and run. With Sampson dead, the money would dry up instantly. The mercenaries wouldn't hang around to face Kaine or answer any police questions. But what about Akers? He wouldn't have run. No way. The nutter had personal reasons to want Kaine dead. Reasons that would be reinforced every time he caught a look at himself reflected in a mirror. He'd have fought to the death. Where the hell had he disappeared to?

Enderby picked up the phone again and dialled the security desk.

"Yes, Commander?" A man asked. Enderby didn't recognise his voice.

"I'm popping out. Need to stretch my legs."

"Very good, Commander. Will you require an escort?"

"Naturally."

As though he'd ever leave the building without close-order protection.

"Very good, Commander."

Time for a quick change of scenery.

Chapter 5

Tuesday 1st June - Gregory Enderby

Sandbrook Tower, Soho, London, England

Enderby replaced the handset, stood, and confirmed he had his backup phone in his pocket. A quick glance through the window showed a watery sun shining on the red-brick wall. At least he wouldn't need his brolly. He removed the Beretta from its safe, checked the load, and slid the gun into its holster. Then he removed his jacket from the hanger hooked to his office door and slipped it on.

In reception, Enderby collected his shadow, another familiar face—Grieves. Enderby liked to know the surnames of the people responsible for risking their lives to protect him. It seemed a reasonable thing to do. Of average height, dark, unobtrusive, and highly effective. He would do well enough.

Grieves stepped through to the foyer.

"Are we driving or going on foot, sir?" he asked.

"On foot. I'll be popping across the road to the café and then strolling to the Gardens. Keep your distance, and stay unobtrusive."

"Of course, Commander," Grieves said without inflection.

Enderby waited for Grieves to step outside and do his bodyguard thing before following him through the revolving doors and into the open air.

Outside, Enderby paused long enough to scan the immediate area for anything suspicious, checking Grieves' handiwork. He buttoned his jacket against a chill wind that picked up the litter dropped by the passing morons, spun it in mini whirlpools, and dropped it in ugly piles in the sheltered corners. His fringe flicked into his eyes, and he brushed it away with his fingers.

Grieves took his position five metres behind, and followed Enderby to the crossing, where he had to wait with a small group of lunkheads for the lights to change and the bleep to activate—Grieves closed the gap between them to one metre. After checking left and right, they crossed the street together and turned left towards The Coffee Shack.

Enderby entered the café and slipped to the back of a short queue. He waited in line for ages until an overstuffed barista, who'd clearly been helping herself to too many of the shop's glutinous pastries, finally filled his order. Eventually, she delivered him an extra-large Americano, black, no sugar in an insulated takeaway mug. He didn't order any food. Grieves remained near the doorway the whole time, monitoring the entrance, doing his job.

Enderby didn't offer his shadow a drink. The man needed to pay attention to his job, and he could hardly do that when slurping on a mug of takeaway coffee. Besides, it wasn't Enderby's job to subsidise the hired help. The Coffee Shack sold overly expensive coffee and snacks to an exclusive clientele. Grieves could make do with instant back in his little office cubbyhole—assuming coffee was his beverage of choice. Enderby didn't care enough about the man to find out.

With the mug in hand, Enderby stepped back out into the blustery wind, turned right, and set off at a brisk pace towards one of the few patches of greenery for miles, Soho Square Gardens. He turned right again onto Dean Street, left onto Carlisle Street, and strode through the open, black, wrought-iron gates. Miraculously, he found an empty bench near the entrance and plonked himself down to enjoy the powerful brew. A careful man, he never ate or drank on the move. That way would likely lead to indigestion and stains on one's clothing. Neither of which would go down well in the rarefied environment he inhabited.

Enderby removed the top from the coffee mug, breathed in the aroma of the Blue Mountain blend, and took a gentle sip. The rich, full flavour hit the mark immediately. Restorative. Delicious.

Grieves started his usual routine—walking laps of the small park, always keeping within sight, patrolling at the maximum distance possible while still being able to protect his client. A professional performing his job well enough.

Enderby pulled the ancillary phone from his jacket pocket and scrolled through the short list of contacts. He dialled and held his breath. The call connected. Thank God. At least Akers hadn't powered down his mobile.

Enderby waited. The double burp of the ring tone droned on … and on.

Come on, man. Answer your bloody calls.

Enderby sank against the back of the bench, feeling every one of the horizontal slats digging into his spine. The ring tone continued for a count of thirteen before it clicked in answer.

"Adam?" Enderby demanded, barely disguising the relief in his words.

"Hello? Who is this?" a female voice asked.

A woman?

Enderby frowned. He considered hanging up, but curiosity beat discretion.

"Who are you, please?" he asked.

"This is Detective Chief Inspector Olivia Strachan, sir. I take it you know the person who owns this phone?"

The police? Jesus wept.

Enderby disconnected the call and powered down the burner. He waited until Grieves looked away before removing the battery and returning the pieces to his pocket. He'd dispose of the bloody thing later.

Shit! What the bloody hell?

Without thinking, he took another sip of coffee. It tasted like acid on his tongue. He leaned to one side and tipped the expensive brew over the grass behind the bench.

Such a waste.

Enderby stood, hurried to the nearest bin, and deposited the empty mug and plastic lid through its gaping mouth.

A shadow appeared at his shoulder.

"Anything wrong, Commander?" Grieves asked.

"No," Enderby snapped. "Why should anything be wrong?" He sounded both aggressive and defensive.

Calm down, Greg.

Grieves shrugged, his light brown eyes still scanning for threats. "You usually finish your coffee, sir."

"Not today, Grieves. I'm heading back to the office." He glanced up at the largely cloudless sky. "Looks like rain."

Chapter 6

Tuesday 1st June - Gregory Enderby

Sandbrook Tower, Soho, London, England

Back in his office, Enderby woke his desktop computer, logged onto the PNC, and searched for any current UK investigations involving a DCI Olivia Strachan. He struck lucky immediately. The case related to a double murder. Two adult males had been shot to death inside the Avonside General Hospital mortuary in Evesham.

Bloody hell.

Enderby read the entry again. A double murder *inside* a mortuary? He didn't miss the irony, but his blood still ran cold. Why was Adam Akers' mobile being answered by a serving police officer? There could only be one answer. It had been found at the crime scene. Akers must have been there. He'd either dropped it leaving the crime scene, or could be one of the victims.

God above!

The case fell within the jurisdiction of the West Mercia Police.

Enderby scrolled through the file, looking for an initial report or crime scene photos, but none had yet been uploaded. The West Mercia Police clearly weren't as efficient as their Northumbrian counterparts. Maybe they had to deal with more crime in West Mercia.

Enderby leaned back in his chair and took a moment to consider his options. Should he contact DCI Strachan or leave well alone? What were the downsides of an approach? For a start, she'd probably try to identify who'd called Akers' phone. She wouldn't be able to link the caller to Enderby, of course she wouldn't, but Enderby didn't like loose ends.

And, damn it, Enderby was a senior member of the intelligence community. He had every right to involve himself in any investigation with a terrorist element, and, as he'd pointed out to Chief Superintendent Slocombe of the Northumbria Police, anything involving a current or previous employee of SAMS fitted the bill.

The NCTA database held a comprehensive list of direct contact details for all the UK's police services. Enderby searched for and identified the direct number for the communications desk at the West Mercia Police HQ and dialled it using his desk phone. Perfectly official. No need to worry.

"West Mercia Control Centre," a man said. "How can I help?"

"This is Commander Enderby of the National Counter Terrorism Agency," he announced, using his most official inflection. "I wish to speak to DCI Strachan." To maintain

his posturing, he pronounced it in the Scottish manner
—Strawn.

"One moment, Commander. I'll see if I can find—"

"Does my phone number appear on your system?"

"Yes, Commander."

"In that case, have her call me as soon as possible. It will
save me waiting."

That's it, Greg.

Enderby could play the self-important arsehole too busy
to wait for a minion to perfection, and he thoroughly
enjoyed doing so.

"Yes, Commander."

"Thank you."

Enderby hung up and leaned against the back of his
chair once again. He read the time off his watch, wondering
how long it would take for Strachan to call. Rain spattered
his office window, streaking the grime on the glass. A large
raindrop hit the top of the pane and gravity took hold. It
rolled down the glass, connected with another and another,
tripled in size along the way, and picked up momentum.
The rivulet wound its way to the bottom of the frame and
pooled in the ridge, leaving its wriggling trail behind. Soon,
other rivulets formed, and Enderby watched them chasing
each other down the glass and into oblivion.

The bodies in the morgue. Who were they?

Enderby repeated the words aloud.

"The bodies in the morgue."

He snorted.

It would work as the title of a horror film, and probably
already had. Two murdered men. Was one of them Adam
Akers? It would definitely explain why his phone had ended
up at the scene.

Nervous tension started working its way through Enderby's guts, twisting his bowels into tight knots. He didn't like the feeling one little bit. If it got much worse, he'd have to race to the loo and risk missing the call.

"Who are the bodies in the morgue?" he asked the rain-splattered windowpane.

The sharp buzz of his desk phone broke him from his musings, and he reached out to snatch up the handset.

"Enderby."

"Commander? This is DCI Strachan. I understand you wanted to speak to me, sir." She delivered the words brusquely, as though annoyed at the interruption to her day, and pronounced her surname in the English manner, emphasising all the consonants. The woman couldn't even pronounce her own name properly.

"I did. Thank you for contacting me so quickly."

"What's this all about?"

Strachan came across as curt and aggressive. Enderby could hardly blame her. In Strachan's situation, he'd have felt exactly the same way about an interloper disturbing her at the beginning of a new investigation.

"Are you still at the Avonside Hospital Mortuary?" Enderby asked, reverting to type. He'd long since learned that to keep the upper hand in a conversation, it always paid to answer a question with another question.

"What?"

"Please answer me, Chief Inspector."

"Yes, I am," she answered, her dull Midlands accent coming to the fore. "Why is the deputy head of the NCTA interested in a double murder at a hospital mortuary?"

Good question.

"That, I'm afraid, must remain confidential for the moment. As I understand it, two men were shot to death. Is that correct?"

"It is," she answered after a short delay.

"Did either of the victims have a damaged nose? An old injury?"

"Yes, Commander. One did," Strachan answered, the angry response softening as she showed signs of intrigue. "How do you know that?"

"Blond hair, blue eyes?"

"Yes again. That is true for both victims, Commander. But one did have a pre-existing injury to his nose. You clearly know him. Wait a moment," she said, the penny finally dropping, "was it you who called the victim's phone a short while ago."

"Yes," Enderby said, "it was. I apologise for hanging up on you so abruptly. I was a little … indisposed."

Hopefully, she'd interpret that as a call of nature.

"I understand, Commander," she said. "On the phone, you asked for 'Adam'. Is that the man's name?"

Enderby couldn't help but be impressed by the woman's memory. She might not know how to pronounce her own name, but she could, at the very least, remember someone else's.

"I'm not certain. When are you going to upload the crime scene photos and video walkthrough to the PNC?"

"Not until after we're finished at the scene, which won't be for a while." She paused for a moment before adding, "Well?"

"Well what?"

"Are you going to give me *Adam*'s full name?"

The anger and impatience had returned. Enderby could picture a fiery redhead with dark freckles and a red, masculine face trying to rein herself in.

"Dial back on the aggression, DCI Strachan," Enderby

barked. "I'm not one of your subordinates." He paused long enough to let the message sink in.

Strachan broke the pregnant silence with a reluctant, "Forgive me, Commander, but we have discovered four dead men in the past thirty-six hours in what is not usually a high-crime area. I don't have time to play nice."

"*Four* dead men, you say?"

"Yes, Commander. I was about to report to my superintendent, but I find myself talking to a spook from London instead. A spook from London who seems happy to withhold vital information on one of the victims. I think I have every right to be angry. Don't you?"

Enderby smiled at her response. The woman showed spirit. Maybe he'd arrange to meet her one day, to find out whether the spirit was housed in a frame that looked a little less masculine than he imagined. For a moment, he considered running a quick interrogation of the West Mercia Police's personnel files to find an ID photo, but dismissed the idea as a ridiculous waste of his time.

"When you put it like that, Chief Inspector," he said after a moment, "I can see your point." He took a breath before continuing. "Before I can say anything further, I need to know a little more. As I understand it, two men were discovered shot to death in the mortuary. Yet you're telling me you found *four* bodies. Would you care to elaborate?"

Strachan hesitated before launching into an explanation.

"Yesterday morning, the bodies of two men were found in woods to the northwest of Evesham, near a village called Spetchley."

"Were both men also shot?" Enderby asked, interrupting her flow.

"No, Commander. One suffered blunt force trauma to the

head. The other had a lock knife buried in his neck. I'd say he bled to death. Their bodies were taken to the nearest mortuary, which happens to be where I'm standing right now. Their post-mortems were scheduled for today. However, this morning, two more bodies were discovered in the mortuary by the day shift. Both had been shot to death. One through the back of the head, the other through the right wrist and the chest. Now, I don't know about you, Commander, but I'd say in all likelihood these four deaths are linked. Wouldn't you?"

"Without further information to the contrary, that hypothesis seems reasonable at this stage."

Enderby shot the window a self-satisfied smirk. Sometimes, he could impress himself with his grasp of the English language, especially since he'd performed so badly in his school exams.

"Okay, Commander," Strachan said, exaggerated patience flowing down the phone line. "Are you prepared to tell me Adam's surname now?"

After so much hedging, Enderby thought it prudent to lob the feisty Midlander a bone. A small bone.

"If your victim is who I *think* he is, the man's name would be Adam Akers."

"Adam Akers?" Strachan asked slowly, probably repeating the name to commit it to memory. Either that, or she was dictating it to a subordinate.

"If it is Adam Akers, he used to be Vice President of Internal Security for SAMS, the arms manufacturer. Which explains my agency's interest in this case, does it not?"

"Yes, it does. Thank you for that, Commander. Do you have any further information for me?"

"I may have, Chief Inspector," he said, smiling as he prepared to lob a second morsel. "Akers was found with another blond man, you say?"

"Yes, Commander."

"Did they look alike?"

"No. Apart from the fair hair and blue eyes, they looked nothing alike. However, one of the other two bodies we found yesterday could pass for Adam Akers' brother."

Bloody hell.

Sampson's people were dropping like flies. Along with Sampson himself.

"In that case," Enderby said, pulling himself together, "the lookalike might be André Akers, who is Adam's younger brother."

"Thank you again, Commander. Is there anything else you can tell me?"

"In fact, there is, DCI Strachan. The last time I spoke with Adam Akers, he was at a place called Belham Castle, Tumblethorpe Lake, Northumberland. I suspect your investigation is going to have to expand somewhat."

"Excuse me?"

Again, Enderby felt the urge to smile. Helping the police would earn him loads of Brownie points—not that he needed any.

"If I were you, DCI Strachan," he said, "the next call I'd make would be to a Chief Superintendent Slocombe of the Northumbria Police."

"Why?" Strachan snapped.

"Call him, Chief Inspector. You will find it useful to compare notes."

"What's happening here, Commander Enderby? Are you holding out on me? Do you know what happened?"

"No, Chief Inspector," he said, with all the firmness he could generate, "I'm afraid I do not. Good day to you."

Enderby ended the call. He stood, crossed to the corner, and made himself an instant coffee with powdered milk and no sweeteners. Pacing the thin carpet in front of the rain-spotted window, he sipped the inadequate brew and tried to determine the best way to proceed. So far, he'd been reacting on instinct when he should have been working to a plan.

Eventually, the coffee and the pacing sparked some life into his brain, and he finally started thinking clearly.

Malcolm Sampson had died overnight. Murdered. His men had disappeared, melted into the atmosphere. Now it seemed as though the Akers brothers were lying dead in a mortuary alongside two others. John Abbott of T5S had also been killed. So much peripheral damage.

What the hell happened?

The whole thing had degenerated into a bloody cluster-fuck. Enderby's carefully constructed plan to isolate Ryan Kaine had failed miserably, and where did that leave him? Out on a limb, but … no. He still had Guy Gordon in his pocket, and Gordon's role would prove pivotal. In fact, it would prove to be the only game in town. Enderby needed to move the action forwards. No more prevarication.

But first, Jay needed a news update.

Enderby considered holding off reporting in, but that wouldn't work. Jay gathered information the same way as a black hole sucked in light. The news of Sampson's death would reach him soon enough, and it would be better for Enderby to deliver it personally. That way, he could retain some sort of control over the situation.

Enderby reached for his landline again but changed his mind and dragged the burner from his pocket. Casting caution to one side, rather than leave 'the building, he stepped into his private rest room and dialled the number.

"*Identification required,*" Jay's electronic security system announced.

Enderby cleared his throat before speaking, making sure his words were slow, clear, and quiet.

"Commander Gregory Enderby."

The phone clicked. *"Repeat the following sequence. Alpha-Bravo-Charlie-Delta-five-seven-eight."*

Enderby obeyed the instruction, as usual.

"Voice identification confirmed." The line clicked again.

"Gregory, dear boy," the Minister of State said, his urbane delivery recognisable to anyone who'd watched TV news bulletins in the previous two decades. "What do you have for me?"

Yes, that's right, Jay. It's always about you, isn't it.

"Hi, Jay. Um, I thought you should know that I've just finished speaking to two members of the UK police force."

"You have, dear boy?" Jay asked. "I do hope you were able to help them with their enquiries." Jay's familiar, booming laugh launched itself down the phone line.

"This is serious, Jay. Malcolm Sampson is dead."

The laughter stopped abruptly.

"Natural causes?" the UK Government's Minister Without Portfolio asked.

"No. Definitely not natural causes."

Keeping his voice down, Enderby described the images he'd witnessed on the Northumbria Police's video walk-through of the crime scene. Jay remained silent throughout.

"But that's not all," Enderby said after he'd finished. "When I tried calling Adam Akers' mobile for a ... sitrep, it was answered by a DCI Strachan of the West Mercia Police. It would appear that Adam Akers is also dead ... as is his younger brother, André."

He told Jay what he knew and waited for an explosion that didn't happen.

"So," Jay said, his voice calm, quiet, "let me see if I have this correct. Malcolm Sampson is dead. His security detail has disappeared, and his right-hand man, Adam Akers, has been found—dead—in a mortuary in deepest Worcestershire along with his baby brother. Is that about the size of it?"

"Yes, Jay. It is."

Jay followed a drawn out, "Hmm," with, "That is most unfortunate. People seem to be dropping dead all over the place. I've already lost the services of John Abbott. This really is most disconcerting. I assume that Ryan Kaine is responsible?"

"That's impossible to say for sure, but I imagine he might have had a hand in it," Enderby answered, deliberately keeping it as noncommittal as possible.

"Do you have any plans to rectify the setback?"

"I'm working on it, Jay. I don't suppose you can suggest a way forwards."

"That's not my responsibility," Jay snapped, his voice instantly as hard as nails. "Show some initiative, man. Clean up your own mess. What does your friend, Gordon, have to say for himself?"

"I haven't spoken to him yet. I thought it best to brief you first," Enderby fawned.

And I'll speak to Gordon as soon as the miserable bugger returns my calls.

"As I understand it, GG Cleaning Systems won three of the … contracts we were discussing earlier."

"They did," Enderby said, nodding to the grimy window.

"In which case, Gordon ought to be able to throw some light on the matter."

"I would hope so, Jay."

"Good," Jay said. "Together, you and Gordon *will*

develop a workable solution. And Gregory … you know what happens to people who don't find solutions, don't you."

Enderby shivered against the cold wind gnawing at the back of his neck.

"I'll call him right away."

"Good idea, Gregory. If you need financial assistance, I might be able to offer some support."

"Thank you, Jay. That would be appreciated."

"It's nothing, dear boy. Nothing. Make sure you keep me in the loop."

The phone clicked into silence without Jay offering so much as a farewell.

Enderby puffed out his cheeks and slumped into his chair. Again, he shuddered. He'd delivered the miserable news and lived to tell the tale. Although Enderby didn't need the money—he had plenty of his own—the offer of financial support was welcome. It showed how highly Jay thought of him. It would stand him in good stead when Sir Ernest Hartington finally moved aside.

Enderby took another sip of his fast-cooling coffee. His hand trembled—with excitement. Despite the reams of bad news he'd received that day, things were actually looking good. With Jay Wyndham onside, his life plan continued to move in an upwards trajectory. All he had to do now was convince Gordon to act and everything would work out as he'd always planned.

He raised his cup to the rain-spackled window and smiled.

Chapter 7

Sunday 6th June - Midday

Heading South, M1, Buckinghamshire, England

Ryan Kaine narrowed his eyes as the blinding sun burst between the glowering, dark clouds and seared through the windscreen. He flicked down the visor and stretched his neck, his eyes reaching towards the shade. Heavy rain one moment, dazzling sun the next. The weather refused to make up its mind. A typical English summer.

In no real hurry for once, he tapped the cruise control button, clicked the speed down to sixty-five mph, and eased into the inside lane. Surprisingly heavy Sunday traffic—the M1 motorway rarely slept—raced past on his outside. People charging towards the next traffic jam.

Let them.

Kaine yawned long and hard, filling his lungs, trying to drive some life into his dull mind and his weary bones. The disaster in France had taken it out of him, left him torn up inside. Angry. Distraught. He could have saved Molly Williams. *Should* have saved her. But he'd been too late. Too bloody late. And Rollo ... He would have liked time to process Molly's loss and Rollo's injury, but when Will phoned, Kaine answered. He had no alternative.

He yawned again, covering his mouth with the back of his hand.

"Wake up, you dozy bugger!" he growled at the bleary-eyed man blinking heavily in the rear-view mirror.

The mobile phone vibrated in his pocket and the dash-board display announced an incoming call from, "Whiskey One".

Ah, the man himself.

Kaine pressed the phone button on the steering wheel control cluster and accepted the incoming call.

"Hi, Will," he said. "What's happening?"

"The Commander," Will answered, referring to Commander Gregory Enderby, one of two targets for the ~ration, "is at home, and has been all weekend. No sign ¹eaving the apartment anytime soon. Huntsman has ⁿn and will let me know if he moves."

ᑎele Hunter—the most recent and, as yet, ⁻ion to their team—being out on ⁱne certain cause for concern, ⁻Ⱳhat choice did he have?

⁻rt   Pagnell

"Ninety minutes, give or take traffic delays."

"Okay," Will said, "I'll have the kettle ready."

"Excellent. What are you up to?"

"Doing a spot of DIY," Will answered after a slight delay.

"Really?"

"Yep."

"Care to expand on that?"

"I'm prepping the house for our guest's arrival. We wouldn't want his stay to be too comfortable, now, would we."

Kaine laughed. "You can be a nasty piece of work, my friend. Has anyone ever told you that?"

"Once or twice."

"So," Kaine said after a momentary pause for thought. "You've definitely worked out a way of scooping him up without risking damage to his security team?"

"I think so, but it means getting up close and personal, and I can't do that myself. The Commander and I have met a few times, and he'd recognise me. You'll have to do it. I'll brief you fully when you get here. We'll have plenty of time. See you in ninety."

"Roger that."

Kaine pressed disconnect and settled in for a long and tedious drive.

Newport Pagnell Services rolled by in a slow blur of signage, an overhead walkway, and a tailback of vehicles waiting on the access road.

Seconds later, Kaine indicated right and eased into middle lane to allow a sleek, black BMW M3 to filter the motorway via the services' slip road. The driver dark hair, grey steam from a vape exploding from window—barged his way into the inner lane a panel van and immediately tailgated a large Volvo towing a large caravan. Hemmed in by the passing nose-to-tail traffic in the middle lane, Vape-man flashed his headlights at the rear of the caravan, urging the driver on in a show of angry impatience. The Volvo driver—a grey-haired man in his sixties—refused to be pressured and maintained his restricted speed limit of sixty mph. Vape-man continued his intimidatory flashing.

In his Range Rover, Kaine overtook the black M3 and the caravan slowly enough to catch the rage on Vape-man's fuzzy-jawed and reddened face. The angry man kept glancing into his offside wing mirror, searching for non-existent gaps in the middle-lane traffic. At one point, he slammed his open palm into the steering wheel, blaring the horn at the hapless Volvo driver.

"Easy, mate," Kaine muttered. "You'll give yourself a coronary."

Another cloud of nicotine-infused mist billowed from the vape. With so much mist, Kaine wondered how Vape-man could see the road ahead.

The man at the wheel of the car directly behind Kaine, a Nissan Qashqai, slowed enough for a decent gap to form between them, and flicked his headlights. Without waving his thanks or indicating right, Vape-man tugged sharply on his steering wheel. The M3 jagged right and filled the newly created space. This time, he chose to tailgate Kaine's Range Rover, driving so close, their bumpers weren't far off kissing.

Kaine shook his head and waved the man away. The moron wouldn't take the hint and edged the M3 even closer.

"Keep your bloody distance," Kaine growled. "Idiot."

With the outside lane as full as the middle, it didn't take Vape-man long to work his headlights again. They flashed three times. Each longer than the last. Kaine leaned to his right and pointed through his windscreen, showing Vape-man the heavy traffic ahead.

"Hold your bloody horses. Where can I go?"

It didn't help. Vape-man flashed his lights and blared his horn again. Kaine ground his teeth. Vape-man's bullying tactics had started to annoy him. What the bloody hell did he think he was doing?

Ignore him, Kaine. Ignore him.

Five minutes passed without a let-up. Headlights kept flashing, the two-tone horn kept bellowing, and the steam clouds around Vape-man's head kept thickening.

Unable to use much of the M3's high-performance straight-six petrol engine, with its 510 horses and its 8-speed transmission, Vape-man grew ever more irate. He drew to within a hair of kissing the Range Rover's bumper again, then backed off a metre or two.

Glancing in his rear-view mirror, Kaine shook his head. What was it about drivers these days? So bloody angry. So damned impatient. His mind slipped back a couple of days to the White Van Man who'd rear-ended him in a stationary queue in London. In response, Kaine had climbed out of his car, and they'd faced each other down. "Don't do it, son," Kaine had said quietly, staring the man in the eye. "It really isn't a good idea." That driver had eventually wilted under Kaine's clear-eyed stare and his calm words.

If Vape-man bumped the Range Rover at sixty-five mph, Kaine wouldn't have the opportunity to use the same calming tactic. Wouldn't have been inclined to do so, either.

Without indicating, Vape-man howled, stamped on his accelerator, and bullied his way into an impossibly narrow gap in the outside lane between a bright green Fiat Ducato and a dark blue Vauxhall Corsa. The Corsa driver braked sharply, the car's nose dipped, the front wheels locked up, and black smoke billowed from the tyres. The car behind the Corsa narrowly avoided a rear-end shunt.

"You bloody moron!" Kaine yelled.

Horns blared and headlights glared. Traffic slowed and concertinaed dangerously.

The Fiat Ducato indicated left and pulled into the middle lane. Vape-man's M3 burst forwards, pulling close to the next car in the lane, a red Ford Fiesta.

"How far did that get you, fool?" Kaine growled.

Under pressure from Vape-man, the Fiesta's driver pulled aside, and the high-sided Ducato blocked Kaine's view of the fast-disappearing M3. He relaxed his cramping jaw muscles.

Arsehole.

Half a mile later, the first countdown sign indicated three hundred metres to Junction 14, and an overhead gantry announced the turn off to Milton Keynes and Newport Pagnell.

Ahead, the Ducato indicated right, pulled into the outside lane, and cleared the view for Kaine. Vape-man's M3 had been held up by yet more traffic. Without indicating his intentions, Vape-man darted left into the middle lane, and left again into the inside lane, cutting between a tourist coach and a Ford Focus. He continued his line, aiming for the slip road.

The Focus' brake lights blazed, and its front end dipped. The back wheels lost traction, and the rear end slewed out into the middle lane, narrowly avoiding being sideswiped by a small van. The Focus' driver fought the wheel and regained control, but the red Tesla Model 3 directly behind slammed into its rear end. The two cars spun. Hopelessly out of control.

Kaine slammed on the anchors. The brake pedal shuddered underfoot as the antilock braking system took over. He steered around the car in front and squeezed into a tiny gap in the inside lane. All around him, brake lights blazed, tyres squealed, and vehicles screeched to a halt. In the outside lane, a big Mitsubishi slammed into the car in front and shunted that one forwards, but most stopped in time.

The BMW M3 sailed onto the slip road. Vape-man, either oblivious to the carnage he'd caused or totally unconcerned by it, roared away up the hill.

"Oh no you don't," Kaine bellowed, "you bastard."

Rage flooded Kaine's system with adrenaline. The image of Molly Williams lying on the filthy bed flashed into his head alongside a pained Rollo, with his smashed and bloodied shoulder. This time, Kaine wasn't too late. This bastard, Vape-man, wasn't getting away.

No bloody chance.

Kaine skirted behind a coach filled with stunned and white-faced passengers, filtered the Range Rover onto the hard shoulder, and thundered onto the traffic-free slip road.

Naughty, naughty, but it's for a just cause.

The M3 had reached the unexpectedly clear roundabout on the brow of the hill and taken the first exit onto the A509. The heavy Range Rover couldn't hope to match the M3 for base speed, but Kaine knew the area. Traffic snarl-ups on the single-carriageway road were notorious and frequent. Kaine stood a decent chance of catching the bugger.

He engaged *dynamic* mode to stiffen the Range Rover's suspension, tighten the steering ratio, and ramp up the speed of the gear shifting, and stamped on the accelerator. The increased power punched him deeper into the driver's seat.

The Range Rover powered up the slip road, entered the

roundabout at pace, and took the first exit. Kaine added more pressure to the throttle as the two-laned road straightened. In short order, the speedo clicked up past a hundred. Ahead, the black smudge of the M3 overtook a red van, narrowly avoiding a head-on collision with an oncoming coach—its driver wide-eyed and terrified. The sports-tuned M3 darted left, clinging limpet-tight to the road. Kaine reached the red van, slowed for the coach, overtook, and slammed on the brakes to avoid running into the back of a Fiat Punto.

Hedges climbed high on each side of the road. A humped grass verge ruled out a nearside undertake, and oncoming traffic blocked the right lane, preventing an overtake. Forced to slow, Kaine watched the black M3 pull inexorably away. He eased his foot off the throttle. Race over.

Bugger.

Somehow aware of the situation, the Fiat's driver indicated left and pulled in tight to the verge, allowing Kaine just enough room to filter down the middle of the road. Thanking the driver with a wave, he stomped on the throttle, and powered between the Fiat and a stream of oncoming traffic. He took a tight right-hander at increasing speed.

Four hundred metres ahead, held up by a skip loader and a lane full of oncoming vehicles, Vape-man tried his old trick, but flashing his lights had less effect than it did on the motorway. Kaine smiled, eased back on the accelerator, and closed on the M3. They slowed to forty-five, the gap reduced to thirty metres, twenty, ten, and Kaine took his turn to flash his lights. He added a little wave.

Vape-man stared into his rear-view mirror, snarled in recognition.

Smiling, Kaine pointed two fingers at his eyes and turned them to face Vape-man.

"I'm watching you, arsehole! You're going nowhere."

Vape-man toked on his e-cigarette, spewed out yet another cloud of white vapour, and shot Kaine the finger. He tapped on the brakes, trying to intimidate Kaine into backing away, but Kaine shook his head and threw Vape-man another grim smile.

"You're mine, arsehole. All mine."

One mile later, as they approached a double round-about, the skip loader slowed. Their speed dropped rapidly from forty-five to thirty, and then to twenty. Still, the oncoming traffic filled the right-hand lane, preventing Vape-man's escape.

Kaine glanced in his rear-view mirror. The Fiat Punto had caught up, but maintained a decent gap. Its driver, a stocky, middle-aged man with grey hair, careful and considerate, seemed content to take his time.

Eventually, the skip loader rolled to a stop, held up by temporary traffic lights servicing inactive roadworks ahead of the double roundabout.

Vape-man slammed his fists into the steering wheel, reached for something on the passenger's seat, and cranked open the driver's door. He climbed up and out of the cabin, pulled back his shoulders, and turned to face Kaine. A snarl screwed up his square-jawed, stubble-darkened face.

In his left hand, he held a zombie knife. The weapon's curved blade had a razor-sharp lead edge, a serrated, saw-toothed back, and filled the manufacturer's design brief to perfection—assuming the design brief included the words "evil" and "threatening".

Sweating freely, Vape-man gripped the knife in two hands, and pointed it at Kaine. He whipped it in a tight circle, arms and wrists working together—supple, strong. He looked comfortable doing it. Practised. The knotted, white drawstrings on his dark blue hoodie danced and flicked as his shoulders moved and his upper body swayed.

"You want something from me, shithead?" he snarled, pausing his movements. Arms thrust out at chest height, he pointed the blade at Kaine.

With his eyes fixed on the immobile blade, Kaine threw open his door and slid out of the Rover. He left the door ajar, stepped around it, and strode towards the man pointing the evil-looking weapon. He stopped far enough from Vape-man to keep a healthy, stabbing-lunge distance between them.

"Yep," Kaine answered, nodding, "I do want something, actually."

"What?" Vape-man sneered.

"I want you to go back and hold your hands up to causing that pileup."

Vape-man edged closer. The zombie blade carved a large X into the air between them, swishing with each diagonal swipe. Intimidating. Vape-man had clearly practised the move—probably in front of a mirror.

"What fucking pileup?" he barked.

"The one you caused on the M1 when you cut across two lanes of traffic. A multi-car pileup."

"So fucking what?" Vape-man snarled, adding a sneer.

"You might have killed someone."

"I don't give a shit," he said, stretching out a harsh smile that didn't reach his dark eyes.

"I do."

"So fucking what?" he repeated, a man of limited vocabulary.

Ahead, the traffic lights changed. The skip loader's

engine revved, gears meshed, and it pulled slowly forwards. Oncoming cars stopped rushing past them, held up by the roadworks' filter lane.

Vape-man glanced over his shoulder.

"Don't even think about it, son," Kaine said, shaking his head slowly. "You're going nowhere."

"Fuck you, dickhead."

Vape-man shimmied closer to Kaine, leading with his left foot.

He sliced another X through the air. At the end of the second swish, he flicked his wrists and cut the blade back and across at the level of Kaine's belly, turning the tale of the X into an L. The blade swiped less than a metre short of Kaine. He held his ground, hands raised, waiting for an opening. Adrenaline coursed through his system, increasing his heartrate, warming his muscles, dilating his pupils, preparing him for action.

Fight or flight?

Sod flight. Not happening.

Zombie knife or not, Vape-man was going nowhere.

Vape-man bellowed again. Pinprick pupils suggested his e-cigarette contained something stronger than nicotine. The man was high on something, out of control, unpredictable. Too dangerous to talk down.

A woman behind Kaine shouted, "Oh my God!"

"I'm calling the police," a man shouted.

Without turning his back on Vape-man, Kaine held up his hand and pushed it behind him.

"I *am* the police," he shouted. "Keep back. I have this under control."

Really, I do.

Excitement gleamed in Vape-man's dark eyes.

"A pig, huh?" he asked. A menacing chuckle burst from

deep within his throat. "I'm gonna enjoy gutting you for market, little piggie."

Kaine held out his hands, beckoning with his fingers. "Hand over the machete, mate."

"Why should I?"

"If you don't," Kaine said lowering his voice, making sure his words didn't carry to the people behind, "I'm going to take it from you."

Vape-man snorted, and his lips stretched into an evil smile.

"How you gonna do that, little piggie?"

Still gripping the machete in both hands, he waggled the point at Kaine's face.

Kaine sidestepped around to his left.

Vape-man grinned and also circled left, moving in a wide arc. Kaine continued moving, keeping his arms up, hands outstretched.

"Come on, little piggie," Vape-man jeered. "Come take this little old knife from me."

Vape-man lunged, slicing diagonally downwards, right to left.

Kaine sidestepped. The flashing blade sailed past his right shoulder. Arms lowered, Vape-man spun, swept a backhanded swipe. The blade carved upwards through the air. The knotted drawstring flicked upwards, snapping into Vape-man's right eye.

He yelled. Jerked his head back.

Kaine darted forwards, grasped Vape-man's wrists in both hands and swivelled. He drove his hip into his opponent's midriff and continued the rotation, simultaneously pushing out and around with his hands and arms.

Vape-man flipped over Kaine's outstretched hip, howled, and slammed into the tarmac. The zombie knife flew from his grasp, skittered towards the M3, and came to rest beneath the rear offside tyre.

Kaine twisted Vape-man's right wrist, flipped him onto his front, and wrenched the arm high behind his back. Vape-man screamed, struggled, kicked out hard. Kaine rammed his knee into the small of Vape-man's back and forced the bugger's hand higher up between his shoulder blades.

"Bastard!" Vape-man screamed. "Fucking bastard!"

"Keep struggling," Kaine hissed into the downed man's ear, "and I'll pop the shoulder!"

To Kaine's right, traffic rolled slowly past. A tiny part of his brain became aware of drivers and passengers staring through windows, open-mouthed, wide-eyed. None stopped to help.

Vape-man's shoes scraped the road. He tried to squirm, tried to twist out from the armlock.

Still rotating the wrist, Kaine used his other hand to lever the arm even higher. Gristle crunched, the joint popped.

Again, Vape-man screamed. He stopped shouting, stopped struggling, started panting.

Kaine released the wrist and snaked his right arm around the man's neck. He reinforced the sleeper hold with his free hand, squeezed the throat and neck, and compressed the carotid arteries. Driving his knee into Vape-man's back, Kaine pulled, and started counting.

One ... two ... three ...

Vape-man gargled, gagged, kicked, wrenched, trying to buck Kaine off his back. He reached up with one hand, the other useless. Nails scratched, clawed at Kaine's forearm. Panic added strength to the efforts.

Seven ... eight ...

Vape-man gurgled. Gasped.

The scratching, gouging, clawing weakened. The writhing slowed. The bucking stopped. Vape-man's hands slipped away. He lay still.

Nine ... ten ... eleven ...

Beneath Kaine, Vape-man's head fell limp in his arm. Neck cartilage flopped and stretched.

Thirteen ... fourteen ... fifteen ... sixteen.

Kaine released the choke hold. Any longer and the restriction of blood flow to Vape-man's brain would have risked serious damage. As it was, he'd wake to a vicious headache.

Kaine swallowed, took in a deep breath, and wiped the sweat from his face.

Now what?

Vape-man groaned, raised his head. Groggy, but recovering quickly.

With his knee still jammed into Vape-man's back, Kaine ripped the knotted drawstring from the hoodie, and used it to tie the man's wrists together behind his back. Kaine stood.

Vape-man groaned again. Swore. Tried to roll onto his side. Kaine raised a foot and pressed it down on Vape-man's shoulder, driving it into the road. Vape-man stopped struggling.

A spontaneous round of applause erupted from behind Kaine. He spun to face what had become a small crowd of drivers who'd climbed from their vehicles to watch the action. The cars in the oncoming lane had finally stopped, the drivers' curiosity overpowering their need to reach their destinations.

"Bloody hell!" one man said, his stunned voice carrying on the momentary stillness. "Never seen nothing like that."

A woman—long, dark hair whipped around her head by the wind—looked on, mouth agape. Silent.

Beside her, two smiling, giggling youngsters held up their mobile phones, filming the action. For what? To show their friends down the pub?

Some people.

A wide-shouldered man climbed from a Fiat Punto and hurried forwards.

"Excuse me ... Officer?"

"Officer?" Kaine paused, then shook his head to clear the momentary brain fog. "Oh, yes. Right."

"Are you okay?"

Kaine smiled and added a cheery nod. "Yes, thanks."

"That was so ... so ..." The man gulped. "I don't know."

"Stupid?" Kaine suggested.

The grey-haired man nodded. "I was going to say brave, but stupid will do. In fact, stupid's probably better. Unarmed and facing a madman with a machete ... not the smartest move I've ever seen."

"My blood was up," Kaine said, shrugging and tilting his head to one side.

Not much of an explanation, but it was all he had to offer, and true enough. He'd seen red and almost lost control. Almost.

"Are all police officers trained to do that?"

"What? Sorry, no. I doubt it very much." Kaine shrugged again. "But then again, I wouldn't know. I'm not really a police officer."

"But you said—"

"Sorry. I lied," Kaine said, adding what he intended to be an apologetic smile.

The man tucked in his chin and frowned in confusion. "Why?"

"It was the only way I could think of to make him give up the zombie knife."

The grey-haired man arched an eyebrow.

"Didn't work, though. Did it."

Kaine sighed. "No, not really."

Vape-man squirmed and raised his head from the tarmac.

"Get the fuck off me, you bastard!" He kicked out, and struck nothing but empty air.

Kaine added more weight to his foot, grinding Vape-man's popped shoulder hard into the road. Vape-man howled.

"Mind giving me a hand?" he asked the Fiat driver.

"Not at all. What d'you need?"

"I need to restrain this fool before he hurts himself—or attacks someone else."

Kaine bent and hooked his hand under Vape-man's right armpit—his damaged armpit. Vape-man whimpered and stiffened. The Fiat driver did the same on the other armpit. Together, they dragged the groaning Vape-man to the back of the M3.

"Hold him still for me, would you?"

"Happy to."

The Fiat driver grabbed Vape-man by the scruff of the neck, and forced the struggling man's head into his knees, using the whole of his imposing bodyweight. Kaine smiled, impressed by the man's enthusiasm and his technique, and ripped the hoodie's second drawstring—the one at the waist —free. He used it to secure Vape-man's tethered wrists to the M3's towbar.

"You can let him go now, mate," Kaine said.

"You sure?"

"Yes thanks. He's going nowhere."

The Fiat driver leaned heavily on Vape-man's head to push himself to his feet. He bent, wiped his hands on the back of Vape-man's dirt-and-gravel-covered hoodie. Then he turned towards Kaine.

"I'm Jack," he said, pushing out his right hand. "Jack Hargreaves."

"Hi, Jack," Kaine said, grasping the hand and pumping hard. "Thanks for your help."

Kaine released his hold, retrieved the zombie knife from beneath the tyre, and placed it on the M3's roof, taking care not to scratch the pristine paintwork. No one could accuse Ryan Kaine of wanton vandalism.

Vape-man screamed a curse and kicked out, narrowly missing Hargreaves' shins. Kaine stepped out of range, beckoning Hargreaves to follow.

"Alan Thompson," Kaine said, picking a name out of the ether. "By the way, thanks for pulling over back there and letting me through."

Hargreaves tilted his head. "It looked like you were in a hurry, and I wasn't. So why not? Mind if I ask you a question?"

Kaine shot him a thin smile. "No, please do."

"Why were you chasing him? Road rage, is it?"

"Pretty much, but not on my part," he said. "That arse-hole"—he nodded towards the still-raging, but properly secured man—"cut across two lanes of traffic on the M1. Caused a multi-vehicle pileup. I saw it all. Nearly came a cropper, too. Thought I'd try to catch him."

Hargreaves nodded his understanding. "I called the police while you were, you know, dealing with your man. They're on their way. Be here soon, I imagine."

Kaine pulled in a few deep breaths, trying to pay back some of the oxygen debt he'd generated during the fight.

"I like what you did with Vape-man's head. Made it easy for me to tie the knots."

Hargreaves tilted his head and sniffed. "I learned a thing or two in the Gunners."

"You were a footballer?" Kaine asked, eyes-wide, acting the fool.

"Don't give me that," Hargreaves said. His face crinkled into a scowl. "You know what I mean."

Kaine smiled. "Royal Artillery."

"That's right." Hargreaves said. "Sergeant in the Gunners until a few years back. Retired on a full pension. You served, too?"

Kaine dipped his head at the old soldier.

"Royal Marines," he said, lowering his voice.

Finally, the truth. Jack Hargreaves deserved that much— and no more.

Hargreaves threw in another nod and added a knowing smile.

"Thought as much," he said. "The way you carried yourself had 'bootie' written all over it. Maybe even *special forces*?" He whispered the last two words.

Kaine winced and glanced over Hargreaves' shoulder at the earwigging audience. The last thing he wanted was to hang around gassing while the police raced towards them on blues and twos.

Hargreaves frowned and lowered his head. As a fellow military man, he knew the rules. Special forces operatives kept their identities secret.

"Listen, Jack," Kaine said, leaning closer and lowering his voice even further. "I'd rather not be here when the police arrive." He scratched his beard. "It could prove a little awkward."

"Why? If what you say is true, you were well within your rights to make a citizen's arrest. Nobody would argue you were in fear of your life."

"Yes," Kaine said, "but the police will tie me up for hours. I'm already late for … my sister's wedding."

"Really," Hargreaves said, curling his upper lip and turning it into a smile. Not believing a word of it.

"Yes, really. Kate's going to kill me if I'm late. I'm giving her away. She's expecting me to be in Newport Pagnell by two o'clock." He pointed towards the road sign and its double roundabout pictogram. "I don't suppose you could do me a favour?" He lowered his chin, then shook his head. "No, no. It's too much to ask."

Hargreaves dropped his smile.

"I'm not about to lie to the police," he said. "Not even for a … a bootie."

Kaine pressed his right hand over his chest. "Wouldn't ask you to, Sergeant. Wouldn't dream of it. Just tell them exactly what I told you. No more, no less. You can even give them my car's licence number if you can remember it."

Hargreaves pursed his lips.

"I reckon I can do that," he said, nodding slowly.

"And tell them I promised to call them and make a statement after the wedding."

"I can do that, too. After all, I'm hardly in a position to stop you, am I?"

Kaine reached across and clapped the former Royal Artillery sergeant on his shoulder.

"Thanks, Jack. I appreciate it," he said and added a smile, "as will Kate."

A twinkle reached Hargreaves' eyes. "Oh I'm sure she will. Give her my regards."

"Thanks, Sergeant. Mind how you go, now."

"How do you plan to get out?" Hargreaves asked, pointing to the M3 and the tailback of stopped traffic blocking the right-hand lane. "Want me to clear a path?"

Kaine nodded. "If you could."

Hargreaves jerked up his chin. "Leave it with me, Bootie."

He brushed past Kaine and headed towards the leading stopped vehicle—a small panel van.

"C'mon man," Hargreaves shouted, waving the van driver forwards with all the authority of a man who'd spent his whole adult life issuing orders and having them obeyed. "Nothing more to see here. Move along."

The van driver flicked a hand at him, engaged first gear, and crawled away. The second vehicle in the queue, a dirt-encrusted Kia, followed the van, as did the Citroën C5 behind it.

Kaine raced to his Range Rover, dived in, and pulled the door shut. He fired up the engine, indicated right, and nudged forwards.

Risking life and limb, Jack Hargreaves stepped out into the active lane and threw up his right arm to stop an oncoming DAF truck. Air brakes whooshed, the front of the cab dropped, shuddered, returned to the horizontal, and stopped no more than three metres in front of Hargreaves.

Bloody hell. That was close.

The narrow gap between the DAF and the M3 looked tight, but would be wide enough if Kaine sucked in his breath.

Kaine nudged the Range Rover forwards, nodded his thanks to Hargreaves as he rolled past, and—breath held tight—nosed into the crack between truck and sports car. Once through, he nipped into the empty lane and trundled away. Ignoring the red light, he skirted past the roadworks, heading towards the double roundabout and the road to Bedford.

In his rear-view mirror, Jack Hargreaves raised his arm again and smiled while the people grouped around him looked on in puzzlement. The two youngsters with the raised mobile phones kept filming. They'd have plenty of footage to show their mates down the pub—and maybe even the police.

Not to worry.

He'd be miles away by the time the police had a chance to arrive and work their way through the witness statements.

In the distance, the ululating wail of sirens marked the approach of the emergency services.

Kaine approached the first roundabout at a gentle forty-five mph, took the third exit to Bedford, and slowly increased his speed.

━━━

FOUR FAST MILES LATER, Kaine pulled into a lay-by and climbed from the Range Rover. The slipstream tugged at his hair and his clothes as traffic roared past on the A422, Newport Road. He walked to the back, raised the tailgate, and removed the two magnetic licence plates he'd brought along for emergencies. He retraced his steps around the SUV, casually covering old plates with new along the way. The new plates registered the car to a breakdown service in Coventry, which would confuse the people operating ANPR cameras, giving Kaine time to reach London without having to find a clean vehicle. It paid to be prepped for all eventualities—even angry Vape-men armed with zombie knives.

Housekeeping completed and back behind the steering wheel in his comfortable, leather seat, Kaine pressed the phone button and asked for Whiskey One. Will accepted the call quickly.

"Hi, Will," Kaine said cheerily. "I'm going to have to revise my ETA, I'm afraid."

"Traffic?"

"Pretty much." Kaine winced. "The M1's a nightmare. I had to take a bit of a detour. I won't be with you for"—he read the revised numbers on the infotainment screen's GPS —"another couple of hours."

"Not a problem."

"How's the DIY coming along?"

"Getting there, mate. See you when I see you. Don't go breaking any speed limits."

"I won't."

Kaine smiled, fired up the Range Rover, and pulled into a surprisingly empty carriageway.

Chapter 8

Monday 7th June - Gregory Enderby

Sandbrook Tower, Soho, London, England

Enderby stared blankly at the Kaine file, reading the same paragraph over and over, unable to concentrate long enough to make anything of the words swimming on the screen. Had he covered his tracks well enough? The last thing he needed was for the evil bugger to learn about the Grey Notice and Enderby's part in its creation. Christ knew what the man would do. He'd target Enderby for sure. Enderby swallowed hard. He needed to keep his eyes peeled and his guard all the way up. Not that he ever allowed his guard to fall. Not a chance of that ever happening. Better chance of West Ham winning the premiership next season —not without spending millions on a whole new squad, and that wasn't on the cards with the state of their bank balance. Enderby had more money salted away than the Hammers.

He closed the file on his computer, sat back, and swivelled his chair to face the unappealing view. The dull, red-brick wall stared back at him, as depressing and mute as ever.

Where are you hiding, Kaine? Who are you coming for next? How the fuck am I going to kill you first?

A sharp, double rap on the office door snapped him out of his thoughts. He read the time from the clock on the computer screen. 15:00. And there she was. Bang on time, as always and as expected.

"Come in, Ms Harper," he called, switching on the smile, and dialling up the charm. "Come in."

The door opened and the timid but pretty, little creature, Claire Harper, stood in the doorway. Business-like in her grey twinset and below-the-knee skirt, clutching a buff-coloured folder to her chest—her large but hidden chest. A twinset, for pity's sake! Such a change of style from the temptingly dressed woman who attended her interview. How long ago was that? Three months? Four? How things could change in so short a time.

A severe fringe cut into shoulder-length hair did absolutely nothing for her. What on earth was the woman thinking? Twenty-nine years old and decked out like a grandmother. What a waste of a perfectly decent bod. So different from her early days. If she'd looked so daggy early on, he'd never have showed any interest in her. He'd never have tried it on. And as for the time in the lift. Bugger it. All he'd done was admire her silk blouse. He loved the way it clung to her skin. Translucent. Delightful. He didn't tell her that part, though. That would have been a highly inappropriate way for a superior to talk to a junior member of staff.

Not Enderby's style. Not in the slightest. He used much more subtlety than that. After all, he wouldn't wish to suffer the consequences of indiscrete actions. Not again.

"Good afternoon, Mr Enderby," she said, prim and proper with her clipped, northern accent. She entered, leaving the door wide open and his office in full view of the corridor.

Bloody woman.

She knew he preferred it closed when he had visitors.

"Good afternoon, Ms Harper. Please, take a seat." Enderby opened his hand and waved it at the visitor's chairs.

"No, thank you, sir. I'd rather stand."

Of course you would, bitch. Suit yourself. No skin off my nose.

Her free hand reached up to clutch the gold chain hanging around her throat, fingers searching for the tiny, gold cross that usually hung from it and occasionally glinted under the office strip lights. Her single piece of jewellery. These days, the bloody woman didn't even wear earrings.

"What's wrong, Ms Harper? Did you lose your cross?"

"Er, no, sir," she said, avoiding eye contact. "It sometimes works its way up the chain."

"Would you like to take a moment to find it?"

"No, sir," she said, looking over his head. "It's fine. Thank you."

Oh dear, what an ungrateful cow.

And he was being so helpful. So friendly. Clearly, his charms were wasted on her. Why bother?

"So, Ms Harper, what do you have for me?"

He held out his hand for the folder she clutched so tight to her chest. How could a woman with such little poise and confidence be so good at her job? A rapier mind that missed little, he could set her any desk-based investigation and she'd ace it. On the other hand, ask her to perform a simple job that involved personal interaction, and she'd melt into a puddle of her own sweat.

Ah well. Horses for courses.

Others could handle the face-to-face stuff. The physical activities.

"It's the report on Abdul Hosseini you asked for, sir."

Without stepping closer, she stretched out and dropped the folder on the desk, still refusing to look him in the eye.

Enderby took the heavy file, placed it on the desk in front of him, and squared up the edge. He left it closed.

"Management summary, please. Is he clean?"

Harper released the gold chain and clasped her hands together, holding them at the height of her midriff. A defensive posture. So timid. Crying shame in a good-looking woman with so much potential.

"Yes, sir. I think so. I couldn't find anything that warranted us continuing the investigation."

"You're certain?"

"As certain as I can be, Commander."

"So, Hosseini is clean?"

"Yes, sir. According to the surveillance reports, Mr Hosseini hasn't met anyone outside his immediate circle of friends, all of whom have been thoroughly vetted. Apart from the occasional shopping trips, he rarely leaves his bedsit. His only other outside interests involve his mosque and the local food bank."

"He visits a food bank, you say?"

"Yes, Commander." She dipped her head in a stiff nod. "As both a volunteer and a client."

"The same food bank as the one used by Hamid Ansari?"

"No, sir. I did check."

He graced her with another warm smile. "But you don't think it interesting that two of our subjects visit food banks? It's nothing more than a coincidence, you feel?"

"Given that neither men are permitted to work while their asylum claim is being assessed, using a food bank would hardly be unexpected, sir."

Did she just sneer at him?

No, probably not. She wouldn't dare. A trick of the light.

Enderby opened the folder and rested a hand on the paperwork inside.

"Okay, Ms Harper. Leave this with me for now. I'll review your notes and make my recommendations to the Home Office in due course."

"Yes, sir."

"Carry on. And thank you for your input. Most impressive."

"Thank you, sir." She rushed from the room as though reacting to a starter's pistol and finally closed the door behind her.

Fucking woman.

For fuck's sake. All he did was compliment her on her silk blouse, and maybe stand too close a few times. Perhaps he did accidentally brush up against her once or twice. Nothing more than that, and all completely innocent. He was only being friendly, welcoming a new member of staff like any decent superior. Any decent boss would do the same thing.

Enderby closed the Hosseini file and set it to one side. It could occupy his in-tray for a while, along with all the others. Bloody immigrant riffraff could damn well wait. No skin off Enderby's nose if they suffered as a consequence. Damn people with their hard-luck stories, sniffing around, waiting for a handout. Insufferable creatures. Let them wait.

His desk phone's intermittent buzzing indicated an external call. Enderby let it ring five times before leaning forwards and hitting the speaker button, leaving the handset in its cradle.

"Enderby," he said, aiming for cool and efficient, but probably coming across as officious. Not that it mattered. Enderby didn't give a damn.

"Commander, it's me, Guy Gordon." He sounded rushed, breathless.

Fuck's sake. What's he doing?

"Hello, Guy," Enderby said, leaning forwards in his chair. "I've been expecting your call. How are you, old man?" He forced himself to sound friendly.

"I tried calling you earlier," Gordon announced, "but I couldn't get through on your … mobile. You haven't changed your number by any chance?"

"Ah, yes," Enderby said, wincing. "Sorry about that. The old one died on me. Dodgy battery. I forgot to let you know."

After the nightmare with the Strachan woman, he'd crushed the old burner and had yet to broadcast the replacement number to his selected contacts. No wonder Gordon had called on the land line.

"Still," Enderby continued. "You managed to call me … at the office." He paused to emphasise the point to the often-thoughtless Gordon. He was prone to blurt out proprietary information that Enderby didn't necessarily want to end up being recorded for posterity.

"I'm … returning your call," Gordon said, being only slightly evasive. "How can I help?"

You can't. Not on the bloody office line. Moron.

"It's nothing, Guy. I just wanted to find out how you were doing, old friend."

"I ... er, well," Gordon stuttered, having difficulty forming his words. "I've lost a few members of staff recently."

"Natural wastage?"

Now tell me something I didn't know.

"In a manner of speaking. I'm having to recruit."

"Oh dear," Enderby said. "I imagine recruitment's a struggle in your industry. To find people with the right qualifications, I mean."

"You wouldn't believe it, Greg."

Oh, I would.

"Following the untimely and unfortunate demise of John Abbott," Enderby continued, "I wouldn't be surprised if you'd find some T5S staff on the job market in the next few weeks. You might be able to attract some of them at a budget rate. Consider it a business development opportunity."

"I do, and I've already put out a number of feelers," Gordon said. "However, with GG Cleaning Systems' strong client base and thriving business portfolio, we will need to act swiftly if we are to take advantage of new opportunities."

Enderby smiled.

The man couldn't help himself. Despite the recent losses —six dead staff members including Will Stacy and the Reilly woman—Gordon still had the absolute gall to pitch for more work. And pitch for it on the bloody landline.

"That's the spirit, Guy. It always pays to look on the positive side," Enderby said, trying not to clench his jaw.

"I trust we can count on your support moving forwards, Commander?" Gordon asked.

The brass neck of the man. As though Enderby could show an obvious bias in favour of one particular private company. It simply wasn't done. At least, not officially.

"You can't expect me to answer that question, Guy. However, you *can* rest assured that the agency will look even-handedly on *any* bid that meets the five core principles of public procurement."

Enderby allowed his smile to broaden. He loved the sound of pomposity in the afternoon.

"That," Gordon said after a brief pause, "is all I can hope for, Commander. As you know, GG Cleaning Systems prides itself on offering a premium service coupled with great value for money."

Bullshit.

"Indeed," Enderby said, refusing to go beyond the limits of propriety.

"Might I ask if there are any contracts in the pipeline?" Gordon asked.

"You can ask, Mr Gordon. However, all I am able to tell you is that the agency *may* be about to issue an invitation to bid on a packet of work that is absolutely vital to the nation's security." Enderby allowed the information to dangle for a moment before adding, "Forgive me, but I've already said more than I should have. I can add no more. You will have to keep your eye on the on-line procurement notices. Just like all the other preferred contractors."

"Of course, Commander. Thank you," Gordon said, with a lightness to his voice that hadn't been there earlier. "I'll let my people know to do that."

"Good, good. Very good," Enderby said. "Now, on a more personal matter, what are you doing this evening?"

"This evening?"

"Yes, this evening. It's been quite some time since we got together socially. Are you free?"

Come on, Gordon. Take the bait.

"Well," Gordon said, drawing out the single word. "Truth be told, there's nothing pressing that I can't postpone."

"Excellent. Let's meet at my gym. Tonight. Seven o'clock sharp. I'll sign you in as a guest. Come ready to spar."

"Ready to spar?" Gordon said, sounding alarmed. "Boxing, you mean?"

"The noble art. Why ever not?"

"But," Gordon gasped, "I haven't sparred in … forever."

"Nonsense. According to your website profile, you spend two hours in the gym most days training for your MMA bouts."

As if!

"That's pure hype and you know it, Greg. I haven't been able to train properly since damaging my knee a few years back."

Your damaged knee, right. Not since stuffing so many puddings into your fat face, more like.

"Never mind that," Enderby said, laughing. "I'll go easy on you. It'll be a great way for you to blow off some steam, and I'll treat you to a meal afterwards. The club does a wonderful line in vegan salads. What do you say?"

"Er, right. Okay. That sounds … lovely. See you at seven."

"Brilliant. I'll be looking forward to it. But mark my words, we won't be discussing business matters. Oh no. That would be out of the question."

"Of course not, Greg," Gordon said, a smile in his voice. "That would be unethical."

"Cheerio, Guy."

Enderby leaned forwards, hit the disconnect button, and could not help smiling.

That's the way to do it, Greg.

He'd dangled the promise of a lucrative packet of work in front of Gordon and would let him stew on it for the rest of the afternoon. By the time he landed the bombshell, Gordon would be far too desperate to refuse.

Yes. He'd played it perfectly.

As to the Kaine issue. That could bloody well wait. With the Grey Notice still in place, the matter would work itself out eventually. In the meantime, he'd concentrate on other things. Things such as career development. Enderby's career development.

Enderby found himself smiling at the window and the uninspiring view through it.

Chapter 9

Sandbrook Tower, Soho, London, England

In the corridor outside Enderby's office, Claire Harper peeled her ear away from the door panel. Breathing slightly easier, she hurried towards the stairwell and the lifts. She'd been standing in the open corridor way too long.

Loitering outside her line manager's door, eavesdropping, had constituted a monumental risk. If caught, she'd have faced so many awkward questions, maybe even summary dismissal. Standing near his door, trying to look innocent, she'd nearly wet herself every time the lift bell rang, or footsteps clattered in the stairwell behind the fire doors, but she'd held her nerve.

Worm, the sleazebag, was up to something dodgy. His

phone call with Guy Gordon couldn't have sounded any more suspicious if it tried. No way should Worm be fraternising with a public contractor. And as for the reference to John Abbott's death … it sent warning bells ringing through Claire's head.

She reached the bank of lifts without passing anyone in the corridor, pressed the down button, and paced the tiled floor while she waited. She kept her eyes peeled and her ears open for approaching worm-shaped figures.

Your word against mine, is it?

At the start, his interest had seemed innocent, friendly even, but after weeks of sly looks, inappropriate comments, and standing too close, he'd caught her alone in the lift. He'd forced her up against the wall and groped her. He'd squeezed her breasts hard, but not hard enough to leave bruises. No proof. Bastard. Worm saw her as prey. A target. Well, no chance, buddy. Not Claire Harper. She'd be damned if she'd fall victim to sexual harassment again. Workplace bullying. Not her. Not again.

Your word against mine, be damned.

Claire would wait and she would watch until he did something she could use against him.

Her three-month probationary assessment had been lukewarm at best. Worm had watered down her line manager's high praise just enough to hold her back, but not to have her dismissed or transferred out of her job. No, that would have given rise to too many questions. Claire might have been able to defend herself, argue a case against constructive dismissal. After all, before joining the NCTA, she'd received nothing but glowing performance reports from every one of her previous line managers. In fact, her star quality had been one of the prime reasons for her sideways promotion to the NCTA in the first place.

Ever since the final incident in the lift, Enderby had given her every grunt job going, holding back any chance of her being able to shine. But she wasn't about to hand in her notice or ask for a transfer. She'd worked too long and too hard to start again with a black mark on her record. Six long years. Three as an admin officer, three more as an executive officer, and then she'd been "cherry picked" by the agency. At the interview, they'd more or less assured her fast progression up the pay grades. Higher executive officer within two years, and senior executive officer within five more. After that? No promises, but a move to director level wouldn't be out of the question.

That was before the lacklustre performance review. Fat chance of rapid promotion now.

Well, damn you, Worm. Damn you.

Claire would find a way to survive and thrive. She would find a way to pay the creep back for making her wear such daggy clothes at work. Clothes that made her look like a grandmother. And as for the God-awful fringe …

Don't go there, Claire. Your time will come.

The light above the lift lit up and an electronic bell chimed its warning. Five seconds later the metal doors slid apart to reveal an empty cube. Before entering, Claire checked the corridor in each direction.

Once bitten.

Inside, she hit the button for her floor and the "close door" button and held her breath for the seven seconds it took the bloody doors to move. It would take Enderby less time than that to reach the lift from his office, should he choose to do so.

The brushed-metal doors slid together, and Claire breathed again. What bloody right did Enderby have to make her worry about entering a lift unaccompanied? What bloody right did he have to make her feel the need to carry a one-hundred-and-forty-decibel personal alarm to the office?

Ignorant pig.

She released her hold on the alarm and pulled her hand from her pocket.

Moments later, the lift dinged to announce the imminent arrival at her floor. The carriage slowed to a stop, and the doors retracted again. Claire stepped out into her open-plan office where fifteen souls—eleven men and four women —toiled throughout the working day. None of the other women felt the need to carry personal alarms. Claire knew. Without reference to Worm, and in the strictest confidence, she'd asked them all in turn.

Claire nodded to Barry, the fifty-something, only openly gay man in the department. He always acknowledged her when she entered the office. A nice, quiet chap who lived in the suburbs with his husband of ten years and grew prize-winning orchids. He rarely missed an opportunity to show her photos of his gorgeous and delicate blooms.

She strode to the acoustic-panelled cubicle that passed as her office and collapsed into her chair, surprised at how exhausted the clandestine activities had made her. She would never have succeeded as a spy. Claire reached out for her flask and drank. The lemon and lime mixture refreshed her dry mouth and helped her recover from the stress of eavesdropping.

She replaced the flask in its designated niche and nudged the mouse. Her desktop woke to the page she'd left it on—the management summary of the Hosseini file. An innocent man held in limbo by a system that didn't give a damn, and kept there by a man who cared even less.

Claire sighed. She'd done her best. Hosseini's fate now

rested in the hands of Enderby, a sexual predator, a sexist pig, and maybe even something more sinister.

Sitting at her desk, Claire reviewed the little she'd been able to overhear through the man's office door. He and Guy Gordon had mentioned John Abbott's "untimely and unfortunate demise". Claire knew exactly who and what they'd been talking about. The gun battle at Abbott's home had been all over the media for days. Even in such violent times, a gunfight in the quiet Cambridgeshire countryside—a gunfight resulting in multiple deaths and leaving a solitary survivor—rated huge media interest. And how had Worm and Gordon reacted? Rather than lament Abbott's sad loss, they'd seen it as nothing more than a business opportunity.

The cold-hearted, evil … bastards.

Claire pulled her keyboard closer, opened the internet browser, and typed, "John Abbott and gun battle", and stopped before hitting return.

Idiot. What are you doing?

The spy bots in the operating system monitored all the searches as standard operating protocol.

Big Brother is watching.

She raised her index finger one centimetre, held down the backspace key, and watched the search string disappear. Claire smiled. How much easier her life would be if she could do the same thing and erase Worm from existence.

What about the CCTV?

She swivelled her chair and casually looked up at the nearest camera in the ceiling. Its lens had swung on its maximum rotation and pointed towards the lifts, not towards her desk.

Oh dear, Claire. Paranoid much?

Claire shuddered, grabbed her handbag, and stood. She needed a break. Time to think without the worry of being watched. The loo. Sanctuary. No government agency could get away with installing surveillance cameras in the rest rooms, not even the NCTA. She retraced her steps to the office entrance.

As she reached his desk, Barry swivelled his chair and glanced up at her.

"Are you okay, dear?" he asked, concern written all over his kindly and expressive face. "You look a little peaky."

"Upset tummy," she lied, adding a slight grimace.

"Women's problems?" he whispered, glancing around to make sure they weren't being overheard.

She nodded, hoping that would be an end to it.

"I understand, dear. Sorry," Barry said and flapped a hand in the air between them, "I really shouldn't detain you."

"Won't be long," Claire said and continued on her way to the ladies.

Inside the plain but sanitary rest room, she confirmed that all three stalls were empty before entering the one furthest from the door. She worked the lock and sat on the lowered seat, placing the handbag on her lap. Only then did she remove her mobile and access the internet browser. She typed "John Abbott and T5S" into the search box and hit enter. The search found an obit that confirmed that Abbott had died in a gun battle at his home a couple of weekends back. She read the details.

John M Abbott, a fifty-three-year-old, former army officer, unmarried. He'd formed Target 5 Security a decade ago. T5S had won their first high-profile security contract for SAMS the same year and had gone from strength to strength. The obit's photo showed a handsome, strong-jawed man with dark hair and eyes, that looked straight at the camera with supreme confidence. An old photo of

Abbot as a much younger man. The bio neatly glossed over T5S' financial troubles following Malcolm Sampson's fall from grace and the near bankruptcy of SAMS.

Claire closed her browser, opened the news app, and searched "Cambridgeshire Gun Battle". She skimmed through the most recent articles but learned nothing new. The reports contained little but rumour, speculation, and a hundred unanswered questions.

After fifteen minutes' fruitless searching, Claire lowered the phone and stared at the back of the stall door, asking herself the same unanswerable questions. Who killed Abbott and why? Did Worm and Guy Gordon have anything to do with it?

Don't be ridiculous.

But she wasn't being ridiculous. She couldn't put anything past Worm. If he saw a way to benefit from the demise of a government contractor—to promote another perhaps, and one in his pocket—he wouldn't hesitate. And given the way Guy Gordon reacted during the phone call, he wouldn't hesitate either.

Crap. You're sounding like a conspiracy theorist.

Claire couldn't discount the idea that her hatred of Worm biased her against anyone he talked to, and anyone he called a friend. And without evidence, she definitely couldn't go voicing her suspicions to anyone. She was swimming in murky waters. Perhaps she should leave well alone.

Or, perhaps not.

If Worm *was* doing something underhanded or illegal— and at the very least, his relationship with Guy Gordon reeked of collusion—finding proof and dropping an anonymous line to the police would do Claire's position no harm at all. She would be able to remove Worm from her life without resorting to the risk of an employment tribunal.

Finding proof might be difficult, but at least she knew where Worm and Gordon would be that evening at seven o'clock. She could start there and see where her investigations led.

She stood, flushed the toilet for show, and exited the stall.

As she pushed through the main door, she almost walked straight into Alison Holt.

Claire jumped back, startled.

"Oh, you nearly gave me a Connery," Alison said, throwing a hand up to her mouth.

"Sorry," Claire said. "Miles away."

"Don't look so upset, girl. I'm only kidding." Alison opened her hand and pressed it firmly to her enormous chest. "I've just had my annual medical. My heart's as strong as an ox."

Claire took another pace backwards, into the toilet, and turned sideways to allow Alison room to pass.

"Are you okay, love? You look as though you've seen a—"

"Yes, yes. I'm fine. Honest. Upset stomach. Must have eaten something that disagreed with me."

Alison pushed fully into the rest room, shepherding Claire inside with her. She made sure the door had closed properly before turning to face her, concerned showing on her round face.

"I get that all the time, love. Never could resist a fancy pastry, as you might be able to tell by my waistline." She smiled.

Claire opened her mouth to protest but Alison interrupted.

"No. Don't bother with the platitudes. I have no delusions. I'm heavy and I'm resigned to it. You're not …?"

"Not what?"

"In the family way?"

Claire shook her head firmly. "No. Definitely not."

No chance of that happening any time soon.

She didn't even have a boyfriend.

"Okay, just making sure. In that case ... here, just a moment." She dug a hand inside her handbag, pulled out a packet of pills, and held them up. "Antacid tabs, love. Best on the market. I swear by them."

"Thanks," Claire said.

Alison popped two tablets from their blister bubbles and dropped them into Claire's open hand.

"Take both and drink plenty of water. You'll be right as rain in no time."

"I'll take them at my desk, with my drink. Thanks ever so much."

"It's nothing, love. Us girls have to stick together, right?"

"Right."

Claire smiled as enthusiastically as she could and turned away, delighted to exit the sanitised rest room.

Back at her desk, she dropped the tablets into her bin, covered them with a crushed sheet of scrap paper, and took another drink from her flask.

She added what she'd learned about Worm to the database growing in her head. Information was power and the new data would help her find a way to exact revenge on the evil slime bag.

The road to payback started at seven o'clock that evening.

For the second time that day, Claire Harper smiled.

Chapter 10

Sandbrook Tower, Soho, London, England

Enderby stared at the unopened and unactioned Hosseini file and shook his head. He'd tried to concentrate on finessing his proposition to Gordon. A difficult balancing act, he needed to pitch it just right, playing to Gordon's greed and his need in equal measure, but the Hosseini file kept drawing his attention away from the task. It kept nagging at him. Not the file itself, but the woman who created it.

The Claire Harper situation kept niggling away at him. At its worst, it had the potential to destroy everything he'd worked so hard for these past twenty-five years.

What a bloody idiot.

He should never have made the moves on her. Pissing on his own doorstep like that had been a dreadful error of judgement. That day in the lift, he'd let himself down badly. A boozy lunch had contributed to his lapse. Three large glasses of a rather nice Fluette Gamay 2013, with its silky, bright taste and cherry-and-blackberry bouquet had done it for him. The alcohol had increased his libido but decreased his self-control. He must have been out of his tiny, little mind, but the bloody woman had looked so good in her clinging, see-through, silk blouse. He should never have entered the lift with her, but her welcoming smile had sent him entirely the wrong message.

Stupid, stupid woman. Why dress that way if you're not up for it? Why send out the wrong message?

She looked up for it. Gagging for it, even.

It had been all her fault. If she hadn't smiled at him, hadn't egged him on. Damn it all to hell. How could he know she was frigid? A bloody dyke.

The bitch hadn't said anything at the time. She hadn't screamed, hadn't reacted, but the sidelong looks she kept throwing him, and the subsequent changes she'd made to her wardrobe told a tale. A sorry tale.

Ah well, water under the bridge.

He'd weathered that potential storm at sea and had spiked her guns with the slight amendments to her performance review. Should the worst happen in the future, he could explain away her accusations as spurious—an underperforming employee's spiteful reaction to a less-than-glowing report.

It wasn't as though he'd ever done anything like it before. At least not recently. No, his current record on the employee relations front could not have been more perfect. One or two past blemishes couldn't be allowed to affect his future adversely. After all, Harper was a mere executive officer, for pity's sake. Two up from the bottom rung of the ladder. Bloody woman didn't matter worth a damn.

If it came down to a contest between Enderby and Harper, there could be only one winner. He'd see to that. In any event, should Gordon agree to his proposal tonight—and why wouldn't he—the name Claire Harper might find itself appearing second on the list of stains for GG Cleaning Systems to wipe away.

Time would tell.

Enderby's heartrate increased at the thought of "owning" his own personal "cleansing operation". The heights he could achieve in the realms of sanitisation. First, Sir Ernest Hartington. Second, Claire Harper. Third, who knew? The power of initiating a deep cleanse could be such an aphrodisiac.

Such a blast.

He pulled in a deep breath and looked up. The shadow of Sandbrook Tower finally eclipsed the red bricks on the building opposite, and the wall clock clicked over to six-thirty.

That'll do. Time waits for no director of operations.

Enderby powered down his desktop computer, hefted the Hosseini file—still unopened and unactioned—and dropped it into the groaning pending tray on his desk. Hosseini could damn well wait. Enderby had better things to do than rubber stamp another towelhead's entry into the Promised Land. The gym beckoned. As did his upcoming meeting with Guy Gordon.

With so much riding on Gordon's reaction to his

proposal, he couldn't afford to keep the man waiting. Nor could he afford to treat the man with anything other than respect. He would roll out the welcome wagon and greet Gordon like a dear and cherished friend.

Ha. The very idea.

Enderby reached for the gym bag he always stored on the floor beside his chair out of sight of visitors, stood, and locked the office behind him. He marched along the corridor, swinging the bag as he went. Ignoring the open lift as usual, he strode through the swing doors and skipped down the stairs. Eight floors worth of staircase descended at a decent lick would contribute to his pre-exercise warm-up. Minimising his use of the lifts also helped to counteract an increasingly sedentary work lifestyle.

The higher he climbed the promotion ladder, the more he seemed to be tied to his desk. Still, the pros far outweighed the cons. The opportunities to pad his bank account were a definite pro. In any event, he always had the gym and the boxing ring to work out his frustrations and stave off any potential softening to his midriff.

Taking his shadow with him, Enderby negotiated the revolving door, stepped out into the evening sun, and turned left. The shadow followed, keeping her agreed ten-metre distance. Far enough away to avoid getting under Enderby's feet, but close enough to intervene if required.

The brisk, fifteen-minute march to his gym would augment the staircase warm-up and leave only a short programme of stretches to complete before the bout could begin.

⊏⊐

"YOU'RE GOING to kill him for me," Enderby whispered in Gordon's ear.

"Are you fucking serious?" Gordon gasped through his gumshield. He grabbed hold of the ropes and stared, wide-eyed, through the headguard. They'd been in the ring less than three minutes, yet the sweat leaked out of Gordon, streamed down his forehead, and ran into his eyes. More sweat dripped from the tip of his nose.

Enderby tapped Gordon's shoulder with the side of his glove, released the sweaty clinch, and backed away, holding his gloves high.

"Why not?" he asked, dancing away and adding his modified version of the Ali shuffle. Just as fast and just as slick as the self-proclaimed "greatest heavyweight champion of all time", he used the routine to impress and befuddle. It rarely failed.

During the shuffle-dance, he switched from orthodox to southpaw and back again, lightning fast. The move usually confused the hell out of his sparring partners, but was wasted on Gordon, who stood flat-footed, guard up high, exposing his sagging belly to any punch Enderby chose to throw—straight right, uppercut, hook, jab. Whatever.

Too easy. Not a fair contest. But who said life had to be fair?

He could have finished the bout in seconds, but that wasn't the object of the exercise. In the ring, they were alone. No one could overhear them.

"Why not?" Gordon echoed, gasping. "Are you … fucking mad? You want me to *kill* the … head of the NTCA?"

"Got it in one." Enderby winked, keeping his voice low.

He darted forwards, feinted left, threw a fake right jab, and ripped an uppercut under the open guard. As glove connected with jaw, he pulled the punch a fraction and danced back and away. Gordon barely had time to react. Enderby shot him as wicked a grin as he could manage with a gumshield stretching his lips.

Too damned easy.

Gordon had a full ten kilograms weight advantage over Enderby and a longer reach, but he could use neither. The man didn't have the skills, the power, or the speed to match Enderby.

Outside the professional circuit, few people did.

Enderby slid closer and allowed Gordon to pull him into yet another clinch.

"Hartington's ... protected," Gordon wheezed. "He's ... guarded day and night. Just like you are."

Enderby snorted. "If you had his schedule in advance, would it help?"

Gordon frowned, gulped in another huge breath, and nodded.

"It ... might."

Gordon released the hold and stumbled back and to the right, leaving himself open to a flurry of Enderby's best shots. A pair of lightning-fast left jabs to the face, a straight right to the gut, a left cross to the side of the head, and an uppercut to the chin. He pulled every punch but the last, which snapped Gordon's head back, and planted the big man on his fat arse.

Knockout!

Or it would have been if any of the blows had landed full force. As it was, Gordon lay on his back, trying to shake the daze from his head and the glaze from his eyes. Enderby gave him a few minutes recovery time before tapping his gloves together.

"C'mon, Guy. You're not hurt. I barely touched you."

A few seconds later, Gordon rolled onto his front and pushed off the canvas with his gloves. He stayed down, on hands and knees, gut hanging close to the canvas, chest heaving, sucking in great lungfuls of air.

Enderby sauntered across the ring, reached out, and helped Gordon to his feet. He tapped the man on his hairy shoulder and slid away.

Gordon stood, head lowered, shoulders sloped, arms hanging loose at his sides, in a sorry state.

"Keep your guard up at all times, Guy. It'll help. And don't forget to clean your gloves. I don't want you smearing canvas dust in my eyes."

Gordon grunted and wiped the front of his unused gloves on his creased and sweaty vest. He pulled in another gasp of air, snarled, and shot out a fast, snaking right cross. Enderby ducked, and the glove whistled over the top of his head.

"Nice one, Guy," Enderby said, smiling and backing further away. "A little spirit. Didn't know you had it in you."

"I told you," Gordon wheezed, "I'm ... ring rusty. Don't like ... being used as a punching bag."

Gordon lumbered to his left, sidestepped right, and snapped out a solid left jab to the head followed by a rear hook to the body. He grunted with each thrown punch, telegraphing the moves, making them easy to avoid.

"So," Enderby said, bobbing and weaving around Gordon's wild lunges, "what do you say?"

He popped out a left jab to the head and a left hook to the body. Both blows landed well, rocking Gordon back on his heels. The fat man staggered away until held up by the ropes.

"Enough!" he cried, holding up his arms and waving his gloves in front of his face. "I'm done."

He spat his gumshield into his right glove in a sure sign of surrender.

Gloves still high, guard up, Enderby prowled closer, staring Gordon deep in the eye, his breathing normal. So far, he hadn't needed to draw a breath in anger, and he'd barely broken a sweat.

"Do we have a deal?" he whispered.

Gordon broke eye contact and dipped his chin in a nod. "Don't have much choice, do I?"

Gotcha! Game, set, and match.

"None," Enderby said smiling. "Not if you want to avoid bankruptcy." He removed his gumshield and tucked it into the waistband of his boxing shorts.

"Okay," Gordon said, still gasping, "how do you … want to play it? Does it need to look like an … accident?"

Enderby shrugged. "Accident. Foul play, it doesn't matter as long as it's done soon, and I have an ironclad alibi."

"Will anyone suspect you of—"

"Unlikely, but I'm a careful man. Now, have you really had enough?"

Gordon nodded, blanched, and clapped a glove to his mouth. He turned his head and ripped out a deep, loud belch. "Think I'm … going to throw up."

Enderby stepped back. He'd only just bought his red-leather boots. The last thing he needed was for some fat tosser to puke all over the shiny things. He waved his right glove in the direction of the changing rooms, where his shadow for the evening, Winters, sat. She watched his moves, trying not to show how impressed she was with his ring work. One of the two women on the team. Ellen? Helen? Whatever. He never could be bothered to learn their first names. After a while, even the women became faceless.

Blunt instruments whose only reason to exist was to jump in front of a bullet to protect their clients.

Bodyguards. Sheesh. What a ridiculous career choice.

While he and Gordon sparred, Helen or Ellen, dressed in loose gym gear to hide her sidearm, focused on the gym's other occupants. After she'd sized up Enderby's opponent and no doubt found him wanting, she'd paid scant attention to the ring and focused on the other gym bunnies.

"Go find yourself a drink of water," Enderby said to Gordon, for once playing nice. "Ask Michael to give you a massage and put the bill on my account. You'll feel better for it, I promise. If you don't mind, I'll do a little work on the heavy bag. I need a *real* workout." He leaned forwards and lowered his voice again. "We'll work out the details of our arrangement over supper. Off you go, old man. And well done. You've made the right decision."

Gordon, all colour drained from his face, tore off the leather head guard. Breathing deep, he nodded, distinctly unsteady on his pins.

Magnanimous in victory, Enderby stepped on the middle rope and held up the top one to make it easier for Gordon to leave the ring. Groaning, the big man climbed through the opening and stepped down to the gym floor.

"I won't be long," Enderby said as Gordon hurried to the changing rooms, no doubt to hang his head over a toilet bowl.

Enderby managed to hold back a belly laugh. With Gordon's agreement, things couldn't have worked out any better.

Back in the centre of the ring, he danced back and forth, shadowboxing in front of the floor-to-ceiling mirror. He looked good doing it, but needed more. Taking five minutes to pummel the crap out of Guy Gordon had done little to satisfy Enderby's need to work off his frustrations. It had only whetted his appetite. Punching empty air helped even less.

Time for the heavy bag.

He glanced over at the corner. The three speed bags were free, but someone was hogging the heavy bag. For pity's sake, how many times had he told management to install a second. What self-respecting boxing gym only gave its members access to one heavy bag?

Enderby stopped shadowboxing and stood, hands on hips, watching a member he didn't recognise monopolising the gym's only heavy bag. Slim, short, bearded, and with shaggy, fair hair. The man wore a loose tracksuit and patted away at the leather bag, barely making it swing on its chrome chain. Although generally flat-footed, the forty-something man's punches were accurate and sharp, but ineffective. Powderpuff punches from a middle-aged man who might have been halfway decent in his prime, but the passage of time had weakened him. Probably slowed him down, too.

Enderby snorted.

Time for a little more fun.

Snapping out random air combinations, Enderby shuffle-glided towards the corner post. He used it to help him vault over the top rope and landed light on his feet before heading towards the bags. The new guy watched him through the wall mirrors, but he didn't miss a beat. He just kept patting away at the heavy leather, panting with the effort, but hardly breaking a sweat. Maybe he was one of those people who didn't sweat much.

Enderby stood behind the stranger, arms crossed and glowering, trying to make a point. At least ten centimetres taller than the vertically challenged stranger, Enderby had to look down on the man. He waited. Three minutes passed according to the clock hanging on the wall over the door to the changing rooms, and still the diminutive idiot, Shorty, didn't let up. He refused to defer to the superior athlete.

Halfway through the same combination of feather-weight head and body shots—a combination he'd repeated several times already—Shorty stopped and hugged the barely moving bag.

"Can I help you?" he asked, deep blue eyes staring up at Enderby through the mirror.

"I don't recognise you. Are you a member here?"

Shorty released the bag and turned to face him. A thin smile stretched out on a bearded face that looked vaguely familiar. Enderby studied the microfine creases around the unmarked eyes and revised the man's age down by five years. Thirty-eight, thirty-nine maybe.

Still a powderpuff though. The frame hidden inside his baggy sweatshirt would have been scrawny.

"Trial membership," Shorty said, breathing slow and even. "I'm checking out the facilities."

Enderby expanded his chest and tightened his abs. He considered pumping up his guns, but thought better of it. No need to put on too much of a show. He didn't want to terrify the poor idiot, just intimidate him a little.

"Far as I know," Enderby said, "the club doesn't offer trial memberships. And the last I heard, there was a three-year waiting list."

Shorty's smile broadened, and the creases around his eyes crinkled.

"I had my people contact the owners." He shrugged a pair of scrawny shoulders, head tilting to one side, fair hair dangling. "Money talks."

"And what do you think ... of the facilities?"

Shorty sniffed and looked around him. "Not bad. Impressive even, but the place could do with a few more heavy bags."

"Yes," Enderby said, nodding. "I keep telling them that. Will you be long?"

Shorty's bright smile faded a little. "Ten, fifteen minutes. I'm just warming up."

He raised a hand to wipe his mouth. For the first time, Enderby caught a good look at the man's gloves. Fingerless.

Interesting.

"You're into mixed martial arts?"

A frown deepened the creases cut into Shorty's brow. "Sorry?"

"Your gloves. They're used by MMA fighters."

"Are they?" He pushed out his arms and studied the gloves, turning his hands over and back again. "I borrowed them from a friend. I had no idea." The relaxed smile returned, and a twinkle flashed in his eyes.

"Are you taking the piss?"

Shorty frowned and flattened his right hand over his chest.

"Who, me?"

"Yes, you!"

"And why on earth might I want to do that? You and I have only just met."

"Are you certain? You look familiar. I'm sure I've seen you before someplace. Just can't—"

"Not possible. This is my first time in London for donkey's years. I've been … abroad."

The stranger who looked vaguely familiar swept the messy hair out of his eyes, tucked the stray lock behind his ears, and turned his back. He raised his gloves and curled his fingers into fists, preparing to throw more of his feeble punches.

Arrogant sod. How dare he turn his back?

"By the way," Shorty said, looking at Enderby through the mirror again, "I watched you in the ring with the large fellow."

"You did?" Enderby puffed out his chest once more. "What did you think?"

"I was heartily impressed."

Enderby grinned.

And why wouldn't you be.

"You really outclassed him. However …"

Shorty started to say more but shrugged, shook his head, and left the word dangling. He addressed the bag in an orthodox stance, switched to southpaw, and returned to orthodox, leading with his left, frowning as though unsure of which to choose. He threw an arcing, head-high left cross. It scraped across the front of the bag. Shorty lost balance and toppled to one side, barely moving his feet in time to stop himself falling. Covering his error, he jagged closer to the bag and rolled out a lead hook to the body. The blow connected, the bag deformed slightly and swung away.

Don't turn your back on me, you ignorant prick.

Enderby leaned in and tapped the little jerk on the shoulder. Shorty stopped weaving and throwing punches, and turned to face him.

"Oh, are you still here?" he asked.

The offensive little git.

"'However', you said," Enderby growled. "What were you going to add?"

"Oh, don't mind me," Shorty said, hitching his right shoulder and flapping the back of his left hand towards Enderby. "What do I know?"

"If you have something to say, say it."

The short man winced and shook his head.

"Nah, it's nothing. I wouldn't want to insult a man with your obvious skill set, but ... well ..." He winced and tilted his head again.

"Tell me!" Enderby snarled, leaning closer to the runt.

Shorty scratched his bearded chin, and threw his arm around the bag.

"Okay. The way I see it, you overreach with your left, especially with the lead uppercut. It leaves you unbalanced and open to a counterpunch to the body. A better sparring partner would have exploited the weakness in your defence." He released his hold on the bag, opened his hands, and held them out to the side. "Sorry, but you did ask. Now, if you don't mind, I'd like to continue my workout."

"So," Enderby snarled, "I have a weakness in my defence?"

Shorty nodded. "A small one, but it's there alright. Clear as day."

Enderby placed his feet shoulder width apart and planted his gloves on his hips. A challenge nobody could dispute ... or ignore.

"Care to try exploiting this weakness of mine?"

"What, me?"

Shorty's eyes widened and he searched the gym for what? Help? A way out? In the free weights corner the three musclemen had stopped throwing dumbbells around the place to watch the confrontation. Arman, the gym's inhouse trainer, had his back to them, adjusting a static bike for a sixty-something tub of lard with a hilarious combover.

Helen or Ellen, on an inclined bench, stopped in the middle of an abdominal crunch with double twists. She arched an eyebrow in question. Enderby shook his head and waved her back down. He didn't need her help. Not for this. She nodded and carried on with her faux exercise routine, keeping watch, but from a distance.

"Yes, you," Enderby answered.

"Oh no. We're in a different class."

Too right we are, arsehole.

"If you don't want to spar, get out of my way. I'm cooling down and want to use the heavy bag."

"The speed bags are free," Shorty suggested, nodding to his left, towards the three unused bags.

"They're no good. I need the heavy."

Shorty shook his head.

"Sorry, I haven't finished with it yet."

"Yes, you have."

Enderby took a stride closer, stepping within straight jab range.

Shorty released an exaggerated sigh and stepped aside.

"Okay, you win."

Enderby sneered. "You've finished with the bag?"

"The bag?" Shorty tilted his head to one side in confusion. "No, I mean you win. We can spar if you like. Only trouble is, I don't have a headguard, and I won't use a hire. To be honest, I don't fancy wearing something someone else has sweated into." He shivered. "I have my standards."

Enderby took the hint.

"Suits me," he said, releasing the Velcro strap under his chin and tearing off his headguard.

"We work the body only?" Shorty asked. "I don't have a gumshield, either."

Such a wimp.

"Okay, friend. Body shots only."

Shorty shrugged and held his arm out towards the ring. "After you, old sport."

Enderby punched the palm of his left glove with the right. The slap of leather on leather drew the attention of those members working out close to the ring. He stood taller, wallowing in the attention.

This'll be fun.

Chapter 11

Monday 7th June - Early Evening

Body-Ring Limited, Soho, London, England

Kaine stretched out his arm, showing Enderby the way to the ring.

"After you, old sport," he said, trying not to smile at his triumph.

After days in the planning, largely by Will, he'd finally managed to finagle his way inside Enderby's guard. Now to finesse the opportunity.

Enderby punched his gloves together, attracting the notice of the three members closest to the ring. The message spread to the rest of the gym's clientele and the majority stopped exercising to watch.

The only woman in the place, Enderby's bodyguard,

Ellen Winters, peeled herself away from the inclined bench and strode closer, ignoring her client's waved instruction to keep her distance. The professional in her probably sensed something out of the ordinary.

So much the better.

It suited Kaine's plans.

Kaine sidestepped around Enderby and climbed the three steps to the ring. He held the ropes open in exactly the same way as Enderby had done for Gordon.

Enderby shot him a superior glance, said "Thank you," and climbed through onto the canvas. The ring floor deflected slightly under his weight. Light heavyweight, bordering on cruiserweight. No matter, Kaine had faced bigger—and uglier—and he held a major advantage. He'd seen Enderby spar. It taught Kaine a great deal.

Kaine peeled off his hooded top to reveal a loose-fitting, long-sleeved shirt which hid everything—his scars, his toned body, his sinewy arms. He left the baggy tracksuit bottoms on. They wouldn't hamper his movements in any significant way.

"Would you like to warm up again?" Kaine asked, being ever so helpful. "Only, you just complained about having to stand around, getting cold."

"Yes, I would."

Kaine retreated to his corner, relaxed against the padding, and rested his elbows on the top rope.

Enderby took his place in the centre of the ring. He rolled his neck, shoulders, and head, shuffled his feet, and threw a dozen rapid-fire combinations. They looked rather impressive. He kept half an eye on Kaine to make sure his moves were being studied. By the time he'd finished posturing, the sweat shone on his shoulders and face, and he'd started blowing a little.

"Ready?" Kaine asked.

"Yes. You?" Enderby said from the middle of the ring, beckoning Kaine closer with both gloves.

"I'm ready. What d'you say? Three three-minute rounds?"

Enderby snorted. "I won't need that long."

"Humour me. I like working to a clock. It gives me focus."

Enderby tutted.

"Okay. If you insist. Three by three."

"Rest intervals of one minute?"

"Okay, okay."

Enderby closed the gap between them, leading with his left.

Kaine raised his right hand to halt the advance. Enderby grunted in frustration.

"What now?"

"Who's running the clock?"

"What?"

Kaine tapped a finger to his left wrist. "Who's timing the rounds?"

"She can." Enderby nodded towards the bodyguard. "Helen, you're up."

"It's Ellen, sir," Ellen said, her delivery cool but guarded. She'd obviously seen Enderby in action and didn't appear too impressed.

Enderby swatted her words away. "Whatever. Time the rounds, will you? Three minutes each."

"And one-minute rest breaks," Kaine said, smiling down at the heavily put-upon bodyguard.

"What about your headguards and shields?" she asked.

"We're working to the body only. No head shots allowed," Kaine said, letting his smile stretch wider.

"Fair enough," she said. "In the absence of a bell, I'll just shout 'box' at the start and 'stop boxing' at the end of each round, okay?"

"Works for me," Kaine answered. "You?"

"Yeah, yeah. It works," Enderby snapped, showing his impatience.

"Okay, Ellen," Kaine said. "Whenever you're ready, please."

Kaine backed into one of the neutral corners. Enderby held the centre of the ring.

"Box," Ellen called and slammed the flat of her hand to the canvas.

Kaine raised his guard and stepped towards his opponent. He switched from orthodox to southpaw and back again, maintaining the charade. Enderby advanced, swaying from side to side, looking for an opening. Kaine allowed him to close within range of a well-aimed jab to the ribs before sliding to the right and stepping out of the way. Enderby grunted as his jab missed by a country mile.

"Nice shot," Kaine said, sidestepping further to the right. He breathed slowly, through his nose. "Well done."

Enderby tried to close again. He reached out with his left and followed with a right cross to the jaw. Kaine jagged backwards and the cross met empty air.

"Naughty," Kaine said, wagging his right index finger towards the ceiling. "No head shots, we said."

"Sorry," Enderby gasped, blowing hard. "Forgot."

Someone in the crowd booed. Others followed. Nobody seemed to be supporting the tall, well-muscled civil servant in the tight-fitting workout vest, the three-quarter-length shorts, and the shiny, red boots.

One by one, the other gym members gathered closer to

the ring, standing in small groups, muttering quietly to each other.

Enderby closed rapidly. He threw a double left jab to the chin, a right cross to the body, and a lead hook with his left. Kaine glided to his left, and each shot missed its mark, the hook not by much.

Boos rippled around the crowd, which grew more agitated with each head shot thrown. To that point, Kaine had done nothing but rock and sway and dance and shuffle, easily avoiding the increasingly wild and angry blows. He hadn't thrown a single punch.

Enderby attacked. Kaine danced and backed away. He could have kept up the same high-intensity skirting all night. Enderby, red-faced from the exertion, breathed heavily and the sweat poured out of him.

"Stop boxing!" Ellen called and slapped the canvas.

Enderby stretched forwards and threw a raking lead cross. Kaine twisted at the waist. The shot brushed his left ear, the friction of leather on skin burned.

Too close, Kaine. Wake up, idiot.

"Stop boxing!" Ellen shouted.

The crowd echoed her call.

Enderby tapped his gloves to his ears as if to indicate he hadn't heard the first call. He turned to Ellen and shouted, "Speak up, woman."

Kaine backed away to his corner, holding the top of his stinging ear. One of the gym members, a black man with a gold ring in his right ear and a damaged nose, approached Kaine's corner. He cracked the seal on a bottle of water and held it up together with a bucket. Kaine swilled his mouth with the water and spat it into the bucket.

"Thanks," he said.

"No problem, man. Can't stand that supercilious prick.

Struts around the place like he owns it. Cock o' the walk, y'know. His bodyguards make sure we know he's protected. I'm surprised the woman's let you anywhere near him. Name's Denny."

"Hi, Denny. Pleased to meet you. Mine's Peter."

A towel appeared in Denny's hands, and he wiped Kaine's face.

"You plan on wearing that baggy shirt for the whole bout? Got to be hot in that, man."

"Pretty much. I'm shy, and it's cold in here."

"Cool, man." Denny offered his right fist, and they bumped.

"Hey, you! Shorty," Enderby called from the other side of the ring. His breathing had settled, showing a half-decent recovery rate. "Planning on running all night?"

Kaine smiled and kept his mouth shut.

"Too scared to throw a punch?" Enderby brayed, when he should have been catching his breath and saving his energy.

Nobody in the crowd offered Enderby a drink. Ellen stood back and watched.

"I thought my guard was open?" Enderby mocked. "What's wrong. Can't find a way through my defences?"

"You're waiting for him to punch himself out?" Denny whispered, hiding his mouth from Enderby.

"Something like that," Kaine answered.

Something like that.

"The way he's blowing, it won't take long," Denny said, tapping Kaine's shoulder.

Kaine double hitched his eyebrows and smiled.

Halfway through the first round, the doors to the changing room had opened and Guy Gordon, wearing one of the gym's monogrammed dressing gowns, stood in the opening, studying the proceedings. Kaine couldn't read the expression fixed to his reddened and bloated face, but the man didn't seem inclined to offer any vocal support to his friend. Assuming he and Enderby *were* friends.

"Ten seconds," Ellen called.

Enderby punched his gloves together and strode into the centre of the ring. "C'mon, Shorty. Time to hit the canvas."

Round two turned into a rinse and repeat of the first. Enderby attacked, throwing rapid combinations to the body and head. Each failed headshot received the full-throated condemnation of the spectators. Kaine backtracked, kept out of range, and avoided every blow. As the round progressed, Enderby's blows became less frequent and grew increasingly wild, flailing, and less convincing.

"Stop boxing!" Ellen yelled.

Enderby, breathless and wheezing, his shoulders sloped, dropped his guard and returned to his corner without throwing another after-round flurry. Kaine pulled in a deep and satisfying breath and backed into his corner, keeping his eye on his opponent and his guard raised. He wouldn't trust Enderby to behave himself if the man's life depended on it.

Again, Denny offered him the bottle and bucket. This time, Kaine sipped the water and swallowed a little before swilling and spitting.

"You know," Denny whispered, "if this fight was being judged, you'd be losing on points. Although he hasn't laid a glove on you, he's doing all the attacking, and you haven't thrown a single punch."

"I know." Kaine threw Denny another wink.

"You gonna end it now?"

"Haven't decided yet."

Denny nodded towards the opposite corner. Someone had taken pity on Enderby and handed him a bottle of water. He'd downed half the bottle in one slurp, dribbling a rivulet down the front of his muscle vest.

"He ain't taunting you this time, my friend," Denny snorted.

"Doesn't have the spare energy."

Ellen extended her arm under the bottom rope and slapped the canvas.

"Ten seconds," she called.

Kaine met Enderby in the middle and held out his gloves for Enderby to touch. The man slapped them away.

"That's the first time you've raised your gloves," he gasped. "You going to keep running all night?"

"Throw another headshot and I'll be really miffed," Kaine said, keeping his voice so low only Enderby could hear it.

"Bite me."

Ellen slapped the canvas again.

"Box!"

Enderby leaned in and threw a lead hook to the body and followed it with a right cross to the chin.

Kaine ducked inside the cross and threw an uppercut to the chest—with the knuckle of his middle finger extended. The blow sneaked under Enderby's non-existent defence and drove into his midriff, below the sternum. Enderby grunted, the air rushed from his lungs, and he collapsed to his knees. Dazed, gasping for breath, his arms dropped to hug his chest, leaving his head unprotected.

The crowd fell silent.

Kaine stepped close, whirled his right arm in three wide, anticlockwise circles, winding up for a stunning blow, before tapping Enderby on the nose with his left index finger. Enderby folded, curled into a tight ball, and his forehead touched the canvas.

The ten-man crowd groaned.

One shouted, "Finish him!"

Another called, "What are you waiting for?"

"Bloody hell," a third said to his mate, "did you see that? One punch. One single punch."

"Bugger deserved it. Big-headed prick," his mate replied.

"Is he alright, d'you think?"

"Who the fuck cares?"

"Should we call an ambulance?"

"Nah. The bugger's already recovering. The blonde bird can deal with it. C'mon. I'm missing my workout."

Ellen climbed into the ring and approached her client, who hadn't moved. He remained curled into a ball, intermittently coughing and panting.

Kaine stood back and let her do her thing. She dropped to one knee beside Enderby and rested a hand on her client's back.

"Breathe slowly, sir," she said quietly. "You'll be okay in a minute. You're just winded."

She glanced up at Kaine and nodded, her expression unreadable. If pressed, he might have interpreted it as disappointment.

With nothing of interest happening, the audience dispersed and returned to their various exercise stations. Kaine waved a thank you to Denny, who showed a set of pearly white teeth in a broad grin and fired him a quick salute. He turned away and headed to the changing rooms, carrying the spit bucket. As he passed one of the free weights stations, a guy he'd been working out with before the bout called him over and they started chatting. From time to time, they shot appreciative glances in Kaine's direction. He'd developed an unexpected fan club.

Kaine closed on Ellen and the fast-recovering Enderby.

"Is he okay?" Kaine asked, already sensing the answer.

Although he'd landed a knuckle punch, he'd pulled it slightly at the moment of impact. Without the significant reduction in force, the blow could have delivered serious damage. As it was, Enderby would know he'd been on the receiving end of a beating. He'd see and feel the bruising below his sternum for a good, long while.

Enderby unfurled and pushed himself off the canvas, ending on his gloves and knees.

"Bastard," he gasped, "what the hell ... kind of a ... punch was that?" He raised his head and looked up, eyes glazed, face as white as Gordon's had been when he'd left the ring.

Kaine held up his right hand, showing the MMA gloves. He curled his fingers into a fist but left the first knuckle on the middle finger slightly raised.

"Knuckle punch," Ellen said. "Didn't see you throw it."

"You weren't meant to," Kaine said, showing her a grim smile.

Enderby reached up to the top rope and used it to haul himself to his feet. He swayed, turned his back to the ropes, and leaned heavily against the padding covering the corner post as Kaine had done earlier, but with much less finesse.

Enderby stared at Ellen, a plaintive expression on his pallid face.

"Why didn't you stop him?" he whined.

"Your standing instructions are not to interfere when you're in the gym."

"But he could have killed me!"

Enderby tugged himself away from the ropes, an angry scowl replacing the expression of defeat.

"You're paid to protect me. I should—"

"You threw another head punch," Kaine said, stepping closer.

"What?"

"I did warn you not to. I think you should apologise."

Enderby's chin trembled. He lowered his head. "Yes, yeah. Sorry, I lost control."

"Not to me," Kaine said, "to your minder." He jagged a thumb towards the clearly exploited Ellen. "It's really difficult to run close-order protection for a man who doesn't want it."

Ellen nodded her wholehearted agreement, and Kaine felt sorry for what he was about to do to her.

"Feels as though I've been kicked by a horse," Enderby grumbled.

He tried to take a deep breath in, but aborted the process halfway through, winced, and pressed his right glove into his chest.

"What do you know about 'close-order protection'?" Enderby asked after a momentary pause for recovery.

Kaine smiled. "It's how I make my living, Commander Enderby."

Enderby stiffened. "You know me?"

Kaine dropped the smile. "Yes, sir. And we've been following you for the past couple of weeks."

"'We'? What do you mean, 'we'?"

"My associates and I."

Enderby shook his head in defiance.

"I don't believe you."

"I have proof."

Enderby sneered, recovering some of his pre-sparring bluster.

"Okay," he said. "Prove it."

Kaine sighed. "How far do you want me to go back?"

"As far as you like," Enderby answered and straightened. Again, he winced at the movement.

"Okay," Kaine said, frowning in thought. "A week ago, mid-afternoon, you tangled with a man called Merlin Handy and his friend, Robert 'Spike' Powell. My associate has the photos on his mobile phone. I'd be happy to have him show them to you."

"You were there!" Enderby punched his right glove into his left—an action he apparently enjoyed. "The long-haired man in the scruffy clothes. That was you!"

"No, sir," Kaine said. "That was one of my associates. I'll introduce him to you at some stage. Depending upon how things progress."

Ellen faced her client, a thunderous look darkening her eyes. "You left the Tower unaccompanied and without notifying my team?"

"No, of course not." Enderby flapped a glove to dismiss her concerns. "Grieves was with me."

"But the death threats—" She shot Kaine a glance and broke off. "We're trying to keep you alive … sir."

Enderby turned his blue eyes on Kaine.

"Why?" he asked.

"Why what?

"Why were you following me?"

"It's part of my company's MO. We like to know all about our prospective clients before we pitch for their trade."

"Your company is in the personal protection business?" Enderby asked, his breathing still shallow and rapid, but slowing.

"Yes, Commander. A&W Associates has selected the NCTA as its first target client in the UK public sector."

"Nonsense," Ellen said, dismissing Kaine's statement with a sharp shake of the head.

"What is?"

"In the UK, government ministers and senior civil servants are guarded by the Metropolitan Police's Protection Command. The government isn't about to privatise its own—"

"The same way it hasn't privatised any of its prisons or its prisoner escort services, Ellen?" Kaine asked, eyes wide, innocent.

"That's preposterous."

"No," Kaine said, shaking his head, "it isn't. We have it on good authority that the Cabinet Office has been discussing ways to reduce the size of the state for many years. One of the recent proposals is to privatise the MPPC. I'm surprised you haven't heard the rumours, Ellen. Truth be told, the Home Office is even now working on a change in the law to allow civilian protection officers to carry weapons under special license. A radical idea for the UK, but not one that would raise any eyebrows in other countries. Australia and Canada for example. We—and by 'we', I mean my company—have always tried to be ahead of our competitors. Which is why we're making this somewhat … pre-emptive approach."

Ellen Winters frowned the whole way through Kaine's explanation.

"Yes," she said. "I have heard the rumours, but the government has always denied them."

"Given how controversial and sensitive the plans would be, are you surprised?"

"*I'm* not," Enderby said. "You can't get a straight word out of any of the beggars."

"What's your company called again?" Ellen asked.

"A&W Associates. The 'W' stands for Wingard. That's me, Peter Wingard. At your service." Kaine dipped his head in a slight bow.

"Peter Wyngarde?" Enderby scoffed. "Like the actor?"

"Not quite. Different spelling. But my mother *was* a fan of the TV series."

"A&W Associates?" Ellen repeated. "I've never heard of you."

Kaine turned to face her. "You wouldn't have. We like to keep a low profile. We don't advertise our services. Nor do we have a website or a social media presence, Ms Winters. Or may I still call you Ellen?"

She ignored the question and studied Kaine's face, no doubt looking for signs of evasion. "Whatever the politicians of the day decide, the MPPC is currently in charge of the NCTA's personal protection and that is unlikely to change for the foreseeable future."

Kaine showed her a superior smile. He expected to impress Enderby with it.

"Perhaps," he said, "perhaps not. You never know how fast the government can move with the right motivation. Isn't that right, Commander."

"Yes," Enderby said, still rubbing the middle of his chest, "that's, er ... correct."

"And ..." Kaine added, moving in for the final attack, "given how lax the MPPC has been in its duties, I think the case for change has already been made. Maybe in an advanced pilot study. Do you agree, Commander?"

Enderby frowned in bewilderment.

As expected, Enderby clearly hadn't paid any attention to the rumours Kaine had outlined. Rumours and speculation that had been making the rounds for years.

"We have *not* been lax in our duties!" Ellen hissed, glancing around to make sure they weren't being overheard.

"Really, Ms Winters?" Kaine took a half-pace closer to Enderby, approaching to inside arm's length. "This evening," he continued after a short pause for breath, "you, Ms Winters, stood by while an unknown subject entered the ring with your client and came within a single thrown punch of ending his life."

"Now hang on a moment," Enderby said. "You were nowhere near—"

"With the greatest respect, Commander," Kaine said, keeping his expression calm and professional. "When you were on your knees, defenceless, you were at my mercy, and Ms Winters did nothing. She didn't even try to save you, sir. That, I find unacceptable. Furthermore, if it isn't grounds for changing the official protection system, I don't know what is. Don't you agree, Commander?"

"How do you know all this?" Enderby demanded. "All this is rumour and speculation."

"It's my job to know these things, Commander." Kaine reached out and gripped the top rope, centimetres away from Enderby's right arm. "Even now, I'm within touching distance of you and she still does nothing to protect you. I mean, I could kill you right now with a punch to the throat, or a knife through the ribs, and she could do nothing to prevent it. Am I right, Commander?"

Ellen bridled. "Now wait just a minu—"

"No, Ms Winters," Kaine snapped. "*You* wait. Both you and the MPPC have been woefully inadequate in your duty to protect Commander Enderby. He deserves better security than you are currently providing. What say you, Commander?"

"Well, I'm ... I don't know." Confusion deepened the creases on Enderby's flushed face.

"Would you care to discuss this ongoing issue over an evening meal, Commander? I currently have rooms at the Savoy."

"I really—"

"If you're worried for your safety, please bring Ellen with you to vet the room and validate our credentials. But I'm afraid she won't be privy to our negotiations. I have no intention of discussing confidential business in the hearing of any would-be competitors. And you will, of course, be asked to sign a non-disclosure agreement."

Enderby turned away from Ellen and faced Kaine, showing his preference.

"Unfortunately," Enderby said, "I have a prior engagement." He nodded towards the doors to the changing room, where Guy Gordon still waited, watching them, curiosity written all over his bloated face.

"I'm afraid I can't allow Mr Gordon to join us, Commander. GG Cleaning Systems would also be a direct competitor moving forwards."

Enderby paused for a moment before answering.

"You have rooms at the Savoy, you say?"

"Yes, Commander. The Burlington Suite."

Kaine dropped a hand on Enderby's shoulder and removed it when Ellen twitched. He didn't want her to provide a belated response and hated the idea of hurting an innocent.

"Sounds like a marvellous idea to me," Enderby said without hesitation. "I'll tell Gordon that our meeting can wait."

"Commander Enderby," Ellen said, "I really don't think—"

"That's just it," Enderby barked through her warning. "You don't *think* at all, do you! Mr Wingard has demonstrated that he knows more about personal protection than you and your MPPC. I'm inclined to at least give him the chance to state his case. I'm also inclined to stand you down for the evening. What do you say about that?"

"That is your prerogative, Commander. But it would be against my advice."

Enderby lowered his hand from his chest and stood taller, stretching to his full height.

"Nevertheless," he said, "you are dismissed … for the evening. Mr Wingard and I have business to discuss. Good evening to you."

"But, Commander, I really must insist—"

"Enough." Enderby waved her away. "Go."

"Right," she said, glancing sideways at Kaine. "He's an arrogant pain in the backside, Wingard. He never listens to advice, which makes him nigh on impossible to protect. You're welcome to him." To Enderby, she said, "I'll be making a full report about this to my superiors and copying it to Sir Ernest."

"I'm sure you will, Helen," Enderby said, lifting his nose and turning away.

Ellen climbed down from the ring and marched through the gym, ponytail swinging. She stormed through the changing room doors, brushing past an open-mouthed Guy Gordon.

"Shame," Enderby said.

Kaine nodded. "Agreed. I hated to badmouth a fellow professional."

"That's not what I meant."

"No?"

"No. I meant, it's a shame I won't be seeing her again

tonight. She has a magnificent arse. So firm, you could bounce tennis balls off it." He laughed, winced, and pressed the glove more firmly to his chest. "Bloody hell, for a small man, you don't half pack a punch."

For show, Kaine laughed along with him.

"Sorry about that, Commander," he lied, "but it was the only way I could think of to introduce myself correctly."

He held up the top rope for Enderby to climb through, and target number one of two duly obliged.

Chapter 12

Church Avenue, Soho, London, England

Claire clung to the shadows and shivered. The wind whooped between the surrounding buildings, driving down the temperature. The next time she decided to follow the worm, she'd dress more suitably. Her thin top and baggy jumper didn't offer nearly enough protection for hanging around outside in the evenings. She cupped her hands, breathed warm air over them, and rubbed them together vigorously. It did little to ward off the numbing, finger-stiffening cold.

Stop being so stupid, woman. Go home.

She'd followed Worm and his blonde minder from

Sandbrook Tower to the gym, where he'd met Guy Gordon, who'd been waiting for him outside. Worm nodded a formal greeting, but neither offered to shake hands. Definitely not friends. Barely even friendly. She'd taken pictures of the meeting on her mobile just in case it turned into something interesting.

"What are you up to, Worm?" she'd muttered.

No one answered.

With her curiosity piqued, Claire vowed to wait them out. How long could they be? One hour? Two?

According to her internet search, Body-Ring Limited advertised itself as "an exclusive facility for serious athletes". It provided no sidebar services. No colonic irrigations. No pedicures or manicures. No salad bars with nutrition experts to guide its members through the minefield of fad diets. BRL's ethos dominated its corporate image: KISS, "Keep It Simple, Stupid". Their primary site in Soho offered free weights, fixed weights, endurance exercise machines, boxing bags, a boxing ring, and "first-class coaching". Members could have an exercise routine designed for them by their own personal coach or workout to their own plan if they pleased. The final line on the home page of their website proudly announced a three-year waiting list for new members.

How exclusive was that?

After thirty minutes, when the sun dipped below the tall buildings and the temperature plummeted, Claire searched the immediate area for a coffee shop with a direct line of sight to the gym. No luck. The only place still open turned out to be the gym itself, but there was no point asking a business with a three-year waiting list for a tour of the premises. They probably had a waiting list for tours, too.

Keeping out of direct view of the gym, Claire paced a side street one hundred metres from the gym's subtly lit entrance with its maroon sign and stylised outline of a man and a woman, both with impossibly well-defined bods. The perfect human specimens.

As if there were such a thing.

She preferred her men to be more real. Narcissistic bodybuilders like Worm were too self-absorbed to make good partners. Again, she shivered, but it had less to do with the cold than the thought of shackling herself to a creep the likes of Worm.

"Hello, darling," a man said—a quiet, smarmy voice behind her in the dark.

Claire jumped. She hadn't heard him approach.

"How much for a blow job?" he asked in a breathless whisper.

"Go away," she said, shuffling into the light and reaching into her pocket for the personal alarm.

"Twenty quid?"

"Go away," she repeated. "I-I'm waiting for my boyfriend."

"Thirty?"

Claire pulled out the alarm and pushed it towards the man's face. Five o'clock shadow, fifty-something, tall, dressed in a smart business suit. He held up his hands and backed off.

"Easy, love," he said, stopping at a safe distance away. "Honest mistake. This is Soho, after all. If you're not touting for business, you shouldn't be hanging around the streets out here in the dark, alone. It's a dangerous place."

"Go on," she called, voice breaking. "Keep moving. Lance is twice your size and he'll be here any minute."

Claire had no idea where she found the name Lance, but it flowed well and sounded natural.

The disappointed potential client dropped his arms. "Alright, love. Alright. I'm going, I'm going. Keep your hair on. Just take care, huh. Not everyone around here is as nice as me."

He turned and hurried into the night, leaving Claire breathing hard and struggling to slow her racing heart.

"What the hell are you doing, woman?" she muttered to herself. "That's it, I'm off."

Claire buried the alarm back into her pocket and turned in the opposite direction to the grubby member of the "dirty mac brigade". She hurried past the front of the gym and narrowly avoided colliding with Worm's rapidly departing blonde bodyguard.

"Sorry," Claire mumbled and turned away from the entrance, expecting Worm to exit the building at any moment. The last thing she wanted was to bump into the evil creature.

"That's okay," the blonde said. "My fault for not looking where I'm going." She looked closely at Claire, and her eyes narrowed in recognition. "Ms Harper, isn't it?"

"That's right. Do I know …? Ah yes, you're one of the agency's personal protection team, aren't you?"

"What are you doing here?"

"Heading for home," Claire said, nodding straight ahead. "Oxford Circus Underground Station. Why?"

"Sorry," she answered, "force of habit. But you're heading in the wrong direction. Oxford Street's that way." She pointed back in the direction from which Claire had come.

"I-I know," Claire said, searching for a reason and

finding one much more quickly than she expected. "I'm going the long way around."

"Why?"

"A man back there …" Claire glanced behind her. "He propositioned me. Asked me for a price to … well, you know. He thought I was a *prostitute!*" She whispered the final word.

"Ah, yes. I see. This isn't the safest place to walk home from work, is it?"

"I wasn't … walking home from work, I mean. I stopped for a coffee with a friend. A work colleague."

Easy, Claire. Don't over-elaborate.

In the words of Body-Ring's website, she needed to KISS.

The protection officer nodded and looked around her. Checking her perimeter? Claire learned the phrase from reading crime thrillers and watching TV dramas.

"Are you working?" Claire asked.

"I was, but not anymore."

"Off duty?" Claire nodded and waited for her to move off, but the bodyguard didn't seem in that much of a hurry.

"Something like that," she said, frowning.

Claire latched onto the opening.

"You look upset. Is everything okay?"

The woman winced. "I might have just lost my job."

"Oh dear. Can you talk about it?"

She shook her head. "Not really."

"Ah, right. I understand. Didn't I see you with the commander earlier?" She couldn't help asking and hoped she hadn't sneered too much when using Worm's actual title.

The woman chewed on the inside of her lower lip. "Do

I detect a little friction between you and Commander Enderby?"

Claire grimaced. "Is it that obvious?"

"Just a bit," she answered, nodding.

"Would it shock you to learn that I call him 'Worm'?" Claire said through a pinched smile.

"Not in the slightest. It's nothing compared to the names I call the bas—the man. I'm Ellen. Ellen Winters. Nice to meet you, Ms Harper."

"Claire," she said.

Ellen offered her hand, and they shook. Ellen's hand was warm, her grip firm.

At that precise second, the gym doors swung outwards, and Worm stepped through the opening along with Guy Gordon, and a bearded man with wavy hair.

On spotting the women, Worm stopped and sneered.

"Are you still here?" he asked Ellen, then turned towards Claire. "And you, Ms Harper. You're not following me, are you? I'm very flattered, but you know stalking is a crime these days." He laughed and punched Guy Gordon on the upper arm. "See you later, Guy."

Two taxis arrived. Guy Gordon dived into the back of the first cab, and it pulled away. He seemed delighted to leave, and he didn't wave goodbye.

"Now," Worm said to Ellen, ignoring Claire, "if you don't mind, there's a filet mignon with my name on it, and I wouldn't want it getting cold. Lead on, Mr Wingard." He turned to the man with the long, fair hair and held out a hand towards the taxi.

Unlike his companion, Wingard had the good grace to appear uncomfortable. He nodded to Claire and Ellen, and ushered Worm into the second taxi, which whisked them off, southbound.

The moment the second cab indicated left and turned into Mansfield Street, a memory sharpened into focus.

"That man, Wingard," Claire said, pointing towards the taxi. "He looks familiar. I'm sure I've seen him before somewhere."

"You might have," Ellen said. "Apparently, Wingard and his firm have been following the commander for weeks."

"And you're okay with that? As one of his bodyguards, doesn't it worry you?"

"Not particularly. As I said, I'm not on call anymore. It looks as though Mr Wingard is keen to take over protection duties. And bloody good luck to him."

"Mr Wingard's a bodyguard? Really? He doesn't look … imposing enough."

"Don't let his size fool you," Ellen said. She shook her head and her ponytail flicked behind her. "That man knows how to handle himself. He's just taken 'Worm' apart in the boxing ring. Love that name for him, by the way. Highly appropriate. Anyway, I've never seen anything like it. Wingard ran him ragged. Worm, the egotistical blowhard, huffed and puffed, but couldn't lay a single glove on him. Brilliant to watch. An absolute masterclass in boxing as an art form. Wingard ended it in the third round with a single punch. Only problem was …" She read the time off her watch and smiled. "Damn. Sorry, must dash. If I leave now, I'll make it home in time to read my daughter her bedtime story. Come on, I'll escort you to the underground. We can always hope that someone tries to accost us. Right now, I'm in the mood to do a pervert some serious damage."

Unable to think of a suitable excuse, Claire accepted the invitation, and they headed in the direction of her earlier lookout post.

After a brisk march along a deserted Duchess Street,

they turned right onto the brightly lit and much busier Port-land Place, heading south. Ellen kept up a remorseless pace, rattling on about her seven-year-old daughter's latest escapades. During the outpouring, Claire made the appropriate noises and asked what she hoped were suitable questions.

Dodging the heavy, pedestrian traffic, they descended an underpass and crossed to the far side of Regent Street before Ellen stopped talking to draw breath. Claire took her opportunity to pounce.

"Mind if I ask a question?" she asked, slightly breathless due to the pace Ellen had maintained.

The bodyguard wore trainers, while Claire had on a new pair of leather court shoes. Although they had low heels, she'd yet to break them in properly. Blisters had already started to form on both feet.

"Feel free."

"Back at the gym, you said something about a problem."

"Did I?" Ellen frowned and nearly missed her step.

"Yes. You were saying how one punch ended it and the only problem was … What? What was the problem?"

"Oh yes," Ellen said, smiling. "I meant, the only problem was that Wingard didn't finish the job and beat the arrogant prick to a bloody pulp." She raised her index finger —short nail, clear lacquer. "Only you didn't hear that from me."

"Wow," Claire said. "Wish I'd been there to see it."

Ellen smiled. "It's a shame the gym doesn't have CCTV. If it had, I'd have commandeered the footage and posted it on social media. Anonymously. It would be an absolute hoot. Show Worm his place."

Within sight of Oxford Circus station, Claire had little time left to pump her unexpected ally for information.

"Yes. Such a shame. I have another question."

"Go ahead."

"If Mr Wingard embarrassed Enderby so badly, how come they've become best buddies and are going off for a meal together?"

They reached the steps leading down to the underground station, and Ellen paused and placed a hand on Claire's forearm.

"This goes no further, okay?" she said. "If you tell anyone, I'll deny it."

"I swear, this is between you and me."

"Wingard is schmoozing the commander for a future protection contract. Right now, they're on their way to the Savoy Hotel for a slap-up meal. It's part of the Old Boy's network. Excuse my language, but those effing bastards make me sick. Anyway, here's where we part. Look me up at the office. I'm on rotation tomorrow morning. You can tell me why you call the arsehole 'Worm'. Okay?"

Claire smiled. "It's a deal."

At last, she'd found someone she could open up to. A kindred spirit. Someone who hated Worm as much as she did.

Ellen nodded farewell and skipped down the steps, leaving Claire at the top of the staircase, wondering what to do next.

A taxi pulled up to the kerb alongside her and disgorged its fare—a young couple dressed for an evening on the town. The woman wore a skimpy, off-the-shoulder dress, all glittering sequins and four-inch stilettoes. Her partner wore a light grey suit with a Nehru jacket. Very smart.

With her decision made on the fly, Claire dived into the

back of the taxi ahead of an elderly lady who wasn't best pleased at her place being usurped.

"Excuse me!" the woman snapped.

"You're welcome," Claire answered, smiling. "The Savoy Hotel, please, driver."

"Right you are, love."

The cabbie flicked off his hire light and pulled into the slow-moving traffic.

Chapter 13

Mansfield Street, Marylebone, London, England

The "cabbie"—Dele Hunter, in a black cab borrowed from a mate—turned left onto Mansfield Street, continued to the end of the road, and took another left onto Portland Place, heading north. He turned right on Park Crescent and carried on along Park Square East.

Enderby stared through his window, frowned, and twisted in his seat to face Kaine.

"Wait a minute. This isn't the way to the Sav—"

He stopped talking when his eyes found focus on the SIG P226 in Kaine's right hand—the SIG P226 pointing at the centre of his bruised chest. He blanched, his jaw dropped, and he held his arms away from his body.

"Wh-What are you doing?"

"Isn't it obvious," Kaine said, through a tight smile. "We're abducting you."

"We?"

Hunter stopped at a set of red lights, reached over his shoulder, and slid open the privacy panel.

"Him and me," he said, matching Kaine's smile. "Sit back and enjoy the ride, Commander." He turned to face front, leaving the privacy panel open.

The lights flipped to green, and Hunter pulled away. They made a left turn and rolled anticlockwise around the Outer Circle. The open green space of Regent's Park, lit by wrought-iron, "Victoriana" streetlights, stretched out to their left. Town houses and apartment blocks rolled past on their right.

"What's going on here?" Enderby demanded. He tore his gaze from the muzzle of the SIG and locked it on Kaine. His blink rate slowed.

"I've already told you," Kaine said. "Don't make me repeat myself. It's annoying and you really don't want me annoyed. I can turn rather nasty when I'm annoyed."

"Not green though, eh, boss?" Hunter said, staring through the rear-view mirror, his grin widening.

Kaine threw Hunter a deep scowl and made sure Enderby saw it. "Concentrate on your driving."

Hunter dropped his smile and glowered into the rear-view.

"Yes, boss," he growled.

"Where are you taking me?" Enderby demanded.

"As you so rightly said, we aren't going to the Savoy Hotel," Kaine answered, calm and slow. "Oh dear me, no. I have no intention of wasting twelve hundred pounds to impress the likes of you, *Commander* Enderby."

Kaine reached across and removed the Beretta from the holster under Enderby's left armpit. He checked it for safety before sliding it into his jacket pocket.

"For this operation, I thought dropping the name *Savoy* into the conversation would be enough to entice you away from your rather attractive minder. Turns out I was right." He endowed the prick with a mirthless smile.

Enderby swallowed hard. "Who are you?"

"Well, I'm certainly not Peter Wingard. In fact, I understand you've been looking for me for the last few months. You and thousands of others."

"What?" Enderby's confused frown deepened. He stared harder at Kaine, trying to put a name to his face.

"Not having a good night, are you," Kaine said. "First, you're humiliated in the ring by an elderly lightweight when you're at least a cruiserweight. How embarrassing for you. Now, that same lightweight is taking you at gunpoint to who knows where? Nope, not a good night for you at all."

"Who are you!" Enderby repeated, anger flaring and momentarily overcoming his fear.

Kaine reached up, tugged the blond wig from his head, and raked his fingers through his overlong curls. The cool air dried the sweat on his scalp.

Bliss.

"You know what the absolute worst part of the evening was?"

Enderby didn't answer. He simply sat still, blinking in silence.

"The wig," Kaine said. "I hate wigs. Too damned hot. I considered ending our little sparring session in round one, but I was having so much fun at your expense. Ah well. I'm a bad man. Really bad." He shrugged. "So, sue me."

On witnessing Kaine removing the wig, Enderby's anger melted away and the fear returned.

"Yes," Kaine said. "You're right to worry. I'm revealing what I really look like. Can't be good for you, can it." He paused, and added, "Not good at all."

"D-Do I know you?"

"Why, do I look familiar?"

"Y-Yes, but ..."

"Can't remember where from?"

Enderby shook his head. "No ... No, I can't."

"Try to imagine me with short-cropped hair, without the beard, and with brown eyes rather than blue." He brought two fingers to his face and pointed. "These are cosmetic contact lenses. A little uncomfortable to begin with, but it doesn't take long to get used to them. They make my eyes a fetching shade of baby blue, don't they."

The colour drained from Enderby's face and his jaw dropped.

"Kaine," he gasped. "Ryan Kaine!"

Ignoring the gun pointed at his chest, Enderby twisted at the waist, grabbed the door handle, and pulled. Nothing happened. He yanked on the handle again and again. Same effect. Eventually, he sagged back against his seat, defeated.

"Don't you just love child-proof locks?" Kaine said, allowing the thin smile to return.

"Yeah, it's a real boon," Hunter growled. He indicated right and filtered onto Avenue Road where London plane trees shone bright under more faux-Victorian lampposts.

"So, Commander," Kaine said, lowering the SIG and pointing it at the stunned man's right thigh, "can we be serious for a moment?"

"I'm a dead man," Enderby groaned. "Get it over with, why don't you? Shoot me."

"And have your blood make a mess of these nice, clean seats?" Kaine shook his head. "Not likely. My associate"— he used his free hand to indicate Hunter—"would have to clean up. He'd never forgive me. No, no. There are many more ways to kill you without using this SIG. Bloodless ways. Would you like me to name a few?"

Enderby raised his hands and used them to scrub his face.

Hunter took them left onto Adelaide Road and maintained a decent lick. The thinning traffic allowed them to reach close to the speed limit, a rare event in London. They made a sharp right onto Finchley Road and slipped into the bus lane, passing shop after shop on either side. All were closed.

To give Enderby time to stew over his fate—a well-trusted tenderisation process—Kaine passed the time by watching the shops slide past. A clothes boutique displayed retro dresses. The windows of an optician's shop showed photos of smiling people wearing expensive-looking, designer glasses. A downmarket gym promised the perfect body in three months. A brightly lit pub filled with happy drinkers.

"Where are you taking me?"

Kaine ignored the question.

A betting shop flashed past, its doors closed and its windows dark. Another pub. A supermarket, its lights shining bright, offered twenty-four-hour opening for people with the desperate need to restock their larders at three in the morning. A pizza place doing good trade.

"Where are we going?"

Kaine took pity on their captive, but not enough to provide a proper answer.

"You'll find out soon enough."

The shops changed to houses and apartment blocks, and the A41 widened into six lanes, three in each direction, separated by a narrow safety barrier. After negotiating a wide junction and dipping under a walkway, they veered onto Hendon Way.

Not far now. Time to ratchet up the pressure.

He reached across and tapped Enderby's shoulder with the back of his free hand. The commander jumped.

"Ask yourself this," Kaine said. "Why would a man like Ryan Kaine, a man who's been a fugitive for nine months, suddenly break cover and come for you."

"I-I have … no idea," Enderby whimpered.

"You don't?"

"No."

"The bugger's lying," Hunter announced.

"I know," Kaine said, "but concentrate on your driving. We don't need an accident."

"I'm not lying," Enderby whined. "I'm not. I-I have no idea what you want with me."

"Oh dear. Starting off with a lie is not a good idea. You need to try to build my trust. Such are the rules of hostage negotiations."

Behind the streetlights' bright bloom, the detached homes of the wealthy elite flashed past. Multi-million-pound houses with fewer than three bedrooms a piece. Shockingly expensive, but hardly surprising for the UK's capital city.

Hunter took the slip road signposted, "Wood Green, Brent Cross, and The North". They dropped under the Brent Cross Flyover, turned left onto Cooper Way, and slowed right down to negotiate a busy roundabout. After taking the third left at the roundabout onto Haley Park Rise, Hunter pulled the cab into the drive of Number 85.

"Here we are," Kaine said, smiling again. "Home at last. Weary the traveller."

Enderby twisted in his seat. "Money? You want money? I have a … little put away. A few thousand. I-I can give you cash."

Kaine sighed. "Please stop that. You know I don't need your money."

He flicked the man's shoulder with the back of his hand. Enderby flinched.

"We'll continue this chat in the house. First, the ground rules. Are you listening carefully, Commander?"

Enderby dropped his head in a nod.

"My driver is going to release the locks and you are going to sit right where you are without moving until he opens the door for you. If you so much as twitch, I'm going to forget about my promise and shoot you in the right knee. Hang the blood on the leather seat. The wound won't be fatal, but you will be in a great deal of discomfort. Do I make myself clear? And don't think I wouldn't want to draw attention to myself. This taxi will act like a silencer. There are no pedestrians and none of our new neighbours will hear the gunshot over the traffic noise." Kaine paused to add emphasis. "Do you understand me, Commander?"

Enderby nodded.

"Say it!"

Enderby increased the speed of his nod and added, "Y-Yes. I understand."

"Good man."

Kaine made the signal and Hunter disengaged the door locks. Enderby remained immobile. Hunter stepped outside, strode around the bonnet of the cab, and pitched up at the nearside passenger's door.

"Well done, Commander," Kaine said. "So far, so good. Keep this up and you might even survive the night."

After another nod, Hunter opened the rear door, slipped a hand under Enderby's left armpit, and "helped" him out. Kaine slid across the bench seat and climbed from the back. He slammed the door behind him and followed them to the house Corky had rented through an online booking service.

The front door to Number 85 opened inwards before they reached it and had to knock, and Will Stacy stepped back to allow them all inside. He didn't smile a greeting.

Enderby looked up and shot a rapid-fire double take.

"Stacy!" he gasped. "Will Stacy."

He tried to back away, but Hunter's grip on his upper arm held him firmly in place. Their captive was going nowhere.

"In you go, *Commander*," Kaine said, digging his un-cocked SIG into the middle of Enderby's back. "No hysterics, please. That would be unseemly for a man of your standing, and we wouldn't want to use violence so early in the piece."

"No," Will said, showing Enderby his patented, dead-eyed stare. "The violence can come later."

Hunter pushed a staggering Enderby over the threshold and Kaine shut the door quietly behind them.

"Hello, Commander," Will said, his face stony. "How nice to see you again."

"B-But ... we thought you were dead."

Will snorted. "Reports of my demise were a tad premature. As you can see"—he wafted his hands in front of his body—"I'm still breathing."

Will turned and led them through the hallway. He opened a door and descended a set of wooden stairs to a cellar that, despite all the work, still smelled of damp and mould. He threw a switch. An old-fashioned, fluorescent, strip light flickered and caught, bathing the near-empty space in a harsh, white glare. Heavy carpeting covered the ceiling and walls. Hunter and Enderby had to duck to avoid the low ceiling. Will and Kaine didn't.

Kaine nodded at Will. He'd done an excellent job. The thick carpeting would offer pretty decent soundproofing.

In the centre of the cellar, a strong metal chair bolted to the concrete floor, sat waiting. Chains lay in small piles on the concrete, one attached to each leg with a pair of stainless-steel handcuffs. With no upholstery on view, the arrangement looked decidedly uncomfortable. The chains reminded Kaine of a different chair, in a different building, some nine months earlier. He didn't remember the arrangement with any degree of fondness.

Enderby kicked and twisted, making a desperate attempt to back away from the chair.

Hunter stilled him with an open-handed blow to the back of his head. The crack made Kaine wince, but the thick carpeting absorbed the sound and killed any echo.

With Kaine holding the SIG on Enderby, Will helped Hunter force him into the chair and attach the chains. They wrapped one around his chest, one over his thighs, and a third around his ankles, all cuffed to the chair legs. Finally, Will looped the fourth chain around Enderby's neck and attached it to the back of the chair with a padlock, making it loose enough to allow him room to breathe—assuming he didn't struggle too much, or lean too far forwards.

He didn't look entirely comfortable. Kaine knew exactly how it felt. Still, he didn't care.

Enderby looked up, eyes pleading.

"Money," he gasped, "I-I can pay you. Twenty thousand … No, fifty—"

"Don't be ridiculous, Commander," Kaine snapped. "You know I stole millions from the SAMS slush fund."

"You did?" Hunter asked, eyes widening.

Enderby stopped struggling. He lowered his eyes for a second before raising them again. "You did?"

"You've read my file and seen the video."

"Video?" Enderby asked. "What video? I-I have no idea what you mean. Honestly."

"Dear God, man. You must be the worst liar in the country. How did you reach the lofty heights of director in the National Counter Terrorism Agency without being able to lie through your teeth?"

"Okay, okay. I've read your file. I know all about you."

"So, you've seen the video."

"What video?" he repeated.

Kaine stepped closer. Enderby tried to squirm away, but the chains allowed him very little movement.

"The video showing me chained to a chair a little like this one," Kaine said, keeping his voice low and calm. "The video where Sir Malcolm Sampson's hired thugs are trying their best to pummel me through the chair's carbon-fibre mesh. The same video where Sir Malcolm admits to having me set up to shoot down Flight BE1555. *That video!*" He ended with a shout. Enderby flinched in expectation of a blow that Kaine didn't throw, even though he really wanted to.

"No," Enderby squealed. "I-I didn't. I haven't seen any such video. I-I promise."

Kaine shook his head. "I don't believe you." He glanced across at Will, who nodded and left the cellar.

"Sir Malcolm Sampson," Enderby said, frowning. "He was to blame for Flight BE1555? A-Are you serious?"

He made a half-decent effort at appearing shocked. Perhaps his best attempted lie yet.

"Stop it, Enderby. You're being absurd."

Kaine stood up straight. His hair brushed the flock carpet screwed to the arched ceiling.

Enderby took as deep a breath as the chains would allow him.

"Okay, okay," he said. "Let's say you *do* have a video showing you were set up. Why not release it to the press? Why not post it on social media? Why not hand yourself over to the police and stand trial? If you're so bloody innocent, prove it!"

Kaine clenched his fists and edged closer to his captive.

"I've tried the official approach. The Home Office has had the video that will clear my name for months, but they refuse to take me off the most-wanted list. Refuse to offer me any protection. So, you think I should hand myself over and sit in a remand cell for months on end, waiting for someone to set up a court date? In the meantime, I'll have to defend myself from any inmate who fancies claiming the reward on my head."

"What reward?"

"The reward Malcolm Sampson offered for my death. Half a million euros at the last count."

"But Sir Malcolm's dead now," Enderby shouted, eyes glinting under the white light. "It's been all over the news. Without him there *is* no reward."

"How many of my fellow inmates would believe that? One sniff of that kind of money and they'd turn rabid."

Enderby lowered his eyes and shook his head. "The authorities would put you in special measures."

"Solitary confinement in a small, windowless cell for months on end? Relying on the protection of underpaid prison guards who are just as likely to try to take me out? No, thanks." Kaine shook his head. "Nope. I'm sort of happy with the status quo ... at least, I *was* happy until I learned about the Grey Notice."

Enderby jerked his head forwards and gagged as the chain bit into his throat. He scrunched back down in the chair to release the tension.

"No denials, this time?"

Enderby's chin dropped to his chest.

"No. No denials," he said, staring up at Kaine through bushy brows, pleading. "But the Grey Notice has nothing to do with me. I-I don't have the authority to raise one. I'm not high enough up the chain of command."

"I know that, Enderby," Kaine snapped. "You're just the first rung of the ladder. The easiest place to start. After you tell us all you know, we'll target the next rung up. And the next, and the next. All the way to the top. And do you know what, *Commander*?" He paused, waiting for a response.

"No," Enderby said, lowering his eyes for a second before looking back up.

"I'm going to enjoy every moment." Kaine smiled and made it a little manic.

Will returned carrying an open laptop and a footstool. He placed the footstool on the floor in front of Enderby—well out of reach—and set the laptop on the footstool. The laptop screen showed a still of the video in question. A black triangle inside a white circle appeared over the centre of the image.

"This is the video we were discussing a moment ago," Kaine said, closing on the laptop. "A friend of ours has set it to run on a loop. I'm going to play it now and let you absorb all the intimate details. Doesn't make good viewing, I'm afraid. Still"—he smiled and hovered his index finger over the keyboard—"it'll help pass the time for you. It might even give you an idea of what to expect when we return."

He dropped the smile and tapped the space bar.

The action opened with the late Adam Akers, former interim VP of Internal Security of SAMS, raining punches down on a chained and defenceless Kaine. Standing over the laptop, Kaine shuddered at the remembered onslaught. He allowed his tongue to work over the dental implant a friendly orthodontist had used to replace the incisor he'd lost during the beating.

Enderby watched, his eyes glued to the small screen, grimacing at every blow, no doubt anticipating the same treatment.

Kaine waited for the part where he'd bitten off the tip of Adam Akers' nose—his favourite part of the recording—before leaning forwards and pressing the spacebar to pause the action again.

"Poor Pinocchio. He paid dearly for getting too close."

Enderby tore his eyes from the screen and looked up at Kaine. He frowned.

"Pinocchio?"

"It's the name I gave him after biting off his nose. You've heard about his demise?" he asked.

Enderby hesitated, then nodded.

"The p-police found his body in the mortuary in Evesham," he said. "That was you, I suppose."

Kaine smiled. "Pinocchio wanted to retrieve his brother's body before the autopsy. At least they ended up together. Rather poignant, don't you think?"

"You killed Adam *and* his brother?" Enderby gasped.

"No, no. A friend of mine killed the brother. Self-defence, as it happens, but I did execute the man Pinocchio brought with him. An American named Treat, would you believe? Treat Dixon. Don't forget him. The bodies are piling up around me, eh? Another added to the list won't bother me. It won't bother me one little bit."

Kaine smiled, pressed the spacebar again, and turned away. He signalled for Will and Hunter to precede him up the stairs.

"Enjoy the show," he said. "I'll be back after supper."

On his way up the stairs, Kaine flicked off the light switch. Darkness fell, broken only by the flickering image on the laptop's small screen. As he shut the door, Kaine looked back. Enderby's eyes never left the screen.

Chapter 14

Monday 7th June - Claire Harper

Mozart Wine Bar, The Strand, London, England

"What are you doing?" Claire mumbled, staring through the plate-glass window of the Mozart Wine Bar.

The overpriced bar's decent view of the grand entrance to the Savoy Hotel was her only reason for setting foot in the place. It also enabled her to soak in some welcome warmth even though she'd had to fend off the unwanted, amorous approaches of more than one of its drunken clients who offered to ply her with more drink than she needed or wanted.

No, thank you very much.

She wasn't interested.

Claire took another tiny sip of the ridiculously expensive

Chardonnay she'd been nursing for the previous two hours, and glanced at her watch for the hundredth time. Eleven o'clock and still no sign of Worm. Surely he couldn't be staying the night, not with work in the morning.

Was the creature even in the posh hotel? Could he have left by another exit? Could there be a rear exit to such a high-class establishment?

How long did she intend to wait for the supercilious git? She'd chased Worm and Wingard to the Savoy in order to take a photo of them together—something she'd been unable to do outside Body-Ring. Why? To add the photo to her growing surveillance file on Worm. Why? God alone knew.

She was being preposterous, but something about Peter Wingard bothered her. She recognised him, but had no idea from where. And Guy Gordon's presence at the gym didn't sit well, either. She could be reading too much into it, but a relationship—any relationship—between Worm and Gordon would be wrong.

How could it be acceptable for them to socialise? The way Gordon reacted when they'd met outside the gym confirmed that they were definitely not friends.

As a member of the panel that decided the agency's bidding process, Worm shouldn't have been fraternising with a contractor. If they *were* friends, Worm should have registered the relationship. At the very least, he should recuse himself from the panel to avoid a potential conflict of interest. And he should have added the meeting to his online diary. Maybe he'd done all those things. She'd check in the morning.

No. Something was wrong. Really wrong.

And why had Worm allowed himself to be taken to the Savoy?

After a moment, she smiled as a scene from a movie she'd watched ages ago worked its way into her mind. A movie where a team of conmen had convinced a millionaire industrialist to change hotel suites and ended up holding him for ransom.

Claire almost hugged herself as she allowed the image to build in her head. She giggled into her wineglass.

If only ...

As if such a thing would ever happen in real life. Worm wasn't worth the effort. After all, the creature was nothing but a civil servant.

But what a wonderful dream.

Then again ...

What if the mysterious Wingard *didn't* have a suite at the Savoy? What if he *had* kidnapped Worm for some other reason. A reason other than ransom?

The idea of Worm being terrorised by a gang of armed and vicious kidnappers gave her a warm glow inside. Worse still, she didn't feel the least bit guilty about it, which went against her Roman Catholic upbringing. Sister Mary Andrew, head of Claire's convent primary school, would have been horrified by such a fall from grace.

Oh stop it, woman.

She was being silly. Nobody had kidnapped Worm. It was nothing short of wishful thinking. That sort of thing happened in Hollywood movies, not in England.

She drained the last of her warmed wine, set the glass down on its coaster, and sighed.

C'mon, Claire. That's enough. Off you go.

There was nothing for her here. Never had been.

At the far end of Savoy Court, the exclusive entrance to the five-star hotel, one of the revolving doors started spinning. Maybe ... No. A middle-aged couple—the man in a dark suit, the woman in a form-fitting, electric-blue dress—stepped out. They were followed by a man in a long coat and a top hat, the taller of the two concierges, who wheeled a heavy-looking suitcase. He waved the leading black cab of three forwards, which parked, by custom, on the wrong side of the road to make it easier for the cabs to enter and exit the court.

The concierge opened the taxi's rear door and helped the woman climb inside. The man scooted inside without needing assistance. After depositing the suitcase in the back of the cab, the concierge tipped his top hat to the couple—no tip was given or expected. The cab performed a neat U-turn and rolled serenely away. It exited the court, turned right onto The Strand, and disappeared east.

Claire sighed at the pomp, but admitted to being a little jealous. For once in her life she'd have loved to be pampered like that.

"Fancy another, love?" a man asked. "White wine, wasn't it?"

Claire looked up to find a red-faced man in his forties, leering at her chest and standing close. Way too close. His breath smelled of wine, and he swayed slightly.

"No, thanks," she said. "I'm just leaving."

He reached a hand towards her shoulder, but her deep scowl made him snatch the hand away and back off.

"You sure, love?" he asked, wafting more alcohol-laced breath into her face. "The night's still young and, if you don't mind me saying, you're looking ever so lonely."

"Go away," she said.

"Really?"

"Yes."

"If you insist."

"I do."

The man sneered at her, mumbled something under his breath that called into question her sexual preferences, and turned away. He swaggered towards a nearby table where three other equally red-faced men sat watching and waiting. As he reclaimed his seat, his companions burst into loud jeering, rating his performance in the only way they knew how. One of the men, the quietest and youngest of the four, shot her an apologetic smile. Claire didn't react to it.

Enough of this nonsense.

She retrieved her mobile from her bag and tapped it awake. After watching the comings and goings of the Savoy for the previous two hours, she fancied treating herself to a cab rather than use a night bus and risk even more unwanted attention from late-night revellers.

Her evening had been such a monumental waste of time.

She'd followed a man she hated to a gym, and then chased him to a posh hotel and waited for what? The Lord alone knew. She was becoming a stalker. What had she hoped to learn?

Claire shook her head. She knew exactly what she wanted. Ammunition to put an end to Worm's career. Maybe even an end to his freedom. The creature was up to something. She knew it deep in her gut, but without evidence, she could do nothing.

Evidence, pah.

After weeks of listening at keyholes and following Worm, she'd produced almost nothing.

A total waste of her time. A waste of her life.

What life? She had no life.

Still, the wicked idea of Wingard having kidnapped Worm persisted. It refused to leave her. If it were true, she could let things rest and maybe resume a normal existence.

On the merest whim, she opened her phone's web browser, searched for the Savoy's number, and dialled.

"Savoy Hotel, London," a man said brightly. "How can I help you?"

His effusive delivery made him appear totally delighted to receive her call.

"Hello," she said, hesitant, unsure of what to say. "I'm in a bit of a dilemma. I … need to contact my friend, Anabelle, as a matter of some urgency, but she's not answering her phone and my texts aren't getting through."

"Yes, madam? And how might I help?"

Keep going, woman.

"You see," Claire continued, "Anabelle went out on a blind date with a man who claims to have booked a suite at the Savoy. She was supposed to contact me with a password if everything was okay, but I've heard nothing."

"Oh dear. This man has a suite with us, you say?" the receptionist asked, showing real concern.

"That's what he claimed," Claire answered, allowing a slight catch to enter her voice. "I'm really worried about her. I was thinking of calling the police, but I thought I'd try you first. I don't want to make a fuss."

"I completely understand, madam. This man, what name do you have for him?"

"Wingard."

"And do you have a suite number for Mr Wingard?"

"No. I'm afraid not."

"Hmm. I see," he said, over the clicking of a keyboard. "Do you spell Wingard with a Y or an I?"

"I've no idea. Can you try both?"

Claire heard more clicking followed by silence.

"Well?" she asked.

The receptionist cleared his throat.

"I'm afraid I am unable to help you, madam."

"You can't?"

"No, madam. The Savoy has a strict confidentiality policy in place. I can neither confirm nor deny the presence of a guest in the hotel."

Claire relaxed her shoulders. Had he given her an answer?

"So he *is* booked—?"

"However," the receptionist interrupted, "you might wish to revisit your first option."

What?

"Are you telling me Wingard *isn't* booked in, and you think I should call the police?"

"No, madam," he said, aghast. "I'm saying nothing of the sort. Really, I'm not. Good evening and good luck, madam. I hope your friend is safe." He ended the call and the phone fell silent in her hand.

Wingard hadn't booked a suite at the Savoy!

An electric trickle of excitement ran through Claire's body. The kidnapping possibility still existed. It really did.

Hell!

Of course, Claire may have misunderstood the recep- tionist. After all, the man hadn't exactly made it obvious. He hadn't actually confirmed that Wingard didn't have a suite, but he had implied it. However, if Wingard *didn't* have a suite at the Savoy, there were other explanations for the confusion. Ellen could have misheard the location. Maybe Wingard said the Dorchester or the Ritz rather than the Savoy. An easy mistake to make, wasn't it? Ellen might have been so angered by Worm's behaviour that she'd made a mistake. Unlikely, but all things were possible. Worm had strange effects on people. On the other hand, given Ellen's chosen career, would she really have misheard?

Claire reviewed the phone conversation in her head.

No.

She hadn't misunderstood. The receptionist had been perfectly clear. In a roundabout way, he'd advised her to call the police.

Wingard *had* lied about booking the hotel room. But why? Once again, the very real possibility of it being an attack on Worm reared its very welcome head.

How exciting.

No, not exciting. Scary.

No, not scary. Exhilarating.

Her interpretation of the facts put her in a difficult position. It gave her a moral dilemma. If Worm faced imminent danger, she should call the police. Raise the alarm. She brought up the number pad on her phone and hovered her thumb over the 9. On the other hand, what could she tell them?

She ran through an imaginary phone conversation.

"Hello," she'd say. "Is that the police?"

"Yes, madam. How can I help you?" the operator would ask.

"I think my abusive boss may have been kidnapped."

"Really, madam? What makes you think so?" he'd ask, remaining calm and professional.

"I've been following him, and he's disappeared."

"You've been following your boss?"

"My abusive boss."

"And you admit to stalking him?"

"No, not really. I have been following him, but not as a stalker."

"Do you know it's a chargeable offence to use the emergency number for making hoax calls? Have you been drinking by any chance?"

"Yes. No. Not really. I've had a glass of wine, but …"

Claire snorted and shook her head. The woman staring back at her from the window's reflection didn't look drunk, but her breath probably did smell of wine, like the idiot at the nearby table.

No. She wasn't about to dial 9-9-9 and ask for the police, not even anonymously. Sod the moral issue. The last thing in the world she wanted to do was help Worm. As far as Claire was concerned, the slithery creature could rot in hell.

An important question remained. What was she going to do about her ludicrous suspicions? The answer? Nothing. Absolutely nothing.

Decision made, it was time for her to head home, take a shower, and jump into her nice, comfortable bed. Again, she glanced at her reflection in the restaurant's window. This time, an evil smile had stretched the lips of the woman with the severe fringe and the daggy clothes.

You are wicked, Claire.

What would Sister Mary Andrew say?

Who the hell cares?

Hopefully, Worm wouldn't be sleeping much that night. At least not in a comfortable bed.

Enough. Off you go now, woman.

Claire stood and pushed her way outside, where the cold, night air sliced right through her light jacket. She shivered, worked the zip up to her throat, and glanced right to check the lane for traffic before rushing, with a skip to her step, to the pedestrian island. The other lane cleared quickly, and she crossed to the other side of the street much faster than would have been possible earlier in the day.

Instead of turning right and searching for the nearest bus stop, she headed into Savoy Court.

Rather than return through the rotating doors, the tall concierge had strolled to the head of the taxi rank and stood chatting to the cabbie, a smile of recognition on his craggy face.

She marched to the head of the rank and stood still, waiting. The concierge smiled at her and tipped a finger to the rim of his top hat.

"Can I help you, madam?"

"Am I allowed to take this cab?"

"Why wouldn't you be?" the concierge asked, smiling.

"I thought it might be on hold for the hotel."

"Not at all, madam. That would be against all the rules." Still smiling, he opened the passenger door for her, and she dived inside.

"Thank you."

"You're welcome, madam," he said. Tipping his hat to her once again, he closed the door.

"Where to, love?" the round-faced cabbie asked.

Claire gave him her home address and sank back into the soft, leather seat, unable to wipe the evil smile from her face.

Sleep tight, Worm. Wherever you are.

Chapter 15

Monday 7th June - Gregory Enderby

Haley Park Rise, Brent Cross, London, England

Enderby had sat through the same bloody video—in living colour and stereophonic sound—four times already and still nobody came. Not that he wanted them to, necessarily. Hell no.

But the waiting … God, the waiting.

According to the screen time, he'd been in the chair for eighty-two minutes and counting. Cramp knotted his muscles and shot lances of fire into every part of his body each time he tried to move. His shoulders, arms, wrists, hips, buttocks, and legs throbbed and screamed in time with each pulsing heartbeat. The stainless-steel cuffs encircling his wrists cut the flow of blood to his hands, causing untold agony whenever he flexed his numb and tingling fingers. Worst of all, he needed the loo. His bladder was ready to burst. How embarrassing it would be to wet himself and ruin his expensive but deeply wrinkled suit.

He'd seen the video before. Of course he had. The full version, not the edited copy currently repeating on the interminable loop in front of his eyes. All those months ago, when he'd seen it for the first time, Enderby had actually laughed at Kaine's discomfort. He'd hooted when Kaine had bitten Akers' nose off, too. He wasn't laughing now, though. Not one bit of it.

He ground his teeth as another spasm of cramp tore through his body.

Once again, the video reached the part where Sir Malcolm Sampson left the room to fetch his baseball bat, and Kaine picked the locks to the handcuffs holding his chains in place. Although he explained how he did it to the blubbering knight of the realm later in the show—with a ceramic lockpick buried in the palm of his right hand— Enderby still couldn't imagine how Kaine had managed the feat with tingling, lifeless fingers. The man was either a freak with unnaturally good circulation, or Sir Malcolm's goons hadn't tightened the cuffs as much as Will Stacy and the black cabbie had done to his.

Bastards. Fucking evil bastards.

And what about Stacy?

Not only alive but working with Kaine. What the shit was that all about? How many people were on Kaine's side? No wonder the bugger had avoided capture—and death— for so long. He had help. So much help. Even more than they'd suspected. The man gathered people around him like a bloody Messiah. And money. He'd stolen millions of euros from Sir Malcolm Sampson's deep pockets. Hundreds of millions. The bastard should be sunning himself in the Bahamas, not kidnapping honest civil servants like Greg Enderby.

Then, it hit him.

That's how he's stayed alive for so long.

Kaine had bought himself a whole load of help.

Money could buy loyalty by the bucketload. And three hundred million euros could buy a hell of a lot of buckets.

If Kaine had bought Stacy and the black driver's loyalty, maybe Enderby could buy them, too. He had plenty of "rainy day" cash set aside for situations such as this. A damn sight more than he'd told Kaine about, too. He snorted to himself, suffering the angry fire of his bruised chest and his oxygen-starved muscles in return.

If anything constituted a rainy day, this did. He had access to more if he needed it, too. Loads more. If he could only wangle the use of a phone … One short phone call would save his life. He even knew where they were keeping him. So bloody confident in their superiority, they'd let him see where they'd taken him. A swift phone call would summon the wrath of the world down on Kaine's shoulders.

When the video rolled through to the sixth showing, Enderby wanted to scream, but he held it in. Nearly two hours he'd been chained to the chair. Two bloody hours. And still no sign of them.

God, how he needed the toilet.

Bastards.

They'd come when they were ready and not before. Nothing he could do would change it. Enderby had never felt so helpless in his entire life. Tears of fear and frustration pooled in the corners of his eyes and his nose started running.

Fuck you, Greg. Man up. You can survive this. You will *survive this.*

Part of him *wanted* them to come. Part of him prayed for the cellar door to open and for someone to burst in and release the growing tension. The rest of him wanted nothing of the sort. When the door opened, it might be Kaine, the man who'd felled him with a single punch to the chest in the boxing ring. What would he do? Enderby had helped send people to kill Kaine and others to kill his team. One of those same people, Will Stacy, now stood alongside him. Bought and paid for.

Money.

Everything boiled down to money. It always did.

Jesus, when will it end?

If Kaine arrived first, Enderby would die. He knew it with absolute certainty. Stacy, too. He'd met Stacy twice before and knew his record. A cold, calculating killer. No chance of turning Stacy. But what about the black guy, the driver? Kaine spoke to him like the hired help. Treated the man like a servant. He might be open to a payoff. If he had the chance, Enderby would risk it. He had no other hope.

Enderby stared through the dark towards the staircase, looking over the top of the laptop screen, praying for the black man, Midnight, to come. And to come alone.

THE VIDEO LOOPED THROUGH AGAIN, and Kaine bit off the tip of Adam Akers' nose for a seventh … no eighth … no, that's right, the seventh time. Pinocchio raced from the room, screaming, cursing, and holding his bleeding snout, heading for Sir Malcolm's guest bathroom.

Above and behind the laptop's screen, the cellar door remained resolutely closed.

God help me. I'm dead. Why don't they get on with it and kill me?

The sweet torture of waiting had to be worse than the actual punishment. Didn't it?

On the screen, Sir Malcolm left the room to collect his baseball bat. Kaine released himself from the chair and followed Pinocchio's route to the bathroom. Seconds later, he emerged shaking his hand and flexing his fingers. Bloodied and beaten, his face a battered and swollen mess, Kaine returned to the centre of the room, crossed his arms, and stood, waiting.

Footsteps clumped above Enderby's head. The cellar door creaked open, and a shaft of dazzling, yellow light from the hallway seared his retinas. He squeezed his eyes tight shut.

Let it be Midnight. Please let it be Midnight.

Cautiously, Enderby peeled open his lids. A pair of legs descended the wooden stairs. Legs encased in black chinos, the feet wearing black hiking boots. A sweatshirt appeared next, dark blue, no logo. The man stopped halfway down the stairs and bent at the waist, peering into the darkened cellar. The black man's shaved head glistened in the half-light.

Midnight! Thank God.

"Still enjoying the show?" Midnight asked, smirking.

"Please, I need the loo!" Enderby called out. "Please!"

Midnight sucked air through his teeth. "Piss yourself for all I care, bro."

"I-I have money," Enderby called in a stage-whisper. "Lots of it. Make one phone call for me and it's yours. All of it. Fifty grand. Think about that. Fifty thousand pounds in cash, and it's yours for the price of a phone call."

The black man's eyes narrowed, and he canted his shiny head to one side.

"Cash?" he whispered.

A noise in the hallway made Midnight turn at the waist.

"All okay, Hunter?" Kaine called out from above and behind him.

"Yes, boss! All secure. He's asking for the latrine."

"Let him soil himself."

Midnight, Hunter, laughed. "That's what I said."

He faced Enderby again, winked, and lifted a finger to his lips, before turning and climbing back up the stairs.

Enderby's heartrate leaped. The wink and the raised finger. What did the signals mean? Had the promise of money worked again? Did he have an ally?

Oh my God. Is it true?

Two thirds of the way through the tenth repeat, the cellar door screeched open again and the strip light flickered into bright, momentarily dazzling, life. This time, Kaine led Stacy down the stairs. They strode into the centre of the room and stood upright. Neither had to duck.

"Seen enough, Greg?" Kaine asked, sounding light, almost friendly.

He reached forwards and closed the laptop during Sir Malcolm's self-incriminating speech. The room descended into a silence that Kaine let stretch out forever.

Enderby held his breath.

"Who authorised the Grey Notice?" Kaine asked, getting to the point immediately.

Enderby swallowed. How could he answer without incriminating himself? Try another lie first. They'd be expecting one.

"I-I don't know."

Chapter 16

Monday 7th June - Evening

Haley Park Rise, Brent Cross, London, England

Kaine wrinkled his nose at the smell of warm urine which added to the underlying reek of mould and damp.

"Seen enough?" Kaine asked, staring down at his trussed captive without pity or regret.

Enderby lowered his head and kept silent.

The man had sent killers after Kaine and his friends. Killers who cared nothing about any innocent bystander who might wander into the line of fire. To reach Kaine, Maureen Reilly would have happily murdered Rhodri Pierce on the cliff face in the Beacons. Without Will's intervention, she might well have succeeded in ending Kaine's life. And he suspected that Enderby had a hand in helping

Pinocchio point mercenary strike teams towards his people. Teams from T5S and GG Cleaning Systems. Lara had been caught up in the fallout, too.

No. Enderby deserved every scrap of the pain he suffered and would continue to suffer.

Kaine leaned forwards, closed the laptop in the middle of Sir Malcom's confession, and the cellar fell silent. He let the silence stretch out for a few charged seconds.

"Who authorised the Grey Notice?" he asked.

No point hanging about. Enderby had had more than enough time to stew.

The captive closed his eyes for a moment. When he opened them again, he met Kaine's steady gaze full on.

"I-I don't know."

Will eased forwards.

"Want me to give him a slap, Ryan?" he asked, his stage whisper plenty loud enough for Enderby to hear. "He's taking the piss—if you don't mind the pun."

Kaine allowed himself a thin smile.

"Dear me, Will. That was dreadful."

"Yeah, well. The best I could come up with at short notice."

"Try harder."

"No, really. It's true," Enderby whined. "I don't know. A-All I know is my boss"—he gulped—"Sir Ernest Harting-ton, announced it in a private briefing a few weeks ago. I don't know who authorised it, but a Grey Notice has to come from people at the top. Very few people carry that much authority."

"The Home Secretary?" Will asked, stepping around Kaine and showing himself fully to Enderby.

"P-Possibly." Enderby lowered his gaze as though unable to meet Will's icy stare.

"The PM?" Kaine asked.

Enderby shook his head, flinching as the rusty chain bit deep into his throat.

"I-I doubt it. He'll be insulated from the process in case it leaks. Plausible ... deniability." Enderby swallowed and scrunched lower in the chair. The chain around his neck slackened. "Hartington will know, though. As Permanent Secretary to the NCTA, he'll have been part of the final decision-making process. Hartington. You need to talk to Sir Ernest."

Kaine nodded, digesting the information that confirmed what he already suspected.

"How does it work?"

"Sorry?"

"What's the process for initiating a Grey Notice?"

Again, Enderby gulped.

"I-I'm not sure, but ... someone high up in military intelligence writes a report. The head of the department in question, which would be MI5 in this case, makes the recommendation and passes it up the line."

"It's as simple as that?" Kaine said. "Someone files a report. Someone else signs a sheet of paper, and just like that"—he snapped his fingers—"I'm on the government's hit list?"

Enderby shrugged as best he could, given the chains. "There are supposed to be all sorts of checks and balances ... you know, investigations and reviews, but ... I don't imagine that ever happens. Don't forget, this is highly classified. No one wants to stick their heads over the ... parapet. No more than three or four people will have been involved in the process. Ask Sir Ernest. He'll know all about it."

Kaine nodded.

"Okay," he said, "thank you for that."

"You ... believe me?"

The brightness of hope shone in Enderby's pale blue eyes.

Kaine gave him a nod. "Your information tallies with the intel we've already gathered. I am inclined to believe you."

"Will you ... let me go now?"

"Soon." Kaine smiled.

"Really?" Enderby asked, breathless.

"After you give us Sir Ernest's schedule for the next three days. I'll also need a rundown of his personal security arrangements."

"Yes," Enderby barked, "I'll tell you everything I know, but please loosen these chains. I-I've lost all feeling in my fingers."

"We can manage that." Kaine half-turned towards Will and nodded.

Will winked and strode forwards.

"Don't try anything silly," Will said, holding up a key. "Ryan told me all about how well you can fight. Believe me, it would be no contest."

"I-I can't feel my fingers or toes," he whimpered. "I'm in no fit state——"

"Fair enough. Stop banging on about it. You brought this on yourself."

Will released the first cuff and the chain around Enderby's neck slipped away and rattled to the floor. The bound man pulled in a huge breath, stretched his neck, and rolled his shoulders.

"Thank you."

Will released the other three chains. While Kaine stood and watched in silence, Enderby slowly flexed his fingers and rotated his joints, whimpering the whole time.

Straight faced, Will backed away to a dark corner of the cellar where a brick wall jutted out to form a small recess for coal deliveries. He ducked behind the wall and returned with a bucket of soapy water and a scrap of towel, which he placed on the floor in front of their captive.

"You'll find another bucket and a change of clothes behind the wall, but don't bother trying the coal chute. It's too small, and I've blocked the access to the street."

Pale faced, sweating, and in obvious discomfort, Enderby nodded his understanding.

"We'll give you fifteen minutes to recover and clean yourself up. Then we'll be back to ask a few more questions. If you behave yourself, I might even bring you some refreshments. Will cheese sandwiches and a cuppa do?"

Again, Enderby nodded. "Y-Yes. Yes, please."

"Excellent. There's no need to make this more unpleasant than it absolutely has to be. Don't you think?" Kaine smiled and hiked his eyebrows.

Will shot out a hand, grabbed Enderby's left wrist, and enclosed it in a handcuff attached to one of the shorter chains.

"No, please," Enderby pleaded. "I won't try anything. How can I change clothes with this on?"

Will reached up and tousled Enderby's fair hair. "If you try hard enough, I'm sure you'll find a way."

"But I stink."

"Yes. You certainly do."

For the first time in ages, Kaine heard Will Stacy laugh. A pleasant enough sound, but it made Enderby squirm.

"C'mon, Will. Fancy a cuppa?" Kaine asked.

"Sounds good to me."

Kaine led the way up the wooden stairs and, in an apparent show of magnanimity, he left the light on.

Chapter 17

Monday 7th June - Gregory Enderby

Haley Park Rise, Brent Cross, London, England

Enderby hid a thin smile behind his hand. Kaine believed him! The arrogant prick had fallen for it. Fallen for the lie. It proved one thing. The "great man" wasn't infallible. He made mistakes.

In a whole world of physical pain, but buoyed by the slightest touch of optimism, Enderby held his breath while his captors climbed the wooden staircase, laughing. The bastards were laughing at him.

Keep going. Don't look back. Oh God. Please don't look back.

He expected the light to go out, but it stayed on. It stayed on as the cellar door creaked shut, the key turned in the lock, and the bolt slammed into place. Footsteps on the floor upstairs creaked, heading towards the back of the house.

The laptop!

Enderby couldn't believe it.

The arrogant, overconfident bastards had left the laptop behind!

It sat on the footstool, a shining beacon of desperate hope.

Another sign of Kaine's fallibility.

The abduction might yet prove Kaine's undoing.

The conceited arsehole!

All thoughts of the pain and of the damp patch in his groin, that had grown cold and pushed the rank smell of his own urine into his nostrils whenever he moved, disappeared into the back of Enderby's mind.

He released his breath slowly, forcing himself to keep still, when his whole being wanted to dive forwards and open the laptop, the potential key to his rescue. The last thing he needed was to draw their attention to a rattling chain. His throbbing and useless fingers wouldn't answer his mental commands anyway. He only had one chance, and moving before he could type would ruin it.

But no. Wait.

They'd *expect* him to be moving about. They'd *expect* the chain to rattle. As far as Kaine and Stacy were concerned, Enderby would be desperate to wash away the filth and change his soiled trousers and underpants. After all, Stacy had presented him with a bucket of water and promised some dry clothes to change into.

Move, Greg. Do it.

Slowly, he curled the fingers into fists, driving past the throbbing, pounding agony. Desperate to increase the blood flow and improve their mobility, he rotated his wrists, extended the fingers, and rippled them in sequence. Gradually, the harsh, drubbing ache eased and changed to pins and needles as sensation returned. Thank God.

Now move!

Grinding his teeth against the agony in his stiffened hips and legs, he straightened. The chain clattered against the chair leg. He stopped, held his breath. Listened.

From upstairs, nothing. In the cellar, only the incessant buzzing of the fluorescent tube broke the silence.

Enderby relaxed his jaw muscles and breathed again. He inched forwards, working his buttocks against the metallic seat, bent at the waist, and slowly stretched out his left arm.

Please don't let it be password protected.

Again, with his tingling left hand, he reached out and opened the laptop. It burst into life, showing a bright blue desktop, but no password dialogue box.

Yes! Thank you, God.

Icons glowed along the taskbar. One of them, an envelope. The Wi-Fi connection showed three bars. A full signal.

The internet. It's connected!

Working against numb fingers and with an unfamiliar left hand, he operated the trackpad, slid the cursor over the envelope icon, and double clicked. Gloriously, the app opened to an empty inbox.

Without hesitation, he clicked the "compose new message" icon and typed in the email address. In the subject field he keyed in the emergency code, *Red 121*. In the message area he typed his name, his ID, the address—Number 85, Haley Park Rise, Brent Cross—and added, "In the cellar." He hovered the cursor over the send button and hesitated.

If this was a trap …

Sod it.

If it worked, he stood a chance. If not, he was dead anyway. How many times could they kill him?

He pressed "send" and started praying. The message hung in the outbox.

Come on. Come on!

The grey dialogue box appeared and sank his hopes.

CANNOT SEND *message using the server.*
Connections to host on the default ports failed.

"NO!" he yelled. "No, no, no!"

Above, a metallic click made him snap his head up.

"You didn't really think we'd forgotten the laptop, did you Commander?" Kaine's gloating, metallic voice rattled through a speaker above his head—a speaker hidden behind the brightness of the fluorescent light. *"Really?"* Kaine added.

"Can't believe he fell for it," Stacy said, following up Kaine's words and laughing.

Footfalls padded on the floorboards.

The message remained in the outbox. Unsent.

For God's sake!

Eyes tearing, Enderby shot out a finger and hit "delete".

"Don't bother, Commander," Kaine's voice crowed. *"We've mirrored that laptop with ours. We have all the information we need for the moment. Thank you very much. I've sent Hunter down with your refreshments. Enjoy."*

The cellar door opened. Hunter descended the stairs, carrying a tray and slouching to avoid scraping his head on the drooping carpets. He pointed at the speaker in the ceiling and raised a finger to his lips.

Another trick?

"Sit back, *Commander*," he ordered, speaking loud enough for the hidden microphone to pick up his words.

Enderby did as he was told, and the chain cuffed to his right wrist clanged against the chair's metal leg.

Hunter removed the laptop from the footstool and replaced it with the tray which contained a steaming mug of something that looked like tea and a sandwich on a plate— two slices of thin, white bread, cut diagonally. He mouthed something Enderby couldn't interpret and pointed to the plate. After pressing a finger to his lips again, Hunter turned and left.

He left the light on, locked the door, and the overhead speaker clicked into silence.

Enderby lifted the plate and found a single square of tissue paper, folded in half. He cast his eyes around the cellar, searching for a camera, but couldn't find one. Hiding his movements as best he could, Enderby picked up the paper, peeled the leaves apart, and read the scribbled message written in blue pen.

GET READY.
I'll come for you tonight.
H.

NO, he didn't believe it. Wouldn't believe it. He wouldn't fall for another trick.

Mind games. They were playing mind games. They wanted to break him, but he wouldn't let them.

Bastards. Bloody bastards.

Enderby picked up the cup and sipped. Tea. Weak. No sugar, but at least it would offer some warmth. The sandwich looked unappetising, but he needed to keep his strength up, needed the energy. He bit the corner off the triangle and chewed. Dry and tasteless. Processed cheese. No butter. Practically inedible. So different from the filet mignon he'd promised himself earlier that night.

He chewed and chewed and swallowed the bolus down with a mouthful of the cooling, insipid tea.

Enderby fought back the tears.

He'd never felt so alone.

Chapter 18

Haley Park Rise, Brent Cross, London, England

The muscles in Enderby's neck cramped, sending a knife thrust of agony up into the back of his head and down into the gap between his shoulder blades. His tongue adhered to the roof of an arid mouth. He tried to peel open his eyes, but they stuck together and wouldn't work. Ignoring the kernel of a migraine and the rattling chain, he rubbed his eyes with the heels of his dirty hands. Grains of dust from inside his lids grated against his eyeballs, flooding them with tears.

He tried again. This time, his eyes opened—to total blackness.

Christ, no. Oh God.

Enderby hated and feared the dark. Half-imagined cellar walls covered in dirty carpet closed in around him, cutting off the life-giving air, crushing him, choking him.

"Jesus!" he croaked. "Hel—"

He cut off the scream, the cry for help, with Kaine and Stacy's dire warning of what they'd do to him if he tried to raise the alarm still ringing in his head. The non-surgical removal of each finger in turn rode high amongst the threats.

Stop it, Greg. Cut it out! You're better than this.

Biting down on the terror threatening to overwhelm him, Enderby fought to bring order to his racing mind. Order brought calm and calm allowed him to think.

Where was he? Chained in a cellar. Number 85, Haley Park Crescent … No Haley Park *Rise*, Brent Cross. That's right, Haley Park Rise.

He'd been abducted. They'd taken him.

He'd fallen for it so bloody easily.

Kaine had played him like a twenty-pound pike on a fifteen-pound line. He'd been a fool and succumbed to the flattery of being targeted by Kaine's fictitious, personal protection company. So much the fool, he'd even dismissed his own bodyguard, the luscious, firm-arsed Ellen Winters, leaving himself wide open to the abduction in the process. Fuck's sake. He'd made it so easy for them.

Greg, you are a total moron.

Were there any positives?

He still breathed. They hadn't killed him yet. That was something. Apart from the psychological torture of the endless video loop and the vile trick with the laptop, they hadn't dragged out the thumbscrews. At least, not yet. He still had all his fingers and toes, so far. They must have wanted him alive and physically unharmed for now. More positives.

Anything else?

The black man, Hunter. He seemed to offer hope. But was he for real? God alone knew. Could he take the risk of trusting the man? Was there an alternative? He'd decide in the moment—assuming the moment ever arrived.

Calmer and better able to think, Enderby breathed more easily, and rolled his head and stretched his shoulders to work some warmth into his muscles. The bones in his neck clicked and creaked, but the movement eased the cramp a little.

Enderby squeezed his eyes tight shut again. Dull images floated behind his lids. What else did he remember?

Sometime after he'd finished the tasteless crap Kaine had laughingly called "refreshments", Enderby searched the cellar and found the change of clothes that the stone-faced Stacy, the former MI6 killer, had left for him in the coal chute. He'd peeled off the urine-soaked trousers and under-pants, washed himself in the freezing water, and dried off using the ragged towel. Stacy had provided a faded but clean tracksuit one size too small, but a definite improvement. Enderby gratefully tugged on the bottoms and slipped his shoes back on, delighted to be free of the soiled clothes.

Unable to work his shirt and jacket past the handcuffed wrist, he'd crawled into a corner, and used the tracksuit top as a makeshift blanket. Listening for any signs of movement overhead, he leaned against the carpeted wall and curled himself into a tight ball to ward off the biting damp and the numbing cold.

Sometime during the unending night, he must have dozed off. Thank God. By falling asleep, he'd missed the time when the bastards had turned off the light. If he'd been awake, the instant and total darkness would have tripped a switch in his head. He'd have screamed for the light. Begged. Pleaded. He'd have broken down, told them anything, everything. No lies, no obfuscations, everything. Just so long as they turned the fucking light back on.

At least the sleep and the natural wakening had helped restore some semblance of sanity. But for how long? When would they drag out the thumbscrews? The tin snips? The box cutters?

Stop it, Greg. Things will work out. They have to.

It couldn't end this way for him. Chained up in a cellar, tortured to death. He had things to achieve. Great things.

THEY'D TAKEN his watch and his mobile. And the laptop.

Enderby lost all track of time. The hours stretched on endlessly. He didn't know whether it was day or night. He woke. He slept. He woke again.

Occasionally, traffic rumbled outside, the noise vibrating up through the damp, concrete floor, irregular, unpre-dictable. Morning or evening rush-hour? He couldn't tell, but it had to be daytime. Didn't it?

At some stage, the fluorescent tube flickered on, searing his eyes with an agonising, blinding light. Enderby squeezed his lids together, ground his teeth, and blinked hard and fast. Above him, the cellar door creaked open, and Hunter descended the wooden stairs, carrying a tray and again holding a finger to his lips.

Hunter placed the tray on the footstool in front of Enderby and mouthed something indecipherable.

"What?" Enderby whispered, barely able to force out the word through a parched mouth.

The black man bent at the waist and leaned close to whisper in his ear.

"Last night," he said, "the bastards had me running errands. I couldn't do nothin'. Keep your shit together. I'll try again tonight."

Hunter straightened.

"What ... what time is it?" Enderby asked, begged.

The black man who was Enderby's only hope for escape turned away and started climbing the stairs. Halfway up, he stopped and crouched low enough for Enderby to see him below the carpeted ceiling.

"The light stays on for 'alf an hour. Make the most of it."

He held up eight fingers and continued the climb, locking the cellar door behind him. His footsteps creaked on the ceiling, again heading towards the back of the house.

Eight fingers. What did that mean? Eight o'clock? Morning or evening? Morning, surely. It had to be eight o'clock in the morning. Enderby couldn't explain why, but knowing the time somehow improved his mood.

He pulled the tray towards him. It contained the same thing as the night before—a dry cheese sandwich and a mug of lukewarm, sugarless tea. This time, Enderby wolfed down the unappetising food and savoured the tea. The cheese tasted better. Fresher.

The fluorescent tube clicked off and pitch black returned to cut a jagged slice into Enderby's guts and jolt his heart. Too soon. Far too soon. It couldn't have been half an hour. Could it? No way. He'd barely had time to finish the delicious sandwich.

He started tapping his hand against his knee, trying to count the passing seconds. He reached three hundred. Five minutes. Did that make it eight thirty-five?

Was he going too fast? Too slow?

Shit!

He'd lost count.

Useless. Bloody useless.

Start again.

No. Why bother? What was the point? For all he knew it was eight o'clock in the evening. Or Hunter could be lying. Messing with his head.

Trust no one.

He had to fend for himself. No one else would do it for him.

Minutes later—or was it hours—the tube flickered on again. No, it couldn't have been hours. He still felt the weight of the sandwich in his stomach.

Hunter reappeared with another tray, and they repeated the same performance.

"What time is it?"

As he left, taking the first tray with him after leaving the fresh one, Hunter glanced up at the fluorescent tube and held up five fingers.

"Lights off in 'alf an hour," he growled and closed the door again. The rattle of a key in the lock, and the clunk of it fastening shut hurt Enderby more than he could put into words.

How long?

How long would they keep him chained up like a dog? How long would they torture him?

Again, he reached for the tray.

This time, they'd spoiled him. The white-bread sandwich had been smeared with butter and a thin slice of ham added to the processed cheese that wasn't cheddar. Luxury. As an added bonus, the mug contained hot coffee with milk and sugar. It tasted out of this world.

Enderby savoured every bite and gloried in every sip.

With his life in the hands of others, he had to make the most of anything on offer and value every single second remaining to him.

After finishing every morsel and drop of his ... supper, he didn't bother trying to count the time, but soaked in every single lux of light—or was it lumen? What did it matter? Either way, he was going to absorb it, appreciate it, bask in it.

Hunter had held up five fingers, indicating the time as five o'clock ... in the evening.

Really? How could that be possible? Had the time really flashed by so quickly, yet at the same time so excruciatingly slowly? It didn't seem possible.

If so, they'd held him for the best part of a day. Enderby should have been in the office all day. He'd be missed. People would be searching for him. Police, Special Branch officers, members of the security services would trace his steps. Using ANPR, they'd be able to track Hunter's taxi from outside the gym all the way to Brent Cross. London had rightly become known as the surveillance capital of the world. According to recent research, there were close to seven hundred thousand surveillance cameras watching the citizens of London. It worked out as being close to one camera for every dozen people. No one could walk the streets of the city without being filmed. And that number didn't include doorbell cameras or dashcams. The moment a work colleague raised the alarm, the police would launch a massive search operation. They would stop at nothing. They'd find him in no time. All he had to do was sit tight and wait.

Enderby's gaze landed on the footstool.

Dear God.

His hopes fell away quicker than water running down a drain.

His passcode. His access code.

Shit!

He'd given the bastards his identity code. If they knew what they were doing, they'd be able to use it to cancel the alarm. A simple email or text message sent, apparently by him, would explain his absence, stop the search. Enderby gasped. The acid roiled up from his stomach. He gagged. Swallowed. Bile scorched the back of his throat. Tears blurred his vision. They'd played him again.

Hunter. The only hope left. Hunter.

Moments later, the harsh, unyielding blackness returned.

Enderby wanted to scream, cry out, beg for light, but they might come down and silence him—silence him forever.

Instead of screaming, he clamped his jaws together, and he dropped to his knees. For the first time in his adult life, Greg Enderby prayed.

Chapter 19

Sandbrook Tower, Soho, London, England

Claire ducked through the revolving doors to Sandbrook Tower, surprised to hear Big Ben striking for the ninth time. The rumbling traffic usually drowned out the bell's off-key dong.

Must be a southerly wind.

She took the empty lift to her floor and briefly paused at Barry's desk for the usual morning pleasantries.

"Morning, Barry. How's tricks?" she asked, willing herself to sound cheerful. After such a sleep-deprived night she needed to force it.

"Everything's fine, thank you. Such a lovely morning.

How about you, dear? If you don't mind my saying, you look a little jaded."

Claire smiled. "Thank you, Barry. I can always rely on you to tell it like it is."

Barry's eyes widened, and he flapped a hand against his chest.

"My dear girl," he gasped. "I didn't mean to … I'd never want to upset you."

Claire held out a hand.

"Barry. It's okay. I'm kidding. Truth is, I didn't sleep very well last night. One of my migraines."

Barry grimaced and leaned closer.

"Another one?" he whispered. "Poor you. That really is awful. Have you made an appointment with your GP? You know, I did tell you to."

"I've been trying, but have you any idea how difficult it is to book a consultation these days?"

"Tell me about it, girl."

They exchanged medical scare stories for a few minutes before Claire tore herself away and dropped into her chair.

It took the usual age for her ancient desktop computer to boot up, but gave her time to sort through her morning post. Nothing urgent.

The moment the agency's logo appeared on the computer screen, she logged in, accessed the global calendar, and searched Worm's appointments. Surprisingly, the evil creature *had* registered the previous evening's meeting with Guy Gordon. He classed it as an after-hours conference to debrief a contractor on previous work. Legitimate, if a little unusual, but nothing she could add to her growing list of evidence related to Worm's sharp practices.

She checked Worm's upcoming appointments. He had a full schedule for the day. First up, a ten o'clock meeting with

Sir Ernest. They were prepping for a visit to the House of Commons. Sir Ernest was due to answer questions from a sub-committee regarding the upsurge in illegal immigration and the government's delay in clearing the backlog of asylum applications.

Her desk phone chirruped with an internal call. Claire jumped, snaked out a hand, and snatched up the handset.

"Claire Harper," she announced, her heart fluttering. Her desk phone didn't ring often.

"Ms Harper, this is Nancy Goodview, Sir Ernest Hartington's PA."

Bloody hell.

Claire sat up a little straighter.

"Hello, Ms Goodview," she said, her throat dry. "How can I help?"

"Sir Ernest would like to see you in his office in … fifteen minutes. He'd like you to brief him on the latest asylum figures."

What?

"He would?"

"Yes, Claire. He understands you've been collating the numbers for Commander Enderby. At least, it's your name on the quarterly report."

"Well, yes. It is, and I have."

"Good, then you'll have the numbers to hand?" she asked.

"I delivered the report to, er … Commander Enderby last Friday. I'll have to print a hard copy unless you want me to bring my laptop."

"That won't be necessary," Ms Goodview said, stiff as a starched shirt. "I've already printed a copy for Sir Ernest. He prefers to read from the printed page." She sounded sniffy.

"Will Commander Enderby be joining us?"

"No, Ms Harper. He won't. The commander hasn't arrived this morning. It really is most unlike him."

Claire's heart skipped two beats. Once again, the prospect of abduction reared its joyous head. Could it be possible? Had Wingard abducted Worm? The idea spread through her in a deep, warm glow.

Stop it, woman.

"I'll be there in fifteen minutes."

"And make sure you're prepared to accompany Sir Ernest to the House."

"The House?" Claire asked.

"Of Commons, Ms Harper. The House of Commons. You'll need your security pass and a comfortable pair of shoes. Sir Ernest prefers to walk, and it's a little over a mile."

THE MORNING and early afternoon had flashed by in a blur of excitement and nervous tension. Claire had only ever visited the Palace of Westminster once before, and then as a member of the public, not as a part of an official civil service delegation.

Despite the restoration work going on all about the Palace, the noise, and the hanging dustsheets, the House of Commons, with its carved stone walls, vaulted ceilings, and ornate, oak panelling, impressed the bejaysus out of her. The committee room itself, however, one of the smallest on the Committee Corridor, filled with hard-backed visitors chairs and walls hung with grey, pockmarked, acoustic panels, couldn't have been more of a disappointment. Not that her role had anything to do with critiquing the décor.

Her role was to support Sir Ernest and furnish him with the data he needed to answer the barrage of questions fired at him by members of the sub-committee. As far as she could tell, she'd acquitted herself reasonably well on that front.

By the time she'd marched back to Sandbrook Tower with Sir Ernest and his bodyguard, a stern-face man called Perry Grieves, nervous exhaustion had set in, and she could hardy stop herself yawning.

A true gentleman, Sir Ernest allowed her through the revolving doors ahead of him. He followed her inside and Grieves brought up the rear. Once they were all safe inside the protective walls, Grieves took his leave of Sir Ernest and disappeared behind the reception desk and into the security office beyond.

Claire smiled at Sir Ernest and waited, wondering what to do next. Gentleman or not, she didn't fancy the idea of being alone with him in the lift.

"A brief word before you go, Ms Harper," he said, dipping at the waist in a bow and lowering himself to her height.

"Yes, sir?"

"I understand that was your first time in the House." He smiled.

"Yes, sir. It was."

His smile stretched wider.

"I must thank you for your assistance. You handled the situation well. Very well indeed. Especially given how little notice you had."

"Thank you, Sir Ernest."

"When Commander Enderby returns, I shall rebuke him for hiding such an asset to the agency."

Claire took the opening.

"Is the Commander unwell, Sir Ernest? I haven't seen him today."

Please say you haven't heard from him. Please say he's disappeared. Please.

"Yes," Sir Ernest said, nodding sharply. "I'm afraid so. Apparently, he ate something that upset his stomach. Poor man."

Damn. Not kidnapped, then.

Deep down, she knew the kidnapping fantasy had been just that—a fantasy. Far too much to hope for. A crying shame.

One thing surprised her, though. She hadn't detected any sympathy in Sir Ernest when he'd mentioned Worm's illness. None at all. Clearly, there was no warmth in their working relationship. None at all.

Interesting.

"Unfortunate for the commander," Sir Ernest continued, "but at least it gave me the opportunity to watch you in action, Ms Harper. And as I said. Most impressive."

"Thank you, Sir Ernest," she repeated, hardly daring to look at the man who towered over her.

Before she could work out what to do next, Sir Ernest's mobile rang to the SOS morse code signal. He sighed and withdrew the phone from his pocket.

"Please excuse me, Ms Harper," he said, smiling. "I have to take this." He leaned closer and lowered his voice. "It's my wife, you see. For her to call me at work it must be an emergency." He winked and turned away to answer. "Hello, Gill, how are you, my dear? … Yes, thanks. It went very well. The committee were as abrasive as usual, but I had able assistance and fought my corner well enough." He wandered towards the lifts and pressed the call button.

Claire took her chance and headed for the staircase. As

she passed the reception desk and received a warm smile from the bottle-blonde receptionist, the door to the security office swung open. Ellen Winters stepped through the opening and beckoned her closer.

"Claire," she said. "Do you have a moment?"

Claire glanced in the direction of the lifts, one of which had opened. Still talking to his wife, only much more quietly, Sir Ernest stepped inside. The doors closed and Claire breathed more easily.

"Is anything wrong?" she asked, noting Ellen's serious expression.

"No. Not at all," Ellen said, slipping around the reception desk and out into the foyer. "Fancy a coffee?"

"Er, yes. That sounds like a great idea. I'm gasping."

Ellen nodded to the receptionist, ushered Claire through the revolving doors, and then stepped out into the pleasant, afternoon sunshine.

Claire shot the bodyguard a surreptitious glance. Ellen Winters studied her surroundings, watchful, professional, always on duty, her expression unreadable.

Nerves rippled through Claire's stomach and the breath caught in her throat. What did Ellen want? Had she been found out? Was she going to be branded a stalker?

Chapter 20

Sandbrook Tower, Soho, London, England

The tall bodyguard marched towards the pelican crossing. As with the previous evening, Claire had to hurry to keep up with the pace Ellen set. At least this time, Claire was wearing more comfortable shoes, and fortunately, the blisters hadn't fully formed.

"I hear you've been to the House," Ellen said as they waited for the red man to turn green.

A crowd gathered around them on the pavement.

"Have you been checking up on me?" Claire asked, the alarm bells ringing.

Ellen shook her head. "Not at all. Perry Grieves had to

sign out and leave his destination when he escorted you and Sir Ernest. It's SOP. Standard Operating Procedure."

The green man started flashing, the warning bleeped, and they crossed the road with the nameless pedestrians. On the other side of the street, they turned back on themselves, marching towards the sun. Ellen paused and slowed her pace, probably taking pity on her new friend. Her short-legged, conspiracy theorist, new friend.

"Was there any fallout from last night's … incident?" Claire asked.

Again, Ellen shook her head, and her ponytail flicked.

"Nope. If a client doesn't want protection, we can't force it on them. My governor accepted my report without kicking up a fuss. The whole unit knows what it's like to work for Commander Worm." She smiled again. "The team love your name for him, by the way. It'll stick."

They reached The Coffee Shack. Ellen held the door open, and Claire entered first. So late in the afternoon, there were plenty of spare tables, and Claire chose her favourite—the one with the best view of the street. Excellent for people watching, usually.

Ellen sat to the side, back to the wall, keeping her eyes and ears open, on the lookout for threats, clearly unable to switch off. In Ellen's presence, Claire couldn't help but feel safe.

Marco, the highly attentive barista, took their orders—two extra-large lattes and a slice of banoffee cheesecake for Claire—and swaggered back to the counter. He really did like to strut his stuff.

"I missed lunch," Claire said when Ellen looked aghast at her order.

"Don't know where you'll put it, girl. There's nothing of

you. If I ate a cheesecake in the afternoon, I'd have to spend an extra hour in the gym tomorrow morning."

Marco returned with their order and, despite Claire's offer, Ellen paid the bill.

"My invite, my shout," she said, absorbing the aroma of her latte with obvious relish. "You can get the next one."

Claire cut off the nose of her cheesecake, forked it into her mouth, and closed her eyes to savour the delight.

"Good?" Ellen asked.

Claire swallowed before answering.

"Heavenly."

"Wish I'd ordered one for myself, now."

"Go for it," Claire said. "Spoil yourself."

"Better not." Ellen took another small sip. "This'll do me."

Claire cut off another large piece and demolished it just as quickly as the nose. She stared at the top of the latte, studying the milky artwork—a perfect love heart underlined three times.

How do they do that?

She raised the mug to her lips and sipped. The creamy coffee tasted as delicious as the pie.

"Okay," Ellen said, crouching closer to the table. "You promised to tell me why you call him 'Worm'." She lowered her voice to a near whisper. No one at the nearby tables could have heard.

"So," Claire said, "I have your curiosity to thank for the coffee and cheesecake?" She tried not to let the relief show in her voice.

"You do. C'mon, fess up."

Claire pushed her plate away. For some reason, the cheesecake had lost its appeal. She cupped her hands around her mug as though needing to soak in its warmth.

"I don't really like talking about it." She raised the mug, but lowered it again without drinking.

"He attacked you?"

Claire nodded.

"Tell me," Ellen urged. Her left hand formed a fist, the knuckles bleached white under the tension.

"It's nothing I can take further or make a complaint about. I have no proof."

"It doesn't matter. I'd like to know."

Tell her, girl. Tell her.

Claire took a deep breath. She dragged her eyes away from the foamy heart and met Ellen's fierce and steady gaze.

"A few weeks after I joined the agency, the commander and I were alone in the lift. Looking back, I think he engineered it. ... It was after lunch ... he reeked of alcohol ..."

She told it all. It took a while. Ellen listened in silence to the story, including Claire's suspicion that Worm had downgraded her probationary report just enough to spoil her chances of a rapid promotion. As she related her accusation, it sounded so thin. Nothing she could take to an employment tribunal. Not a single shred of evidence.

"You know what he said when I'd fought him off?" she asked after she'd reached the end of her pitiful tale. "After he tried to laugh it off as a bit of fun."

"Go on," Ellen said.

"'It'll be your word against mine,'" Claire answered. "And he was right. Nobody would have believed me. There are no cameras in the lifts, and I had no proof of anything. The time in the lift, when he pressed against me. Squeezed my breast. Reached under my skirt. He didn't leave any bruises."

Ellen jutted out her jaw.

"I bloody knew it," she said. "That's what they all say.

214

The bastard got his jollies by frightening you. He probably replays the scene in his head whenever he wants to jerk off."

"Yes." Claire nodded. "I can see it when he looks at me. He has this smirk, like he owns me." She swallowed and looked sideways at Ellen. "You're a beautiful woman. Has he ever tried anything with you?"

Ellen snorted.

"Not a chance," she said, her jaw set firm. "I'd break both his arms and slice off his todger."

Claire wished she could have done the same thing. It would have made such a difference to her life.

"The incident scared me, but I love this job. I've taken to wearing these daggy clothes"—she waved a hand in front of the tweed jacket—"and carrying a personal alarm."

Ellen's sympathetic smile made Claire well up, but she succeeded in holding back the tears.

"I thought that was a fashion statement. I thought you were going for the fifties, librarian look. Didn't do much for you, though."

"It's my anti-Worm outfit. I hate it."

Hate the God-awful fringe, too.

Ellen nodded. "Ever since I met the creep, I had the feeling he was a wrong'un. When we were first assigned to the agency, I searched his work record. Both civilian and military."

Claire sat up straighter.

"Did you find anything?"

"Nope. Not a thing. It's pristine. Spotless." She shook her head in frustration. "Too perfect, in fact. No complaints, no demerits. It's as though it's been whitewashed. And we both know what the arrogant prick's like. He's guaranteed to have upset someone."

A restriction formed in Claire's throat, and she fell

silent. To hide her teary eyes, she lowered her head and took another sip of coffee.

"Are you okay?" Ellen asked. Stretching forwards, she lay her hand on top of Claire's.

"Y-Yes," she answered, her voice tight. "Yes, I am. Thank you."

Claire nodded and smiled when she really wanted to burst into tears. The acceptance and understanding she saw in Ellen's eyes forced the buried emotions to the surface, and the warmth of Ellen's hand on hers gave her the strength to continue.

"I ... I have a confession to make," she said after fortifying herself with another gulp of latte.

Ellen released her hold on Claire's hand and picked up her cup.

"Go on."

"For the past few weeks, I've been following him."

"What?" Ellen straightened. "Are you completely ..." She lowered her cup and fixed Claire with a stern look. "Wait a minute. Is that the real reason you were outside Body-Ring last night?"

"Yes." Claire lowered her eyes, unable to return the look. "I've been trying to find something I can use to take him down. He's up to something. I just know it."

Ellen's harsh glare softened.

"Did you find anything?"

Claire shook her head. "No, not really. Nothing I can use." She allowed her shoulders to slump and released a deep sigh. "I even followed him to the Savoy last night, after you and I separated."

Ellen frowned and shook her head. "That's beginning to sound like stalking. You need to be careful."

Claire placed the flat of her hand on the table.

"But that's just it. Worm didn't reach the Savoy. The man he was with … What was his name?"

"Wingard."

"That's right, Wingard." Claire leaned closer. "He claimed to have a suite at the Savoy, right?"

"That's what he said. It impressed Worm enough to dismiss me for the night."

"He was lying!" Claire said, so excited she almost shouted, earning her another frown from Ellen. "I checked. No one called Wingard was booked into the Savoy last night."

"How do you know that?" Ellen asked, sounding doubtful.

Claire recounted her conversation with the Savoy's receptionist.

"Clever," Ellen said, raising her eyebrows and nodding. "I'm impressed."

"You know what I thought at the time?"

"Do tell."

Claire puffed out her cheeks.

"It sounds ridiculous, but I actually thought … well, hoped, really … I hoped that Wingard had kidnapped Worm and was …" She raised her hand to cut off Ellen's interruption. "Yes, I know. Completely mad, but it made me feel better. I actually slept quite well last night for a change. Evil aren't I."

"Delusional, perhaps," Ellen said, smiling, "but not actually evil. Not really. Not considering what he's put you through."

"Truth is," Claire continued, "this morning, I'd convinced myself that I'd created an absurd fantasy. I mean, Wingard's company could have reserved the Savoy suite in *their* name, not Wingard's."

Again, Ellen nodded her agreement.

"That's what I was thinking. A&W Associates, the company Wingard works for, might well have booked Wingard under a pseudonym. After all, they're trying to keep their interest in the NTCA under wraps."

"But," Claire said, not to be shaken, "when Sir Ernest asked me to stand in for Worm at the House this morning, the hope returned. For a moment, I really did start to believe that Worm had gone missing, but ..." Claire sighed. "When Sir Ernest told me he'd phoned in sick, it burst that particular bubble. Such a shame. Life isn't fair, is it?"

"No," Ellen agreed. "It isn't. But you're wrong. Well, half wrong. Worm *didn't* call in sick this morning."

"No?"

"No. He emailed. But don't get your hopes up. His email has been validated. He used the correct identification code and protocol. No, with any luck, Worm is hanging over his toilet bowl, throwing his guts up. We can but hope."

Claire's mood lifted a little.

"You never know, Wingard might have poisoned Worm's filet mignon," she said, managing a hopeful smile. "Someone should call the poor man and check that he's okay. What d'you think?"

"Sod that, girl. We're going to let the arsehole suffer in peace." Ellen finished her coffee and signalled to Marco. "I'm having another. I need an extra caffeine hit. How about you?"

"Good idea. But this time, I'll pay."

Marco hurried over, cleared the table, and returned with fresh coffees.

"So," Claire said, after sampling the new latte, which seemed a little stronger than the first, but just as nice.

"Other than the fact that he's a complete arsehole, have you noticed anything off with Worm?"

"In what respect?" Ellen asked.

"Has he met anyone else he shouldn't?"

"What do you mean?"

"Did he explain who he was meeting at the gym last night?"

"No, he just gave me the destination." Ellen shook her head. "You need to understand what we do. Our role is to protect the client and stay in the background. Clients don't have to explain themselves to us. Whatever we see, wherever we go, we're supposed to keep it to ourselves."

"See no evil, speak no evil?"

"Something like that," Ellen said, dipping her head. "But don't forget, we were only attached to the agency when the terrorist threat level increased from 'substantial' to 'severe'. That was the end of April."

"Six weeks?"

"About that, yes."

"And you've witnessed nothing to pique your interest in all that time?"

"Not really, no."

Claire drank a little more coffee and looked across at Ellen.

"Okay, so what next?"

Ellen frowned and pulled in a breath.

"I don't think there's much we can do except keep an eye on him—from a safe distance."

Claire frowned. "You mean I should stop listening at his office door?"

Ellen's eyes widened and she lowered her cup to the table.

"What? Are you completely mad? If you're caught—"

"I know, I know," Claire interrupted, raising her hand in apology. "Instant suspension and eventual dismissal. I've only done it a couple of times. It was really scary, too. Heart in mouth stuff. Didn't learn much for my troubles, either. But I do think he's up to something with Guy Gordon. He was the other man with Worm at Body-Ring last night. The tubby one."

"Yep," Ellen said, nodding. "First time I'd met him."

"Gordon runs GG Cleaning Systems. A security firm with preferred-bidder status. As it is a government contractor, Worm shouldn't be socialising with him. Not without declaring a personal interest. Don't you see?" Claire said, allowing urgency into her voice. "It's all kinds of wrong."

"Suspicious, certainly. But he'll have a reasonable explanation for it. His sort always does."

Claire sighed. "Yes I suppose so. What happened in the gym? What did they do?"

"Nothing much. Sparred for a few minutes." Ellen sighed, and shook her head again. "Pitiful it was. Gordon's useless, he made Worm look like a pro, and he's not. Just thinks he is. *I* could take him apart in the ring. Wingard showed him up for what he is—a rank amateur, all flash and no bite. I really enjoyed the way Wingard wiped the floor with him, too. It was really classy."

"Yes, you told me," Claire said, nodding.

"Yep." Ellen stretched out a dazzling smile. "Like I said last night, you'd have loved it. Wingard made Worm look silly. Finished the bout with a single blow. I nearly burst out laughing, but that would have been *so* unprofessional." She chuckled and shook her head. "Oh dear, the things I see at work."

"Wish I could have been there to see it."

Ellen took another drink and fixed Claire with a stern

look. "I'm sure you do, but listen to me. No more peering through keyholes, and no more following Worm through the streets of Soho at night. Agreed?"

Claire nodded, but did it with some reluctance.

"Agreed." She released a heavy sigh. "So, we're letting him get away with what he did to me?"

"Oh no," Ellen answered, "I didn't say that. I'll be the one following Worm—while I'm protecting his sorry arse. Assuming he recovers from his poorly tummy." She stretched out another smile, this one pure evil. "And ..." She pursed her lips and let the thought hang.

"And?" Claire prompted.

"I'll be telling my colleagues, Clay and Perry what Worm did to you."

"But," Claire said, shaking her head, "I told you in confidence."

"Don't worry. I won't mention you by name. Clay and Perry are good guys. They need to know, and they'll help. I promise. They dislike Worm as much as I do. We're not going to let him get away with what he's put you through. He's likely done the same to others, too. Evil pig."

Claire paused to think things through. By breaking her silence and opening up to as strong a woman as Ellen Winters, she'd gained a powerful ally, but she'd also lost some control. She'd known it would happen and she still opened up.

So be it.

"Okay," she said, through another deep sigh. "Tell Clay and Perry and only them. For now, at least."

Ellen pressed the flat of her hand to the table surface between them.

"We'll get the arsehole, Claire," Ellen said, her blue eyes steely. "One way or another, he'll pay."

For some reason, Claire had no doubt. For the first time in months, she didn't feel totally alone. She'd seen Clay Upton around, but hadn't really met him. As for Perry Grieves, he'd protected her and Sir Ernest during their trip to and from the House of Commons. He'd impressed her with his professionalism and his calm confidence. Not the sort of man who played to the gallery. Not at all like Worm. He and Clay Upton would be good to have onside. Perry was nice looking, too. In a strong and silent sort of way.

She almost asked Ellen if Perry was single, but that would have been wrong and completely out of the question. Besides, Worm had put Claire off men.

Well, maybe not *all* men. And maybe not forever.

Chapter 21

Haley Park Rise, Brent Cross, London, England

Blackness. Total blackness.

Silence, inside and out. Night? It had to be night.

What time is it?

Enderby had lost all track ... all bloody track.

Shit!

A creaking floorboard above his head made him jump, hold his breath. He looked up into the pitch blackness and imagined following the footfalls as they approached the cellar door.

His heart raced, slamming against his ribs. It beat so loud, it threatened to rouse the whole bloody house.

Be Hunter. Please be Hunter.

He focused everything he had on the squeaking floor-boards. His whole world pinpointed on the groaning wood-work of a grotty, old house.

Metal scraped on metal, the lock mechanism clunked, and the cellar door creaked slowly open. An almost-imper-ceptible paleness lightened the blackness. Dim, but acting as a beacon of hope. It was dark outside. Still night. Definitely. He hadn't been asleep that long.

A silhouette, legs, materialised in the dimness. They descended the staircase, the wooden treads grinding as they deflected under the man's bulk. The cloth of his trouser legs rustled against each other.

Enderby shielded his eyes ahead of the expected blaze of the fluorescent tube, but it didn't happen. For once, he gave thanks for the blessed, blessed darkness.

The silhouette stopped at the foot of the steps.

"You awake?"

A whisper in the blackness. The voice unrecognisable. Hunter?

Please let it be Hunter.

"Y-Yes," he croaked. He coughed. Tried to swallow past a rasping throat. Couldn't.

"Keep quiet. Protect your minces—your eyes. Light comin' on."

Enderby looked away and the narrow beam of a penlight sliced through the blackness. Wonderful, warming light. The light of hope.

In the backwash of the penlight, the silhouette's outline sharpened into the shaven-headed form of Hunter, his potential saviour. Dressed head to toe in black, he still looked like a silhouette.

Hunter approached his dark corner, his rubber-soled

walking boots barely making a sound on the uneven concrete.

"Hold out your 'and."

"What?"

"Do it."

Enderby complied with the instruction, unable to let himself believe what was happening.

"Hold the chain. Stop it rattlin'."

Hunter placed the penlight between his teeth and keyed the cuffs. The bracelet parted and the chain fell from his wrist. Enderby stopped it clattering to the floor and gently lowered it into an uneven coil.

Hunter recovered the penlight and whispered, "Fifty grand, you said."

"Yes, yes. Fifty grand in cash. All yours."

At that point, he'd have agreed to anything. To escape the hideous darkness, he'd have sold his mother. If she'd still been alive.

"Follow me," Hunter breathed. "Keep the noise down. They're light sleepers."

"Where are we going?"

"Shut up or I'll leave you 'ere," he whispered.

He turned and ghosted up the staircase. Enderby followed, trying not to stagger on numb, lifeless legs.

At the top of the staircase, Hunter paused, and Enderby nearly blundered into him in his hurry to leave. The black man held out an arm to hold him back. They paused for an interminable moment, listening to the groans and creaks of a house settling and cooling after the relative warmth of the day. Hunter dropped his arm and turned left, making for the front of the house.

A mere six paces separated them from the front door, its

glazed upper panels backlit by amber streetlights that repre-
sented the outside—freedom.

Only six paces.

Even though they hugged close to the wall, the floor-
boards still creaked underfoot. No, they didn't creak, they
groaned, howled, screamed.

Oh God.

Two paces.

Nearly there. So close.

Enderby could barely believe it.

Upstairs, someone snored. Sharp and loud, but only
once. He and Hunter froze. Stood immobile for endless
seconds. Enderby feared his heart might explode under the
strain.

Hunter started again. Two more steps.

They reached the front door. Hunter slid back the chain
—another bloody chain—and turned the lock. It clicked
loud enough to wake the snoring man overhead, loud
enough to wake Enderby's dead mother.

Please let me out.

Hunter tugged the handle, and the door opened on
silent, recently oiled hinges. Cold air rushed through the
opening. The icy air of freedom, of escape. Enderby shivered with cold and delight.

The black man marched through the opening. Enderby
followed closely behind.

Outside. They were outside.

God. We've done it!

Hunter rushed along the short and empty drive, darted
through the open gateway, and turned left when he reached
the pavement. Enderby followed as quickly as his weakened,
cramping legs could carry him. Every muscle and joint in

his body cried out for him to stop, but he had to carry on. He had to get away.

At the third junction, Hunter took another left and slowed to wait for a lagging Enderby, who struggled to breathe through the pain in his chest. Bloody thing still hurt from Kaine's stunning knuckle punch. After two days it still bloody hurt.

Eventually, he pulled alongside, bent at the middle, and clasped his hands to his knees. Ignoring the blowtorch flame that seared his lungs with every breath, he whooped in great gulps of chill, night air.

"Where are we going?" he gasped. Sweat poured out of him, chilling him to the bone.

"My wheels, bro. It's just over there." Hunter turned and marched towards a black BMW 3 Series parked under a streetlight. The car had a crumpled rear bumper and had seen better days—about ten years earlier.

"I-I was expecting the black cab."

Hunter snorted and sucked air through his teeth. "Stands out too much in this area, bro. I prefer the Beemer. Can't beat the power under that bonnet. Get in."

He pressed a button on his key fob, the Beemer's hazard lights flashed twice, and the interior courtesy light filled the cabin with its welcoming, yellow glow.

Enderby yanked open the front passenger door, dived into the seat, and melted into the worn, but soft, leather upholstery. Glorious. Never again would he take the comfort of a beautifully padded seat for granted.

Hunter slid behind the steering wheel, fastened his seatbelt, and pressed the ignition button. The engine rumbled into life. A red warning light flashed and bleeped on the dashboard.

"Belt up," Hunter said.

With shaking hands and trembling fingers, Enderby pulled the seatbelt over his aching shoulder and around his waist, and slid the buckle into the lock. The warning light and buzzer extinguished.

Hunter checked over his shoulder for traffic before pulling gently away from the kerb. Keeping well inside the speed limit, he took the second exit at the roundabout they'd negotiated two evenings earlier and followed the signs to the Brent Cross Flyover.

Enderby clenched his right hand into a fist and bit his knuckle, desperate not to cry out in delight. Desperate not to show any emotion, any weakness.

They were heading back into town. He'd made it. He'd actually escaped. Only then did the fears surface and the questions start forming. The paranoia set in.

Why? Why had Hunter broken ranks and risked all to save him? It surely couldn't be for the money. Would he risk his life and betray a man like Ryan Kaine for a mere fifty thousand? Would he demand more?

Stop it, Greg. You're out. Make the most of it.

The digital clock on the dash clicked over to ten past two. He'd had so little sleep in the previous two days. With that and being chained to the metal chair, it was no wonder his body and mind were shutting down. Only the fear-driven spike of adrenaline kept him from falling asleep in the comforting warmth of the Beemer.

They drove two miles along the A41 in silence before Hunter indicated left, slowed, and turned into the first side street they reached. He stopped under a streetlight.

"Why have we stopped?"

"I want my money."

"What, now?"

"Fifty grand, you said. In cash, you said. But I want a hundred, and I want it tonight."

Bastard. Fucking money-grubbing bastard.

Enderby stared at the man's wiry frame. Lean, toned muscles. A middleweight, not a cruiserweight like Enderby. Before he could work out whether he could take the black man apart in his weakened state, Hunter dipped a hand inside his open jacket and withdrew a gun. In an instant, he racked and released the slide, and slid his index finger through the trigger guard. A SIG, judging by the diagonal striations running down the outside of the slide. A serious weapon in the steady hands of a professional skilled in its use—the way Hunter held it—not sideways like a Hollywood *gangsta*.

"One hundred," Hunter repeated. "We got a deal?"

Enderby nodded.

"One hundred," he said. "It's a deal."

"Don't even think of stiffin' me, bro," Hunter said, showing his gleaming, white teeth in a snarl. "Cash money, you said. I want it now, or I'm takin' you back to the house."

"What? Take me back?" Enderby said, folding his arms across his bruised chest. "Don't be stupid. You'll be in as much trouble as me. You can't go back now, and we both know it."

Hunter dropped the snarl and replaced it with a sly smile.

"We *can* go back, bro," he said. "With you in a body bag. If they wake up, I can always say you escaped, and I recaptured you, but you put up a fight. They won't mind you bein' dead. Not since you've already given up your emergency protocols. Dummy."

"How the hell would I have escaped? I was handcuffed to a chain."

Hunter laughed. High-pitched and manic, it made Enderby's stomach churn and the hairs on the back of his neck quiver.

"Simple, bro. After I shoot you in the head, I'll smash your right hand with the butt of this here gun." He pointed the SIG at the roof and showed him the butt in question. "Easy to slip out of a pair of cuffs when the bones in your hand are crushed, innit."

Enderby stared into the dark brown eyes of his rescuer and read nothing but certainty. The man would do what he'd threatened. He was looking into the eyes every bit as much of a stone killer as Ryan Kaine and Will Stacy. Enderby swallowed past a dry throat.

"Why?" he asked, taking the risk of antagonising the steely-eyed black man pointing the gun in his face.

"Why what?"

"Why betray a man like Ryan Kaine?"

"I got one hundred thousand reasons, bro. 'Sides, you saw the way he kept dissin' me. I drive him aroun' like a snottin' chauffeur. I fetch an' carry for 'im. I make fuckin' sandwiches. And he pays me peanuts. You know what I got for this job? A monkey. Five hundred smackers, yeah? A monkey for jackin' a government bigwig? A monkey for a job as carries a life sentence, yeah? I call that an insult, bro. An' you know why he only payin' me a monkey?" He paused and opened his eyes wider, expecting an answer.

Enderby shook his head.

"It's 'cause I'm black an' he's a racist prick." He curled his upper lip and sucked air through his teeth. "I know for a fact that Stacy's gettin' five grand a day, and all he did was bolt a chair to the floor an' nail some carpet to the walls. I mean ... Kaine's a racist, man. You feel me, bro?"

He held out his left fist, but Enderby didn't have the energy, or the inclination, to bump it.

"Okay, bro. You can leave me hangin' if you like. No skin off of my hooter. If you's got the cash, I ain't worried 'bout the chill factor."

Enderby relaxed but didn't let it show. Despite looking down the barrel of a 9mm cannon—not something he would ever grow accustomed to—he had things under control. The black man's greed would work in Enderby's favour. Enderby understood avarice. He would use it for as long as he had to. All he had to do was reach home. The apartment was his sanctuary. His safe haven.

"So," Hunter growled, "where the money at?"

"In a wall safe in my apartment."

"Where's that?"

"Holborn."

Hunter whistled.

"You got a crib in Holborn? Man, you is filthy rich. Maybe I shoulda axed for more money." He laughed. "Nah, don't fret, bro. I'm happy wi' the hundred."

"Good."

You won't live long enough to see it let alone spend it.

Hunter decocked the SIG and stuck it back into his pocket. He shifted the stick into first gear and pulled away from the kerb.

Chapter 22

Wednesday 9th June - Gregory Enderby

Bideford Avenue, Holborn, London, England

They made good time on near-empty roads, and it only took them twenty-five minutes to reach the blessed relief of familiar territory. Home territory. Enderby directed Hunter down Sandford Street and left onto Bideford Avenue. On finally catching sight of the white rendering on the ground floor of his Edwardian terrace, he nearly cried with joy.

"We're here," he said, regaining total control. "Park anywhere you can. We won't be long."

Not long at all.

Hunter would be dead before the traffic wardens were up and about. The fucker had played a role in the most humiliating period of Enderby's life. Nobody embarrassed

Gregory Enderby and lived to boast about it with his mates. The big, black bastard was going to die. And Enderby would be the one to do it. No one else but him. For his self-esteem, he'd do it himself.

Enderby glanced at the man who thought he was in control.

Not long now, you arrogant prick.

Hunter—the dead man driving—found an empty place opposite Number 41 and parked badly, hanging the front wheels over the edge of the bay. He killed the engine, pulled the SIG before Enderby had time to release his seatbelt, and flashed his white teeth.

"No funny business, bro. I don't trust you no further'n I can spit. You feel me?"

Yeah, I 'feel' you, arsehole.

Enderby raised his hands in surrender.

"All I want is to go home, pay you what you deserve, and take a hot shower."

"One hundred grand. In cash, yeah?"

"In cash. In my safe. It's all yours."

Hunter flashed another bright smile.

"Stay right where you are, bro. Don't you move a muscle."

Hunter opened the driver's door, slid outside, and hurried around the front of the BMW. He reached the passenger's door and tugged it open. At no stage did the SIG's muzzle point anywhere but at Enderby's face.

"Out you get, bro."

I'm not your fucking brother!

Enderby climbed out of the car and closed the door quietly. Hunter stepped close, lowered the SIG, and hid it in the folds of his black-denim jacket.

"Just think on this, bro," he whispered. "Although I ain't

as good a shot as the Captain—few are—I won't miss. Not at this range. You feel me?"

"Yes," Enderby said, trying not to sound annoyed by the man's attempted intimidation.

Enderby led the way back to his building, Number 3. As they approached the slate-grey, arched door, Hunter edged even closer.

"Nice gaff you got here, bro," he whispered. "Plenty of security goin' on in a place like this? Surveillance cameras an' shit?"

"Concierge-protected entry. It's manned twenty-four-seven. But Lord knows who'll be on station tonight. The security company can't keep hold of its staff. They send a different idiot almost every week."

Hunter grabbed Enderby's upper arm and pulled him closer to the railings. His grip tightened.

"What the fuck, man?" he hissed. "Is you leadin' me into a trap?"

Yes, I am.

"Of course not."

"What's the bloke gonna do when you arrive with a brother at your side?"

Enderby screwed up his face. "He won't do anything. I press the bell, he runs the facial rec, and buzzes me inside. And that's that. No problem."

"And how's you gonna explain me?"

Enderby shook his head. "If he asks, I'll tell him you're one of my old schoolmates. I often have friends crash in my spare room."

And if you believe that, you're thicker than you look.

"Just don't speak," Enderby added.

"What? You think I can't pass for one of your home boys?"

You said it, dickhead.

Enderby clamped his mouth shut and waited.

Hunter tilted his head to one side, eyes narrowed, deep in what passed for thought in his empty head. Eventually, he nodded.

"Okay, bro. But don't do nothin' stupid. Remember who's got the gun when *we're on the inside.*"

The lure of money had won out over the arsehole's natural caution.

Greedy prick.

Hunter released his iron hold on Enderby's upper arm and nudged him towards the entrance.

Ahead, a big, silver Range Rover, headlights dipped, turned left into the avenue from Sandford Street and rolled quietly past. The driver, a tough-looking man in his late twenties, stared straight ahead. The SUV's blacked-out rear windows hid the occupants of the passenger compartment. Nothing unusual there. Bideford Avenue housed dozens of high-flyers who paid through the nose for bodyguard-chauffeurs and to maintain their anonymity.

Enderby reached the gap in the railings which would once have housed a pair of gates and turned into the covered entrance of the corner plot. The arched doorway with blast-proof glass and steel double doors stood between Enderby and safety. He stopped, held his breath, and stared into the camera lens.

"Morning, sir," the doorman said through the surveillance system. He sounded wary. No doubt, he'd clocked Hunter on the surveillance camera. "How are you?"

"Buzz me in, man," Enderby barked. "It's cold out here."

"Please look at the camera, sir."

Enderby lifted his head and scowled at the security

camera for the five seconds it took the facial-recognition system to scroll through its automated process. The worse the weather, the longer it seemed to take.

"Come on, man!"

Eventually, the lock released, and Enderby pushed open the door. Familiar, subdued lighting told him he'd reached a place of safety. He'd reached home. Hunter's right arm moved against Enderby's side, reminding him about the gun. The bugger was starting to feel antsy.

Wouldn't be feeling anything soon.

"Good evening, sir," the doorman said from behind his oak counter. A real bozo this one. Pudgy, grey-haired, late fifties, dull expression on his rounded face. "It's cold tonight."

"Now tell me something I don't know," Enderby growled.

"Have you had an accident?" Bozo asked. He stared pointedly at the tracksuit bottoms and lifted his gaze to take in the wrinkled suit jacket and heavily creased, silk shirt, missing a tie.

Shit, he must have looked a total mess.

"An arsehole in the pub spilled a glass of red wine over me." He held up his right fist. "Bugger won't be doing that again in a hurry. Another suit ruined, but what the hell." He shrugged. "I have plenty of suits."

The small office behind Bozo housed a kitchenette, a bed, and a toilet. All the comforts of home. Of greater interest, the open and readily accessible shelf under the counter hid a big, red panic button. At the first sign of trouble, Bozo's standing instructions would tell him to hit the button. Once struck, the security locks would activate, rendering the building impenetrable to everything short of a missile attack. On top of which, the nearest police station would receive the silent alarm, and send an armed response unit around to send the attackers into oblivion.

Enderby toyed with the idea of tipping Bozo the nod, but there was no telling how Hunter would react to being caught inside a mantrap. He might just open up with the SIG and that would be disastrous. Besides, if he did that, Enderby would lose his chance to take personal revenge. He'd be damned if he couldn't overpower a semi-literate guttersnipe like Hunter.

"Who's your guest, sir?" Bozo asked.

"None of your damned business."

"Do I need to book him in, sir?"

"No."

Bozo stared blankly at him.

"Understood, sir."

No love wasted between them, and why should there be? Bozo was nothing but the hired help. After such a shitty time—undoubtedly the worst two nights of Enderby's life—he saw no reason to be nice to the staff.

Enderby led Hunter into the staircase, and they climbed ten flights of stairs to the fifth floor, the penthouse. His next place would have a dedicated lift which would open directly into his apartment's main living area. And that would happen soon. As soon as Gordon held up his end of their deadly bargain and eliminated Sir Ernest.

Enderby pressed his index finger to the touchpad, keyed in the five-digit access code, and his front door clicked open.

"Fingerprint access, huh?" Hunter asked, sounding suitably impressed.

"Naturally."

"What's wrong with keys?"

Enderby allowed himself a derisive snort.

"Keys are heavy, and they spoil the line of a nicely cut suit."

Hunter sniffed. Unimpressed.

Enderby entered his apartment and hit the main light switch. The wall sconces flicked on, throwing their warm and subdued glow around the lounge-diner. Hunter brushed past him and moved to the centre of the room, keeping the SIG levelled at Enderby's head.

Not long now, arsehole. Not long.

"So, how d'you get into your car, bro?"

The *bro* was growing old so bloody quickly.

"I have an iris-recognition system fitted to my Maserati."

"Well now. Ain't that fancy."

Hunter pushed close, skirted behind Enderby, and shoved him in the back. Enderby stumbled and caught himself on the wingback chair in front of the state-of-the-art, curved screen TV.

"Enough gabbin', where's my money at?"

Enderby turned and raised his hands. "The safe's in my office. It's through there." He pointed towards the door he always kept closed.

"Go on, then," Hunter snarled. "Let's do this."

Enderby pushed himself away from the wingback and led the way to the office, rehearsing the action in his head. He only had one chance and had to make it count.

Open the safe door. Remove the cash and the fully loaded and ready-cocked SAMS P29 semi-automatic. Turn and fire.

Simple. Nothing difficult.

Enderby couldn't wait. He shuddered in anticipation.

Hunter wasn't wearing body armour. That much, Enderby had learned from the drive. He could afford to aim centre mass, which reduced his chance of missing the target.

"Don't try nothin' clever, bro," Hunter said. "Remember what I'm packin'."

Enderby opened the oak-panelled door, pushed it wide, and strode into the cosy office.

"Stop right there. Lemme see what you got."

Hunter stepped closer. So close, his breath warmed the back of Enderby's neck and made him cringe.

Slowly, to avoid startling his "captor", he stretched out an arm and threw the wall switch. The ceiling lamp shot a bright light around the room. His desk faced the door, the office chair behind it, and on the wall behind the chair, hung the landscape painting of his family's holiday home in the Cotswolds. A stone cottage he hadn't set foot inside for the better part of a decade.

"Where's the safe, bro?"

"Behind the painting."

"Well, get to it, bro. I don't got all night." He flicked the SIG at the painting.

"Okay, okay. I'm doing it."

Enderby skirted around the desk, reached out, and pressed the hidden button on the right side of the picture frame. The catch released, allowing the painting to swing free.

Enderby moved slightly to his left to hide the safe and pressed his thumb to the pad. He punched in the number—the same one he used on the front door—and the safe's door popped open.

"Thank you, Greg," a man—not Hunter—said. "That's all we need." He spoke quietly.

Enderby froze.

No! Oh God. No. It can't be!

Acid bile roiled in his stomach, threatening to burst into his throat.

So close. So close he could almost smell the gun oil, but now ... Oh God.

"Turn around," the quiet man said. "Do it slowly, and make sure your hands are empty. If they're not empty, this won't end well for you."

Enderby's left hand gripped the safe's open door, his trembling right hovered over the primed P29.

So close.

He wanted to cry.

Enderby retracted his hand and turned, slow and steady.

Three armed men stood inside the open doorway, pointing their guns at him. Hunter to the left, a toothy smile spread all over his dark face. To the right, a carved-from-stone Will Stacy, dead eyes narrowed, Glock steady and pointing at Enderby's chest. In the centre, stood the shortest of the three. Long, wavy hair, full greying beard, brown eyes hidden behind thick-rimmed glasses, and as stone-faced as Will Stacy.

Kaine.

Oh God.

Ryan Kaine!

Chapter 23

Finchley Road, Golders Green, London, England

Kaine stretched out and half-dozed on the comfortable back seat of Will's Range Rover. It had been a long few days, and he'd had very little in the way of sleep, snatching nothing but catnaps when he could. In the BMW ahead, Hunter and Enderby hadn't spoken since hitting Finchley Road, and Kaine could barely keep his eyes open.

Enderby was taking Hunter to his home. With another fifteen minutes at least before they reached Holborn, Kaine settled back and let his eyelids droop. He allowed his thoughts to drift …

"We're here, Captain. Bideford Avenue's just around the corner," Stefan said from the driving seat.

Already?

He'd dozed off.

Kaine sat up straight, yawned, and rubbed some life into his face.

Time for the special glasses.

With some reluctance, he removed the comfortable earpiece, pulled the glasses from their protective case, and slid them on. Much heavier than standard specs—the frame contained a mass of electronic tech—the damn things tended to pinch his nose and give him a headache, and he'd put off wearing them as long as possible. Kaine tapped the left arm once.

"Alpha One to Control. Are you receiving me? Over."

"*Hi there, Mr K. How you diddling?*" Corky asked. He never seemed tired or stressed.

"We'll be heading in soon. How are the glasses? Over."

"*Perfect. Corky can see whatever you're looking at. Zoom in and everything. Recording now.*"

"Excellent. Won't be long now. Alpha One, out."

Kaine had used the camera-glasses once before, in Arizona, and still had no real idea how they worked. Corky had tried to explain the concept to him, but Kaine had glazed over at the first mention of bifocal, eye-tracking sensors in the arms feeding signals to a fish-eye camera built into the frame. Still, it didn't matter *how* they worked, just that they did.

He stretched out on the back seat, prepping for imminent action.

Stefan rolled the Range Rover to a stop alongside the darkened Old Nick, a pub whose traditional, green-and-gold paintwork looked in keeping with the street's red-brick, Victorian terrace, but not with the grey-steel-and-smoked-glass, multi-storey monstrosity opposite. A classic example of the local planning department's inability to balance the new and the old.

"Want me to wait here for the signal, sir?" Stefan asked. "We're only a few metres away."

Kaine nodded and glanced at Will, who sat alongside him in the back seat. "Anything?"

"They've parked the Beemer," Will said. "Won't be long now."

Kaine tapped the left arm of the specs twice to pick up Hunter's comms and they listened together.

"...*I'll tell him you're one of my old schoolmates,*" Enderby said, speaking quietly. "*I often have friends crash in my spare room. Just don't speak.*"

"*What? You think I can't pass for one of your home boys?*" Hunter snarked, playing the streetwise heavy to the hilt. Kaine worried that he might be overdoing the act, but Enderby seemed to be falling for it. "*Okay, bro. But don't do nothin' stupid. Remember who's got the gun when* we're on the inside."

"That's it—the signal," Kaine said. "Cough, out you get. You can make it on foot from here. I don't want it to look as though you're riding shotgun. Stefan, take us around the corner. Nice and slow."

Kaine wanted to run a live recon of the ground ahead of the attack. The satellite run-through had told them a great deal, but the area might have changed since the images had been taken. Something as simple as road works or building maintenance could compromise their approach. Hunter could be walking into a trap, and Kaine would rather abort the operation than increase the risk.

"Walk all that way, boss?" Cough asked, opening the door and climbing out onto the pavement. "All on my own?"

"Poor you," Stefan mocked. "It must be all of a hundred metres."

Cough grinned at his mate, pushed the door closed, and headed off towards the turning into Bideford Avenue.

Stefan added a little pressure to the accelerator and the big Range Rover pulled away. Smiling, he flicked Cough a dismissive wave as they rolled past and indicated left. They made the turn in time to see Hunter push Enderby through a gap in the railings in front of Number 3. Enderby glanced at the Range Rover but didn't appear spooked by their passing.

Bideford Avenue hadn't changed from the satellite images. Kaine nodded to Will. The operation was a go.

Stefan carried on until they reached the turning into Princeton Way, and double parked the second they were out of sight of Enderby's building.

"*Morning, sir,*" an electronic voice said in Kaine's comms. "*How are you?*"

"*Buzz me in, man. It's cold out here.*"

"*Please look at the camera, sir.*"

"Okay, that's it," Kaine said. "Let's go."

Kaine and Will jumped out of the Range Rover and marched towards Number 3, while Stefan pulled away to complete as many slow and extended circuits of the block as required. Few things stood out more on a quiet, residential street at night than a double-parked SUV.

Kaine and Will slowed as the stilted conversation between Enderby and the concierge continued. Kaine hated the dismissive and aggressive way Enderby spoke to the man. No need for it. Enderby couldn't have been more of an arrogant prick.

They stopped three doors back from Number 3, hugging tight against the black railings in the deep shadow of one of the many trees lining the avenue. He tugged his snood up over his nose, drew his SIG, and racked the slide. Alongside him, Will followed suit with both snood and his preferred Glock.

"Alpha One to all. Ready?" Kaine whispered.

Will dipped his head. Cough—standing in the shadows on the far side of Number 3, snood also covering the lower half of his face—signalled his readiness by circling his thumb and index finger. He'd clearly picked up the divers' "okay" from the rest of Kaine's troop.

Kaine raced forwards with Will sticking tight to his right flank. He darted through the opening in the railings and shoulder charged the steel-and-glass door. The lock Hunter had blocked with a thin, magnetic strip popped, and the door crashed inwards.

"Hands!" he barked, lining up his SIG at the middle of the stunned concierge's forehead. "Show me your hands!"

Eyes wide, open-mouthed, the man threw up his open hands and glanced down at his desk, undecided.

"Don't even think about it, my friend," Will said, his voice carrying so well he didn't need to shout. "We'd prefer the silent alarm to remain … silent."

Kaine could imagine Will smiling at the man from behind his snood. He didn't often resort to puns, but that one worked well enough.

Blinking rapidly, the security guard eased his body away from the counter, decision made. He'd sized up the situation and wasn't about to risk a bullet to press the panic button. Loaded guns could have a debilitating effect on the bravest of men.

"Stand up," Will ordered.

Hands still raised, the concierge stood, his chair scraped on the hard flooring, and he backed away from the counter.

Sweat formed on his upper lip. Moving slowly, he wiped it away with the back of his hand.

"Who the—"

"Don't be silly," Cough said. "It won't help you to know who we are." He stepped around the counter, grasped the man's shoulders, and spun him to face the rear wall.

"Arms please," Cough said, "and don't fight me. Let's do this nice and easy."

He wrenched the tubby man's arms down and behind his back, and bound his wrists with a heavy-duty cable tie.

"Thank you, sir," Kaine said to the concierge's back. "We won't detain you long."

He nodded to Cough, who pushed the compliant concierge through the door leading into his office cubby-hole. After securing him in the back, Cough would take the man's place behind the counter in the unlikely event of another resident needing to gain entry so late at night.

Kaine and Will left Cough to his predetermined task, and raced each other up the wide stairs, its thick, pile carpet rendering their footfalls near silent. They reached the top floor in a dead heat. Again, Hunter had left the apartment's front door unlocked as agreed, and they entered a subtly lit and expensively furnished room.

They lowered the suffocating snoods, and moved silently towards the bright light shining through an open door on the far side of the room. After stepping into the office, they fanned out next to Hunter.

Enderby had his back to the room. One hand gripped the safe's door, and the other hovered in the opening.

"Thank you, Greg. That's all we need," Kaine said.

Enderby jerked. Froze.

"Turn around. Do it slowly, and make sure your hands are empty. If they're not empty, this won't end well for you."

Arms raised, hands open and trembling, Enderby turned. His jaw dropped and his eyes widened.

"Kaine!" he gasped.

Kaine smiled. "Hello, Greg. How are you, old man?"

"Oh God."

A dark stain spread down Enderby's tracksuit bottoms.

"Oh dear, look at that," Will said. "He's wet himself again."

"Not been a good couple of days for you, has it, Greg?" Kaine said, offering Enderby a sympathetic smile he didn't mean. "Step away from the safe and take a seat."

Enderby staggered forwards and collapsed into the leather chair on his side of the desk. He looked ready to throw up or burst into tears, but Kaine couldn't generate one gram of pity for the creature who'd colluded with Malcolm Sampson and Pinocchio, and helped set up his men to be killed. Not to mention the part he'd played in organising the Grey Notice.

They were reaching the end game, and Kaine had never been more ready.

"Place your hands flat on top of the desk, Greg," Kaine said. "I don't want you reaching for anything in the drawers."

Enderby complied. His fingers spread over the desk's polished surface and pressed down so hard, it looked as though he was trying to hold on and stop himself collapsing into a puddle of his own sweat.

"By the way, Hunter," Kaine said, nodding to the latest addition to his growing payroll, "well played. I almost believed you myself."

Hunter's smile grew even wider. "Thank you, Captain."

"Hmm," Will said, shaking his head, without taking his

eyes off their dejected captive. "I thought you went way over the top with all that 'Bro' nonsense."

"Everyone's a critic," Hunter huffed, still smiling.

"Okay," Kaine said, stepping closer to the desk. "Let's get down to business, shall we?"

Kaine strolled around to Enderby's side of the desk and yanked open each of the three drawers. He found paper, files, and various items of stationery, but nothing that could be used as a weapon, unless Enderby wanted to try attacking three armed men with a loaded stapler or an ink-filled cartridge pen. Or he could try garrotting them all with a length of USB cable. Unlikely.

"Hunter," he said, "time for you to do your thing."

"Remind me again. What am I looking for, sir?"

"Anything of interest … and of value."

Enderby canted his head to stare up at Kaine. "A robbery? Is that why you're—"

"Yes, Greg. That's exactly why we're here."

While Hunter left to start his "search", Will edged around to the side of the small office. He stood in front of a floor-to-ceiling display cabinet that was filled with boxing and golf trophies, taking up a commanding position where he could cover the whole room.

"By the way, thanks for leaving the safe door open," Kaine said, glancing to his right and stretching his neck to see its contents. "Beating the access code out of you would have been fun, but such a timewaster. Messy, too."

"There's money in the safe. Cash. You can take it if that's—"

"How much?" Will asked.

Enderby's haunted gaze shifted from Kaine to Will.

"Fifty thousand … pounds."

Will's eyebrows lifted ever so slightly.

"And everyone's telling me cash is going out of fashion," he said. "How did you lay your hands on that sort of money?"

Enderby lowered his head, refusing to answer.

"You told Hunter you'd give him a hundred," Kaine said, catching the cowering man's eye. "Were you lying, Greg?"

Enderby shifted in his chair, either in discomfort at being caught out in another lie, or from the dampness of his tracksuit bottoms, Kaine couldn't tell. Didn't care much, either.

"I-I hoped that seeing the cash would be enough to … I don't know."

Kaine frowned. "And if that didn't work, the piece of crap SAMS P29 would convince him to accept your revised offer, I suppose?"

Enderby shivered from his core.

"What? I-I don't know—"

"Naughty, naughty, Greg." Kaine leaned closer to the open safe. "You shouldn't keep it loaded and primed. The way those things are put together, I wouldn't be surprised if the damn thing went off on its own."

Kaine decocked and holstered his SIG, reached into the safe, and retrieved the P29. Handling it with great care, he decocked the unreliable weapon, too. For added security, he removed the thirteen-shot magazine, and ejected the round up the spout.

Without removing his hands from the desk, Enderby twisted awkwardly in his chair, watching Kaine's every move.

"Is there anything else in there you wouldn't want me to take from the safe, Greg? Apart from that nicely wrapped bundle of cash, I mean."

Enderby averted his eyes and shook his head.

"N-No."

Kaine grabbed the brick of cash and dropped it on the desk. The see-through, plastic wrapping revealed individual bundles of new banknotes, each held together with a yellow band. Each band contained two and a half grand worth of fifties. A cashier's signature and the bank's rubber stamp certified the bundles as accurate.

"Thanks for the contribution to the cause, Greg," Kaine said, grinning. "Now, what else do we have in here?"

Enderby lifted his right hand from the safety of the desk, realised what he'd done, and slammed it back into place.

"Just household stuff. Legal papers. My will. The mortgage contract on the apartment. My passport. N-Nothing you'd need."

Kaine reached into the safe again and emptied it of the three buff folders. He opened the first and tipped its contents—a thin document bound with a plastic strip—onto the desk beside the cash. The top sheet bore the copperplate title, "Last Will and Testament of Gregory Bysshe Enderby".

"Bysshe?" Kaine scoffed. "You're middle name's Bysshe?"

Enderby lowered his head again. "My ... mother liked poetry."

Kaine skimmed through the second folder. Mortgage and life insurance documents. So far, Enderby hadn't lied on either count. He'd told the truth about the contents of the safe, and his earlier version of the way the government operated tallied with what Kaine already knew.

He opened the remaining folder and emptied its contents—birth certificate, passport, bank account details and statements—on top of the pile. Nothing valuable to

Kaine, or anyone else but Enderby. No sign of the USB flash drive he'd been hoping for. Another blank.

"Why are you here?" Enderby whined. "I've done nothing to you. Nothing."

"Shut up!" Will barked, raising his voice in anger for the first time in as long as Kaine could remember. "You set up the Grey Notice."

"No, I had nothing to do with it. I-I already told you," Enderby blubbed, unable to look either Will or Kaine in the eye. He had to be the worst liar Kaine had seen that year, and he'd seen a few.

"I'm not high enough up the government's totem pole to initiate a Grey Notice," Enderby continued. "Only a government minister has that kind of authority, but … it usually happens when they're acting under the advice of a department or agency head."

"An agency head like Sir Ernest Hartington, you mean?" Kaine asked.

Enderby raised his head and stared at Kaine, hope shining bright in his eyes.

"Yes, that's right. Like I said in the … in the cellar." He squirmed and his lower lip trembled. "Sir Ernest wrote the report and sent it up the chain. It was him, not me. I had nothing to do with—"

"Who to?" Kaine asked.

"Sorry?" Enderby asked, frowning.

"Who did he send the report to?"

"I-I don't know. I never saw the report. Honest. You'd have to ask Sir Ernest."

Kaine glanced at Will, who shook his head.

"I'm afraid we don't believe you, Greg," Kaine said, affecting a display of sadness.

"B-but it's the truth. I-I promise."

Will bunted himself away from the display cabinet and closed on the desk, a predatory gesture not lost on Enderby, who shuddered and backed away. His chair's lightweight castors bit deep into the thick carpet, preventing him from rolling far.

"Liar," Will said, leaning close to the sweating man.

He raised the Glock and mashed the muzzle into Enderby's forehead, forcing his head into the high back of the chair.

"Oh God. Don't. P-Please don't shoot."

"Why shouldn't I, you lying piece of shit?"

Will jutted out his jaw and rammed the Glock harder. Enderby squealed under the pressure. His eyes squinted to stare at the Glock.

"I worked for GG Cleaning Services, remember," Will said, teeth gritted. "I heard you on the phone order Ryan's death. You sounded in control. You sounded like you were enjoying yourself."

"No. No, I ..." Trembling, Enderby squeezed his eyes closed. Sweat exploded from his face, ran down his nose, and dripped from his chin. "I-I was only——"

"Acting under orders?" Kaine asked, keeping control. Barely.

"Yes, exactly," Enderby said. "I was only doing what Sir Ernest told me to do. It's his fault. It's all down to him."

Will yanked his Glock away. Enderby's head bounced forwards. A circular depression had formed in the middle of his forehead. It stood out red against the pale skin and looked painful.

"So, everything's down to Sir Ernest?" Kaine asked.

"Yes, yes. He's the one you need. I only wrote——" He closed his eyes and clamped his jaws together, realising his mistake.

Enderby had started to crack. Kaine pressed harder.

"You only wrote what, Greg?" he asked, drawing away from the safe and standing alongside Will.

Enderby stared up at Kaine, terrified.

"I-I ... only ... did what Sir Ernest told me to do. Honest."

"And what was that, Greg?"

Enderby sank lower into his chair, shook his head, and fell silent.

"Tell us, Greg," Kaine said, smiling his encouragement.

Enderby swallowed and waited a beat before responding.

"I-I helped prepare the report ... on his instructions," he said, his words a gasped whisper.

Kaine smiled. "Now we're finally getting somewhere. And who did Sir Ernest send the report to?"

Enderby gazed up through pleading eyes and shook his head again.

"I-I promise you. I really don't know. It could have been any one of the big hitters. The Home Secretary. The Foreign Secretary. The Chancellor. The PM. Anyone."

Kaine nodded to Will, who backed away and once again took up his watching position in front of the display cabinet.

Given room to breathe, Enderby peeled a hand from the desktop and rubbed at the mark on his forehead before dropping it back into place.

"And now for the obvious question, Greg. Why?"

"Sorry?" Enderby stopped rubbing and looked up. "Why what?"

"Why did Sir Ernest create the report? What did he have to gain from it?"

"I-I have n-no idea. He might have been prompted to

prepare the report by someone who didn't want to be directly associated with its creation."

"What do you mean?" Kaine asked.

Again, Enderby swallowed.

"Well ... sometimes a request for action comes down from on high. An unofficial ministerial instruction, it's called. I-I think that's what might have happened here."

"Explain," Will ordered, glowering down at Enderby from his side of the office.

Enderby glanced up at Will, his eyes glistening under the dim lights.

"If someone in authority ... someone like, say, the Foreign Secretary ... wants something done on the quiet ... unofficially, they might prompt an agency director to investigate and issue a recommendation. That way, it would be couched as the agency's initiative, not the government's. Things like that happen all the time when the security of the state is challenged."

"So," Kaine said, "let me see if I fully understand what you're telling me. The Foreign Secretary or one of his cabinet colleagues asked Sir Ernest to find a justification for putting a Grey Notice on my head. Is that the way it went?"

"Yes! Yes. Exactly." Enderby's repeated nods could not have been much more enthusiastic.

"And ..." Will said, drawing out the word and letting it hang in the air between them.

Once again, Enderby cowered under Will's gimlet stare.

"And?" he asked, barely able to force out the word.

"Hartington ordered you to write it for him," Will said.

"I-I had to. Don't you see? It was my job, but I hated doing it." Enderby bunched his hands into fists, but kept them pinned to the desktop.

"Sorry, Greg," Kaine said. "I'm afraid I don't believe you."

Enderby jerked up his head. "But you must. It's the truth."

Kaine glanced at Will.

"What d'you think, Will?"

"I think it's total bullshit."

"Yep. Me too."

Enderby looked at each of them in turn but showed the good sense to keep his mouth shut—the first bit of good sense he'd shown since they'd taken him.

"What now?" Will asked, levelling his Glock at Enderby's chest. "Want me to kill him?"

Enderby recoiled and closed his eyes in anticipation of a bullet smashing through his sternum.

"I don't know," Kaine said. "Give me a second."

"We don't have all night."

In the ensuing silence, Hunter arrived at the doorway, a look of delight spread across his chiselled face. He held up a small bag.

"Look what I found," he said.

"Anything of value?" Will asked, lowering his Glock, to Enderby's obvious relief.

"A load of goodies. Two Hublot watches, three pairs of gold cufflinks, a nifty pair of Ray-Bans. A couple of gold rings. One with an inset diamond. Lovely."

"Leave them," Kaine said.

"Excuse me?" Hunter said, the triumphant expression crumpling into a frown.

"It's small change, and that stuff's too easily traced."

"I know a good fence."

"Hunter," Kaine said, "put the trinkets back."

"Yes, sir."

Hunter lowered his head and turned away, muttering something indistinct. Kaine smiled. He'd get over it, and he had plenty of other things to do.

Kaine turned and peered into the open safe. He must have missed something.

The safe, nothing more than an empty, stainless-steel cube the size of a shoebox, peered back at him. Seamless. He knocked the top, bottom, and sides with a knuckle, but each clunk rang back as solid.

Enderby, head down, tried not to look, but a furtive sideways glance gave him away.

Interesting.

Kaine tapped the back panel. Hollow.

"Really, Greg?" Kaine said, turning to face Enderby. "A secret panel?"

No response.

"How does it open?"

Enderby shook his hanging head.

"I'll ask you once more before letting Will loose on you. How does it open?"

Will eased closer to the desk once again, a dead-eyed smile stretching his thin lips. This time, he pressed the Glock into Enderby's left knee.

"Three seconds," Will said. "Three ..."

His index finger tightened on the trigger.

Enderby pulled in a sharp breath.

"Two ..."

"Okay, okay," Enderby squealed, holding up his hands. "Press ... press and release the top right corner."

"Thank you, Greg," Kaine said. "You've just saved yourself a great deal of discomfort. Sorry, Will. Maybe later."

Will glared at the man in the chair and pulled the Glock away.

"Next time, no countdown," Will muttered, showing what looked like genuine disappointment. "I'll just shoot."

Kaine reached into the safe and followed Enderby's instructions. The stainless-steel back plate popped out on hidden, flush-fitting hinges and revealed a space half as large as the first. It contained a sleek, black box and nothing else.

"Well, well, Greg," Kaine said, smiling. "What do we have here?"

Chapter 24

Wednesday 9th June - Pre-Dawn

Bideford Avenue, Holborn, London, England

Kaine reached into the safe and removed the black box from its hiding place. He turned it around in both hands, inspecting it carefully. Solid, black, and unmarked apart from a capital "W" imprinted into the top. The only other indications as to its function were the USB socket and the LED power light cut into the back edge.

"An external hard drive," Will said, stating the obvious.

Kaine placed the drive on the desk, strolled around to the front, and slid into the spare chair opposite Enderby.

"What's on the drive, Greg?" he asked, keeping his tone conversational. "Knitting patterns? Your grandmother's Christmas cake recipe?"

"No, of course not," Enderby answered, trying not to look at the drive, trying to make it seem as though the device held nothing of importance. "It's an external backup for my desktop. The safe is fireproof."

Enderby nodded towards the state-of-the-art computer.

"I don't think so," Kaine said. He leaned forwards and tapped the top of the drive with his index finger. "I've a feeling this is what's called a smoking gun."

"I have no idea what you mean," Enderby said.

Kaine smiled. A grim smile intended to turn Enderby's stomach.

"Yes, you do. We've been looking into your background, Greg. There's no way you made deputy head of the NCTA so quickly on your own merits. You see, you're simply not that talented."

He paused to let the insult sink in before continuing.

"I've an idea that you're the type of man who gathers information and ferrets it away on devices just like this one," Kaine said. "I think you're a man who misses nothing, and knows how to use information to press the right levers."

He crouched forwards and rested his forearms on the desk either side of the drive.

"And on top of that," he continued, "I think you like to document everything you do and keep copies of incriminating evidence on your desktop and on this here drive. The sort of evidence you use to encourage certain high-powered individuals to help you climb the ladder. I've no idea where you keep the originals. Perhaps in your safe deposit box in Barnhardt's Bank on the High Street in Holborn. How am I doing?"

Enderby's gaunt face registered shock. He definitely had no idea how they'd found out about Barnhardt's. Then again, he had no idea that Kaine had friends the likes of Corky and Frodo.

Enderby breathed deep, no doubt trying to stop himself from throwing up.

"I see from your reaction that I'm hitting the mark. This"—Kaine tapped an index finger on the drive—"is your treasure trove. Your ace in the hole. *My* ace in the hole now, though."

Enderby swallowed and launched into it. His final desperate act of defiance.

"If you're right—and I'm not saying you are—I'll never give you access to it. You can let Stacy loose on me if you like, but I'll never give up the password."

He clenched his hands into fists, but kept them pinned to the desktop.

"I wouldn't bet your life on that, Commander," Will growled, and shook his head. "I really wouldn't."

Will padded around behind Enderby, rested his empty hand on the sweating man's shoulder, and squeezed. Enderby winced under the pressure. Will didn't look particularly strong, but Kaine would never challenge him to an arm-wrestling contest. The outcome wouldn't have been in doubt.

"Don't touch me," Enderby shouted. "I'll tell you nothing, unless ..." He allowed the words to trail off into silence.

"Unless what, Greg?" Kaine asked, hiding a yawn behind his hand.

"Unless ... I get some assurances."

Here we go.

Kaine couldn't wait to hear the man bargaining for his freedom—and his life.

"What kind of assurances?" Kaine asked.

"I want your word of honour, as a fellow military officer,

that you'll let me go. Promise to let me live, and I'll tell you everything I know."

Kaine arched an eyebrow and allowed a thin smile to play on his lips.

"You'll take the word of an alleged terrorist who shot down a passenger plane, killing eighty-three people?"

Somehow, Enderby tore his shoulder out from under Stacy's iron grip and leaned so far forwards, his chest dug into the edge of the desk.

"Everyone here knows you were set up for that ... that horror," he said, speaking quickly, speaking for his life. "We've all seen the video. You showed me the damn thing on a bloody loop for hours on end. We all saw the evidence linking Sir Malcolm Sampson, *the late* Sir Malcolm Sampson, to the atrocity. Christ, he admitted it on the recording. *Sampson* was the one ultimately responsible for that disaster, not you. You were just the trigger man. As much an innocent victim as the poor souls aboard that doomed plane."

He paused for a moment to take a deep breath.

"Sir Malcolm had help. The support of people in power. That's why he was convicted of corporate fraud and tax evasion, not mass murder. And that's why he was released from prison on compassionate grounds when he was as healthy as a racehorse. The whole thing was a bloody stitch up right from the start, and I know who orchestrated it." He paused long enough to swallow before continuing. "These are powerful people who would rather see you dead than face trial as a terrorist. They are terrified the truth will come out during a public court case." Ignoring Stacy's looming presence behind him, Enderby pushed away from the desk and leaned against the back of his chair. "I know who they are. You can have them all. All the names. All the way to the very top. And you can have the proof that tears down the government and puts them all behind bars. It's all on that drive," he said, forcing out the words. "I'll give you access to it, but I want your word that you'll let me go. I want to live, free and safe. That's all. Let me go, and I'll disappear. Let me go, and you'll never hear from me again."

"Hmmm," Kaine said, frowning up at Will. "What d'you think, Will."

Stacy folded his arms and pointed the Glock to the ceiling.

"You know what I think, Ryan. I think he's as much to blame for this as the people he's protecting. I think he's a coward who'll give me the password in a heartbeat. Let's find out if I'm right."

Kaine scratched his chin.

"Well now, Will. I'm actually considering his proposal. I've killed too many people in my time. I've had enough. But first, we'll give Mr C a chance to interrogate this nifty, little gadget." Kaine tapped the external drive.

Stacy turned his back to Enderby. "What if Mr C can't access the data?"

"In that case, Will," Kaine said, "we'll take Greg and the drive back to Brent Cross, and you can torture the access codes out of him at your leisure."

"No one can access that data but me," Enderby said, interrupting the discussion. "If anyone tampers with the drive, the data will be lost. Go on"—he nodded—"be my guest. Plug the drive into any computer without my direct access code, and... and it'll self-destruct after ten seconds."

Enderby stopped talking and held his breath. His expression of triumph suggested he could finally see a way out of his predicament.

Sorry, buddy. That's not happening.

Chapter 25

Bideford Avenue, Holborn, London, England

The arm of Kaine's heavy glasses clicked once, the sound penetrating into his ear through the same bone-conducting interface that powered the much lighter and more compact earpieces.

"*Whatcha, Mr K. How you diddling?*"

"I'm okay, Mr C. What do you have for me? Over."

"*The commander's talking twaddle about the drive.*"

"I rather thought he might be, Mr C. Would you care to explain? Over."

Although Kaine looked at the drive most of the time, he shot the occasional glance at Enderby, who had started to look less composed. Less confident.

"*That there device,*" Corky began, "*is a Westbury International, Rugged Mini, solid state hard drive. An Easy-Access 30TB, by the size of it and running a USB 3.2 Gen 2x2 access port. A decent bit of kit, actually. Corky uses them from time to time. And, there ain't no such thing as a built-in self-destruct system, by the way. If you want to know what's on it, plug it into any computer with an internet connection, and Corky can access it for you.*"

"I didn't understand half of what you just said, Mr C, but thanks. I appreciate it. Over."

"*Corky rather thought you mightn't. Plug it into Enderby's desktop computer.*"

"I see it, Control. Hold on a second. I'll power it up. Over."

He reached for the desktop and hit the power button.

"It's password protected," Enderby said, sweating profusely again. "You won't get in."

"*Don't worry 'bout that password nonsense, Mr K. Let it boot up and leave the rest to good, ol' Corky.*"

After a few seconds, the computer's screen glowed blue. A password dialogue box appeared in the middle, cool and defiant.

"I told you," Enderby said, growing more uncomfortable by the minute—judging by the way he squirmed in his seat.

"*Right, Mr K. Hold down the alt key, hit F1, and type in the following code. Asterisk-three-two-three-seven-asterisk. You got that?*"

Kaine followed Corky's instructions, pecked out the code with two fingers, and the password dialogue box disappeared to reveal a busy desktop filled with a jumble of folder icons.

"You can see the screen? Over," Kaine asked.

"*Yep. Corky has access from here. You don't need to keep looking at it so hard. Plug in the drive now. There'll be a USB cable somewhere."*

Kaine slid open the desk's middle drawer and retrieved the cable he'd noticed during his earlier search. He plugged it in, and the Westbury drive's power light glowed green.

"Got that? Over."

"Yep. Give Corky a couple minutes to download the files. Watch the download bar. When it's reached one hundred percent, Corky'll sanitise the drive and wipe the machine. Corky and Frodo will need time to trawl through the data and let you know what we find. Does that work for you?"

"Yes thank you, Mr C. Over."

Corky chuckled and the comms unit built into the glasses clicked into silence.

Kaine angled the desktop's screen to allow them all to see the red line on the download bar slide to the right and the percentage numbers above it climb.

The remaining colour drained from Enderby's already pale face.

"How?" he gasped, barely able to force out the word.

Kaine shrugged. "Beats me. I just let Mr C and Frodo work their magic."

"Frodo?" Enderby gasped. "You've got Frodo?"

"Yes, Greg. We're looking after him now. In fact, he much prefers Mr C's company to the Akers brothers and Malcolm Sampson. It makes him a much more willing volunteer. He's much happier, too."

The countdown ended, the drive's power light faded, and the folders on the desktop disappeared, one by one.

Enderby stared at the blank screen as though willing the icons to return. His lower lip started to tremble.

Will pulled in a deep, slow breath.

"That's it," he said and moved behind Enderby. "All done. Can I kill him now?"

The quaking man couldn't see Will's sly wink.

"Patience, Will. Patience. I might still have a use for him."

The glasses clicked.

"*Whatcha, Mr K. Corky's downloaded the folders, but it's just like you thought. The important files, the ones you need, are encrypted. It's a decent encryption algorithm, too. It'll take Corky and Frodo a little while to decrypt. Sorry 'bout that.*"

Kaine sighed. "Only to be expected, Mr C. Do what you can. Alpha One, out."

"Problems?" Will asked.

"The files are encrypted."

"I told you," Enderby said, puffing out his chest.

"Bugger," Will said. "Want me to beat the code out of him?"

Kaine snorted. At times, Will could have a one-track mind.

"Yes, Will, but there's no time. We need to go."

Enderby tore his gaze from the desktop's blank screen and turned it towards Kaine. Hope shone renewed. He opened his mouth to speak, but shut it again when Kaine held up a finger for silence.

Hunter appeared in the doorway, looking a little glum at having been ordered to relinquish the shiny goodies.

"Are you finished?" Kaine asked.

Hunter nodded.

"Yes, sir," he answered, shooting Enderby a knowing glance. "Didn't find anything of real value."

Kaine picked up the bundle of cash from the desk and lobbed it towards the door. Hunter caught the package left-handed and hugged it tight to his chest.

"Look after that for a while, will you? We'll divvy it up later."

"Happy to, sir," he said, brightening the room with a high-wattage smile. "All done here?"

"Nearly," Kaine said. "Why not pop downstairs and see if Alpha Three needs a hand."

"Happy to, sir." He threw the room a smart salute and sloped away, hugging the cash as though it were his baby.

Kaine turned back to face a cowering Enderby.

"Okay, Greg, we'll be leaving now," Kaine said.

He stood and nodded to Will, who stopped hovering over Enderby and joined him at the near side of the desk.

Will waved his Glock at their horrified captive.

"What are we going to do with him?" he asked, quietly.

Enderby raised his hands. "Don't kill me, please."

Kaine frowned and turned towards Will. "Did you hear that, Will? He thinks we're going to kill him."

Will frowned. "Whatever gave him that idea?" he asked, lowering the decocked Glock, and sliding it into his shoulder holster.

"No, Greg. We have the files. We own you now. Why would we want you dead when you still have your uses?"

Enderby leaned forwards in his chair, disbelief written all over his face.

"What?" he gasped.

"You're ours, Greg. To do with as we see fit. Remember, the evidence on that drive ties you into the whole conspiracy as much as it does Sir Ernest. Go back to work and act as though nothing's happened for the past couple of days. When we're ready, we'll call you with your instructions. When I call, I'll still be using the name Peter Wingard. Got that?"

"What?" Enderby repeated. His expression fluctuated

from disbelief to relief and ended up at total confusion. "Wingard? Right, Yes. Peter Wingard. I've got it."

"Oh, and keep your mobile fully charged. And we'll be really upset if you try to disappear. Won't we, Will."

"Oh yes."

"But …" Enderby said, then shook his head and stopped talking, probably for fear of saying something that might make them change their minds.

"Spit it out, Commander," Will said.

"How do I explain what happened to me? And what happened here tonight? I-I mean you broke in at gunpoint and … God, what did you do with Bozo?"

"Who?"

"The concierge."

Will sighed and turned to Kaine. "Took him long enough to ask, didn't it."

"Don't worry, Greg," Kaine said. "He's perfectly safe. He's having a lie down in his cubbyhole. As for an explanation"—he shrugged—"why not tell him you set up a security test, which he failed? Will that work, d'you think?"

"And as for your bodyguard, Ellen Winters," Will interrupted. "You can tell her A&W Associates didn't come up to scratch and she's forgiven. Tell her to carry on doing what she does."

"That sounds like a good idea," Kaine said, nodding.

Kaine tapped the arm of his glasses. "Alpha One to Alpha Three. Anything to report? Over."

"*Alpha Three here,*" Cough answered immediately. "*Quiet as the grave, boss. Over.*"

"Excellent. We're on our way. Alpha One to Alpha Four, come in. Over."

"*Alpha Four here, boss. Want me to come and collect you? I'm getting dizzy driving around in circles. Over.*"

"Yes, please, Alpha Four. Alpha One, out."

Chapter 26

Bideford Avenue, Holborn, London, England

What the fuck?

Enderby sat in his comfortable chair with the piss drying on his second-hand tracksuit bottoms, trying to understand the complexities of what had just happened. One moment he'd been certain that death had arrived in the shape of a bullet from Will Stacy's Glock, the next, they'd let him go. He hadn't even been interrogated or tortured. At least not properly. Not physically. Mind games. They'd been playing mind games the whole fucking time. In the end, they'd offered him a lifeline. Kaine and Stacy made out that he'd be told what to do. For the rest of his life, he'd be their puppet. However long that might be.

Would he fuck.

They didn't know it yet, but the arseholes had nothing on him. Sweet fuck all. Enderby smiled.

Nobody told Gregory Enderby what to do. Nobody.

Time to cash in some markers. Time for Jay, the ponce, to work off some of his debts. Enderby reached for the landline, but snatched his hand away.

Bloody idiot.

Kaine, Stacy, and the mysterious "Mr C" were bound to be monitoring his landline and work mobile. They practically told him as much before leaving. He needed to work things through for a while. Contacting Jay could wait a few minutes.

First, a shower. He needed to remove the stink of the cellar and the stench of the piss-soaked tracksuit bottoms. He'd bin every stitch he'd worn in the cellar. Every bloody stitch. Then he'd shower and scrub himself free of the humiliation.

Enderby stood and stared down at the seat of his expensive office chair. It didn't look or feel damp, but it would smell of dried urine if left untouched. He shuddered at the idea of having a permanent reminder of his embarrassment in the apartment. A cleaning spray might mask the smell, but it would never scrub out the memory of his failure. The chair would have to go.

Enderby hurried from the office, shuddering each time his inner thighs brushed against the stinging, urine-saturated cloth of the tracksuit bottoms.

In the kitchen, he tore off all his clothes, stuffed them into a black bin liner, and tied a secure knot into the top. Then he dropped the black bag down the rubbish chute and wished he could do the same to the office chair. Stark bollock naked, he grabbed the spray bottle of rose-and-wild-mint, multipurpose cleaner and a cloth from the counter, and padded back to the office. He squirted a liberal coating of the liquid onto the seat, scrubbed it into the leather with the cloth, and repeated the process twice more. It smelled better, but God knew what the cleaner would do to the leather. Probably take off the surface and bleach it white, but who cared?

Enderby returned the cleaner to its allotted place in the cupboard beneath the sink, tossed the cloth into the swing bin, and hurried into the bathroom. He turned the electric shower to the hottest setting he could tolerate and stood, scrubbing soap into himself under the steaming water for a full twenty minutes. In the process, he emptied a whole bottle of shower gel and a half-bottle of shampoo.

CLEAN AND DRY, and finally wearing a fresh set of his own clothes, Enderby left the bedroom with its comfortable and wickedly enticing, king-size bed—which he reluctantly had to ignore—and entered the kitchen to make himself a restorative coffee. Only then did he remember the unfinished business downstairs.

What in god's name was he going to find down there? Bozo bludgeoned to death perhaps? His bullet-ridden corpse?

He returned to the office, grabbed the P29 from the desk where Kaine had left it, surprisingly, and slammed in the magazine. He tugged back the slide and fed a bullet into the breech. He released the slide, and it snapped back into position, making a satisfying, metallic clunk. Not the best semi-automatic pistol on the market perhaps, but it had been a present from Malcolm Sampson back in the happy days before anybody had even heard of Ryan-fucking-Kaine. Enderby wasn't the sort to look into the mouth of a gift horse, and certainly not a gift horse with so many billions to his name. He'd accepted the P29 with delight, but had only fired it a few dozen times—in the Met's shooting range. He didn't really like the action or the balance, but it was accurate enough at close range, and with the wind in the right direction.

Enderby crossed the main room, opened the front door, and stepped into the hallway. He stopped and listened to nothing but silence—the building remained dormant—and tugged the door closed, making sure the catch snapped into place and the lock engaged.

P29 extended and held at waist height, elbow tucked into his side, he descended the stairs slowly, his mind racing. So much to think about. So much to do.

He had two immediate priorities. Figure out a way to explain the break-in, and make sure Sir Ernest died before Kaine could interrogate the old fool. The first would likely prove easier than the second. Kaine had provided the answer in his throwaway suggestion. The second required a little more finesse.

At the half-landing above the ground floor he stopped, caught his breath, and listened.

More silence.

It seemed like Kaine and his cronies had left the building, as promised. Enderby allowed himself a small shudder of relief. But what had they done with Bozo? If the buggers had killed him, it might make things easier. Enderby could claim total ignorance—claim he'd slept through the whole event. On the other hand, in a murder investigation, the whole building would become a crime scene, and the surveillance pictures would show him entering the building with Hunter, the slimy, black bastard. The resulting police investigation would throw the spotlight on him, and he couldn't have that. As always, he needed to fly beneath the radar. Only the Good Lord would know what the idiots in the Met Police would discover. In any event, the Boy Scout in Kaine would surely never allow him to kill an innocent— not knowingly. Would it?

The ground floor foyer, lit through the windows and door glass by the orange streetlights and the pale glow of dawn, stood empty. He'd rarely seen the concierge's chair unoccupied, even in the middle of the night. When did they change shift? He had no idea. Eight o'clock, maybe? He peeled back the cuff of his sweater and read the time off his Breitling. 04:17. The sun would be up before long, and with it the early risers, including the dark-haired doofus in apartment three who went jogging around the park most mornings. Assuming this was one of his training days, he wouldn't be long.

Damn it, what would he find inside?

No time to waste.

Enderby slipped behind the counter and opened the door to the doormen's inner sanctum. He'd only been inside it the once, back when he'd first viewed the apartment. The twenty-four-seven security cover had been a strong selling point for the place.

Someone had decorated and refurnished the room since then.

About the same size as Enderby's home office, it had a kitchenette in the corner, a small dining table and two chairs, a bookcase filled with paperbacks to help Bozo and his mates while away the wee, small hours, and one door leading to a small shower room.

"Hello?" he called.

The answer came back as a muffled shout and frenzied thumping from inside the shower room.

Still alive. As expected.

Enderby relaxed. One question answered. At least he'd be able to run with Plan A.

He barged through the closed door and found the unfortunate, wide-bodied Bozo on the floor, wedged between the toilet and the shower cubicle. His hands were hidden behind his back, no doubt bound the same way as his feet—with a thick, grey cable tie.

Eyes wide, sweating profusely, and struggling against his bindings, the tubby doorman kicked out and shouted something through a cloth gag that could have been, "Untie me!"

Enderby kneeled and tugged away the white cloth stuffed into the man's mouth and held in place with a crepe bandage. How very sterile of Kaine and his men.

"Untie me, man," Bozo screamed. "Come on, hurry."

"What with?"

"There's a knife in the kitchen drawer. Hurry, they haven't been gone long."

Enderby patted his hand in the air between them.

"Okay, right. Don't move, I'll be right back."

He slipped outside, returned with a small kitchen knife, and started sawing at the plastic tie binding Bozo's ankles.

"That'll teach you," Enderby said airily, going with Kaine's suggestion, his mind racing.

"What?" Bozo demanded, glowering. "What d'you mean by that?"

"You should have hit the alarm the moment I arrived with an unannounced guest," he answered, making deliberately hard work of severing the tie.

"Your friend, the black guy?" Bozo gasped.

Enderby stopped sawing, and he caught and held Bozo's eye.

"He wasn't a friend, you idiot. He was a contractor. An employee."

"What?"

Enderby shook his head and added a disgusted snort.

"Haven't you worked it out yet?" he asked and resumed his sawing.

"Worked what out?"

"That, my good man, was what we call a 'live-fire security test'," Enderby said, making it up as he sawed. "And you failed it miserably."

"A security test?" Bozo snarled. "A bloody test? I nearly had a heart attack, and it was a fucking *test*?"

"Mind your language, man. It's totally unnecessary."

"Fuck off!"

Enderby smirked at the man's vitriol. Still, he couldn't really blame the idiot. He'd had a hell of a work shift. Not as bad as the shit Enderby had suffered, though. Not even close.

The ankle tie finally snapped apart, and Bozo worked his way forwards, wriggling out of the confined space. Enderby stepped around and behind him, squatted, and started sawing at the wrist bindings. At one point, the knife slipped and nicked the inside of Bozo's wrist.

"Ouch, careful!" Bozo yelped, jerking his arms, and risking another cut.

Enderby didn't apologise, nor did he stop sawing. He'd wasted enough time on the fat fool. He did take greater care with the knifework, though. Slicing through the man's radial artery with a blunt kitchen knife wouldn't be a good idea. All that spurting blood. He'd have to shower and change clothes again.

"So," Bozo gasped. "What's all this about a security test?"

"Oh yes," Enderby said through a smile. "The government has recently upgraded the terrorism threat level to 'severe'. Which means an attack is highly likely. Furthermore, intelligence suggests that the target will be high-ranking government ministers and civil servants. That includes people like me."

Nice one, Greg. He's buying it.

Finally, the wrist tie broke, Bozo's arms popped free, and he groaned.

"What's wrong?" Enderby asked, straightening his aching back.

"Cramp. I've got a dodgy shoulder. Can you give me a hand up?"

Reluctantly, Enderby helped the older man to his feet, half-carried him through to the outer room, and lowered him into one of the two dining chairs. He stood back and watched the doorman massage his injured shoulder. A cup of tea or coffee might have helped the old man's recovery, but sod that. Enderby wasn't about to play the ministering angel. He had better things to do with his time than fuss over the fat oaf.

"I received the threat level notification," Bozo said, licking the blood from the tiny nick on his wrist, "but nobody said anything about the target. I should have been told."

"Would it have made a difference?"

"Yes, it would. I'd have checked out your mate—sorry your 'contractor'—for a start. And I'd have made sure the door was properly locked behind you."

"You should have done that anyway."

Bozo lowered his head.

"Yes, sir. You're right." He fell silent for a moment before adding, "I ... I suppose you'll recommend a disciplinary?"

"That depends."

Bozo looked up from rubbing his wrists, eyes hooded. "On what?"

"On whether you've learned your lesson. Tell me exactly what happened after I went upstairs. I want a full report. Leave nothing out."

"Yes, sir." Bozo took a breath and launched into it, staring at the trembling hands he'd pressed into his lap the whole time. "They crashed through the door a few minutes after you went upstairs. Three of them."

"There were three men?"

Bozo nodded. "That's right. Three men with covered faces. Two of average height, the other much taller. The tall one dragged me in here and tied me up. The other two went up the stairs ..."

He continued the story, ended with Enderby's arrival, and lifted his gaze. "Can I ask a question, sir?"

Enderby nodded. "If you must."

"Who were they?"

"Why do you want to know?"

The doorman grimaced as he rolled his injured shoulder. "They were very good, sir. Efficient, professional. Very convincing. Who were they?"

Enderby shot him a thin smile, taking a perverse pleasure in lying.

"A crack team from GG Cleaning Systems. I'll pass your commendation along. They'll be delighted."

Bozo lifted his head fully. "What did they do? I mean, the two who climbed the stairs after you, what did they do? They were upstairs quite a while."

"We had a pleasant debrief over coffee." Enderby stared at the fat man and couldn't resist adding a dig. "By the way, the team leader recommended your dismissal."

Bozo squirmed in his chair.

"He did?"

Enderby pursed his lips. Time to move things along.

"He did. But I'm not convinced. I think you've learned from this experience. Am I right?"

Bozo straightened his back and twisted at the waist to face Enderby.

"Yes, sir. I have."

"Good, good," Enderby said, nodding, his expression thoughtful. "I'm a great believer in personal development and in giving people second chances."

Greg, you are such a little liar.

"This is a lesson you won't forget. Of course, I'll have to write a full report and submit it to your company, but"—he stared hard at Bozo—"I will recommend you keep your post."

Bozo gulped.

"Thank you, sir."

"That's okay." Enderby waved a dismissive hand. "Email your written report to me by ten o'clock this morning and that will be an end to the matter. You have my work email address, I assume?"

"I do, sir, and I will. And thank you, sir. Thank you."

Done!

He'd played the round well. He'd probably broken par.

Enderby turned to leave the grovelling man in the middle of yet another expression of his heartfelt appreciation. Bozo would be eternally grateful to Enderby for retaining his crappy, little, poorly paid job. At some stage in the future, Enderby might be able to use that gratitude.

As usual, he'd salt the information away to think about later.

Outside, and out of sight of the foyer, he smiled broadly and jogged up the stairs. Time to cover his tracks even further.

———

ENDERBY SAT in his favourite armchair in the lounge, hands cupped around a mug—his largest mug—of heavily sweetened coffee. He took a decent sip, and the instant sugar and caffeine hit could not have been more invigorating. He didn't often add demerara sugar to his coffee, but he needed the burst in energy and couldn't stomach the idea of eating anything yet. The previous two days had been terrifying, but at least his hands had stopped shaking. He'd have to wait a little while for his stomach to settle.

Enderby read the time off the mantel clock. 04:53. Christ. Time to get a hurry on. He grabbed the remote control from the side table, pointed it at the large window, and held down a button. The floor-to-ceiling, blackout drapes split in the centre and rolled apart, letting in a shaft of dazzling, eye-scorching daylight. He shut his eyes tight, released the button, and the drapes stopped moving with the gap at little more than one metre. He opened his eyes again and blinked away the starburst light.

More than enough light for his needs.

Okay, Greg. Let's do this.

He dropped the remote and picked up the second burner he kept hidden deep in the back of a kitchen drawer. Kaine had taken his first burner during the abduction.

Enderby snorted.

So much for Hunter's hunting skills. The bugger might

be able to act the part of a snivelling, lowlife turncoat, but he hadn't found the spare mobile, and he'd taken plenty of time in his search. How useless was that?

Enderby powered up the mobile and punched in the number from memory. Gordon, the useless dick, took so long to answer, Enderby half-expected his messenger service to kick in.

"Hello?" the creep said through an extended groan.

"Guy, my old friend," Enderby said, forcing a smile into his voice. It wasn't easy. "It's me, Greg."

"Enderby? What the f—?"

"No adverse aftereffects from the other night's sparring, I trust."

"What do you want?" Gordon barked, his bad-tempered snarl making Enderby's smile genuine.

"Now, now, Guy. What way is that to greet an old friend and colleague?" Enderby asked, hearing the delight in his voice.

You'll be thanking me soon enough, old man.

The sound of skin scraping on bedsheets suggested that Gordon had turned over in his bed. "Christ on a bike, it's not even five o'clock."

"Do you have a black operative on your books? Preferably ex-military. And I mean black, as in of African descent."

"What?"

More sheet scraping and another groan suggested he'd sat up.

"It's an easy enough question, Guy. Please don't make me repeat myself. I hate doing that."

Gordon yawned before answering, "Yes. Dion Mathews. He's been with us a few months. Former 2 PARA."

"Excellent. Dion and three of your operatives have just broken into my apartment building."

"What the hell—"

"Don't interrupt, Guy. There's an NCTA contract in this for you, and we'll be paying your full daily rate. In essence, your team has just completed a live-fire assessment on the security arrangements in my apartment building. All you have to do is setup the paperwork and backdate your records by a couple of days. Can you do that, Guy?"

He paused and waited for the promise of a lucrative fee to drive its way into Guy Gordon's sleep-furred but avaricious brain. It didn't take long.

"Well, yes, Greg," Gordon said, calmness and friendliness replacing the open aggression. "That can be arranged. Why? What happened?"

"Don't worry about that for now, just organise the backdated audit trail. I'll send you the contract details in the usual manner. I'll also provide a blow-by-blow account of exactly what happened during the assessment. That way you'll be able to prepare your written report and your fully costed and itemised invoice. Think of it as money for nothing, Guy. Any questions?"

Enderby took another sip of coffee. Cooling. He curled his lip and lowered the mug to his side table.

"So, the NCTA will pay for a four-man, overnight incursion in the middle of London, allowing what? A three-day window to prepare the operation?"

Enderby snorted.

"Don't push it, Guy. Allow two days for the prep. The agency's not made of money. And don't forget to add my commission."

Enderby could see no reason he shouldn't earn a little compensation after all he'd suffered.

"Very well, Commander," Gordon said, his tone growing oilier by the second. "Two days, plus the incursion. I'll set it up the moment I reach my office."

"Excellent. I'll email you my review of the security assessment later today."

"Is that all?"

"We need to address the private contract we discussed when we sparred the other night."

A gasp filtered down the phone line.

"You still want to continue with that ... operation?"

"Of course," Enderby said. "Why wouldn't I?"

"Well, since I hadn't heard from you ... I thought ... hoped ... you'd reconsidered the idea."

"No, Guy. I've had other matters on my plate, but that contract's still very much alive. And it's growing more urgent as time passes."

"Oh," Gordon said, disappointment hanging heavy in the single word. "I see."

"Prepare yourself. We'll discuss the matter again very, very soon. Cheerio, Guy. Have a successful day."

He ended the call, dropped the burner phone on the side table next to the coffee mug, and sat back to prepare himself for the next call. A call which would inevitably prove far more challenging.

Chapter 27

Wednesday 9th June - Gregory Enderby

Bideford Avenue, Holborn, London, England

Enderby pulled himself out of the chair by its arms, fought a fatigue-and-sugar-induced headrush, and eventually won. He breathed deeply and started pacing the room, delaying the inevitable.

In the hopes that eating something might finally help to settle his nerves, he detoured around the coffee table, paused long enough to collect the half-empty mug from its coaster, and headed for the kitchen. Two slices of thinly buttered toast and another strong coffee later—taken at the kitchen's granite breakfast bar—he stacked side plate, mug, and butter knife into the dishwasher and stood back.

Enough timewasting, Greg. Do it!

What choice did he have? But how should he play it?

The mantel clock had ticked past five thirty. Still early, but Jay didn't sleep much—not according to his highly paid biographer. A four-hours-a-night man, emulating his idol, The Iron Lady, Jay prided himself on his role as the government's man of action, its prime mover and shaker. The government's fixer. A future prime minister waiting in the wings.

Enderby sloped into the front room, picked up the burner again, and dialled. Unable to relax, he remained standing. The call connected quickly.

"*Identification required*," the electronic security system announced.

Enderby sighed.

Here we go again.

"Commander Gregory Enderby."

The phone clicked. "*Repeat the following sequence. Zulu-Bravo-Kilo-November-three-two-one.*"

Enderby obeyed the instructions, shaking his head the whole time.

"*Voice identification confirmed.*" The line clicked again.

"Gregory, dear boy," Jay said, his voice clear and cheery—and intensely annoying. "This is early, even for you. What do you have for me?"

"Ryan Kaine," Enderby said. "He was here. In my apartment. He broke in. Threatened me. He knows about the Grey Notice. Will Stacy told him." He rushed his words, unable to play it cool when operating under so much pressure.

Fuck's sake, Greg.

Breathe. He needed to breathe.

"Slow the fuck down, Enderby," Jay snapped, not so

refined after the mention of Ryan Kaine. "You're rambling. What happened. Take it from the top."

"Okay, Jay. Okay. I'm sorry, but I've had a horrible couple of days. It started Monday evening at my gym. I was approached by a man who wanted to pitch for a future NCTA's security contract. That man turned out to be Ryan Kaine. He's grown his hair long and is wearing a beard. I didn't recognise him at first ..."

Enderby took Jay through a highly sanitised version of events, where he'd been kidnapped at gunpoint and held in a cellar at an unknown location. He glossed over the part where he'd been deceived by Hunter and played up his stoic bravery. In government circles, they called it "being economical with the truth".

"So," Jay said after Enderby finished his tale of woe, "Ryan Kaine has your files? All of them?"

Enderby coughed out a nervous laugh. "That's just it, Jay. He doesn't have a bloody thing. I let him *think* he owns me, but he's got nothing. The files he took are heavily encrypted dummies. It'll take his 'Mr C' days to crack the code if he ever does. The real files are still here. Hidden *behind* the secret compartment in the safe. It's bloody genius, I tell you."

"You have a second secret compartment hidden behind the first?" Jay asked. "That's very sneaky, Gregory. Very sneaky indeed. Bravo, my good man."

Shit!

Enderby winced. In trying to impress his real boss, he'd gone too far. He shouldn't have told Jay about the second compartment. Foolish thing to do. Not so bloody secret now, damn it. It demonstrated how rattled he'd been by the whole appalling episode. It also showed how much the lost sleep had affected his normally brilliant performance. He'd have to find somewhere else to hide the real files, but that could wait—for the moment.

It had to.

"So, what do you want from me, Gregory?"

"I want you to help me kill Kaine, of course. He's been a thorn in our sides for long enough." He paused to wait for a response that didn't arrive. "Well, Jay? Did you hear me?"

"Yes, I heard you. I was thinking."

"Think faster."

"Cut that out, Gregory. Remember who you're talking to."

Enderby seethed. He'd had enough of playing second fiddle to the obnoxious creep.

"I know exactly who I'm talking to, Jay," he said, trying to remain cool and calm, but failing miserably. "I'm talking to the man who's been curled up tight in bed with the late, and thoroughly unlamented, Malcolm Sampson. I'm talking to the man who arranged for Sampson to have a pass on charges of mass murder. I'm talking to the man who arranged Sampson's release from prison on spurious health grounds." He took a breath and continued. "I'm talking to the man who owns thousands of undisclosed shares in SAMS Plc. *And*, I'm talking to the man whose job and reputation, no, his very freedom, relies on the fact that such information remains outside the public realm. Shall I continue, Jay? Shall I?"

Hell, it felt so good to unload on the slimy arsehole. It had been a long time coming.

"I know who I am, Gregory," Jay barked. "I don't need you to remind me how much you know about me. But remember this, I know all about you, too. I know about the secrets you've been selling to the highest bidder. I know how you helped set up Kaine's men to be killed last week. And a fat lot of good that did. They all failed. We're a partnership, Gregory. If I go down, I'm taking you down with me. Don't you ever forget that."

How the hell could I?

"So," Enderby said, "we have an understanding. Can I rely on your support?"

"What do you need?" Jay asked, after another hesitation, this one more truncated than the first.

"A fully armed team of skilled and trusted men who'll shoot first and ask no questions later."

Jay's heavy breathing huffed down the phone connection.

"What for?"

"I'm going to set Kaine up, but I need a reliable team to take him and his men out. The best team you have."

"Why not use a contractor?"

"Who?" Enderby snorted. "Give me an example."

"Let me see," Jay mused. "T5S is all but defunct since John Abbott's unfortunate demise, although some of their people will probably be available for an ad hoc job or two. There's Arrow Services, who are keen if nothing else. Or how about GG Cleaning Systems? I'll go halves on the contract fee ... if that'll help."

"Oh no," Enderby said, barely stifling a chortle. "Whatever we decide, you're paying the lot. I've lost enough for one night."

"Fifty thousand?" Jay scoffed. "Peanuts. I spend more than that every month on bar fees."

Of course you do, you rich prick.

"GG Cleaning Systems don't have the manpower anymore. Not after that abortion they were part of last week."

No, he couldn't use them. Apart from invoicing for work

he didn't do, Guy Gordon had other things on his plate. One other thing, at least.

"Ah yes. I'd almost forgotten about their part in that debacle. How many people did they lose?"

"No idea. Five? Six? All I know is that Guy Gordon's going to have to start recruiting very soon."

"He might be able to pick up some of the T5S riffraff left after Abbott's demise," Jay offered, unhelpfully.

Fuck you very much.

He'd already had the recruitment conversation with Gordon and didn't need to reprise it with Jay-bloody-Wyndham.

"I don't care about Gordon's employment issues. Can you give me access to one of your strike teams?"

"Hmm," Jay said at last, "I think that can be arranged. What would you say if I put my best team at your disposal? My Praetorian Guard. Hand-picked and raring to go."

"I'd say thank you very much."

And I'd mean it, too.

"Who's the team leader?"

"Alasdair Dresden. *Inspector* Alasdair Dresden."

"Dresden? Never heard of him. How much does he know … our situation?" Enderby asked.

"He knows only what he needs to know. 'China' Dresden is … trustworthy. An honourable man. Totally above reproach." Jay laughed. "China and his unit are on permanent secondment to me from the Met's Special Escort Group, the group tasked with protecting high-ranking government employees. That means people like you and me, Gregory." Jay barked out another coughed laugh. "As it happens, Alasdair Dresden is one of the toughest, most skilful men I've ever had the pleasure of employing. If you wish, I'll task him and his team to provide you and Sir

Ernest with enhanced protection as the targets of an advanced terrorist plot. You will be able to furnish evidence of such a plot, I imagine? I'll need it to keep my official tasking records in order. Bloody bean counters will be all over me if I don't."

Shit. That won't do.

"I always have details of a terrorist plot running in the background that I can wheel out at short notice. And I thank you for your generous offer of protection. I really appreciate it, but do we really have to include Sir Ernest in this?"

"Whyever not, Gregory? A terrorist plot against the NCTA that targets you will inevitably target Sir Ernest as well. There's no avoiding it."

"I suppose so, but this is becoming a little complicated."

"Deal with it, Gregory. Deal with it. I'll have Dresden contact you in due course. Good day to you."

The call disconnected, leaving Enderby alone with his thoughts.

How could he juggle so many balls without dropping any?

The need to remove Sir Ernest from the equation had just become even more urgent. The old man had to die before China Dresden and his unit arrived on the scene and before Kaine had a chance to interrogate him. In addition, Enderby had to modify the fabricated intel on a terrorist plot to target the agency and pin it on someone who couldn't easily defend himself. But who?

Someone who can't defend himself.

The words reverberated around his head.

Who?

The answer hit him so hard and so fast, he couldn't stop himself laughing.

Enderby pulled himself out of his chair by its arms and rushed into the scene of his recent apparent humiliation—his office. He opened the safe, cracked the first secret panel, and accessed the second by the same method. The second Westbury drive remained inside, alongside another thick bundle of cash, as safe as if it were in the Bank of England. Smiling, Enderby removed the second drive, relocked the safe, and dropped into his chair, the chair with the seat slightly faded by the multipurpose cleaner. Faded and not clean enough, but it would have to do for the moment.

Despite all appearances to the contrary, with the second drive safe and sound, he'd beaten Kaine. He'd come out on top. Kaine had nothing. Nothing. If Kaine thought he owned Greg Enderby, he was bloody well wrong. And with China Dresden tasked to guard Enderby's back, he had the ammunition to turn what appeared to be a dire situation on its head. He would survive and thrive. By Christ he would.

Enderby allowed himself a contented smile.

The second Westbury drive held a two-day-old copy of his desktop, complete with the operating system, the apps, and the working folders. Information too valuable and too sensitive to entrust to the cloud. It also contained the only copy of his private database. A private database containing all the information that held the key to Enderby's entry into the big time. A minefield of information that would help propel Enderby to the very top of the Civil Service tree. It also included his personal diaries. Diaries that meant nothing to anyone but him. Diaries into which he poured his heart and soul.

He nudged the mouse to wake his desktop and ran the "reset to factory settings" program. If Kaine's IT man, Mr C, had uploaded any spyware, the reset would surely erase it.

Nobody messed with Gregory Bysshe Enderby and got away with it.

***

AFTER THE FACTORY reset had done its thing, Enderby initiated the reload program. He left it to run through to completion and dragged his weary bones to bed. With luck, he'd be able to snaffle a couple of hours recuperative sleep before heading for work—assuming his racing mind would quieten enough to allow him some rest.

He rubbed the bruise on his chest. Bloody thing still hurt like the devil.

Chapter 28

Sandbrook Tower, Soho, London, England

Sitting at his desk after strolling through the building and running a gauntlet of greetings from sycophantic well-wishers who didn't give a damn about how he really was, Enderby yawned deep and hard enough to crack his jawbone. He'd lost so much sleep during the previous few days, the bennies he'd popped with his breakfast cereal had done little to spark any life into him. In truth, he had no idea how he was going to survive the day.

Suck it up, Greg. There's work to do.

Supping on a mug of instant, he printed the highly critical report entitled, "Updated Risk Assessment, Number 3, Bideford Avenue, Holborn, London", signed, "NCTA

Director". Nowhere near as long as some of the turgid reports he'd created over the years, the risk assessment couldn't have been much more succinct or accurate. He drained the mug of its inferior version of rich-roast coffee while listening to the paper churn through the printer. In it, he'd paraphrased Bozo's prompt and surprisingly well-written report of the break-in and logged the file into the system in the prescribed manner—backdated by four days.

Hopefully, the auditors wouldn't notice the warped time-line, but if they did, Enderby could always lay the blame full square on his current scapegoat, Claire Harper.

"The woman's useless," he'd tell anyone who asked. "Doesn't know what she's doing half the time." So what if she'd performed well at the House when standing in for Enderby—according to Sir Ernest's online review. That rare success would have been forgotten long before the auditors could stick their beaks into his business.

Enderby grinned to himself. Sooner or later, he'd be rid of the miserable bitch. After he'd dealt with Sir Ernest, Guy Gordon would arrange for a little accident to befall the poor thing, and that would be an end to it.

However, first things first.

With a couple of taps on his keyboard, he dropped the file into the private contractor's portal, and made sure to override the time and date stamp. All open and above board and ready for any future scrutiny. All down to the wonders of modern technology—and a prime example of covering one's arse with both hands.

He leaned across to the side table, collected the numbered pages from the bed of the printer, and slipped them into the buff folder he'd already marked with the file number, title, creation date—four days earlier—and time. After initialling the folder, he dropped it into his near-empty out tray, ready for that afternoon's mail collection. Where it went after that, he had no idea and cared even less. Somewhere down in the bowels of the building, no doubt. The electronic folder would reach whoever it needed to reach, but would more likely be ignored until the end-of-year financial audit. He could deal with any questions raised when he was running the department after Sir Ernest's upcoming, shocking, and untimely demise. A demise that grew more necessary and more imminent with each passing hour.

For his part, Guy Gordon would use the file to prepare his reverse-engineered report and invoice, and the information would match that of the official file and the pictures on the overnight surveillance footage. Gordon would also handle the date discrepancy at his end.

Perfect.

One challenge dealt with, he had another to focus on.

Enderby pulled the Hosseini file from the heaving pending tray and opened it for the first time since the miserable cow had delivered it to him. He read the report from cover to cover, looking for a way to use the innocent man to pull his plums out of the syrup.

As expected, Claire Harper had done a first-rate job. Had she succumbed to his advances early on, Enderby would have been singing the woman's praises from the rooftops. As it was she could go boil her head in a large vat of oil for all he cared. Not that he could be obvious about it. No. As far as Claire Harper was concerned, Greg Enderby would be nothing but pleasant and entirely professional, for as long as she lived.

In the lift, he'd been a bloody fool, but he'd learned his lesson. Wouldn't do it again.

Never again.

At least, he wouldn't foul his own doorstep next time.

Enderby shook the musing from his head and returned his thoughts to the challenge at hand.

Abdul Hosseini—Afghani, widower, childless, desperate to start a new life in the Promised Land—would be the perfect instrument. He lived in a fleapit bedsit—paid for by the state—in Tower Hamlets, London's poorest borough. The ideal candidate. But how? How could he plant evidence of a terrorist plot on the man without making it too obvious?

Enderby pushed the folder away and leaned back in his chair, giving himself room to think. Absently, he rubbed the angry bruise where Kaine's knuckle punch had damn near drilled a hole straight through his chest. Much harder and the blow might have stopped his heart. The bruise had blackened and still hurt like a bugger. One day, he'd repay Kaine for that bruise and for the humiliation he'd inflicted on Enderby in the gym. The humiliation Enderby had suffered in front of all his gym buddies. By God he would pay. One day. One day soon.

Concentrate, Greg. Concentrate.

How was he going to use Hosseini to support his case for an uplift in the terrorist threat?

Enderby stopped massaging his chest, gripped the arms of his chair, and turned to face the window without a view. He could force Gordon to plant bomb-making equipment in Hosseini's bedsit, but that would take time to organise. Time he didn't have. It would add another level of complexity to an already convoluted situation. Whatever he did, it had to be simple and had to happen soon. Before China Dresden and his team arrived.

Damn it. He had so much going on it made his head hurt.

Gordon's hired hands could bomb the nearest Christian church to the Tower Hamlets mosque. But again, that would take time. It would also create too much of a mess and involve too many people.

In a blinding flash of insight, he had it. Why complicate matters?

Keep it simple, stupid.

Smiling, he reached for his desk phone and dialled the extension from memory. The bitch answered immediately.

"Ms Harper? It's Commander Enderby," he said, being ever so precise, ever so pleasant.

"Yes, sir?" she answered after a brief pause, surprise and fear ran through both words.

Good.

"I'd like you to arrange an interview with Abdul Hosseini. I want to speak to him face to face."

"Really, Commander? That's rather unusual."

Cheeky bloody cow.

How dare she question him.

Easy, Greg. Play it cool.

"Unusual perhaps, but not unheard of," he said, oozing his well-known charm. "There's a short gap in his work history a decade ago. If he can explain it to my satisfaction, I see no reason to delay his application for asylum. He speaks good English, I understand."

"Yes, Commander. He's fluent."

"In which case, we won't need to book an interpreter. Please set it up."

"When for, sir?"

"I have a slot available at three forty-five this afternoon."

"This afternoon?" She sounded surprised. "That's rather short notice, sir."

That's the whole point, bitch.

"If Mr Hosseini can't make himself available this afternoon, he can't be that serious about his application, can he. It's not as though he has anything else to do with his time." He added, "Apart from his volunteering at the food bank, of course," to prove he'd read the file and remembered her initial briefing.

"Yes, sir," she said. "I'll contact him right away."

What else could she do but agree? She was his underling, after all.

"Very good, Ms Harper. Thank you. Call me when you've confirmed the appointment, and please add it to the agency calendar. We must dot our Is and cross our Ts."

"Yes, Commander."

"I'll see him in the ground-floor reception room. It's so much less formal than the interview rooms on the first floor. I don't see a need for Mr Hosseini to be uncomfortable."

"Yes, Commander," she repeated.

Smiling, Enderby ended the call and brushed non-existent dirt from his hands.

First part done.

With Hosseini on his way into the office, half the battle was complete. If he played his part right, he'd be able to show Harper in a bad light at the same time. After all, the woman had given Hosseini a clean bill of health and recommended his asylum application.

The phrase "two birds with one stone" ran through Enderby's head, and he chuckled to the miserable view through the office window.

Despite the threat of Ryan Kaine hanging over his head, Greg Enderby was still running things. Still making up the rules and playing by them.

Fuck you, Ryan Kaine. You won't beat me.

Now all he needed to do was to finish modifying the

terrorist threat report he'd archived to his home desktop and upload it to the works system. It would take a little time, but he still had an hour or so before lunch. And he certainly didn't want to miss lunch. He had a little errand to run.

AFTER HE'D WORKED HARD for an hour, the desk phone's strident double buzz of an outside call broke his train of thought.

Shit! Can't I catch a break?

He snatched up the receiver.

"Enderby," he announced, angrily.

"Ah, Greg," a man said with a cheery voice he recognised but couldn't quite place. "How are you this fine day? Peter Wingard here, from A&W Associates."

Kaine!

Oh Jesus.

Enderby's heart raced and his mouth dried.

Had they broken the code so soon? Had he been rumbled? Too bloody early. Dresden wasn't in place yet.

Fuck.

"Good … morning, Mr Wingard," Enderby answered, trying to sound relaxed, but not managing it at all well. "How can I … How can I help?"

"I know this is awfully short notice and you are a very busy man," Kaine said, playing the smarmy git to the max, "but do you have some free time this morning?"

"You're right, Mr Wingard, I really am busy. I have meetings all day."

"Oh, that is a shame," Kaine said. "It really is. It's just that I'm in the area, and I'd *love* the chance to continue our recent discussions. I really would. A&W Associates is very keen to offer its services to the NCTA. *Very* keen. Could you spare a few minutes? I understand there's a coffee house across the road from Sandbrook Tower. I could be there in a quarter of an hour. I promise not to keep you long, Commander."

Fifteen minutes?

Sneaky bugger. Dresden would be miles away and wouldn't be able to organise a legitimate operation in time. On the other hand, Kaine would be armed, and he was a legitimate target. The germ of another brilliant idea sprang to mind. Excitement bubbled inside his bruised chest. Maybe Enderby could fix things without the distraction of Hosseini after all. And without the need to involve China Dresden.

I'll bloody well do it myself.

Enderby's heart raced. Sweat prickled his brow and electricity tingled his spine. He *could* do it. He could kill Kaine with impunity. He'd be taking out a known and wanted terrorist—one with a Grey Notice on his head. It couldn't be any more perfect. It would make Enderby a national hero. Cement his place in history.

"Fifteen minutes?" Enderby said, struggling to keep the exhilaration from his voice. "Very well, Mr Wingard. I'm sure I can spare you a short time, but I have to advise you that the NCTA is not currently in a position to change its security arrangements."

"At least you can give us the opportunity to put down a marker for when the situation changes. I'll see you in The Coffee Shack in fifteen."

Kaine ended the call and left Enderby holding a dead handset.

He dropped the phone in its cradle and removed the government-issued Beretta M9 from the gun safe in the bottom drawer of his desk. He worked a round into the chamber, confirmed the safety was engaged, and carefully slid the weapon into his shoulder holster. Not the safest way to carry a gun when walking through the streets perhaps, but he could hardly face Ryan Kaine with an uncharged weapon. That would be pure suicide. He stood and took a steadying breath, trying to calm his racing heart.

He stared at himself in the full-length mirror hanging on the wall alongside the window. Tall, smartly dressed, confident smile.

"Come on, Greg. It's time to make history."

⸺

"I'M POPPING out for a quick coffee. Who's on duty today?" Enderby asked the receptionist, a short woman in her mid-fifties, with dyed-blonde hair—dark roots showing —and too-heavy makeup. He'd never bothered to ask her name.

"Ms Winters, sir," she said, reaching for the phone on her desk. "I'll call her for you."

The luscious, firm-arsed blonde.

Poetic justice.

He'd be able to apologise for his actions of Monday night, and impress the hell out of her when he dealt with a mass murderer without her. Who knew, she might even be inclined to show her appreciation in more intimate ways than a simple, verbal, thank you. Some women were turned on by strong men and violence.

He tried to relax his shoulders, but the growing excitement caused by his upcoming meeting with destiny made it impossible.

The door to the security office opened inwards and the

magnificent woman marched through, looking like thunder. She stopped three paces away and waited.

"Good afternoon, Ms Winters," he said, gracing her with one of his warmest smile. "I'm going for a coffee, care to join me?"

He spoke as though he were inviting her as a colleague, not a shadow. Her answering frown made his smile genuine. She didn't know how to react to his warmth, his friendliness.

Enderby waved her towards the revolving doors. She would lead and put herself in danger to protect him. Such was her role in life.

Outside in the dull, early-afternoon air, they headed for the pelican crossing. He moved alongside her, but maintained a respectful, one-metre distance and broached the embarrassing subject.

"About the other night," he opened. "I have an apology to make."

"Yes, sir," she said, noncommittal, her eyes roving left and right, taking in the scene. Busy road, pedestrian-clogged pavements, potential danger from every angle.

"I was rather hasty," he added. "Shouldn't have dismissed you in such a manner. Most unprofessional of me."

"Yes, sir."

They reached the crossing. She pressed the button, and they waited in the middle of a small crowd of fellow pedestrians.

Enderby edged closer and lowered his voice.

"I'm about to meet with Peter Wingard of A&W Associates."

Ellen Winters' jaw stiffened. He finally had her undivided attention.

"The second man you sparred with, sir?" she asked, her upper lip twisting into a half-sneer.

Enderby dropped his smile. The bitch couldn't help herself. She simply had to give him a dig.

"Yes," he said. "That man."

The lights changed, the crossing bleeped, and the green man started flashing. The crowd around them shuffled forwards. Ellen and Enderby marched with them.

"How did the meeting go at the Savoy?" she asked after they'd reached the opposite pavement and headed for The Coffee Shack. He sensed anger bubbling beneath the surface. Rippling through her whole body.

How delightful.

She was magnificent.

"The meal was lovely, the proposition, pitiful. A&W Associates are nothing more than chancers trying their luck. I turned them down flat."

"So why this meeting? If you don't mind me asking." She paused outside the café and caught his eye for the first time. She'd already scanned the shop's interior and found nothing of concern. Ellen did have rather lovely eyes. Deep, deep blue.

What would it be like to wake up next to a woman with those eyes and that firm arse?

Stop it, Greg.

"No, Ms Winters. I don't mind at all." He smiled and pressed his left arm closer to his side, feeling the comforting solidity of the Beretta nestled in the holster. "Truth is, it's been a long day. I needed a short break and didn't see why Wingard shouldn't pay for the coffees. Will you be joining us?"

"No, sir. I won't."

He shrugged.

"Suit yourself. Oh, by the way. I'll be commending your actions on Monday night to your supervisors. You were perfectly correct in your assessment of the situation. I shouldn't have ignored your advice. Once again, I'm truly sorry."

How magnanimous he could be. One of the good guys. Judging by her lack of response, Ellen wasn't buying it. Still, she'd change her tune when Kaine arrived—and Enderby put a bullet through his forehead.

Enderby opened the door and entered the café, soaking in its familiar warmth. His mouth watered at the enticing aroma of fresh-ground coffee and warm pastries. He strode to one of the few empty tables, and took a seat with his back to the wall, facing the crowded room. They'd made it to the café with five minutes to spare.

He signalled the barista, who sidled forwards and took his order—a tall cappuccino, dusted with chocolate, two sugars for energy, no biscuits. When the barista turned his back, Enderby took the opportunity to draw the Beretta, click the safety to "fire" with his thumb, and hold it in two hands, hidden beneath the table. Scoping the café, Ellen had her eyes on the crowd, not him.

With the Beretta locked, loaded, and ready to fire, confidence flooded through him, and his hands stopped trembling.

C'mon, Kaine. I'm ready for you.

Chapter 29

Wednesday 9th June - Gregory Enderby

Sandbrook Tower, Soho, London, England

The barista arrived with Enderby's drink, including an individually wrapped biscotti. For once, Enderby accepted the inevitable error without reprimanding the young man, who turned away and hurried back behind the counter to help service the latest influx of customers.

Using his left hand—the right remained hidden beneath the table, clutching the Beretta—Enderby stirred the coffee, sipped, and left the biscotti on the saucer. His stomach roiled and he couldn't contemplate eating anything. And besides, almonds tasted rank.

As the minutes ticked slowly by, the pressure built.

Five minutes.

The line at the counter shortened. A man in a business suit left with his takeout cup and a brown, paper bag of goodies.

Six minutes.

A young couple entered and attached themselves to the back of the queue. The woman at the front peeled away with her order and the queue shuffled forwards.

Seven minutes.

Kaine, the arrogant bastard, was late. Keeping him waiting. Keeping Death waiting.

Ellen Winters, standing in the far corner with a commanding view of the room, drank her herbal tea—she only ever ordered herbal tea—constantly scanning the flow of people. Always on guard. As well she should be.

The door opened, the bell rang, and a solitary man entered. Average height, square build bordering on tubby, dressed casually in trainers, chinos, and a grey fleece despite the relative warmth of the day. The peak of his black base-ball cap threw a shadow over his face.

Kaine?

Without looking down, Enderby used his right thumb to confirm the position of the safety and slid his index finger through the trigger guard.

Steady, Greg. Take your time. Don't fuck this up.

He had one chance. One chance only.

The man stretched his neck, searched the café, found Enderby in the corner, and smiled in acknowledgement. He raised his hand in recognition of Ellen and marched towards Enderby, side-stepping between the tables and chairs.

Shit, shit, shit.

Not Kaine. Will Stacy. Will-bloody-Stacy.

Damn it.

Enderby removed his finger from the trigger and activated the safety. Will Stacy wasn't a mass murderer on the run. The police didn't want him for anything. Killing Stacy without just cause would place Enderby in a whole world of pain. As much as he wanted to, shooting Stacy was out of the question, unless he could engineer an attack.

Stacy reached the table, pulled out a side chair, and lowered himself into it. He moved effortlessly. Ghostly. Barely making a sound. The air didn't even seem to move around him.

"Good afternoon, Commander," Stacy said through a bright smile. A bright smile that didn't reach his eyes. "Don't look so disappointed. The captain sends his apologies. He's been detained on other pressing business. Sent me in his place. What's good here?"

Enderby swallowed his frustration and made sure to keep the Beretta out of sight. God, how he ached to use the bloody thing. Pulling the trigger would release so much tension—but cause so much trouble.

"Well?" Stacy said.

"Well what?"

"What's good here?"

Enderby shrugged.

"Don't know. Everything."

As if by magic, the waiter appeared at the table. Stacy ordered an Americano—black, two sugars—and a slice of date-and-walnut cake.

"And you, sir?" the waiter asked Enderby, pointing to his empty cup.

"No, thank you."

"Oh, go on, Greg," Stacy chided. "I don't like to drink alone."

"Okay," Enderby said, forcing a smile. "I'll have another cappuccino."

The waiter, Marco according to the name badge pinned to his waistcoat, cleared the table and minced away, showing his tight buttocks to Enderby and Stacy—and anyone interested in watching the show.

"What do you want?" Enderby demanded, keeping his voice low.

"An Americano, of course," Stacy said, still smiling. "That, and the slice of cake. I hope you don't mind adding it to your bill. I seem to have forgotten my wallet. ... Ah, I see what you mean. Nothing much. The captain just wanted to reinforce our agreement from last night and make sure you understood the position. And we also wanted to ask you a question."

Enderby ground his teeth and squeezed the Beretta's textured grip. One shot. Below the table, into Stacy's belly. Death by a bullet in the guts. A horribly painful way to die, he imagined. That's all it would take. It might be worth the risk. Stacy was bound to be armed. Illegally armed. Enderby could use that in his defence.

"You couldn't do it over the phone?" he growled.

"Not a chance. Couldn't risk it. The NCTA monitors the phone lines. Didn't you know?"

"Yes, I bloody know!" Enderby snapped, barely able to control his voice. "Couldn't it wait until I reached home?"

Marco returned with their order. Stacy waited for the barista to go, watching him the whole way back to the counter, before turning to face Enderby again.

"No," he said. "It couldn't."

The coldness in the words made Enderby shudder.

"Ask your question."

"When I'm good and ready."

Stacy picked up the teaspoon, stirred his drink, and blew across the top before risking a sip. He probably took the same care with everything in his life. He licked his thin lips, nodded, and lowered the cup to its saucer. Still not looking at Enderby, he picked up the fork, cut a piece off the cake, and popped it into his mouth. He chewed slowly. Again, he nodded after swallowing.

"You were right, Commander," he said. "This is very good. I'll probably be coming back."

Stacy pushed the plate away, picked up his cup, and held it close to his lips.

"What were you going to do with the Beretta, Commander?"

Enderby gasped.

"What?"

"The Beretta under the table. The one you're holding in your right hand. What were you going to do with it?"

Jesus! How?

"N-Nothing. I-I … Protection. How did you know?"

"We've had eyes on you ever since you left the Tower. Put it away before I take it from you and *beat you to a pulp with it*." He whispered the final part, lips barely moving, and took another drink of his coffee.

Enderby searched the café. Full of people. None he recognised. He bent slightly at the waist, slipped the Beretta back into its holster, and pulled the flaps of his jacket together.

"Don't bother looking, Commander," Stacy said from behind the cup. "You'll never spot him … or her. We're too good for that."

Good, yes, but clearly not good enough to defeat the encryption yet. If their "Mr C" had broken it, Enderby and

Stacy would be having a very different conversation. He took some comfort in the knowledge.

Stacy sipped again.

"This really is very good, you know," he said. "So, here's the question. Where will we find Sir Ernest Hartington right now?"

Oh thank you, God.

They'd taken the bait. The buggers were going after the old man! What's more, they didn't know where he was. They weren't omnipotent. They didn't know everything.

Rather than jumping in with the answer and appearing too keen, he hesitated, as though reluctant to give up information on his boss.

"Answer the question, Commander," Stacy ordered, glaring at him with those same dead eyes.

Enderby gulped. "At the House ... the House of Commons. He's reporting to the Home Secretary."

"How long for?"

Blag it, Greg. Tell him anything but the truth.

"I'm not certain. He has no other appointments this afternoon. Knowing Sir Ernest, he'll probably hang around in one of the bars for a while, schmoozing the Great and the Good. After that, he'll go straight from the House to his home rather than back to the office."

"His home in Marlow?"

Christ, they know about Marlow.

How the hell did they find out what amounted to a state secret? His throat dry, Enderby swallowed. He was glad to have ordered a second coffee.

"Yes," he answered, taking a sip of his drink.

"And his security detail?"

"Stays with him the whole time he's in London. Once

he's in Marlow, they'll hand over to the local plod and pick him up again in the morning."

"You're particularly well informed," Stacy said, suspicion showing in the normally dead eyes.

"I'm his second in command. It's my job to know where he is at all times, and how well he's being protected. We continually deal with suspected terrorists. It makes us significant targets."

"Hence Ellen Winters' attendance at this meeting?"

Enderby dipped his head.

"Exactly."

"Very well, Commander." Stacy stood and slid the chair close to the table. He signalled to Marco and pointed to Enderby. Marco nodded, taking the message. "We'll be in touch. Don't forget to keep your burner phone fully charged."

He smiled broadly and thrust out his hand. Reluctantly, Enderby took it, and they shook with what would look very much like enthusiasm to any onlookers. Stacy's grip was firm and dry, his palm calloused. Enderby had felt the power of that hand and had no doubt that Stacy could crush his bones to pulp if he had a mind to. How deceptive looks could be.

Once the door had closed behind the killer, Enderby slumped in his chair and downed the rest of his coffee.

He'd come close to wetting himself again. How could a man as soft-looking as Stacy have such a debilitating effect on him? After all, he wasn't the one who'd knuckle punched him. Something about the man terrified Enderby. The utter lack of emotion in his dead eyes, maybe.

Christ, Greg. Man up, will you?

He summoned Marco and paid the bill for them both. Ellen drew alongside and followed Enderby back to the

Tower. Neither said a word. She knew better than to interrupt a man deep in thought.

Stacy had called a face-to-face meeting to prove he and Kaine had Enderby under their thumb—or so they thought. His explanation made sense. Stacy wanted to intimidate him. And it had worked. But the meeting had given Enderby three valuable pieces of information.

Firstly, their much-vaunted IT man, Mr C, had failed to break the encryption. Not even Frodo had been able to help. The dummy files were still intact. It gave him more time to clean house.

Secondly, Kaine and Stacy had asked about Sir Ernest, and they already knew he lived in Marlow. That confirmed they were going to target the old man sooner rather than later. Not good, but he'd deal with that shortly.

Finally, they had no knowledge of Andrea. They couldn't do, or they wouldn't have asked about the old man's movements on a Wednesday night.

It gave Enderby time to extricate himself from the mess he'd been dragged into. The mess *they'd* dragged him into.

It also meant that while Guy Gordon held the key to everything, Abdul Hosseini's role would be pivotal.

BACK IN HIS office and free of Ellen Winters' malign presence—and her prying eyes—Enderby returned the Beretta to its gun safe. Useless bloody thing hadn't been of any help. He locked the outer office door and stepped into his private bathroom where he'd be isolated from the omnipresent surveillance. Time was of the essence.

He dialled the special number. Guy Gordon answered his phone within seconds.

"Hi, Greg," he said, sounding rather chipper, no doubt as a result of having received the paperwork, the chit for an impressively large payday he didn't earn, and the promise of many more lucrative contracts to come. "How can I help?"

"When are you going to kill Sir Ernest?" he asked, keeping his voice down despite the isolation of the bathroom.

Gordon's gasp couldn't have been more clear or more sudden.

"I-I ... don't—"

"It has to be done this evening."

"Fucking hell. Are you completely out of your box? It can't be done. For God's sake, he's an agency head. His protection detail will be all over—"

"This evening, Guy. It has to be this evening."

"Why?"

Because the old man has to die before Kaine gets to him and he tells them what really happened. And before China Dresden arrives.

"Because, he's about to remove GG Cleaning Systems from the approved contractor register. If he does that, I won't be able to undo it after you kill him, not for months. It'll be a dead man's legacy. Do you understand what I'm saying, Guy? If you value your preferred bidder status, Sir Ernest has to die tonight. Don't forget, T5S is defunct. With fewer preferred bidders in the picture, there will be far more contracts on offer for firms like yours. And with me as the new head of the agency ... well, I'll be in your debt, Guy. Heavily in your debt."

Unable to stop himself, Enderby smiled. He'd played a corker. Teed up the ball and driven it down the middle of the fairway, pulling up short of all the sand traps.

"Right," Gordon said, sounding dejected but determined. "But I can't subcontract this. I'll have to do it myself."

"Of course you will," Enderby said. "This has to stay between the two of us."

After all, we are plotting a murder here.

"How am I going to bypass the security team?"

"That's easy," Enderby said, allowing another exultant smile to be wasted on a telephone call. "It's Wednesday."

"So what?"

"Every Wednesday, Sir Ernest dismisses his security team early and spends the night with his long-term mistress, Andrea. As far as his wife is concerned, he's playing poker at his club in Pall Mall. Don't you see? That's why it has to be done tonight. And ..."

"And?" Gordon asked.

"I know Andrea's address ... and her door entry code."

"How the hell—"

"Do I know her door code?"

"Yes. How?"

Enderby laughed. "Sir Ernest doesn't know it, but he's been dipping his wick inside my sloppy seconds for the past three months. And I don't have to pay a penny for Andrea's time. She happens to like younger, firmer men. What can I say?"

Enderby shrugged and it, too, remained unseen.

"'Sloppy seconds', Greg? You always did have a hell of a way with words."

"I know, Guy." Enderby reprised his laugh. "Famous for it, I am. Do you have a pen and paper handy?"

"Just a sec."

Gordon grunted, his phone clattered onto a hard surface, and a drawer slid open. Seconds later the phone clattered again, and he said, "Okay fire away."

Enderby rattled off the address and the five-digit code and had Gordon read the details back to him. In matters of such importance, there was no such thing as being overly cautious.

"Oh and Guy," he said.

"Yes?"

"Kill them both inside the apartment and make it look like a terrorist hit."

"What?"

"You heard me, Guy. Kill them both, and don't be subtle about it. There's no need to make it look like a lover's tiff."

"I don't understand."

No, you don't.

"I'm handling it, Guy. By the time I've finished setting things up, the police will be searching for a terrorist cell, and you'll be in the clear. I promise."

"Are you going to tell me what you're on about?"

"No, Guy. You don't need to know the details. Just do what you have to, and we'll both be in clover. Remember the end game, Guy. Remember what you're doing this for."

"Okay, okay," Gordon said, drawing the words out slowly. "I'll do it, but are you sure the girl has to die?"

You bloody fool. Of course she has to die.

"I'm afraid so, mate. Besides you, Andrea's the only one who knows I have the door entry code. If she lives to tell the tale, I wouldn't want her putting two and two together, and pointing her finger at me. If that happens, we'll both be up to our throats in the mire. Any questions?"

"No. No questions, but I have to say, you are one cold bastard."

"I'll take that as a compliment, Guy."

"Take it any way you want. Wait, I do have a question.

When I'm dealing with Sir Ernest and Andrea, what will you be doing?"

I'll probably be 'helping police with their enquiries'.

"Me?" he said. "I'll be at the gym, punching the heavy bag and making sure everyone sees me doing it."

"Providing yourself with the perfect alibi."

"Precisely, Guy. Precisely."

Still smiling, Enderby disconnected, stood, and flushed the unused toilet. Time to return to the grindstone. He had a very important meeting with Abdul Hosseini due in—he checked his Breitling—a little under two hours.

"Bloody hell," he muttered. "Where *does* the time go?"

Chapter 30

Wednesday 9th June - Claire Harper

Sandbrook Tower, Soho, London, England

Claire paced the pavement outside the Tower. She checked the time again—three thirty-seven. Abdul Hosseini should have arrived already.

Where are you?

In the distance, a lone figure hurried towards her from the direction of the Oxford Circus Underground Station. Wearing a fawn, Pashtun suit—loose-fitting, embroidered jacket with baggy trousers—and a black hat, he cut an impressive figure and stood out from the crowd. A tooled-leather satchel dangled from his shoulder. Lean and with a bushy, grey beard, Abdul Hosseini held his shoulders back, making the most of his lack of stature. As he reached her, his frown of concentration deepened and changed to one of worry.

"You are Miss Harper?" he asked.

"I am."

Keeping his eyes on her, he pressed his hands together and bent slightly from the waist.

"Am I late?" he asked. "My train ... it was delayed and—"

"Not at all. We still have a few minutes."

"Thank goodness," he said and broke out a wide, white-toothed smile. "This is the most important meeting of my life. Tardiness would not be tolerated, I fear."

"I apologise for the short notice."

Mr Hosseini shook his head with enthusiasm.

"I completely understand, Miss Harper. You are very busy, very important people. I am delighted you asked to see me. It means you are working on my case, does it not?"

"It does. Please follow me."

She led him through the revolving doors into the cool shade of the foyer. Hosseini removed his hat and his eyes widened as he took in the marbled opulence.

"Such a beautiful place to work, Miss Harper."

She smiled, but otherwise didn't respond.

They approached the reception desk, and Claire made the introductions. Mr Hosseini completed the signing in sheet, stared into the camera for the security photo, and waited for the receptionist, Anne Jenkins, to produce the laminated card for the visitor's pass.

With the formalities complete, Claire showed Mr Hosseini into the ground-floor reception room as Worm had instructed. Furnished more like a Harley Street doctor's waiting area than an interview room, with a red-leather, three-piece suite gathered around a dark, oak coffee table, the room was more used to receiving important visitors than asylum seekers attending a summons.

Typical of Worm to choose such an ostentatious place to host an interview. He would deem it beneath him to use one of the official interview rooms with their CCTV, recording systems, and emergency strip bar.

"Can I get you a drink, Mr Hosseini? A coffee, perhaps? Or help yourself to water."

She indicated the tray of bottled water and glasses on the coffee table.

"Thank you, Miss Harper. Water will be quite sufficient." He placed his hat and his bag on the floor beside the single chair nearest the window, reserving his place.

"If you'll bear with me for a moment," she said, "I'll let Commander Enderby know you've arrived."

She left Mr Hosseini standing in front of the single tall window, looking out at the passing pedestrians and the crawling traffic.

Outside, she used Anne's phone to dial Worm's internal number.

"Enderby," he said, his voice sharp.

"It's Claire Harper, Commander," she said, trying to be pleasant. "Mr Hosseini has arrived. He's in the reception room on the ground floor as you requested."

"Very good, Ms Harper. I shall be down directly."

The ignorant creep cut her off in the middle of her, "Yes, Commander."

She returned to the reception room and found Mr Hosseini where she'd left him—facing the window. He spun and smiled.

"The commander is on his way down."

She sat in one of the two single chairs that flanked the two-seater sofa, broke the seal on a bottle of still water, and poured herself a glass. Mr Hosseini lowered himself into the other single chair and leaned forwards, resting his forearms on his thighs. He radiated nervousness, and Claire couldn't blame him. The outcome of the upcoming interrogation would determine the rest of his life, and he'd yet to meet Worm.

"Miss Harper," Mr Hosseini said after a long and awkward silence, where they sipped water together and tried to avoid staring at each other, "might I be permitted to ask you a question?"

"But of course."

"Do you know what the commander wishes to ask me? I have already attended many interviews and answered many questions."

"Commander Enderby is concerned about the gap in your work record."

"Ah, I see." Mr Hosseini relaxed his shoulders. "It is quite simple. I had to take a leave of absence to care for my wife who had become unwell." He lowered his head. "Unfortunately, after a long illness, she passed from this world into the next. But I thought I had explained this during my interview at the Home Office. We went through my résumé in great detail."

Claire nodded. She'd read that part of Mr Hosseini's statement and dealt with it in her report. Worm was being his usual, overly obnoxious and overly officious self. Delaying the inevitable simply because he could.

In keeping with that *style*, Worm didn't appear for twenty minutes.

He burst into the room, the buff file she'd prepared held tight to his wide chest, and stood over them until Claire and Mr Hosseini rose and stood before him.

"Mr Hosseini," he said, completely ignoring Claire, "I

won't keep you long. Please sit." He pointed to the sofa and lowered himself into the chair that Mr Hosseini had vacated. He brushed out the creases in his trousers, placed the file on his lap, and opened it to a page marked with a folded sheet of paper.

Mr Hosseini sat bolt upright, hands clasping his knees. A sheen of sweat gathered on his forehead.

"There is no need to worry, Mr Hosseini," Worm said, looking up from the file. "As I said. This won't take long." He lowered his head, scrutinised the open page, flipped over to the next, and carried on reading. A classic, hostile interview tactic designed to make the interviewee even more uncomfortable than he would normally be.

What's he playing at?

Mr Hosseini turned towards Claire, his expression imploring. She nodded at him, trying to transmit encouragement.

Worm flipped over yet another page and cleared his throat.

"Ms Harper," he said, looking at her for the first time, his nostrils flared, "before we begin, I think some refreshments would be in order. I missed my afternoon coffee, and I am sure Mr Hosseini would appreciate something stronger than water." He turned to Mr Hosseini and managed a thin smile. "How do you take your coffee, Mr Hosseini?"

Mr Hosseini blinked rapidly, taken by surprise.

"Black, please. Two sugars."

"Very good. I can't promise you the best coffee in the world, but we can at least provide a better class of instant. Ms Harper"—he turned his pale blue eyes towards her—"if you wouldn't mind. I take mine with cream and no sugar. Have one yourself. The receptionist has been primed."

He dismissed her from the room with a backhanded

wave, and turned to face Mr Hosseini again. He actually sent her away as though she were nothing but a servant.

You arrogant prick!

Cheeks flushed, jaw clenched, she jumped up and forced herself to smile at a confused Abdul Hosseini. She turned her back on the obnoxious worm and marched through the door, thinking twice about slamming it behind her. Instead, she left it slightly ajar, knowing how much Worm hated open doors.

"Now then, Mr Hosseini," Worm said, loud enough for her to hear clearly, "where were we? Ah yes. Here it is. Seventeen years ago, you left your post at Kabul University. Would you care to explain …"

Claire stormed across the foyer to the reception counter, trying not to scowl.

"Calm down, Claire," Anne said, grinning. "You'll give yourself a stroke."

Claire rested her hands flat on the counter and took a deep and slow breath.

"Sorry, just having one of those days." She stopped herself from saying more and shook her head.

"The commander up to his old tricks again, is he?"

"No comment," Claire answered, surprised at Anne's joke. She made a mental note to try to speak to her in private again and keep digging into Enderby's huge dirt pile. "I understand he ordered some refreshments?"

"He did indeed. Coffees all around?"

"Yes, please. They can do their own milk and sugar."

And given half a chance, she'd spit in Worm's mug on the way back.

That's beneath you, Claire.

"I made it fresh," she said. "Nice and strong."

"It needs to be," Claire growled.

Anne turned towards the hospitality corner behind her station and returned carrying a tray with a vacuum flask, a jug of fresh milk, and sachets of brown sugar in a bowl.

"You'll find cups, saucers, and cutlery in the reception room," she said, sliding the tray across the desk. "Enjoy."

"Thanks."

Claire reached for the tray.

A screeched and angry, "*Allahu Akbar!*" echoed through the foyer.

"No!" Worm shouted. "What are you doing?"

A man's scream cut off mid-breath.

Glass smashed. A loud thump erupted from the reception room—the sound of a heavy object hitting the carpet.

"Help, for God's sake!" Worm shouted.

Claire released her hold on the tray, raced towards the part-closed door, and slammed it open.

Worm stood over the prone figure of Abdul Hosseini, his arms splayed.

Mr Hosseini—eyes wide in shock, mouth open, panting —lay on the carpet. His hands clasped the wooden handle of the knife sticking out of his chest. Blood seeped through his hands.

"He attacked me!" Worm yelled. "The bugger attacked me! Attacked me with a knife."

Mr Hosseini turned his head towards Claire. He opened his mouth, tried to speak. No words came out.

She rushed towards him, dropped to her knees at his side.

"I-I did ..." he gasped. "I ... did not—"

Mr Hosseini's eyes lost focus. He stopped breathing. His hands released the knife and his arms flopped to the sides.

Claire looked up. Anne stood in the open doorway, shock etched onto her face. Ellen Winters appeared behind her. She eased Anne aside, squeezed through the opening, and approached Claire.

"Call an ambulance!" she said.

"He attacked me," Worm muttered. "With that knife." He pointed to the object protruding from Mr Hosseini's unmoving chest.

Ellen lowered herself to her knees beside Claire.

"CPR?" Claire gasped, her eyes filling with tears. "Should we start CPR?"

The bodyguard shook her head slowly.

"The blade ... It's near his heart. Chest compressions would do more harm than good."

She reached forwards and pressed the tips of her index and middle fingers into the side of Mr Hosseini's neck.

"Can't find a pulse," she said, so quiet Claire barely heard the words.

Behind them, Worm kept wittering, almost to himself. "He attacked me with a knife. He attacked me. Terrorist. ... A terrorist attack. Here inside the Tower. ... He came at me with a knife. I was only defending myself. You can see that, can't you? Anyone can see that."

By the door, Anne had a mobile phone pressed to her ear.

"Ambulance, please," she said. "And the police. A man's been stabbed with a knife. I-I think he's dead."

Claire slumped onto her haunches and let the tears fall. She couldn't drag her streaming eyes away from the knife handle jutting out of Mr Hosseini's lifeless chest. She expected to see more blood, but ...

Dear God.

Moments before, Hosseini had been alive, breathing, scared but hopeful. Now, he lay dead on the floor.

Nothing made sense.

Anne gave the operator their location and ended the call.

"Police and ambulance are … on their way," she said.

"Who searched him?" Worm asked, stepping closer to the body.

Claire twisted to stare up at him. "What do you mean?"

Ellen helped Claire to her feet.

"He should have been searched," Worm said. "Who did it? Who missed the knife?"

"No one searched him," Claire answered, sniffling. "He was deemed low risk."

"Low risk?" Worm shouted. "Low risk! The man attacked me with that bloody knife! I could have been killed, woman. You should have had him searched."

Ellen stepped between Worm and Claire.

"Oh no," she said, glowering at him. "You're not laying the blame at Claire's door."

Worm leaned forwards and thrust out his jaw.

"How dare you talk to me like that!"

"You put yourself at risk, Commander."

"Wh-What!" he spluttered, fists clenched.

Claire couldn't see any blood on him. Not a mark. Not a single crease out of place on his expensive suit.

Ellen stared him down.

"You should have booked him into a secure interview room. One with full surveillance support. As I understand it from Ms Harper, you insisted on using the non-secure waiting room. If you had any concerns over Mr Hosseini's state of mind, you should have given the protection unit at least twenty-four hours advanced notice of the interview, as per standard protocol. If you had done that, we would have arranged a full security presence. Furthermore," she added with extra force, "we would have screened Mr Hosseini on arrival and accompanied you into the room."

Perry Grieves' broad-shouldered presence appeared in the doorway beside Anne. He slid past her and made his way into the room.

"Now is not the time or the place for a case review," he said, his tone authoritative. "Everyone, please step away from the body. Nobody touch anything. This room is a crime scene."

Worm turned to face Perry.

"He came at me with a knife," he said. "A knife. We struggled. He fell. That's what happened."

"Save the explanation for the police, Commander."

"But you are the police!"

"We're armed protection officers. You need to save your statement for the detectives."

Worm ground his teeth, his jaw muscles bunched.

"Am I allowed to use the rest room?" he asked. "I need to clean up … I mean, relieve myself."

Perry shook his head.

"You'll need to hold it, Commander. It's best if you don't wash up until after the forensics techs have taken their samples."

"But that could take hours," he whined. "I'm bursting, man. I've just had a terrible shock."

Perry glanced sideways at Ellen and Claire and then turned his eyes back to Worm.

"I'll have to accompany you to the toilet, Commander. To make sure you don't wash your hands afterwards."

"That's preposterous," he snapped. "What if I give you my word not to clean my hands. Will that do?"

"No, sir," Perry said, shaking his head once. "It won't."

"What?" Worm's eyes bugged so wide they nearly

popped out of his head. "Are you treating me as a suspect? I'm the director of the agency, man!"

"By your own admission," Perry answered, his voice controlled, "you did just stab a man, probably to death, Commander."

"In self-defence!" Worm screamed, spittle flying. "Hosseini attacked me with a knife."

"So you keep insisting, Commander." Perry shot Worm a silencing look. "At this stage, it might be best for you not to say anything more until you've been read your rights."

Had Mr Hosseini not been lying dead on the floor, not five paces away, Claire would have revelled in Worm's discomfort.

"Okay," Ellen said, working her way around and behind Worm. "Everyone leave the room."

She held out her arms, shepherded them all into the foyer, and closed the door behind them, shutting off the sad view of Mr Hosseini and the knife.

While Perry Grieves escorted Worm to the ground-floor toilets, Ellen eased Claire to one side, out of earshot of Anne and a pair of confused visitors who had wandered into the foyer from outside and stood in front of the reception desk, waiting to be dealt with.

"Anne," Ellen said. "Send them away, please. We don't need any more people in here."

"Yes, right." Anne raised a hand towards the newcomers and hurried towards her desk.

"What happened?" Ellen asked Claire quietly. "Did you see the stabbing?"

"No," Claire answered, shaking her head. "Worm sent me out for coffees. He and Mr Hosseini were alone. I heard screaming and shouting, but …" She pulled in a shuddering gulp of air, trying to tamp down the gorge rising to her throat. The image of Mr Hosseini and the knife sticking from his chest, the blood … it was horrible. She would never be able to forget it.

"But?" Ellen asked.

"I-I don't believe a word of what Worm said. Mr Hosseini didn't attack him. *He didn't have it in him!*" She hissed the last words through clenched teeth.

Ellen reached out a hand and took a firm grip on Claire's shoulder.

"But you didn't actually see what happened."

"No," Claire said, shaking her head. "No. I-I was out here."

Ellen glanced around the foyer before locking eyes with Claire. Anne had sent the visitors packing and had locked the revolving doors until the first responders arrived.

Ellen increased the pressure on Claire's shoulder.

"Listen to me, Claire," she whispered.

Claire blinked and tried to shake the fog of confusion from her head.

"Sorry, what?"

"Listen to me," Ellen repeated. "Listen carefully." She leaned closer, lowering her voice even more. "When the detectives get here, tell them everything you saw and heard today. Everything. No more, no less. Understood?"

Claire nodded.

"Yes, of course."

"And for God's sake stop calling him 'Worm'."

"I didn't. Did I?"

"Yes. You did. More than once." Ellen nodded. "And whatever you do, don't accuse him of being a sexual predator."

"Why not?" Claire asked, frowning.

"It'll muddy the waters."

Ellen glanced away as Perry Grieves and Worm—Enderby—returned from the toilet.

"But it'll show what he's like. I don't want him getting away with murd—"

"You heard the bugger," Ellen said, nodding towards Worm. "He's already tried to shift the blame for the attack onto you. If you mention your grievance, it'll give you a motive for helping Hosseini."

"But that's ridiculous. Nobody would believe—"

Ellen squeezed Claire's shoulder, pressing so hard with her thumb it really hurt.

"I know that," Ellen said, "but don't give Enderby the chance to wriggle out from under this. Let the police investigate. If there's anything suspicious, they'll find it. Promise me, Claire. Don't say a word."

Claire swallowed. Although she wanted to clear Mr Hosseini's name and drop Worm in the mire, Ellen was making sense. She had to keep silent.

"Y-Yes. I promise. Not a word."

"Good."

Ellen nodded, gave her an encouraging smile, and released the grip on her shoulder. Claire rubbed the spot where Ellen's thumb had dug into the flesh. It was going to leave a bruise.

Perry Grieves caught Claire's eye, smiled, and nodded his encouragement. Her heart swelled, and she returned his smile.

Moments later, the strident wail of sirens filled the air.

Chapter 31

Charing Cross Police Station, Westminster, London, England

Perched on a rock-hard bunk and leaning against a cold, tile wall, Enderby forced himself to keep a straight face. This was not the time or the place to be seen smiling even though he really wanted to. Smiling would seem crass. Heartless even. After all, less than three hours earlier, he'd plunged a brand-new kitchen knife—the one he'd bought during his lunch break, for cash in a backstreet shop—into the chest of an innocent man. Not that any asylum seeker could really be classed as innocent. He could generate no sympathy for Abdul Hosseini.

Good bloody riddance to another foreign sponger.

Enderby had to admit though. He'd played it well. An absolute blinder. He'd pitched onto the green and rolled the ball to within a few centimetres of the cup. A sure-fire birdie.

Okay, so he was sitting in a holding cell, after having made an interim statement to a pair of stern-faced detectives, and being stripped and worked over by a man in a white forensics suit. But he did have everything under control. Without the need for a solicitor—after all, who needed a solicitor when they were innocent—he'd taken the detectives through the events, moment-by-moment, blow-by-blow, playing the shocked victim of a terrorist attack to the very limit. He'd trembled at all the right times, and he'd even broken down when reliving the exquisite moment when the knife slipped through the intercostal space between Hosseini's fifth and sixth ribs—a hand-to-hand combat technique they'd taught him in the navy. During the interview, he'd even managed to shift some of the blame onto the Harper woman, which would work out well for him in the long run. She'd dropped the ball, he'd told them. After all, Harper was the one who'd actually escorted Hosseini into Sandbrook Tower without insisting on having the bugger searched. An error that ultimately facilitated an attack on him, the director of the NTCA. The same courageous director who managed to overpower the terrorist and defend himself. The detectives believed him, too. Enderby could tell. They lapped up his version of events. His version of the truth. Lapped it up.

Bloody fools.

Things could not have worked out any better. He raised the cheap, plastic cup to his lips, supped on the disgusting cup of what passed for coffee in the custody suite, and refused to grimace at the bitter aftertaste. The custody officer who'd brought him the brew couldn't help what he provided. The youngster was doing his best. He couldn't be blamed for being unable to provide Blue Mountain Rich Roast. In any event, Enderby would never complain to a man who held the key to his locked cell.

Not ever.

Enderby glanced at his watch. This time, he did smile, but hid it behind the plastic cup in case the custody officer was looking at him through the surveillance screen. At that precise moment, Guy Gordon would be on his way to Andrea's apartment to deliver some much-needed pest control.

Yes.

By the time they released him from the holding cell, free and clear of all guilt, Sir Ernest and Andrea would both be dead, Enderby would have the perfect alibi, and his way would be clear to inherit the crown.

Oh yes.

Greg Enderby had every reason to smile.

Chapter 32

Wednesday 9th June – Andrea Fisher-Smythe

Eaton Place, Belgravia, London, England

Andrea Fisher-Smythe—real name, Mary Jane Smith—added the finishing touches to her eyeliner. Not too much makeup—the old fool preferred the natural look—but the years were starting to take their toll and, these days, she needed all the help she could get. The slight creases around her eyes, laughter lines, were starting to look a little more like full-blown crow's feet, and her once-pert boobs had started to droop. Still, they weren't enormous and would never be pendulous. Never having kids hanging from her nipples for months on end helped. Kids. Dear God, no. The idea of pushing out a gaggle of spawn couldn't have been more abhorrent to a woman who valued her independence. A woman who valued her figure, and made a living from it.

Andrea smiled into the mirror. She'd be able to live off her looks for a few more years yet.

She stood tall and naked in front of the full-length mirror, shaved, perfumed, and primped to perfection. Apart from the softness of her average-size breasts, there wasn't an ounce of spare flesh on her. Trim stomach. Firm, round arse. Long, well-muscled legs—no cellulite. Hours spent in the gym each week and a strict vegan diet saw to that.

Yes, she'd do well enough. She'd "pass muster" as the old chap might say.

Andrea stepped into the white, silk dress and tied the straps in a bow behind her neck. The dress showed off her sunbed tan and clung to her frame in all the right places, allowing her dark nipples to poke out and suggest arousal. A quick trip to the kitchen to stand near the open fridge after he rang the doorbell would help.

The tricks of the trade. She'd learned them well.

He'd be there soon. Always punctual. A gentleman of the old school. He arrived on time, came quickly and without too much fuss, chatted for a while, and left a generous tip. The perfect client. One of many. Not that the old man realised. The poor thing thought he paid her enough to guarantee exclusivity. She caught herself in the mirror, smiling wider. A prizewinning smile, which she used well.

The clock on the mantel gave her fifteen minutes. Time enough for a touch of liquid fortification. She left the bedroom—sheets turned down in readiness—and entered the lounge. Poured herself a stiff vodka and lime which didn't taint her breath and knocked back half a tumbler in one swallow. Alcohol as anaesthetic. Not too much, for that way led down the slippery slope. One large belt only. She'd sip the rest and have one more with him after the non-event which she'd turn into a bravura performance befitting an Oscar.

She sat in her favourite chair, sipping her drink, eyes closed in meditative preparation.

Her mindfulness coach would have had her perform circular breathing and chanting, but she had no time for such luxuries. Not at that moment.

The doorbell chimed. Seven fifty-three. Seven minutes early.

Well now. The old boy must be keen.

Andrea accessed the doorbell camera app on her mobile, confirmed the caller's identity, and hit the answer button.

Showtime.

"Ernest," she gushed. "Come on up. I've missed you so much."

She rushed to the kitchen and stood in front of the open fridge for long enough to obtain the desired result. It would take the old boy a minute or so to climb the three floors to her apartment. Too proud to arrive breathless and sweaty, he would take his own, sweet time.

A gentle double rap announced his arrival, and she plastered a welcoming smile onto a less than willing face.

"Here we go," she muttered to the walls on her way through the lounge to the front door. "Once more unto the breach."

She released the electronic deadlock, turned the handle, and tugged open the heavy security door.

Sir Ernest Hartington, standing tall and lean, and—to be perfectly honest—rather distinguished, filled in the doorway. As usual, he awaited her permission to enter even though he owned the apartment. Such manners. A true gentleman.

"Good evening, my dear," he said, adding a slight bow.

"Ernest," she gasped, hand to her throat. "How lovely to see you. Come in. Please, come in."

Andrea ushered him inside and presented her right cheek for a chaste kiss. He often liked to roleplay, and as usual, she'd take her lead from him.

She pressed the door closed behind him and confirmed the lock had caught. There had been a number of burglaries in the area recently, and one couldn't be too careful. Security mattered. She walked the old man to the settee and invited him to sit.

"Would you like a drink?"

Hartington drank whisky. Single malt. Suitably aged. She kept a bottle in reserve especially for him, but would never have a drink ready in advance. He preferred her to offer it first.

"A wee dram of whisky would hit the spot," he said, eyeing her protruding nipples with unreserved interest. "Thank you, my dear."

At the drinks cabinet, she poured a small measure into a lead crystal glass and carried it to him. He took the glass and knocked the whole lot back in one.

Bloody hell. That's a first.

"That was delightful."

"Another?"

"Yes, please." He returned the glass.

"Really?"

He never had a second until after the performance, when he knocked the stuff back as though it were lemonade.

"It's been a stressful day," he added as if that explained everything away.

She returned to the cabinet and poured him another. This one a double.

Andrea handed him the drink and backed into her single chair directly across from him. She pulled her legs tight into the chair, crossed her ankles, and sat up straight to make sure he caught a good view of her breasts. Even though clearly distressed, he studied her every move.

"Did you catch the evening news?" he asked, eyes lowered, apparently staring at nothing.

"Of course not," she said, flapping her hand over her drink. "I rarely watch the TV news. It's too depressing."

Confused, Andrea tried not to frown. Hartington never made small talk before the non-event. By now, they'd usually be in the bedroom already.

"You should, my dear. It will help keep you informed."

Don't fucking humour me, you decrepit old goat.

He didn't spend money for her conversation.

"There was a knife attack this afternoon in Sandbrook Tower. A man died."

Andrea sat up straighter.

Fucking hell!

"My goodness," she said, placing a hand over her heart. "Actually inside your building?"

He nodded and took another drink.

"An asylum seeker went rogue. Attacked the agency's director with a knife."

Christ!

"Y-Your director?"

"Yes. Commander Enderby," he said. "I've mentioned him in the past, I'm certain."

Greg? Greg was attacked?

Oh please God. No!

"Is he …?" She gulped. "Is he okay?"

"Yes, yes," he said. "I wasn't in the building at the time, but I've been assured he's perfectly fine."

Oh thank God. Thank God.

"What happened?"

"It seems he overpowered the man and … well, stabbed him with his own knife. Remarkable really." The old man paused long enough to knock back the rest of his whisky and added, "Didn't know he had it in him. An act of true heroism. Rumour has it, he saved a female member of staff in the process. One of our executive officers."

Andera closed her eyes for a moment and took a deep sip of her vodka and lime. Her hands trembled and the tumbler rattled against her teeth.

The old man held up his empty glass.

"Another?"

"Yes, please. Another large one. I need the fortification."

She stood on weak and shaking legs and did the honours, adding two fingers of vodka to her glass, but no more lime.

Once back in her seat, she leaned forwards. Nothing suggestive, just a keen interest.

"You're sure Commander, what was it, Endsley? You're sure he's okay?"

"Enderby," he said, holding his glass up to the light and absently twirling the golden liquid. "Commander Enderby, Gregory. Yes, yes. As I told you, he came through the ordeal completely unscathed."

"You saw him, after the … attack?"

Ernest looked at her, eyes narrowed.

"You seem very exercised by this, my dear. Not like you at all."

"Nonsense, Ernest," she said, tossing back her hair. "You know I hang on everything you say about your work. I mean, it's not as though you can tell me much, and you certainly can't take me along to any of your social gatherings. As such, I have to live by what you tell me. So, this Enderby chap, he saved someone's life, you say?"

"It seems so. At least, Claire Harper was booked to be in the interview room with him at the time. Or so I'm led to believe. I haven't had the chance to speak to him yet. Enderby, that is."

"Whyever not?"

"The police whisked him away before I arrived. He's currently what they call, 'helping police with their enquiries', my dear."

"He is?"

What the fuck?

"Of course," he said, shooting her one of his insufferably superior smiles.

Oh no.

"But he was attacked. Why would they arrest him?"

"A man's been killed, my dear. The police have to investigate. I have no doubt they'll release him without charge eventually. After all, he was acting in self-defence and in the defence of others."

"Ernest," she said, stretching her neck out a little, "you're an important man. A man of influence. Can't you exert some of it to help your … your colleague?"

The old man frowned and tucked in his chin.

"Absolutely not. I couldn't possibly do anything of the sort. In fact, it might even do more harm than good." He cut his hand over the top of his whisky. "The investigation must be allowed to proceed without interference."

"They should give him a medal," she announced and meant it.

"And they probably will. In due course. The bugger will probably wangle himself the George Cross out of this."

"Bugger?" she snapped, staring at him across the narrow gap. "Did you just call him a bugger?"

Hartington held up his hand in apology and lowered his head.

"Sorry, my dear, I meant 'beggar'." He licked his lips. "Too much whisky, too quickly. Muddling my words."

The old boy sipped again and stared into his glass for an age.

"It's all going to pot," he said, staring at the rug between his feet. The Persian rug she'd chosen but he'd paid for.

"What is, Ernest?" she asked, not really caring.

Fuck. He's maudlin tonight.

She'd never seen him so full of self-pity. With any luck she'd get away without having to squirm beneath him. If nothing else, Andrea lived in hope.

"Everything." He held out his tumbler again. "Remember what we discussed last week? About Malcolm Sampson and how he died?"

Where the bloody hell's he going now?

A knife attack in his office had segued into the death of an old pervert. It didn't make any sense. Andrea closed her eyes and frowned in apparent search of a memory.

"Ah, yes. The tubby man who owned that weapons company. Imprisoned for theft—no, tax fraud wasn't it?" Andrea answered, being deliberately vague.

She'd been following the story closely as it had all the elements needed to play well in the scandal sheets. A disgraced, former knight of the realm, found dead in his four-poster, tied at the wrists and ankles, and wearing a ball gag. Absolutely outrageous. The tabloids had been full of it. They'd even brought up the air crash and the terrorist, Ryan Kaine. Although she never could quite work out the link between the two stories. Was Kaine supposed to have been working for Sampson?

"Yes," Sir Ernest said, sighing. "Tax avoidance. A bad business. Very bad." Again, he held his glass up to the light and twirled the golden liquid. "At the time, I didn't know how bad. But ... I'm afraid I've ... I've rather let the side down."

Ernest nodded and slurped another mouthful of whisky. She'd never seen him drink so much or so quickly.

"You?" she said. "I don't believe that for a moment."

She did, though. They were all the same. The high-flyers. The movers and shakers. All the damn same. Out to grab whatever they could, and to hell with the rest of mankind.

"I considered cancelling our date tonight," the old boy said, finally lowering the glass and raising his eyes to hers. "Would have done, but I know how you cherish our short time together."

Christ alive. Was he being serious? Could he really be that delusional? If she hadn't been such a good actor, remaining deep in character, she might have burst out laughing. Alternatively, she might have gagged.

"I do, Ernest. I really do." She leaned forwards and pushed her arms together to pump up her breasts and show him all the cleavage she could muster. "Your visits are the highlight of my week," she added.

Easy, Andrea. Don't overegg the pudding.

"Thank you," he said, showing her a sad smile.

He knew. He must do. Sir Ernest Hartington was anything but a fool.

"They only showed me the video recently, you see. The video..." he said, speaking directly to the near-empty whisky glass. "Long after I'd countersigned the report. That report was... it recommended the Grey Notice, of course. But by then, it was too late. Too bloody late. I'd ... over-stepped the mark. Couldn't do a thing about it after that. Not a thing ... Not a bloody thing ..."

"Well now," a deep voice behind them said. "A confession. Isn't that interesting."

Andrea jumped out of her chair, turned, and froze, petrified. A man, dressed in black, mouth and nose hidden behind a scarf, stood in her open doorway. He pointed a gun at her. A scream cut short in her throat.

A gun!

He had a gun.

She stood trembling, trying not to whimper. Trying not to wet herself.

How did he get in? She'd locked the door. She definitely locked the door.

"Please, don't hurt her," Sir Ernest begged.

Using the arms of the chair, he pushed himself to his feet and held out his empty hands, pleading. The crystal glass lay on the floor at his feet, the whisky soaking into the Persian rug. Bloody thing cost a fortune. Did whisky leave a stain?

Christ, girl. What are you thinking?

A man with a gun had broken into her home and all she could worry about was the bloody carpet. What about Sir Ernest? He didn't look too hot. He'd turned a nasty shade of grey. The old boy had been seeing the doctor recently. Something to do with his blood pressure or his heart or something. God knew. When clients started banging on about their health, she tended to tune out the self-pitying arseholes. The only thing she gave a damn about was the health of their bank balance.

Stop it. Stop rambling. Concentrate.

"Sir Ernest," the man with the gun said. "Please sit back down. You don't look at all well."

He spoke quietly, but his voice carried well. Andrea tried not to look at him, but his eyes drew her in. Deep brown they were, and empty, but with the ability to stare right into her soul. If she screamed, he would kill her. She knew it. She had no doubt.

Ernest dropped into the sofa, and Andrea moved to sit beside him.

"No. Not you, love," the man said. "Whiskey Two, in you come." He called.

Chapter 33

Eaton Place, Belgravia, London, England

Cough eased his foot off the accelerator, and they rolled slowly along Eaton Place.

"Pull in there," Will Stacy ordered, indicating an empty parking spot. Although nine doors down from the target building, it had a pretty decent view of the entrance.

"We need a resident permit," Cough said, reverse parking into the tight space.

Once satisfied they were fully inside the white lines and had enough room to leave in a hurry, he killed the engine. The rumble of the city in the late evening grew all around them. Cough loved London. The place hummed with life.

As soon as they'd dealt with Gordon, he'd take Stefan and show him the sights. The kid needed his horizons expanded.

"Traffic wardens don't work this late," Stacy said, searching the area with his all-seeing eyes that rarely stayed still.

"Big Brother's watching us," Cough said, pointing to the blue traffic camera attached to a lamppost less than fifty metres distant. And to the one further along the road. "Big Brother's always bloody watching."

"We won't be here long enough for them to bother us. And the Volvo's registered to a chip shop in Wilsden. We won't be receiving a parking fine."

Cough nodded. Stacy had a point. He was worrying for no reason.

Eaton Place ran ahead of them in a straight line. Rows of identical, seven-storey, Victorian townhouses with twin-columned entrance porches, and all covered in an off-white render, stretched out on either side of the road. All perfect. Each house turned into high-class and very expensive apartments.

"Fancy place for a working girl," Cough said, curling his upper lip.

"Hartington owns the apartment, not Andrea. It's been in his family for decades. He's just installed her in the place."

"Two million quid for a two-bed flat?" Cough said. "Do me a favour." He sniffed. "Wonder what his wife thinks of him giving it over to his bit on the side?"

"I doubt she even knows it exists."

"And," Cough added, "I wonder what he's going to think when we tell him Enderby's been paying house calls behind his back."

Cough caught sight of something so rare he had to mention it.

"Blimey, Major. You almost smiled then."

Stacy ignored his comment and continued his watch.

They waited five minutes and saw nothing but empty pavements.

Cough's earpiece clicked twice.

"*Whatcha, people. How you diddling?*" Corky's cheerful voice broke into their quiet vigil. "*Sorry, meant to say, Control to Whiskey One and Whiskey Two, are you receiving? Over.*"

"Whiskey One to Control," Stacy responded. "I hear you. Over."

Cough smiled. As far as radio protocol was concerned, Corky could do anything he damn well chose, considering he'd developed the comms system and swore blind it couldn't be intercepted.

"Whiskey Two here," Cough added. "I've got you. Over."

"*Corky knew you could, actually. It says so on the system interface. Anyway, GG, er, the subject, left home half an hour ago. He's five minutes out. Control's going to look in on Alpha One, now. Er … Control, out.*"

A click signalled the end of the bulletin.

"Decent bit of kit these things, eh, sir?" Cough said. "Wish we'd hand them in Helmand."

"Okay," Stacy said, ignoring Cough's attempted conversation opener. "I'm going in. I'll let you know when I'm in position."

"Yes, sir."

Stacy cracked the Volvo's passenger door and slid out. Hands in his pockets, he sauntered towards the target house, climbed the steps onto the porch, and tapped the entry code into the keypad as though he'd done it a thousand times.

The movement-activated hall light blossomed, but Stacy ignored it and entered the building as if he had every right to be there.

Three minutes later, Cough's earpiece clicked again.

"*Whiskey One to Whiskey Two,*" Stacy said, his voice as clear as though he were still sitting in the car next to Cough. "*Access gained. I'm in a cleaner's cupboard on the top-floor half-landing. Any sign of the target? Over.*"

"Whiskey Two here. Nothing yet. Over."

"*Keep your eyes peeled. Whiskey One, out.*"

The earpiece clicked again, and Cough shook his head.

"'Keep your eyes peeled', he says," Cough muttered. "As though I'd ever nod off on the job."

In his rear-view mirror, a set of headlights advanced on Lyall Street, shining bright and moving slowly. Indicators flashed orange, signalling an imminent left turn into Eaton Place. Seconds later, a Jaguar XF rolled into view, heading towards him.

"Whiskey Two to Whiskey One. Target in view. Over."

The Jag passed at walking pace, the driver taking time to read the house numbers painted on the porch columns.

"*I hear you, Whiskey Two. Over.*"

"He's driving a dark blue Jaguar XF. Over."

"*Does it have a dent on the nearside front wing? Over.*"

"Yep," Cough said. "Surely does. How did you know? Over."

"*It was me who dinged it. The idiot's using a company car. Complacent bugger doesn't believe he'll be caught. Over.*"

"You had a crash? Over."

"*Long story. Let's leave it for now. Over.*"

Cough provided a running commentary as the Jag continued for another seventy-five metres before pulling into an empty bay on the opposite side of the street. Seconds later, the driver's door opened, and Guy Gordon climbed out on the pavement side. He looked up and down the street, before crossing the road, shoulders hunched, and the peak of his black baseball cap pulled down over his eyes.

"*Doesn't look at all sus, Whiskey One,*" Cough said. "*He might as well be wearing a striped shirt and carrying a sack with a nice big "Swag" marked on the back. Stand by. Over.*"

Ahead, Gordon stopped at the target house, took a long moment to check his periphery, and climbed the six steps to the front door. He keyed the passcode into the entry panel and the lock clicked. After a final and furtive glance over his shoulder, Gordon pushed the door open and disappeared inside. The door swung closed slowly behind him.

"Target's inside," Cough said. "I repeat. The target's inside. Whiskey Two, out."

He climbed out of the Volvo, closed its door gently, and keyed the lock manually. Head lowered, he ambled up to Number 61, and peered through the door's frosted-glass window. The internal courtesy light still shone from Gordon's recent entry. Cough worked the keypad, slipped into the hall, and hurried up the wide staircase. On reaching the half-landing below the top floor, he found the cupboard door shut tight.

Interesting.

He turned the handle, tugged open the cupboard door, and stepped back. Guy Gordon sat on an upturned bucket, head twisted at an unnatural angle, eyes wide, his face contorted in a rictus of death. Stacy had snapped his neck. Fast and efficient. The head of GG Cleaning Systems wouldn't have felt much in the way of pain before Stacy had extinguished his lights forever.

Cough closed the door on the corpse and felt nothing. The evil bastard had sent strike teams after Cough's mates, and he'd done it for money. The man had it coming and deserved no sympathy. If the captain had asked for volunteers to kill the man, Cough would have been the first to step right up.

Above him, a woman's scream cut off sharply.

Cough raced up the final flight of stairs, climbing three at a time. The penthouse door stood slightly ajar, left open for him. At the threshold he paused, waiting for the signal.

"Please, don't hurt her," a man called out. Old and scared, it had to be Hartington.

"Sir Ernest," Stacy said, speaking quietly. "Please sit back down. You don't look at all well … No. Not you, love." He raised his voice and called out, "Whiskey Two, in you come."

Chapter 34

Eaton Place, Belgravia, London, England

Cough raised his snood to cover his nose and mouth, entered the flat, and pushed the door firmly closed behind him. A top-end apartment such as this would be bound to have a decent level of sound insulation—the very least an owner could expect for two million pounds worth of bricks and mortar.

Andrea Fisher-Smythe, as beautiful as her photo, stood with her arms hugged tight to her chest, hands covering her mouth, staring at Stacy—or rather, his Glock—in horror. Her chin trembled and tears rolled down her cheeks, taking some of the dark mascara with them and producing a mask of fear. She wore a white, silk dress so transparent, it confirmed she hadn't bothered with underwear. Behind her, Sir Ernest Hartington sat, half-collapsed on a three-seater sofa, staring up at the major. Grey and sweaty, the sixty-two-year-old head of the NCTA clutched his chest. He looked ready to pass out.

"Take her," Stacy ordered and pointed deeper into the apartment.

"With me, Miss," Cough said, waving her towards an open door that might be a bedroom.

Still staring at the major's Glock, she didn't move.

Cough took her gently by the upper arm and she jolted.

"No! Don't touch me," she shrieked, tearing her arm free. "Please don't."

"Be quiet!" he snapped. "Which one's the bedroom?"

"What? No, no. Please."

She'd clearly misunderstood his intention.

"Shush. We're not going to hurt you. We're here for Sir Ernest."

Andrea blinked, turned towards the grey-skinned, old man, and nodded. "Oh ... I see."

The relief on her tear-streaked face told a tale. As long as they left her alone, they could have Hartington with pleasure.

"Which one's the bedroom?"

"Here," she said and hurried towards the second of four doors in the far wall. He had to rush to keep up with her. The door led into Andrea's workplace, a large bedroom dominated by a king-sized bed, with a metal headboard and footboard.

Perfect.

"Sit and make yourself comfortable."

He didn't have to pat her down. She had nowhere to hide anything in that dress, and the situation certainly didn't rate a cavity search.

Andrea climbed onto the bed, tugged a pillow from beneath the covers, and hugged it tight.

"Right hand, please."

Without hesitation, she held out her arm, meek and mild. She'd clearly been cuffed before.

He secured her wrist to the bedstead with a fat cable tie and made sure it wasn't excessively tight.

"If you start shouting, I'll have to gag you. Understand?"

She nodded.

Before leaving, he searched the bedside cabinet for anything she could use to free herself or call for help, but found only personal care items and a selection of battery-operated toys—which he left in place. She might need something to help her pass the time.

"Remember," he said, raising a finger to his lips. "Keep quiet or I'll be back. This won't take long."

Back out in the main room, the tableau hadn't changed much. Stacy still stood over the cowering Hartington, but he'd lowered the gun to his side. Cough closed the bedroom door and stood guard, his SIG drawn and primed, making sure to keep in full view of Hartington.

"What were you saying about a video before I arrived?" Stacy asked, his tone conversational.

Hartington winced, his breathing rapid and shallow.

"Y-You heard that?"

Sweat popped onto his brow.

Stacy nodded. "Some of it. You said you only saw it recently, but I don't believe you."

Hartington pulled in a deep breath and held it a moment before releasing it and breathing again.

"It … It's true," he said, nodding slowly, as though it took effort. "I-I promise. The video's been kept under wraps. Top secret."

"Why?"

"It's too … in-inflammatory."

Stacy glanced at Cough and nodded.

"Are we talking about the same video?" Stacy asked.

Hartington screwed up his face and rested his head on the back of the sofa.

"I-I … don't know. Are we?"

"The one that exonerates Captain Kaine. The one that shows him chained to a chair in Sir Malcolm's penthouse."

"Y-Yes," Hartington said, dipping his head in a slow nod. "It's incendiary. Jay—I mean, someone in authority, didn't want people to know about it. The distribution list was extremely small. Five or six people only."

"By 'Jay', I imagine you mean Jason Wyndham, MP?" Stacy asked, dropping the bombshell as only he could—with ice-cold simplicity.

Hartington gasped.

"Y-You know?"

Stacy's tight smile didn't reach his eyes. Cough could only imagine what it must feel like being on the wrong end of one of Will Stacy's dead stares.

"Commander Enderby told us," he said. "In a round-about way."

"You got to Gregory?"

Stacy smile faded. "We paid him a visit on Monday night. It took some gentle persuasion, but he became most co-operative in the end."

Hartington straightened. His hand dropped from his

chest and landed on the arm of the sofa. Some colour had returned to his face.

"But ... I saw him in the office ... this morning. He didn't look ... I mean, there wasn't a mark on him."

"None that showed," Stacy said. "And none that would be permanent. Let's just say we are highly skilled at what we do, shall we? And by 'we', I mean me, Ryan Kaine, and our friends."

"Kaine?" Hartington gulped. "You're working with Captain Kaine?"

Stacy tilted his head. "Didn't I make that clear? Yes, we're with the captain. If you haven't worked it out yet, I'm Will. That's Major William Stacy to you, and he"—Stacy nodded towards Cough—"is another associate of ours who prefers to remain anonymous. Isn't that right, Sergeant?"

"Yes, Major. Quite right. I'm happy for Sir Ernest to know my rank, though." Cough smiled behind the snood. Remaining nameless suited him well enough, and it added a little more tension to the situation.

"So," Stacy said, "where was I? Oh yes, the commander. He was very helpful. He told us all about how you wrote the report recommending a Grey Notice be authorised for the captain."

"But ... that's not—"

"You can imagine how the captain reacted to that particular snippet of information."

Hartington released his grasp of the sofa and stretched out his arm but lowered it when Stacy raised the Glock.

"That's not the way it—"

"Commander Enderby was quite keen to point us in your direction. Wasn't he, Sergeant."

Again, he glanced at Cough, and again, Cough nodded.

"Couldn't tell us quickly enough, Major. Pitiful, it was."

"He's a liar!" Hartington shouted, gathering strength from somewhere deep. "That's not what happened. You must believe me!"

"Why?"

"It's the truth."

The major decocked and re-holstered his Glock, but Cough kept his weapon trained on the aging civil servant, and made sure the old man could see it.

"Tell us the truth, then," Stacy said. He dropped into the single chair opposite Hartington and crossed his right leg over his left, making himself comfortable. They looked like nothing less than two old friends enjoying a quiet conversation in comfort.

Hartington rubbed his face hard and collapsed against the back of the sofa.

"Five weeks ago," he said, his voice little more than a gasped whisper, "Gregory presented me with the report in which the NCTA recommended the Grey Notice."

"And you just signed it without question?" Stacy asked, his jaw clenched.

"Of course not," he said, his voice stronger, more decisive. "This is a Grey Notice we're talking about here. I don't take the idea of sentencing a man to death lightly. Of course I asked bloody questions."

"What sort of questions?" Cough demanded, stepping away from the bedroom door and further into the room.

Hartington twisted to look up at him, a pained expression on his grey face.

"I demanded to know who put him up to it. The commander rarely shows so much initiative on his own. The bloody man's workshy, only interested in feathering his own nest. Until very recently, I had no idea how he became my deputy. His arrival at the NCTA came as a complete surprise. It had nothing to do with me. I returned from annual leave a couple of years ago and he was there. Foisted on me. A *fait accompli*."

"And he told you he was acting under orders from Jason Wyndham," Stacy said.

Hartington jerked upright. "Exactly. How did you know?"

"We know a great deal, Sir Ernest," Stacy said. "And what did you do then?"

"After suffering the usual run-around, I eventually spoke to Wyndham directly. I kicked up merry hell—within the bounds of the government-minister-civil-servant relationship. After all, he was, in effect, my boss. In so many words, I demanded to know why he had such an interest in sanctioning Captain Kaine. Tried to get him to change his mind. He prevaricated for a while, as they always do, and then he showed me the video."

"What did you make of it?" the major asked.

"The video?"

"Yes."

Hartington's shoulders sagged. "It made me feel ill. I mean, literally. I wanted to vomit. The beating. The way Malcolm Sampson boasted about everything. I mean, he actually admitted responsibility for organising the destruction of that aeroplane, for pity's sake. He almost gloated about it. All those innocent lives lost … for money. I was mortified. Devastated."

"So why didn't you rip up the report and blow the whistle on the plot?"

"I-I should have. Wanted to, but …" Hartington sat up straighter. "Wyndham's a powerful man with powerful friends. He threatened me. Said I'd meet with an unfortunate accident. My wife, too. And all my children. Grand-children, too."

"And you believed him?"

"Why wouldn't I? You have no idea what Wyndham's capable of doing. He's a psychopath. Untouchable. What could I do?"

Cough snorted. "No one's untouchable, mate. No one."

The slightest light in Will Stacy's dark eyes showed his agreement.

"Wh-What are you going to do with me?" Hartington asked, a pitiful quake in his voice.

"Nothing. This is all about what you're going to do for us."

"What do you want?" he asked. No hesitation.

"A bit of gratitude will do to begin with."

Hartington shook his head and frowned.

"What … What for?"

"We've just saved your life, Sir Ernest," the major said. He uncrossed his legs and leaned forwards, planting his elbows on his knees.

"I don't know what you mean."

Hartington's confused expression matched his words.

"If you look in the cupboard on the landing, you'll find a body."

"Oh my God! Who … Who did you kill?"

"A man called Guy Gordon. You know him, I believe."

Hartington nodded. "He runs GG Cleaning Systems. They're on the government's list of approved contractors. At least for the moment. I instructed Gregory to remove them from the list for being inept. What's he doing here? I mean, why did you … kill him?"

"Gordon was here to kill you and Andrea, and make it look like part of a terrorist attack."

KERRY J DONOVAN

Hartington gasped.

"Why? Why on earth would he do such a thing?"

"You answered that yourself, man. You were going to remove his company from the list. It would have ruined them. Ruined Gordon."

"How did he know? The information wasn't released yet. I only made the decision to ..." Understanding dawned. Colour drained from Hartington's face, which returned to its earlier shade of battleship grey. "Gregory told him!"

Once again, Cough snorted. He hadn't been so entertained in ages. Shame Stefan couldn't be there to witness it. He'd have loved it, too.

"More than that," Cough said, trying to keep a straight face. "Enderby ordered him to kill you tonight. Before we could get to you. He told Gordon where you'd be and gave him the door entry code."

"No, no." Hartington shook his head. "That's not possible. Only Andrea has the code, and she changes it every week. It's part of her ... fee. She likes the sense of autonomy."

"We have a recording of the telephone conversation between Enderby and Gordon," Stacy said. "We've sent a copy of the sound file to your private email address. It'll make interesting listening. It'll also be the proof you need when you contact the police."

Hartington blinked hard, struggling to follow the trail.

"Y-You *want* me to call the police?"

Again, Stacy nodded. "After we've gone, yes. We do. After all, there's a body in your store cupboard. Someone has to report it."

"What ... What do I tell them?"

Stacy shrugged. "I don't know. Tell the police you were defending yourself from an attacker. Tell them you overpowered him. Like I said, you'll have the proof of a threat to you and your ... girlfriend's lives. As I understand it, you used to be quite the boxer in your youth."

"Yes, but that was decades ago."

"Ah, but it'll come back to you. Muscle memory, it's called. The sergeant and I will carry the corpse up here and help you set the scene. Won't we, Sergeant?"

"Yes, sir. Happy to."

"But Andrea ..."

Cough stepped around to the front of the sofa. "Don't worry about her, mate. Andrea will say whatever you tell her to say. She'll do whatever's in her best interest."

Always has, and probably always will.

"She's so young. I ... promised to take care of her."

"Before you get too sentimental, ask yourself who gave Enderby the door code. And then ask yourself why."

Hartington paused. It didn't take him long to work out the answers.

"God!" he gasped. "Andrea and Enderby. They've been seeing each other!"

"Well, Sergeant," Stacy said. "I do believe he's got it."

━━

IT TOOK them fifteen minutes to carry the last remains of Guy Gordon up the final flight of stairs, into the front room, and set the scene to look like the fight had taken place in situ. They propped the body against the sofa, in more or less the same seated pose it had rested in earlier, hoping the blood pooling would match that of its position in the cupboard. If it didn't, Hartington would have more questions to answer. They could only do so much to help him.

"Are you leaving now?" Hartington said. He stood near

the sofa, looking ready to vomit over the corpse. Tears welled in his eyes, although Cough had no idea who or what he'd be crying over. His lost love, perhaps?

"Don't know about you, Sergeant," Stacy said, speaking to Cough, but keeping his eyes fixed on the elderly man, "but I think we've outstayed our welcome. Don't you?"

Cough smiled beneath his snood. "Reckon so, sir."

"But—" Hartington started to say something but shook his head and snapped his mouth shut.

"Go on, Sir Ernest. What is it?"

"What am I going to do about Gregory ... about Ender-by?" Hartington asked, blinking the tears from his eyes. "He sent Gordon to kill me. He can't get away with ... Oh my God"—his mouth flew up to his hand—"Abdul Hosseini. The knife attack. It wasn't a terrorist incident. Enderby set it up. He killed an innocent man!"

Stacy nodded. "Looks that way."

Huntington staggered back and dropped into his chair.

"But why?" he asked. "Why would he do such a thing? It doesn't make sense."

"No idea," Stacy said. "Desperate men do desperate things. I'll ask him when I see him later tonight."

Huntington shook his head.

"You won't be able to."

"Why not?"

"He's in Charing Cross Police Station. Helping the police with—"

"No, he isn't," Stacy said. "One hour ago, he was released on police bail pending further investigation."

"How on earth do you know that?"

"As I said earlier, Sir Ernest. We have our methods."

Cough smiled. He loved the understatement. They did

indeed have their methods—in the shape of two genius hackers.

Corky, with help from Frodo, had hacked the Met's internal comms system, which included the uniformed police bodycams. The pair had been following the investigation into Abdul Hosseini's death from the outset. They'd even recorded the phone call Wyndham made to the Met's commissioner. The one "encouraging" Enderby's swift release from the holding cell on police bail.

Without external intervention—from the likes of the captain and Will Stacy—Enderby would quite literally be getting away with murder.

What it was to have friends in high places.

"In fact," Stacy continued, "the commander is currently at home, no doubt celebrating his freedom and waiting for Gordon to call with the news of your sad demise."

"They let him go so quickly?" Hartington asked.

"Yep. It would appear that Commander Enderby has friends who wield even more influence than you do, Sir Ernest."

"Wyndham?"

Stacy smiled his dead-eyed smile.

"Wyndham," he answered. "Exactly. And now"—he raised both hands—"we'll be going, unless you have any questions."

"Yes, I do."

"Fire away."

"What do you want of me?"

"Nothing."

"Nothing?"

Stacy shrugged. "That's right. Nothing. Just call the police. Report Gordon's death and try to survive the fallout.

I've a feeling you're going to have a great deal on your hands over the next few weeks."

"That's it? You'll leave me alone?"

Stacy barked out a hollow laugh. "Now, I didn't exactly say that. We have all your contact numbers. If and when we want you to do something for us, we'll let you know."

"And the Grey Notice? What do you want me to do? I'm not sure I can——"

"Don't worry, Sir Ernest. We're handling that issue."

Stacy turned to leave, but changed his mind and faced Hartington again.

"Don't even think of trying to warn Enderby or Wyndham. That would make us—make me—very unhappy."

Hartington, shoulders slumped, shook his head emphatically.

"Don't worry about that, Major. I won't contact either of them. Gregory Enderby and Jason Wyndham can burn in hell for all I care."

"Good, but let me make one thing perfectly clear. We own you. Body and soul. Understand?"

Hartington stared at Stacy, his eyes blank, tears dried, unable to speak.

"Do you see this?" Stacy turned his head and showed Hartington the earpiece in his right ear. "This is a comms unit, and it's a very good one. A colleague of ours—a technical genius—has recorded everything you've said from the moment I entered this apartment. If you value your freedom, don't even think of refusing to accept our calls. Do we understand each other?"

"Yes," the old man said, hanging his head and looking up through defeated eyes, "we do."

"Good." Stacy signalled to Cough. "With me, Sergeant."

Cough followed Stacy from the apartment, closed the door firmly behind them, and tugged down the snood. Neither spoke until they'd reached the Volvo.

"Where to, sir? The farm?"

"Holborn."

"Bideford Avenue?" Cough tried to catch Stacy's eye, but the major looked straight ahead.

"Yes, please," he said. "Commander Enderby has outlived his usefulness."

Chapter 35

Eaton Place, Belgravia, London, England

An electric fizz of excitement and anticipation surged through Cough—his standard response to the call to immediate action. He keyed Enderby's address into the GPS and pulled out of the parking spot.

He added a little more pressure to the accelerator, and they rolled along the streets. So late in the evening, the roads were almost free of traffic and made driving a relative joy.

Stacy straightened a twist in his seatbelt and settled back for the forty-minute drive across town.

"Enderby's outlived his usefulness, eh?" Cough asked.

"That's right," Stacy answered, flat and calm.

"We're going to top him?"

"I am. You're on lookout duty."

Shame.

"You're going to ask him a few questions first, of course."

"I am."

"Is the captain okay with it?"

Stacy glanced at Cough for a moment before facing front and watching London's quiet roads roll past.

"Yes. Do you want to confirm it with him?"

"Not necessary, sir. If you say he's okay with offing Enderby, I'm happy with that. I don't think the captain should be disturbed right now, anyway."

Stacy was the coldest of cold fish, but the captain trusted him, and if it was good enough for the captain, it was good enough for old Cough.

"Hartington got off lightly, you ask me, sir," Cough said after they'd sat in silence for a few minutes.

"How so?"

Cough braked sharply to avoid flattening a ginger tabby that darted across the road, then he built the speed again.

Daft cat.

"Hartington's part of this whole bloody conspiracy."

Stacy turned his head to look at Cough through those dark eyes that rarely gave his inner thoughts away.

"Is he?"

"You didn't believe all that guff?"

They rolled along a near-empty Hobart Place and jumped a set of amber lights to reach Lower Grosvenor Place. The pavements were as empty as the roads. No risk of harming a pedestrian.

"What guff?"

"About how he tried to change Wyndham's mind and how the video made him sick."

"Actually," Stacy said, facing front again, "I did."

"I didn't. They're all the same, these government toadies. Out for what they can get."

Stacy held up a finger in contradiction. "Hartington's a civil servant, not part of the government. He's a pen pusher. Does as he's told, mainly."

"The bloke's bent as a paperclip. He set up his mistress in a flat in Belgravia, for fuck's sake. How could he afford a place like that if he wasn't on the take?"

Bressenden Place curved around to the right, double red lines decorating each side of the road. Exclusive tower blocks loomed overhead, the cost of each plush apartment beyond the reach of the vast majority of the UK's population. A socialist at heart, Cough ground his teeth at the injustice of it all.

"According to Corky, Hartington inherited the apartment from his grandfather," Stacy said.

"Okay, I grant you that, but the bugger's cheating on his missus and trying to make out he's a pure as the driven."

"You think he deserves to die because he's having an affair? That's a little harsh, don't you think? That kind of justice would end up wiping out a quarter of the adult population in the country."

"He's still part of the conspiracy. The conspiracy that sent strike teams to kill us all. The boy, Rhodri, included. The doc and Marie-Odile, Rollo's wife, got caught up in it, too. Don't forget that."

"I'm not forgetting it."

"And there's the Grey Notice. An official sanction on the—"

"What would you have done? Kill him, I suppose."

"Might have."

Cough sniffed and negotiated a left turn onto Victoria

Street, following the instructions doled out by the calm voice on the GPS.

"And the woman, Andrea?"

"No," Cough said, "I don't kill women. Not unless they're armed and shooting at me."

"Good point, but she saw us both. Without Hartington to keep her in line, things might have become sticky with the police. See how complicated things can get when you don't think things through?"

Cough knew a dressing down when he heard one and reeled his neck in a little.

"Yes, sir. Certainly, sir."

Stacy shot him a stern look, then relented.

"Okay, okay. Lesson over."

"Thank you, sir."

They eased left onto Horseferry Road, negotiated the roundabout guarding Lambeth Bridge, and crossed the river for the first time. They'd cross back over it again in a mile or so. Bloody city motoring. No chance of driving in a straight line from A to B. Always had to take a circuitous route.

"And besides," Stacy said, "with Enderby about to fall on his sword, we'll find it useful to have a high-ranking civil servant in our back pockets."

"Good point."

They hit Lambeth Palace Road, crawled along behind a double-decker bus, and curved right, heading away from the river.

"By 'fall on his sword', I take it we're going to make it look like suicide? Or rather, you are."

Stacy showed another hollow smile, his second or third of the evening.

"That's right," he said. "Enderby's going to be so over-come with remorse at killing Hosseini and the other evil things he's been party to, he won't be able to live with himself. And while I do the deed, you're going to remove all the bugs Hunter planted last night."

"I am?"

"You are indeed. They're too expensive and incriminating to leave lying around for anyone to stumble over."

"The cops, you mean?"

"I do. A high-placed servant of the state committing suicide so soon after his release from custody won't only have the Met snooping around, it will probably involve the intelligence services, too."

"And how will I find the bugs?"

"You're going to borrow my mobile. Corky installed a neat, little app that will help you locate each one easily."

"Good old Corky. He never lets us down."

"Actually, Frodo built the app. Corky just uploaded it to my mobile."

"Frodo and Corky," Cough said. "What a team. Glad they're with us."

It only took a few minutes to navigate York Road before they passed under the railway tracks, bore left onto Waterloo Bridge, and crossed the river again. After Aldwych, they used the Strand Underpass and emerged at Kingsway. They reached the junction between Southampton Place and the right turn onto Bloomsbury Square before being stopped by their first bit of congestion —a confrontation between cycle and taxi at a set of traffic lights. On his feet and tottering on his cleats, right knee bleeding, the cyclist—in helmet and a bright yellow top— slammed the flat of his hand on the taxi's bonnet.

"You bloody moron," he screamed. "Look at my bike!"

The machine in question lay in the middle of the lane, its front wheel terminally buckled.

The cabbie lowered his window and stuck his head through the opening. "You ought to look where you're going, you dayglow balloon!"

"I had the right of way!"

The cabbie gunned his engine, but the cyclist stood his ground, hands flat on the bonnet, bravely blocking the cabbie's way.

"This'll come to blows," Stacy muttered. "Can you get around them before we're snarled up here for hours?"

Cough waited for the traffic light to turn green and added the slightest pressure to the throttle. By the time they squeezed past the taxi, the cabbie had left the safety of his cab and was facing the "dayglow balloon". If it came to a fight, the cabbie—who had at least fifteen kilos advantage over the slightly built man in the yellow top—would have Cough's bet. On the other hand, how many times would someone have lost money betting against the captain in a ruckus? In a fight, size meant almost nothing. It all came down to skill and determination. The cyclist looked ready to explode, and the cabbie didn't look the sort to back down.

They left the imminent dustup behind them and bore right onto the one-way street running alongside Bloomsbury Square and reached Theobalds Road a few seconds later.

"One minute now, sir," Cough said. "Bideford Avenue's next on the right. We'll be coming at the house from the opposite end of the row from last night."

"Understood."

"Mind if I ask a question, sir?"

"Shoot."

Cough indicated right, made the turn ahead of an oncoming truck, and slowed to little more than walking pace.

"How are we getting in? We don't have Hunter's magnetic strip this time."

"Watch and learn, Cough. Watch and learn."

Stacy smiled. This one shone in his eyes.

A genuine smile from Major William Stacy? Would wonders never cease?

Cough found an empty parking spot on the same side of the row as Enderby's building but fifteen spaces back. He pulled in and killed the engine.

"Ready?" Stacy asked.

Cough stared at the entrance to Enderby's building and hesitated. "You still haven't told me how we're getting inside."

"Just follow my lead."

Yet another smile stretched out on Stacy's round face. Wonders would never cease.

"Yes, sir."

Stacy opened the door and slid out of his seat. Cough followed, and they strolled along the pavement, two old mates shooting the breeze. Stacy led the way through the break in the railings, stepped close to the door, and pressed the bell.

How's this going to work?

"Good evening, sir," a man asked, his voice carrying the deep, rattling burr of a Scotsman. "Please look into the camera."

Unsmiling, Stacy stared into the lens, holding his pose until the lock released. He winked at Cough, leaned against the door, and entered the foyer. Cough followed him inside.

Déjà vu all over again.

"Good evening, Mr Browning," the doorman—not the same man as the night before—said from behind his dark-oak kiosk.

"Who are you?" Stacy asked, adopting a stiff, English accent. "I expected Mr Jackson."

"Mr Jackson took ill, sir. I'm Stevens."

"Oh dear. Nothing serious, I hope."

"Afraid I don't know, sir. I'm just filling in for him."

"I don't recognise you, Stevens. Are you new?"

"Been with the company seven months, sir. First time in this building though. I'm what's called a floater. I fill in as and when required."

"Ah, I see. Very good."

Stevens smiled. "I'll need to book in your guest, sir."

"Of course." Stacy stood to one side and ushered Cough forwards. "This is Alan Philips."

"Good evening, Mr Philips. Please look into the camera."

Stevens pointed to a spot above his head and typed something into his computer, presumably Cough's temporary, new name.

Cough looked up and stared blankly into space for a few seconds—he couldn't see a camera lens anywhere.

"Thank you, sir," Stevens said, exuding the very essence of friendliness.

"Thank you, Stevens," Stacy said, turning away and heading for the staircase. "This way, Alan. Can't wait to show you my latest acquisition. Found it in a bookshop in Brighton. The owner didn't have a clue what he was selling. A first edition *Great Expectations*. Signed by the great man himself. I picked it up for an absolute steal."

"You old thief, you," Cough said, joining him on the staircase.

They trudged up the steps as though climbing a mountain. On the second landing, Stacy finally stopped wittering on about his latest "find" and let Cough get a word in.

"Who the hell's Browning?" Cough whispered.

"Rayne Browning," Stacy said quietly, continuing up the stairs. "He deals in rare books." They reached the third floor and continued climbing. "He owns that apartment." Stacy added, nodding towards the door as they passed.

"Corky fixed the ID photo, I suppose?"

Stacy shrugged. "Corky or Frodo. One of the two."

"What would have happened if Browning had been home?"

Stacy shook his head. "Poor Rayne is currently racing to Yorkshire on the trail of a rare first edition *Pride and Prejudice.*"

"That's a stroke of luck," Cough said, offering Stacy a wry grin.

"Yes. Amazing wasn't it? Apparently, he received an email from a dealer in Harrogate this lunchtime offering him first dibs. Completely out of the blue. Browning wasn't going to miss out on that sort of opportunity."

"Corky's work again?"

"Or Frodo's."

"Or Frodo's," Cough repeated, adding a nod.

Pulling on black, nitrile gloves as they climbed, they reached the half-landing below the fifth floor and stopped. Stacy tugged a mobile from his pocket, selected the locator app, and handed it across. "It works like a metal detector. Sweep the phone and listen to the bleep. Easy as."

"Thank you, sir."

Stacy drew his Glock, worked the slide, and pointed it towards the ceiling.

Safety first.

"Ready?"

"Right behind you, sir."

They climbed the final flight of stairs to the top floor.

Stacy stepped to the side, set his back against the wall, and pressed the doorbell. He waited a few seconds before pressing again.

"Who is it?" The heavy door muffled Enderby's angry shout.

"Stevens from the front desk, Commander," Stacy answered, making a decent attempt at the doorman's rasping voice.

"What do you want?"

"There's a package, sir. My apologies, but I forgot to give it to you earlier."

"Bloody idiot."

The lock clicked, the handle turned, and the door opened a crack.

Chapter 36

Wednesday 9th June - Jason Wyndham

Hill Street, Mayfair, London, England

The Right Honourable Jason Harvey Wyndham—Minister Without Portfolio but with plenty of power and prime responsibility for party discipline—yawned and slapped his cheeks in a desperate effort to keep himself awake. Tasks were piling up. He'd been pushing it recently. Working too hard and missing out on even the minimal amount of sleep he required. He needed a break, but there were too many things going on. Backbench mutinies to quash, uppity ministers to keep in line, wildfires to fight, behind-the-scenes coalitions to foster, people to schmoose. A total ball ache that never ended. And now, this latest complication with Ryan-bloody-Kaine demanded his attention. Such an unholy mess. He couldn't remember when a Grey Notice had taken so long to complete. Nor could he remember when a Grey Notice had caused so much negative fallout. The loss of so many willing mercenaries.

Christ Almighty, in a roundabout way, it had even led to —Abbott's untimely death and the impending demise of his company. T5S had been Jay's go-to organisation for off-book contracts. However, T5S no longer existed in any real sense of the word, which had been the reason Jay offered up Dresden's services to Enderby in the first place. He hated the idea of using his Praetorian Guard in the service of anyone but Jay Wyndham.

But needs must.

Moving forwards, he'd have to foster relations with another defence contractor. Perhaps Enderby's man, Guy Gordon, would be open to an approach. Arrow Services, the new kids on the block, were probably too niche, but might be worth consideration. He'd think on it a little.

Enderby—usually a reliable, if limited minion—should have been able to handle the Grey Notice matter on his own, but Kaine had turned the bloody idiot over. Kaine, the man everyone wanted dead, was still breathing. And while the man lived, he presented a real threat to Jay and his friends … his associates. A clear and present danger. He had to go, and go soon. And to complicate matters, Enderby had gone *off-piste* with the Hosseini thing. What the hell had he been thinking? A total balls-up of the highest order.

Jay shook his head and stared at the glass half full of Macallan. He reached out a hand and quickly withdrew it.

No, Jay. Hold off on the whisky, old man.

He needed to keep a clear head.

Enderby and the dead man, Hosseini. Why had Enderby drawn so much attention to himself? And it hadn't stopped there. Oh no. When the police arrested him for the killing, Enderby used his phone call to instruct his solicitor to ask Jay to pull strings on his client's behalf. Of all the bloody stupid things to do. After all, Enderby had a rock-solid case for self-defence. No two ways about it. He only had to sit back and await his release, but he couldn't even do that.

On the other hand, Jay had been obligated to the cretin. Jay's resulting call to the commissioner had been a simple enough task, but he hated owing anyone any favours, least of all an uppity police commissioner who had his eyes set firmly on a seat in the House of Lords after his retirement.

"Lord Piggy of Pigsty Manor," he scoffed to the Macallan.

The very idea.

Enderby, the pillock, had made himself a total liability. If the man didn't have such a hold over Jay, if they weren't so inextricably linked, he'd have severed their association long ago. Probably would have severed his head from his shoulders, too. Or rather, he'd have had someone do it for him, of course. Jay would never dirty his hands in person. That's what lackeys were for. Lackeys like Alasdair Dresden, who, when correctly primed, would be prepared to end one life in the defence of another—or in the pursuit of a just cause.

Ha! A just cause.

Overcoming his reticence, he reached for the Macallan and wet his lips on the smoky delight. A taste only. Not a real sip.

The TV—set to BBC Parliament—was showing a rerun of the latest horror show. The debacle of the Home Secretary's most recent appearance in the Commons. The massed ranks of the opposition had torn the woman to shreds. Turned her into a quivering lump of jelly who tried desperately not to show it. Whoever thought the woman had the stones to run one of the four great offices of state had been wrong. Dead wrong. Why the PM tolerated such a gormless lightweight was beyond him. Maybe she was good in the sack. Or perhaps her daddy had deeper pockets than most. Either way, the woman had to go. She had to make way for Jay. His time to step out from the shadows and into the light had arrived. Time for political advancement.

Jay paused the TV and dropped the remote back on his desk. The picture froze with the Home Secretary, mouth open, hair dishevelled, a rabbit-in-the-headlights expression on her admittedly attractive face. Not a good look for someone who wanted to appear competent. Perhaps he could have one of Dresden's technically literate subordinates take a screengrab and post it on social media—unattributed, of course. Attaching Jay's name to the post would never do. Showing such obvious disloyalty to a close colleague would be beneath a man of Jason Wyndham's standing.

Quite right.

Sod that. Jay would to anything if he thought he could get away with it. Anything.

He snorted, reached for the intercom, and pressed the switch that connected him to the guard room.

"Yes, sir?" a man answered, his voice strained, scratchy.

"Send Inspector Dresden up to my office."

"Yes, sir. He'll be right with you."

"I don't recognise your voice. Who are you?"

"Hobbs, sir. I've got a bit of a cold."

"A cold?"

"It's nothing serious, sir."

I'll be the judge of that!

"Stay downstairs. I don't want you anywhere near me."

"Yes, sir. Will——"

Jay flicked the switch in the middle of Hobbs' bland assurances and released the pause on the TV. The Home Secretary started moving again, but it made little difference. She still looked like a pitiful lost cause. Although her mouth moved and the words spewed out, her eyes remained vacant.

A double knock on the door announced Dresden's arrival.

"Come in!" Jay called and muted the TV.

The door opened and the commanding figure of Jay's head of personal security entered. He closed the door, approached the desk, and stood at a stiff attention, muscles rippling. The dark blue polo shirt stretched tight across a deep chest, and his biceps threatened to burst the seams of its short sleeves. A powerful man, he exuded confidence and competence, and didn't flap his gums too much, either. An attribute Jay appreciated after having to deal with so many vacuous and verbose morons.

"Evening, Alasdair. Take a seat."

Dresden lowered himself into the visitor's chair across the desk from Jay and sat at attention. The muscles bunched on a square jaw, darkened by a scrub of gunmetal blue—his five o'clock shadow.

On the TV, the Home Secretary dropped into her seat and her shadow, the opposition's most heavyweight bruiser, launched into his vigorous attack. Jay had to admit, the slippery Rottweiler had done a pretty good job of eviscerating the ineffectual woman across the dispatch box. Jay smiled at the memory of her leaving the House, tail tucked firmly between her lovely, long legs, refusing to answer the journalist's howled questions.

Not long now, woman. Your job's mine!

"Are you ready?" Jay asked.

Dresden dipped his chin in a curt nod.

"Yes, sir."

No equivocation. China Dresden would be ready for anything.

"What have you done so far?"

Teasing information out of the man could be like pulling teeth.

"I sent Red Hallam and Graham Paulson to scope out the commander's apartment building this afternoon while we were at the House. The place is pretty secure—"

"It's not that secure," Jay interrupted. "You heard how Kaine finessed his way into the place?"

Dresden nodded and added a grim smile.

"I did. Kaine worked it well. He's a smart cookie. Tough, too. Taking him in won't be easy."

Jay pursed his lips and added a stiff nod of agreement.

Time to prime the pump.

"You're right, Alasdair. Ryan Kaine's not the sort to go down without a fight. To protect Commander Enderby, you might need to use lethal force."

Dresden straightened and the creases on his brow deepened.

"Let's hope it doesn't come to that, sir."

Let's hope it does.

A man in Ryan Kaine's position would never allow himself to be arrested without putting up a fight, and Alasdair Dresden would not back down if he thought innocent people were in danger. Innocent people like Gregory Enderby.

Enderby, innocent. Ha!

Jay leaned closer to his desk.

"Remember this, Alasdair," he said. "Ryan Kaine is a mass murderer. He murdered eighty-three innocent people, and he did it without compunction. If he resists arrest—and he will, mark my words—you will be required to deal with him appropriately." Jay emphasised each word by tapping an index finger on the desk.

"Yes, sir."

"The Grey Notice gives you full, legal justification. I'm instructing you not to take any risks with the lives of your team, or with the life of Commander Enderby. Am I making myself clear?"

"Yes, sir. Perfectly, sir."

"Good. I don't want anyone else hurt on account of this terrorist. Least of all my most dedicated team."

"Assuming Enderby can make a case for it," Dresden said, "I can have a Met covert-surveillance team in place outside his building by nine o'clock tomorrow morning. It'll cost, though. A twenty-four-by-seven stakeout is expensive. Just say the word, and I'll set things in motion."

"That's an idea. I'll consider it. In the meantime, please make sure you're ready to react the moment he screams for help."

Again, Dresden did the head tick thing of his that stood in for a nod.

"If and when Enderby raises the alarm, how many men will you be taking?"

"Excluding me? Five."

"Will that be enough? We've already discussed who you're dealing with here."

Dresden stared blankly back, giving nothing away.

"With respect, sir, my team's the best. I hand-picked them all personally. And Kaine won't be expecting us. We should be able to do it without making too much noise."

Jay nodded. "Very good. Make sure you're ready. I probably won't be able to give you much warning."

"Understood, sir. We'll be ready. Will that be all?"

"Yes."

Without another word, Dresden stood and left.

Jay shivered at the man's broad back. He'd just set up one of the Met's finest to take out Ryan Kaine. He only wished he could be at the dénouement to witness Kaine's death in person. Now, wouldn't that be a delightful thing?

Unable to do any more, he reached for the tumbler and took a deep swallow of the Macallan. It warmed him to the core.

Chapter 37

Bideford Avenue, Holborn, London, England

A blue eye appeared in the doorway's opening. Will Stacy drove his booted foot into the gap, stretched out his gun arm, and pointed the Glock at the nose beside the eye. Enderby cried out, jerked back. The door swung open, and Stacy barged into the room.

Enderby squealed again and threw up his arms.

"Good evening, Commander," Stacy said, speaking normally, and following the stunned man into the room. "Lovely to see you again. Had a nice day? I must say, you've certainly been a busy boy."

Stacy swallowed, trying to soothe his throat. Mimicking Stevens' deep, Scottish voice grated more than he'd anticipated. The lounge hadn't changed much from their previous visit. Still spotlessly clean and tidy. The only obvious additions being a bottle of whisky and a half-full tumbler, each standing on its own coaster on the coffee table in front of the wingback chair.

"Celebrating your early release, Commander?" he asked.

"I-I …"

Cough entered the room and closed the door quietly. He stood beside Stacy, mobile in hand, awaiting instructions.

"Wh-What do you want?" Enderby asked, slowly lowering his arms. He threw back his shoulders and stood up straighter in an attempt to present a brave face, but the quaking voice and quivering chin ruined the performance.

"We've come for the real files, Commander," he said, smiling. "And our bugs."

"What?" Enderby gasped.

"You heard. Lead on."

He pointed his Glock towards the office door, grabbed Enderby's shoulder, and spun him around. Enderby stumbled and caught hold of the wingback chair to steady himself. He glanced around, desperately searching for an opening, a way out.

"Don't be silly, Commander," Stacy said, grabbing Enderby's shoulder again and tugging him upright. "I don't really need you to open the safe. I'm just being polite. Your office, now. Cough, you have ten minutes."

"Yes, sir," Cough answered.

The mobile clicked out a steady beat. He waved it towards the coffee table near the wingback and the clicking increased in tempo and pitch.

"Ooh, this is fun," Cough said, smiling. "Like a treasure hunt."

"You're looking for five bugs. And don't forget to search the bathroom."

"You ... bugged my loo?" Enderby asked, trying to tear his shoulder free.

Stacy released his grip suddenly, and Enderby staggered forwards a couple of paces before steadying himself.

The clicking increased to a continuous bleep and stopped when Cough removed the bug from beneath the protruding lip of the coffee table's top.

"That's one," he said, holding up the bug in evident delight. "Four more."

Stacy forced Enderby into the office and pushed him all the way to the far wall and the picture hiding the safe.

"Open it," he said. "And don't even try reaching for the P29. I'm all out of patience."

"I-It's not in there. The gun. I moved it to my bedside locker."

"How well did that work out for you?" Stacy asked, not expecting an answer.

Enderby worked the catch on the picture frame, swung it away from the wall, and opened the safe. His shoulders stiffened for a moment, then relaxed. He raised his hands again, confirming they were empty.

"Okay, Commander. Very good. Now empty it. Slowly, now."

Stacy edged to his right, making sure he could see Enderby's actions. The commander pulled out the same folders as before, turned, and lowered them to the desk.

"Open the secret panels. Both of them."

Enderby lowered his head.

"You know about—"

"Yes, Commander. We heard you talking to Wyndham this morning and we—"

Enderby screamed and threw himself at Stacy, arms swinging, hands grasping for the Glock. Stacy jagged to the right and threw a short-range, left uppercut. His fist connected with the point of Enderby's chin.

The commander's head snapped up and he collapsed backwards onto the desk. The back of his head slammed into the desktop, and he lay there, panting, glazed eyes staring at the ceiling.

Stacy flexed the fingers of his left hand and shook it out. Damn thing throbbed like the blazes. Bruised knuckles at the very least.

"What the hell was that for? Such a stupid move. Don't you know how inept you are?"

Should have shot the arsehole instead.

He grabbed Enderby's shirt front, heaved him into the swivel chair, and let him slump back onto the desk. Keeping him in sight, Stacy reached into the safe, popped open the first secret panel—empty—and did the same for the second. He reached further in and pulled out another Westbury drive, this one identical to the first. He also snagged the thick bundle of twenty-pound notes he found sitting beside the drive and stuffed it into his pocket.

"Waste not, want not," he said.

The cash would add nicely to the communal pot.

"Very clever, Commander. Two secret compartments. You got us with that one. You really did."

Enderby groaned. He pushed himself upright and rubbed the back of his head.

"What ...?"

He gagged, threw a hand to his stomach, and leaned to the far side of the desk. Head hanging over the bin, he dry heaved and sucked in a number of deep breaths before recovering enough to sit up again, red faced and panting. Mercifully, the bin remained puke free.

"Nicely done," Stacy said, genuinely impressed with the man's ability to hold back the vomit. Not the easiest of tasks.

Enderby raised his head and turned hooded eyes on Stacy.

"What … happens now?"

"Now, Commander," Stacy said, holding up the drive, "we send this drive to the NCA. I'm sure it'll help their investigations into organised crime. After all, we don't need it."

"You don't?" Confusion etched itself into the smug bastard's face.

"Nope," Stacy said, unable to resist smiling. "Initialising the main drive and reverting to factory settings didn't work, I'm afraid." He nodded at the desktop computer. "Our Mr C planted a worm … or was it a virus? A bacterium, maybe? I dunno, that stuff means nothing to me. Anyway, when you recreated your system this morning, he watched the whole process. We've seen everything you've done on the computer since." He gritted his teeth. "Unfortunately, we couldn't work out what you were doing with the terrorist threat data. Not until you murdered Abdul Hosseini."

Enderby shook his head, wincing at the movement.

"That was self-defence. Hosseini attacked me. And the NCA won't do anything. Nor will the police. The people on those files are too important. Too powerful. They're the government, for God's sake. They'll close ranks."

"Enough!" Stacy shouted.

Enderby juddered, clamped his jaws together, and stared at his hands which trembled on the surface of the desk.

Cough appeared in the doorway. Smiling, he held up a clear sandwich bag pinched between finger and thumb.

"Got 'em," he said.

"All five?"

"Yep. And I found this piece of junk in the bedroom." He opened his jacket and removed the SAMS P29 from his waistband. "I checked it was safe."

"Those bloody things are never totally safe."

"Fair comment, but I've emptied the chamber. What should I do with it?"

Stacy held out his gloved hand. "I'll take it."

Cough passed it across, handle first, keeping the muzzle pointing away from them both.

"What now?" he asked.

"We're off. Time's passing."

Cough rolled the sandwich bag into a tube and stuffed it into a jacket pocket.

"You going to deal with him?" he asked, dipping his head towards a sorry-looking Enderby.

"We can't exactly leave him around to warn Wyndham. I'll handle it, though."

"Fair enough," Cough said, shrugging.

He cast an eye over Enderby and backed out of the room, pulling the door closed as he left.

Stacy holstered his SIG and raised the SAMS P29. He chambered a round and turned to face the desk. Enderby shot to his feet, hands raised high above his head.

"No, please! Don't!"

"Sit down!" Stacy barked.

Enderby dropped into his chair, lower lip trembling, eyes streaming. "Please, don't."

"Sit back, Commander."

"Please. Please don't." Enderby stretched out his arms.

"This is for Abdul Hosseini."

⸻

"GOING OUT, SIR?" the gravel-voiced Stevens asked as Stacy and Cough stepped into the foyer.

"We fancied a gentle stroll around the block before popping into the Old Nick. They won't have called last orders yet."

Stevens smiled. "Have one for me, sir."

"Will do. Won't be long. Oh, by the way, I'd like to make a complaint about the man on the top floor."

Stevens frowned.

"A complaint, sir? Why?"

"He's making a hell of a lot of noise. All that banging and crashing. Most annoying. It's why we're going out. Can you do something about it?"

"I'll call him, sir. Ask him if he's okay."

"Thank you, Stevens."

Stacy held the front door open for Cough and they headed out into the rain-spotted evening. On the pavement, they turned left, away from the pub, and strolled along as though they had all the time in the world.

"You used the SAMS on Enderby?" Cough asked.

Stacy nodded. "It seemed only fitting. Bullet under the chin. Quick and easy."

"A bit dangerous though. The way those things are put together, it might have blown up in your face."

"All life is a risk, Cough," he said, sighing.

"Why did you tip Stevens the nod?"

"The complaint, you mean?"

Cough nodded. "Seemed a little unnecessary."

They crossed the road and headed straight for the Volvo.

"Enderby wasn't the most popular man in the world. Few people would have missed him, and I didn't like the idea of his corpse rotting away for days on end. It would be a shame for his bodily fluids to leak through the floorboards and spoil any of Rayne Browning's rare books. It's also why I left Enderby's front door slightly ajar."

"Very thoughtful of you."

"I thought so." Stacy coughed out a short laugh. "Anyway, time to call the captain." He tapped his earpiece. "Whiskey One to Alpha One. Are you receiving? Over."

"*Alpha One to Whiskey One*," Ryan said, his reply clipped and crystal clear. "*I hear you. Over.*"

"All done here. Whiskey One, out." He tapped the earpiece inactive. "Let's go."

As they approached the pearl-white Volvo, Cough hit the button on his key fob and the central locking clunked. They climbed in, Stacy taking his turn to drive.

"Shame we can't hang around to watch the show," Cough said, nodding back the way they'd come.

Stacy shook his head.

"I'd rather not be within five miles of this place when they find Enderby. Keys please."

Cough handed them over, and Stacy inserted the key into the ignition and fired up the old car.

"Mayfair?" Cough asked.

"Mayfair. You're still game?"

"Me, sir?" Cough said, nodding and adding a bright smile. "Game for anything, me. Can't wait to get stuck in."

Chapter 38

Wednesday 9th June - Jason Wyndham

Hill Street, Mayfair, London, England

Jay wet his lips with a fresh tot of whisky, delighting in the flavour and the warmth.

BBC Parliament had moved onto a "talking heads" discussion of the parlous state of the UK economy set against the relative success of its competitors in the G7. A mop-haired environmentalist was holding forth about the government's reluctance to invest properly in green initiatives, which would not only save the planet, but would revitalise British industry.

Jay smirked at the naïvety of the man. Investing in the green initiatives he espoused would also upset the oil companies, which would not do at all.

"Blah, blah, blah," Jay sniped. "Everyone's a critic."

The burner on his desk vibrated. His Rolex told him it was nine forty-one. Did nobody respect the evenings anymore?

He waited for the voice-recognition system to do its thing. Nice bit of kit. State-of-the-art. Not many people could afford such security on their burners.

"*Identification required.*"

"Commander Gregory Enderby." He spoke rapidly, stumbling over his own name.

"*Repeat the following sequence. Mike-Lima-Delta-Bravo-nine-eight-seven.*"

"Bloody hell," Enderby snarled before following the system's instructions.

The man's obvious frustration made Jay snort.

"*Voice identification confirmed.*"

The "line secure" tone sounded.

Jay grabbed the phone and pressed it to his ear.

"Gregory, dear boy," he said, forcing the bonhomie. "I see you were given—"

"Kaine's here!" Enderby interrupted.

He actually interrupted. The gall of the bloody man.

"Where?"

"Holborn. The bastard's sitting in a car outside my home! I can see him. He's right there!"

Bloody hell.

"What's he doing?"

"Talking to his passenger. I can't see clearly, but I think it's the black man, Hunter. They must have decrypted the files. They're back for the real ones. God! They're getting out of the car!"

"Keep them occupied. Dresden will be with you in fifteen."

"Hurr—"

Jay cut the call, pressed a button on his intercom, and slid the burner into his trouser pocket.

"Yes, sir?" Dresden answered, cool, efficient. The perfect tool for the assignment.

"Kaine has surfaced."

"Where?"

"Outside Enderby's building."

The intercom picked up the sound of movement. Bodies standing, weapons being primed.

"Understood. How many men does he have?"

"As far as I know, one."

"We're on our way. I'll leave Simpson and Hobbs here on guard."

"Very well. Good hunting."

Smiling, Jay released the intercom and sat back, listening to the sounds emanating from the ground floor of his fortress home. Men clomping over hard floors, making their way into the garage. The SUV's armoured doors slamming shut, engine firing, bullet-resistant shutters rolling up into the garage. Dresden's hand-picked team were on the move. Heading into the night. Heading towards danger. They wouldn't flinch. Wouldn't back down. They'd take Kaine down or die in the attempt.

Jay nodded. He'd lay his money on Dresden and his three-man assault team. Kaine and Hunter didn't stand a chance. Once again, he wished he could be there to witness the operation in person, but no. He couldn't—wouldn't— take the risk. Danger wasn't for him.

If the operation had any kind of official status, Dresden and his team would be wearing bodycams, and Jay would be able to watch from a Met Police Operations room. The excitement and tension of following a live-fire mission with bullets flying and blood flowing had no equal. He sighed. Such a shame.

He imagined China Dresden's stone-faced strike team racing along the bus lanes—blue lights flashing, sirens held silent—screaming towards Holborn. Screaming towards Kaine. If Jay's dick still worked the way it should, he'd have a raging hard-on by now.

Fucking prostate.

A gentle knock on the office door drew him back into the room.

"Enter."

The door swung open, and the delightful Lauren Simpson entered. She remained near the doorway, holding onto the handle.

"Yes, Simpson?"

"Inspector Dresden and the team are on their way, sir. He wanted me to let you know."

"Don't look so downcast, Lauren," Jay said, smiling, "I'll make sure you're part of the next mission."

"Thank you, sir. Will you be staying in for the rest of the night?"

Of course he bloody would.

With Dresden and the majority of the defence team unavailable, he wouldn't dream of leaving the house and exposing himself to the dangers of London at night.

"I will," he said. "You and Hobbs can secure the house."

"Thank you, sir. Have a good night. If you need me for … anything …" Her wide-eyed smile made it clear what she meant.

Apart from Hobbs, who would stay on the ground floor as instructed, they were alone in the house, two unattached people. By design, Jay's Praetorian Guard only included singletons. Bodyguards with spouses and children were worse than useless. They had too much to lose to be of any value.

He gave Simpson the eye. The power he wielded acted as an aphrodisiac, but only to others. These days, Jay happened to be immune to the weakness of the flesh.

Fucking prostate.

"Thank you, Simpson," he said, "that will be all."

Simpson arched her eyebrows.

"Are you sure, sir?" she asked, unable to conceal her disappointment.

She'd been so certain he fancied her. He *did* fancy her. Who could fail to fancy a beautiful woman with a semi-automatic handgun strapped to her hip—but he could do bugger all about it.

"Yes, Simpson."

He dismissed her with a flick of the hand, and she backed out of the room, closing the door quietly behind her.

"Nothing personal, Simpson," he muttered. "Two years ago, I'd have been all over you like a—"

The door slammed open, and Simpson barged through the opening, eyes wide in shock, hands raised.

Jay shot to his feet. The chair rolled back and slammed into the cabinet behind him.

"What the—"

An electric fizz arced at Simpson's neck. She jolted, cried out, and collapsed to the floor in a contortion of twisted arms and legs.

A slim man wearing black, thick-framed glasses and a cloth covering his nose and mouth, stepped over her body and marched into the room. Dressed head-to-toe in para-military black and armed with a handgun, he held a finger to his covered lips and pointed the weapon at Jay's chest.

Oh Jesus. Fuck!

Jay held his hands out to his sides. The panic button under his desk might as well have been a mile away.

Behind the intruder, a second man—dressed the same as the first, but armed with a stun gun—appeared in the doorway. Crouching low, he straightened Simpson's knotted body, and rolled her onto her front. Without a wasted action, he dropped to one knee at her side and pulled her arms behind her back. He bound her wrists and ankles with cable ties, dragged her away from the doorway, and propped her up against the wall inside the office. Then, he turned and stood still, glowering.

Christ Almighty.

Jay tried to move, but his legs wouldn't work. In any event, where would he run to? His heart raced, and his stomach roiled. For the first time in as long as he could remember, Jay had no idea what to do.

The slim man dug his free hand into a trouser pocket. It came out holding a mobile phone, which he raised to his lips. He spoke into it.

"Good evening, Jay," he said, speaking with Gregory Enderby's voice. "Please sit down and place your hands flat on the table."

Bloody hell!

Jay dropped into his chair and nearly missed. His arse-cheeks barely caught the front edge of the seat. He shuffled backwards, rolled the chair closer to the desk, and spread his hands on the desktop, happy to see the fingers weren't shaking … much.

"What the bloody—"

"Stop talking. And don't even think about pressing the panic button. You'll be dead long before help arrives."

The slim man—with dark brown eyes, partially hidden

behind the incongruous glasses, and speaking with Ender-by's voice—dropped the mobile into the same pocket.

"Do you recognise me now, Minister?"

The voice changed from well-bred Etonian to a strangely familiar, south-coast drawl—the transformation astonishing.

Jay shook his head.

"No."

"Really?" the man said, stepping closer. "Take a better look." He tugged down the scarf concealing the lower half of his face.

Jay's world tilted on its axis. His stomach lurched.

Kaine. Ryan Kaine!

Oh dear God!

Chapter 39

Wednesday 9th June – Alasdair Dresden

Hill Street, Mayfair, London, England

Alasdair Dresden closed his eyes for a moment, readying himself for the work to come.

Not long now.

What was he going to face? He hated being underprepared.

With the blue lights ready to clear the minimal, late-evening traffic out of the way and the BMW's engine roaring, the terraced town houses flew past on either side of their two-car convoy. They'd be on scene inside twenty minutes. Twenty-five tops. Would there be anything left of Enderby by the time they arrived? Would Kaine still be around? Twenty minutes wasn't long in real terms, but it would feel like forever. Taking in Ryan Kaine would be a real feather in Dresden's cap, in all their caps, but Kaine wouldn't go down easily. In all likelihood, there would be gunplay.

Sweating hard in his snug and heavy body armour, Dresden patted the SIG P226 strapped into the holster on his right hip and smiled. Sod the Glock 17s favoured by the rest of the team. Like Kaine, Dresden preferred the SIG for its balance, accuracy, and flat-out stopping power. Couldn't beat it.

Ryan Kaine. One way or another, I'm taking you in. Tonight.

The BMW reached the end of Hill Street and Red Hallam, the designated lead driver for the mission, made a sharp left and merged into the one-way traffic that turned Berkley Square into an elongated roundabout. Dresden twisted in his seat. The second car sat tight on their tail, a stern-faced Graham Paulson behind the wheel, concentrating hard, matching Hallam turn by turn and staying close.

Four of them, including Dresden—each hand-picked, highly skilled, and professional—should be enough to take in Kaine unless the bugger arrived mob-handed. But why would he do that? Kaine had no idea he was being set up.

Or did he?

Even with the might of the UK's police force searching for him, the elusive enigma had remained free and clear for nine months. Why would he let himself be seen by a plonker like Enderby?

"Everything okay, boss?" Hallam asked, flashing his headlights to clear the lane of a cruising black cab. He snapped the wheel hard right, dodged around the outside of the taxi, and floored the accelerator. "You look thoughtful."

"What's the bugger up to?"

"Who, Wyndham?" Hallam indicated right to overtake another slow-moving car.

"No, Kaine. What's he doing back at Enderby's place? More to the point, why would he let the idiot spot him? He's better than that. Much better."

No. It didn't seem likely. Either Enderby was being spooked by shadows, or ...

Shit!

...it was a setup.

Damn it.

"Stop the car," Dresden barked.

Hallam slammed on the brakes and skewered in tight to the nearside pavement, narrowly missing the rear wheel of a woman riding a moped. Paulson, reacting slowly, careered past them on the outside and screeched to a stop ten metres ahead. Traffic backed up behind them and car horns started blaring. Paulson nudged his Beemer forwards to clear the outside lane, and the civilian cars started moving again.

"What the fuck?" Hallam said.

"I don't like it," he said.

"What?"

"It feels wrong. Hold on." He dragged his mobile from his trouser pocket, dialled Simpson's number, and let it ring until the voicemail cut in. "Fuck."

"What's up, boss?" Hallam asked, frowning deep.

"Lauren isn't answering."

Hallam snorted.

"What was that for?" Dresden barked.

"Maybe she's finally getting some action out of Wyndham. She's been giving him the glad eye for months. Didn't you notice?"

"For fuck's sake. She's on duty."

"Eyeing up the main chance, more like. You know how much the bugger's worth, right? And he's single."

"Shit."

So much for his hand-picked team of professionals.

Dresden dialled another number, with the same result. "Hobbs isn't answering either."

"Probably getting his head down in a corner somewhere. He's been banging on about his head cold all day. Been getting on my tits."

"I don't like it."

"You already said that, boss," Hallam mumbled. "What's the plan?"

Dresden reached for the radio mic clipped into his harness and held down the PTT button.

"Dresden to Paulson," he said, "keep going to Holborn. Engage the target if you find him. Red's taking me back to the house. Control, out."

Paulson waved and took off again. He carried along the back end of Berkley Square and peeled left onto Berkley Street, blue lights flashing, two-tone sirens still silent.

Dresden turned to Hallam. "Back to the house. On the double."

Hallam slipped into first gear, disengaged the clutch, and carried on around the square, heading back towards Hill Street.

Dresden snaked out a hand and hit the button to turn off the blues.

"You got one of your feelings, boss?" Hallam asked.

"Whatever gave you that idea," Dresden said. "Pull in here." He pointed to a yellow box marking a bus stop ahead of a stretch of zigzags that defended a zebra crossing.

Hallam jammed on the brakes and parked illegally, but

with its full, day-glow, police livery, who'd argue with the BMW?

"Tailgate," Dresden ordered, cracking open his door and sliding out into the cool of the evening.

Hallam climbed out and joined Dresden at the self-opening tailgate. Dresden unlocked the gun safe and handed Hallam the H&K PSG-1A1 carry case.

"Let's go," Dresden ordered.

"Sniper point one?" Hallam asked, eyes shining with the thrill of the hunt.

"Yes. Protect my back. If Kaine gets past me and you have a clean shot, take him out."

"Really?"

"There's a Grey Notice on him, remember. If he gets past me, I'll be dead, and you'll have the green light on him."

"What if he's mob-handed?"

"Use your best judgement. If it comes down to it, you can take out anyone who's presenting a danger to life."

"Right. Got it."

Hallam shrugged the rifle case onto his shoulder in preparation for the climb.

"You sure Kaine's coming?"

"No, but it's a possibility. The bugger might be there already. Better to be prepared, eh?"

"Roger that, boss." Hallam grinned.

As the best sniper in the unit, Dresden rarely gave up the role of hotshot, but Hallam came a close second and, at the range between OP1 and homebase—inside fifty metres —Red Hallam wouldn't need his best game.

"Let's go," Dresden said, clapping Hallam on the shoulder. "But Red ..."

"Yes, boss?"

"Don't you go shooting me, or I'll be really pissed." Dresden smiled when saying it.

"Wouldn't dream of it, boss." Hallam sniggered. "A bullet wouldn't penetrate that thick skull of yours."

They jogged to the junction where Hill Street broke into Berkley Square and crouched against a set of black, cast-iron railings. Dresden edged forwards, scoping the street, but couldn't see anything to cause him any worry. A high-sided van pulled up at the junction and the driver caught sight of Dresden and Hallam in their full tactical gear, helmets included, and ran through a full-on comedy routine that included a double-take with added jaw drop. Dresden raised a finger to his lips and furiously waved the driver forwards. The shocked man shuddered, gears crunched, and the van jerked forwards and stalled. The driver shook his head, fired up the engine, selected first gear, and barged his way into the traffic on the ring road around Berkley Square.

"Clear," Dresden called.

They entered Hill Street, hugging tight to yet more black railings. After a twenty-five-metre jog along a thankfully clear pavement, they ducked into Hayton Mews, raced past the Fox and Hounds pub, and stopped at the gated alleyway at the rear of the pub. Dresden released the padlock using the key for which Wyndham had paid the publican an exorbitant fee, and the gate squealed open. They sidestepped along the narrow gap between a row of wheelie bins and the neighbouring wall, and stopped below the wrought-iron fire escape.

In a well-rehearsed routine, Dresden placed his hands against the wall and stood with his right leg jutting out from his left. He dropped into a half-crouch and braced himself.

"Go!"

Using Dresden's legs, back, and shoulders as a stepladder, Hallam climbed until he could reach the lower rung of the fire escape. He tugged down the counterweighted extension ladder, stepped around, and scampered up the rungs until he reached the second-floor flat roof. He shot out an arm and gave Dresden a thumbs up.

Dresden wiped brick dust from his hands and retraced his steps through the alley. When he reached the junction with Hill Street, he stopped and pressed the PTT button on his radio.

"Dresden to Hallam, where are you? Over."

"Hallam here, boss. I'm in position. No targets in sight. You're clear to advance. Over."

"Roger that. Keep your eyes peeled. Dresden, out."

He sprinted across the road in front of a slow-moving Ford Focus, using it as a screen, and dived into Farm Lane, slamming his back into the rendered wall on the corner and some ten houses from homebase. Dresden sucked in a deep breath. Running in the heavy gear took it out of him, and being exposed in a well-lit, almost-empty street didn't help his nerves any, but he'd made it so far. He blew hard and waited a moment for his breathing to settle before leaning out a little and looking up. On the flat part of the pub's fourth-storey roof and eight buildings back from homebase—rifle readied and pointed at the target—Hallam threw him another thumbs up. Dresden returned the signal.

Good to go.

Before moving back out into Hill Street, Dresden drew his SIG and racked the slide. Facing a man like Ryan Kaine without a bullet up the spout wouldn't be the best idea he'd ever had.

Chapter 40

Hill Street, Mayfair, London, England

"Wh-Who are you?" Jay asked, although he already knew. The quake in his voice betrayed his utter terror.

Pity's sake, Jay. Be strong.

The whole world knew he could talk his way out of any situation. And they were right.

Smiling, Kaine shook his head.

"Don't go there, Jay," he said, lips stretching into a nasty grin. "May I call you Jay?" He waved his free hand. "Yes, of course I can. Everyone knows how friendly you are. The life and soul of the party. If you'll excuse the pun." He dropped the smile. "I can tell you recognised me right off the bat."

Jay forced his shoulders to relax. He needed to be on his game. If he didn't play it right, things would turn sour in a heartbeat. The huge gun—held rock-steady in Kaine's right fist—both terrified and fascinated him. He'd never been so close to death. Excitement vied for dominance over the fear.

"Very well ... Captain. You're right. I do recognise you. H-How did you get in?"

"That was the easy part. It takes a while for your garage shutters to fully close. Thirteen seconds. Your people should station a guard in the garage when your strike teams leave."

Jay frowned. Shook his head. "Strike teams? I have no idea what you're talking about. What are you doing here?"

"I might have come to kill you."

"Kill me?" Jay said.

Fear turned to rage. An engulfing rage. It roared through his soul. He tore his gaze from the barrel of the gun and fastened it on Kaine's dark brown eyes. The thick lenses of his strange glasses did nothing to minimise the death Jay saw in them.

"Kill *me*! How dare you break into my home and threaten me? I'm a government minister!"

"It's not a threat, Jay. It's a simple statement of fact."

Kaine spoke quietly, his face a mask of calm.

"You can't kill me! I'm a government—"

"You've already said that, Jay. And I did hear you the first time."

Jay held up his hands.

"But why?" he asked. "What have I ever done to you?"

Keep him talking.

The longer he kept the madman talking, the longer Jay would live. And if Kaine was here, he couldn't be in Holborn. Dresden would find out, and he'd be back.

He *would* be back. But how long would it take him? Twenty minutes? Thirty? Forty?

Oh dear God. Keep him talking. Delay the inevitable.

"You signed the Grey Notice, Jay," Kaine said, his words deathly quiet. "You marked me for death."

"A Grey Notice? What's that?" Jay asked. "I've never heard of a Grey—"

"Don't," Kaine snarled, his voice oozing menace. "This isn't the time for lying. You never know, but the truth might save your life. All things are possible."

He straightened his gun arm, pushing the huge weapon over the desk, closer to Jay. The muzzle's black hole grew huge—a cannon ready to spit death into Jay's face. Kaine's index finger tightened on the trigger.

"Okay, okay," Jay shouted. "I do know what a Grey Notice is. But I had nothing to do with the one with your name on it. I don't have the authority. The Home Secretary signed off on it, not me. Go talk to her."

Kaine shook his head. His gaze drilled into Jay's eyes, into Jay's soul.

"Passing the buck won't work, Jay. The Home Secretary's a lightweight. Nothing but a government mouthpiece. You're the power behind that particular throne, and everyone in the country knows it."

The man had a point. If not for the gun pointed into his face, Jay might have blushed at the compliment.

"But why would I do such a thing? Why would I want you dead?"

"If my case ever made it into a court of law, the whole, flimsy house of cards would come tumbling down."

Jay frowned, trying to look confused. "What on earth are you talking about?"

"You own thousands of shares in SAMS," Kaine

announced. "Undisclosed shares. Your government helped save the company from bankruptcy. If SAMS had folded, you and your friends would have lost millions."

Fuck.

Kaine knew. He *knew*. How was that possible?

Don't show it. Play dumb.

"Nonsense," Jay countered, shaking his head. "I refute that as a complete lie. For me to own shares in SAMS without declaring it would breach the Ministerial Code."

Kaine's feral smile sent an ice-cold shiver running up and down Jay's spine. He'd never felt so ... so ... alive. His heart thumped loud in his hollow chest.

"You—the government—took it easy on Malcolm Sampson. Tax avoidance!" Kaine continued. "And you—Jason Wyndham—engineered his early release from prison on compassionate grounds. Compassion! Where's the compassion for all those people? The eighty-three dead souls. Sampson tricked me into killing them, Jay. *Eighty-three innocent people!*"

Kaine shouted the last sentence.

Jay quaked.

Until that very moment, he'd never felt true terror. The end of his life could be mere seconds away. Again, he felt more alive than he had for months. Years.

He saw and heard everything with pinprick clarity. The triple tick of the clock on the mantlepiece. Simpson's ragged breathing. The film of dust on the surface of the TV that the cleaner had missed, again—useless bloody woman. The photos hanging on the wall above the drinks cabinet. In the centre, pride of place, one of Jay shaking hands with the current PM outside Number 10. Next to that, his honorary doctorate from Balliol College, Oxford.

Everything.

Movement caught his eye.

On her backside by the doorway, Simpson stopped wriggling. She narrowed her green eyes and focused them on Jay. He didn't like her expression. It had changed from anger and fear to disgust. The lust had long since died, destroyed by the stun gun, and by what she'd heard so far.

"That's simply not true, Captain. None of it is true."

Kain set his jaw. "Sampson's dead now, and the truth will come out."

Time to change things up.

"You're not making any sense, Captain," Jay said, speaking softly. "You aren't thinking straight. Not that I can blame you after all that's happened. Not after all you've done. The guilt must be unbearable. You need help, Captain. Psychiatric help. Therapy. Let me arrange that for you."

As he reached for the desk phone, Kaine's gun twitched. Jay snatched his hand away and slapped it back onto the desk.

"Good boy, Jay," Kaine said. "You're learning."

"Let me help you, Captain. I can put things right. I really can."

Kaine narrowed his eyes and tilted his head to one side as though seriously considering Jay's offer.

"How exactly are you going to manage that?" he asked.

Jay forced a thin smile onto an unwilling face.

"With the right person in charge, all things are possible."

Kaine shook his head. "I wouldn't trust you as far as I could throw you out of that window." He jagged his chin towards the window—the window filled with bullet-resistant glass.

"But it's your only way out of this mess," Jay said.

"Is it?" Kaine asked. "Is it really?"

Kaine's right index finger whitened as he added more pressure to the trigger.

Oh God. I'm a dead man. I'm going to die.

Chapter 41

Wednesday 9th June - Alasdair Dresden

Hill Street, Mayfair, London, England

On each side of Hill Street, unbroken rows of terraced town houses faced each other, most of the ground floor windows glowing bright behind drawn curtains or wooden shutters. Streetlights bathed the road in a bright orange glow, illuminating the pavements and throwing shadows from the cars parked in dedicated bays, offering Dresden decent cover. He took a moment to scope out the scene. No one hiding in the shadows. No obvious lookouts. No backstops.

Why not?

With Red Hallam as an extra pair of eyes to guard his

back, Dresden darted forwards, keeping his eyes and ears open, searching for anything out of place. At the house next door to homebase, he dropped and crawled beneath an unlit window, past a closed door, and beneath a second window, this one lit. Behind the double-glazed window, a TV blared out the theme tune of a soap so loud, the watchers had to be hard of hearing.

The homebase's garage door appeared exactly the same as they'd left it—rolled down and securely locked. Dresden scooted along, unable to remember the last time he'd felt so exposed. One of Kaine's men could be hiding anywhere, waiting to take a pot-shot at him.

Dresden stopped at the personnel access door to the left of the garage roller shutter and reached for the handle. Locked tight. Had he got things wrong?

How much of a berk would he look if he broke into homebase only to find Wyndham and Simpson dancing the horizontal tango on the office carpet? He'd look even worse if Paulson and Radley bagged Kaine without him. Still, he'd trusted his gut often enough in the past, and it had rarely let him down.

Go on. Do it.

Dresden pressed closer to the house's protective brick-work. Taking care not to rattle the keys, he dragged the keyring from his pocket and released the lock. After waiting for a gunshot from the rear guard that never came, he pushed the door five centimetres open. Silence greeted him. He returned the keys to his pocket, released his breath, and waited for a slow count of ten.

Inside the garage, a soft grunt reached his ears. Thumping followed. The thump of boot heels on concrete.

Dresden raised his SIG, pushed the door wider, and slid

through the opening. Darkness surrounded him. A darkness that smelled of car polish, engine oil, and slowly dispersing exhaust fumes.

The thumping continued to Dresden's left. Thumping and muffled groans. He took a calculated risk, pulled out his mobile, and activated the screen. Its pale glow lit up a wide-eyed, runny-nosed Hobbs, gagged and secured to the leg of a metal workbench with cable ties.

Dresden turned the mobile's screen to show his face to Hobbs, who immediately fell silent and still. Dresden darted closer, dropped to his knees alongside Hobbs, and lowered the mobile to the floor.

"Are you okay?" he whispered.

Hobbs nodded.

Dresden released his dagger from its calf sheath, and its honed blade made short work of severing the plastic ties securing Hobbs' wrists and ankles.

Hobbs tore the gag from his mouth. He turned his head and coughed up phlegm and blew snot onto the floor.

Lovely.

"Bastards sneaked up on me from nowhere," Hobbs grumbled, wiping his glistening nose on his sleeve. "Used a bloody stun gun. I'd forgotten how much that hurts." He rubbed the marks on his wrists where the cable ties had bitten into the skin and rotated the stiffness from his shoulders. The bones in his back and neck clicked and creaked in protest.

Dresden snatched up his mobile and they climbed to their feet, heading towards the staircase. Hobbs barked out a racking cough.

Dresden glowered at him.

"Shut it! For fuck's sake. I should have left you tied up."

"Sorry, boss. I've got a cold."

No shit.

"How many are there?"

Hobbs shrugged. "Dunno. I only saw two."

Only two?

"Where's Lauren?"

Hobbs snuffled, coughed again, but through a closed mouth. He pointed up.

"Upstairs, sniffing around His Nibs. Who are they? Kaine, you reckon?"

Dresden nodded. "Don't know who else would have the reason ... or the balls."

"Are you alone?" Hobbs asked, edging close enough to foul the air with his dog breath.

Dresden elbowed him to back off.

"Red's at OP1 with the PSG."

Hobbs smiled, nodded.

"The others?"

"They should be near Enderby's place by now. Hang on."

He reached for the radio mic and worked the PTT button.

"Dresden to Paulson. Are you receiving me? Over."

He waited three seconds before repeating the call and receiving a response.

"Paulson to Dresden. Receiving you. Over."

"Where are you? Over."

"Thirty seconds from the target. Over."

"Abort, Paulson. Abort. The target is here. I repeat. The target is here. Return to homebase. Over."

Paulson took a moment to respond.

"Message received and understood. Paulson, out."

"Dresden to Hallam, did you hear that? Over."

"Hallam to Dresden. Copy that. Over."

"Okay. Keep your eyes peeled. Dresden, out."

Hobbs rasped out a deep sigh. "We're gonna wait here for Paulson?"

"And leave Wyndham up there with Kaine, unprotected?" Dresden shook his head. "Not bloody likely."

"What's the plan?"

"We're going upstairs. Ready?"

"Not yet," Hobbs snapped. "The bastards took my gun. Hang on a sec."

He turned away and padded towards the far corner of the garage, using the torch light from Dresden's mobile to show him the way. After a few soft, metallic rattles and clanks, he returned armed with a Glock 17. He worked the slide and held the gun in a two-handed grip, pointed at the ceiling.

"Ready?"

Hobbs nodded.

"Ready."

"Slow and quiet. Give me plenty of room and don't you dare cough."

Dresden placed his foot on the first wooden tread, testing for a creak before adding his full weight and starting the climb. Silence filled the house, booming loud through his head. It drowned out Hobbs' rattling breath and the blood pounding through his ears.

He reached the first-floor landing and stopped.

Behind him, several treads below, Hobbs' open-mouthed breathing sounded like the rasping rattle of a petrol lawn-mower running on idle.

"Stay here," he whispered, holding out his left hand. "Watch my six," he added.

Hobbs scowled, but stayed put.

Dresden raised his SIG high, aimed at the place where a lookout might be. He resumed his slow and silent climb, testing each tread as he ascended. Each time he moved, he expected to disturb a backstop, but so far … nothing.

Halfway up the final flight to the second-floor landing, muffled voices threaded their way through Wyndham's open office door.

Dresden stopped and held his breath to listen, trying to work out the location of the speakers from their voices.

From his position at eye-level to the hallway, Dresden couldn't see inside the office, but he could work out where the voices came from. Wyndham sounded slightly clearer. He would be sitting at his desk, facing the open door. He sounded scared. Dresden had never heard him less composed, less arrogant. The other speaker, Kaine probably, sounded a little more muffled. He stood with his back to the door, his voice quiet, controlled. Apart from the shouted, "*Eighty-three innocent people!*"

Dresden frowned. Why would Kaine be so angry about people he'd killed in cold blood. Sadness, Dresden could understand. Regret maybe, but anger? Why anger? And what was that about him being tricked by Malcolm Sampson?

The wanted terrorist wasn't making much sense.

Hugging the wall to minimise creaking, he climbed the last seven steps, listening intently to every word of the stilted, two-way conversation.

With the SIG pressed close to his nose in a two-handed grip, Dresden reached the head of the stairs and stopped. The darkened hallway, illuminated only by the light spilling from the office three paces away, stood empty. Something moved in the light. The outline of a man stood in the opening, his back to the room, facing outwards.

The backstop.

Of course there'd be a backstop. Kaine wasn't stupid.

If Dresden moved, the lookout would see him.

Heartbeat crashing against his ribs, hands sweating, Dresden waited.

Chapter 42

Wednesday 9th June – Jason Wyndham

Hill Street, Mayfair, London, England

"What you said, about Sampson, isn't true," Jay said, an unfamiliar and unwanted tremble in his voice. "I had nothing to do with his sentencing or his early release. Again, that was down to the Home—"

"We have Enderby's files, Jay."

"Enderby?" Jay asked. "I've never heard of an—"

"For God's sake, stop lying. Enderby's the deputy head of the NCTA. The one who keeps calling your unregistered mobile phone. We have his files, Jay. The files that contain proof of your complicity. Proof of your crimes."

Jay snorted. "Rubbish. You've got nothing. You stole the wrong bloody drive!"

Kaine smiled. "So, you *do* know Enderby."

Fuck!

He'd dropped a first-class bollock.

Idiot!

The pressure of the gun pointing at his head had taken its toll.

"Okay, okay. Yes. I admit it. I do know the commander. He's a senior civil servant with hopes of advancement. Forlorn hopes, as it happens. The man's utterly delusional."

"*Of course you know him.* By the way," Kaine said, "we have an audio file of your most recent telephone conversation with him. The one where you offered him the use of your top team. I believe you called them your Praetorian Guard." Kaine shook his head and tutted. The bugger actually tutted. "A tad conceited of you to style yourself as a Roman Emperor, isn't it?"

Christ.

They'd tapped Enderby's phone? How?

"I'd happily play the recording for you," Kaine continued, his right eyebrow arched, "but what would be the point? You already know what's on it."

Jay desperately tried to recall everything he and Enderby had discussed during that call, but it had become a blur. His famed memory had started to fail him. Kaine's arrival—and the gun pointing at his face—had scrambled his brain.

"The conversation was highly enlightening," Kaine said. "Especially the part where Enderby let it slip that his safe had a second hidden compartment behind the first. Ingenious. He really should have kept that little nugget to himself." Again, Kaine tilted his head to one side. He added a grave smile. "As it happens, two of my colleagues have just left Holborn after collecting the real drive. Not that we need it. Not since we gained remote access to Enderby's desktop computer."

Oh God.

Kaine had it all.

The huge gun, in Kaine's right fist—the hand-cannon— remained rock-steady, its aim certain. One gentle squeeze of the trigger and Jay would be dead. He blinked, tried to swallow, failed.

"And speaking of Enderby," Kaine said, gloating, "I imagine Dresden and his team will be approaching Holborn by now. I wonder what they'll find when they arrive?"

He knows about Dresden. He knows everything.

"He's dead, by the way. Enderby, I mean. Took his own life in a fit of remorse after killing Mr Hosseini. Dresden will probably call you in a minute or two. Reporting in."

Jay glanced past the intruders who'd left the office door wide open. Hobbs should have heard the shouting by now. Where the fuck was he?

"Your guard isn't coming, Jay," Kaine said.

What? A mind reader?

"I have no idea—"

"The big bloke in the garage with the runny nose," Kaine said. "Don't know his name, but he won't be coming."

Hobbs!

"You didn't ..."

"Kill him?" Kaine asked. "No, Jay. I don't kill innocent people. I protect them. Or at least I try to. I only end the lives of people who deserve it. People like you, Jay. People like Malcolm Sampson."

Kaine's cold smile faded, and Jay knew. He absolutely knew.

"My God, it *was* you! Belham Castle. You!"

"*Moi?*" Kaine said, placing his free hand over his chest. "I have absolutely no idea what you're talking about."

Again, Simpson's eyes widened beneath a frown. She'd missed nothing. If Jay managed to extricate himself from this unholy mess, he'd have to deal with her—permanently. And quickly.

"So, that's it?" Jay asked. "You're going to murder me … in cold blood?"

Kaine edged closer, and the gun grew larger.

"Give me one good reason why I shouldn't."

Oh God. Tell him. Do it.

He was dead anyway. He might as well burn the house down.

"The prime minister … she was the driving force behind the whole affair. Let me go, and I'll give her to you!"

For the first time since he'd entered the office, Kaine raised his gun. It no longer pointed at Jay, but at the wall above and behind his head. Kaine stared at him, holding his head perfectly still. Concentrating hard.

It was working.

Hope soared in Jay's chest.

He was right. Everyone was right. Jason Wyndham *could* talk his way out of anything.

"You wouldn't be lying to me, would you, Jay?"

Keep going, Jay. You can do this.

His heart raced.

"No, no. I'm not lying. Not this time. I swear it. I can give you proof. Recordings. The PM organised the Grey Notice on you, but she made me sign it. Plausible deniability, it's called. She couldn't be seen to act directly."

"Why? Why did she do it?"

"You know why, Captain," Jay said, leaning forwards in

his eagerness to talk. "You *know* why! The PM was in bed with Malcolm Sampson. Back when she was Defence Secretary, she made sure SAMS won lucrative government contracts even when they weren't best placed to fulfil them."

"Why?" Kaine repeated.

"Isn't it obvious? She had shares in the company, too. Far more than I ever had. Worth hundreds of millions. And then when you shot down Flight—I mean, when the shit hit the fan, she had to protect Sir Malcolm, or he'd have gone public. If that had happened, she would have lost everything. Her seat in the House. Her freedom. Everything. That's why Sir Malcolm got off so lightly."

Jay paused and stared into Kaine's eyes. Was it working? Was he getting through?

"It was all down to the PM," he continued. "I just helped her arrange things. The tax avoidance charges were a smokescreen. You know that. Everyone in the inner circle knows it, too. And Sampson's early release on compassionate grounds was part of the deal to stop him talking. Don't forget, if the PM had been disgraced, the government would have fallen, too. We couldn't let that happen."

Jay finally managed to swallow. He stared at Kaine, who apparently hadn't moved a muscle since Jay had started dishing the dirt on the PM. Did he believe it? He had to. It was the truth! Every single word of it.

"Think about it, Captain. An early election would have been a disaster for the country. It would have let the opposition in. Left-wing lunatics. Christ Almighty, it would have been a catastrophe. The markets would have collapsed. Billions of pounds would have been wiped off the economy. Billions. Inflation would have soared. Unemployment would have rocketed. We'd have faced another recession so soon after the last one. People would have lost their homes. They'd have starved. We couldn't allow that to happen. You see that, don't you?"

Kaine finally moved. He shook his head slowly.

"It was all done for the good of the country?"

Jay leaned even closer to the desk, closer to the cannon.

"Yes. Exactly. The good of the country."

And the good of the party.

"And the eighty-three people who died on that plane? What about them?"

Jay hesitated. On the floor by the door, Simpson shook her head in … what? Disgust?

Fuck her. Her time was limited.

Jay struggled to find a response. "Their deaths were unfortunate—"

"Unfortunate?"

Kaine's jaw stiffened, but Jay couldn't stop. He had to keep going.

"Yes, unfortunate. A terrible tragedy, but they were already dead. Bankrupting the country wouldn't have brought them back."

Colour darkened Kaine's cheeks.

"What about justice? Don't the families of the eighty-three deserve justice?"

Jay shrugged.

"Vengeance you mean. What good would that do anyone?"

"It would vindicate me."

"Ah, yes. That's what this comes down to. It's all about you." Jay sighed, he'd moved onto shaky ground and needed to ease off. "Okay, I understand. You're an innocent man. You were set up by Sampson and your friend, Major Valence, to kill those poor people. You know it, I know it, and the senior members of the cabinet know it, too. But that means nothing. The country—your country—is more important than the individual. You're a soldier, Captain Kaine. You've risked your life for your country often enough. You understand how things work."

"No. Not a soldier," Kaine said, shaking his head. "I'm a marine. A Royal Marine."

"Okay, you're a Royal Marine. So what?"

"It makes a difference."

"Yes, yes. I'm sorry. It does," Jay said, raising his hands, trying to mollify. "But where does that leave us? You can't kill me in cold blood. That would be murder. You don't have it in you."

The young man standing by the door looking out into the darkened hallway, the one who'd tied up Simpson so efficiently, spun. He stomped forwards, towards Jay, thunder darkening his face. Kaine threw out an arm, stopping him centimetres short of the desk. The fire of the man's anger pulsed out of him in red-hot waves. If Kaine hadn't stopped him, the youngster would have torn Jay apart.

Jesus!

Something moved in the doorway behind the youngster. Someone was out there! Jay looked away, looked at the youngster, tried not to gasp, tried not to react.

"Want me to shut the bastard up for you, Captain?" the younger man snarled, nostrils flared, working hard to control his breathing. "His shit's doing my head in."

Kaine shook his head.

"Get back to your post."

Jay shuddered as the youngster glared hotly at him for a moment, then spun and returned to his place by the door looking out. Who was out there? Hobbs?

A gun appeared from the right side of the doorway. Its

muzzle jabbed into the side of the youngster's head. He stiffened and threw up his arms.

"Kaine!" a man called out. "Lower your weapon!"

Dresden! China Dresden!

Thank God.

Chapter 43

Wednesday 9th June - Richard Hallam

Hayton Mews, Mayfair, London, England

Red Hallam climbed the final wrought-iron flight to the top of the fire escape, stepped out onto the flat part of the pub's roof, and dropped to his knees. He slid the rifle case from his shoulder, lowered it carefully to the roofing felt, and released the catches. The case opened to reveal the beautifully crafted PSG-1A1, a first-class, NATO assault rifle with few equals. After removing the lethal darling from her snug, foam cavity and unfolding the stock, he confirmed the selector was set to safety, tugged the charging handle all the way back, and locked it into position. He inserted the full, thirty-round mag into the magazine well, smacked it home, and hit the bolt release lever inside the trigger guard. The charging handle slid into place with a satisfying clunk. Visually, he confirmed the bolt was fully seated, and there she sat, in his lap, loaded and ready to spit death.

An object of pure, refined beauty.

The power of sudden, explosive death held in Red's hands. Some of the hotheads he'd trained with at sniper school called such firepower an aphrodisiac, but not Red Hallam. Oh no. Red Hallam considered himself a cool-headed professional.

Yeah. Right.

Again, he smiled into the night.

He hadn't had so much excitement in months. Guarding Wyndham, the dickhead, had proved to be nothing but hour after hour of unmatched boredom. Apart from the regular visits to the House or to Downing Street, the lazy git rarely left home.

Not tonight, though. Tonight, things were getting tasty.

Crouching low and hugging the deep shadow cast by the sloping roof and the tall chimney, Red worked his way to the low wall running around the edge of the roof. He leaned over the lip, looked down, and surveyed the scene.

Hill Street, with its long row of multi-million-pound, terraced houses, stretched out below, running northeast to southwest. Parked cars lined the far side of the road nose to tail, providing plenty of hiding places to anyone who needed them. He ran his eye over each car in turn, searching for any likely looking shadows or bulges, but found nothing out of place.

Red raised the rifle, snapped open each leg of its fitted bipod stand, and propped the rubber feet on the wall. He lined up the sights on homebase, and the three-times magnification enlarged the target so well, he could make out individual rivets holding the slats of the roller door together.

"Dresden to Hallam, where are you? Over."

Red lowered the volume on his radio and worked the PTT button.

"Hallam here, boss. I'm in position. No targets in sight. You're clear to advance. Over."

"Roger that. Keep your eyes open. Dresden, out."

"Thanks, boss," Red muttered. "Like I'm planning to fall asleep any time soon."

Moments later, China darted across Hill Street in front of a slow-moving car, ducked into Farm Lane, and stopped around the corner, out of sight of homebase. Blowing hard, he popped his head out and looked up towards the pub roof. Red shot him a thumbs-up. Dresden returned the signal and stepped back out onto Hill Street. SIG raised and hugging tight to the black railings that guarded the front of each house, he advanced towards homebase at the crouch.

Keeping one eye on homebase, Red watched China's halting, crawling progress the whole way to the garage roller shutter, and his disappearance through the personnel door.

Entry gained and without incident. Phase one completed.

"Good luck, boss," he whispered and slumped back onto his haunches.

Red sucked in a deep breath and released it slowly to lower his heartrate.

It had been a while since he'd pulled sniper duty. Six months at least, but he never forgot how challenging it could be to take all the variables into account—target acquisition, framing the shot, windage, bullet drop, humidity. Even though few of those particular variables came into play with this shot, he still worked through his process. Routine was everything, and Red was bloody well going to make the most of any fleeting opportunity to put a bullet between the eyes of a legitimate target, and a first-class bad guy.

If China Dresden's gut feeling proved accurate and Ryan Kaine did turn up, Red would shoot the evil bastard the first chance he got. No question. No hesitation. The Grey Notice gave him the legal justification, and he'd be buggered if he'd pass up the chance. Taking out Ryan Kaine would earn him kudos. Earn Red his place in history.

He paused a moment to reconsider his shot.

With the evening dead calm, and homebase forty metres out and eighteen down, he didn't need to worry about windage, or bullet drop even with the SAI G3 suppressor attached to the barrel. He'd deliberately left his marksman scope in the carry case. For a close-range shot under such benign conditions, the rifle's built-in sights would be plenty good enough. He certainly didn't want a laser sight giving away his firing position to a man like Kaine, whose reputation as a world-class marksmen meant he deserved plenty of respect. If Kaine did show his face in the street, the last thing Red wanted was to give the bugger time to get off a shot. Even with a snapshot from a handgun, at so short a range, Kaine would hit his target.

No, Red had to be ready at a moment's notice.

The low wall running around the edge of the roof, capped with sand-coloured coping stones, formed a perfect rest for the PSG's bipod stand, giving him a solid platform for the shot.

Sensing he wouldn't be on the roof long, Red settled into his preferred firing position—seated, cross-legged with his back propped against the chimney. He pulled the butt in tight to his shoulder, testing the comfort.

Not bad. Close to perfect.

He rested his trigger finger along the trigger guard and

lined up the first shot, training the X of the scope's duplex reticles on the garage personnel door at eye level for a man of average height.

Slowly, he eased to the left and back to the right, swinging the PSG's butt in a ten-degree arc. The rifle moved freely, no snags, no obstructions.

Perfect.

He repeated the action, this time looking through the built-in scope. The image rolled from personnel door, to garage roller shutter, and on to the reinforced front door, then reversed along the same route.

Again, perfect.

All set.

He peeled his eye from the scope and took in a global view of the familiar, four-storey frontage of homebase—Number 20, Hill Street. Its imposing, black-painted façade stood out in stark contrast to the cream-rendered, red-bricked houses stretching away on either side. The ground-floor brickwork comprised three openings, all finished in matt black. To the left, a reinforced, panelled front door gave access to the main staircase leading to the accommodation on the three upper floors. In the centre, a double-width roller door led into the triple garage and the rest of the ground floor—which included what would once have been the servants' quarters, but currently housed the armoury, the team's rest rooms, and services. Finally, to the right, a black-steel personnel door—the door China had used—allowed the staff and the security team to enter the house and change into the appropriate clothing without disturbing His Nibs, the insufferable arsehole.

Five tall, sash windows in each of the upper three floors —all glazed with bullet-resistant glass—allowed plenty of daylight into the building. First floor—kitchen, dining room, and one reception. Second floor—lounge, two more receptions, rest room, and office. Third floor—three double bedrooms, all with ensuite bathrooms. Finally, a rooftop garden, with artificial grass and plastic pot plants, completed the monstrosity.

Red snorted.

How many palms did the Right Honourable prick have to grease to gain planning permission for such a conversion?

A shedload of shekels must have passed through so many hands.

For the current operation, Red ignored the windows on the upper storeys and concentrated his attention on the ground floor and its three exit points. His money was on the main door to the left of the roller shutters. It would be the obvious point of egress for anyone unfamiliar with the layout. With Wyndham settled in for the night and the servants dismissed, the only other people on station would be Hobbs, Simpson, and China Dresden. If they left the house, it would be via the personnel door, but they wouldn't leave Wyndham unprotected. Not with Ryan Kaine on the loose and potentially in the area.

Red thumbed the fire selector to single operation and settled back to wait.

Chapter 44

Wednesday 9th June - Evening

Hill Street, Mayfair, London, England

Kaine snap-turned towards the door but kept his SIG trained on Wyndham.

Crap!

Stefan, with a steel-grey SIG P226 pressed against his right temple, stood facing out into the corridor, his arms raised. From behind the door, a hand grabbed his right shoulder and spun him around. Then, a black-clad arm encircled his neck, and they shuffled into the room. Half a face showed behind Stefan and the gun, its unblinking, brown eye fixed on Kaine.

"Lower your weapon," the man repeated, his voice firm and authoritative.

The female officer on the floor gasped, surprise and relief showed on her face. She saw a quick end to her discomfort.

"Boss?" a man called from the stairwell. Footsteps pounded up the stairs.

"Hobbs," the man called out. "It's okay. Stay there. Watch my six. I've got this."

The footfalls stopped. A rasping voice, thick with cold, called out, "Roger that!" He coughed, and the heavy footsteps backed away.

Kaine edged closer to Wyndham, trying to earn a better view of the gunman, but he'd covered himself well. All Kaine could see were the arm wrapped around Stefan's neck, the hand holding the SIG, and half a face. A face he finally recognised from Corky's dossier as Inspector Alasdair Dresden.

"Stop moving," Dresden called.

Kaine froze and gritted his teeth.

Stefan winced.

"Sorry, boss," he said, close to tears. "I screwed up."

"Dresden," Kaine said, "shoot Stefan and your boss dies."

The brown eye behind Stefan crinkled into a smile.

"Do it, Captain," Dresden said softly. "I really don't give a damn."

Wyndham gasped.

"What?" he said. "What did you say?"

Half-hidden behind Stefan, Dresden threw his boss a contemptuous glare and shook his head.

"I've been standing here for a little while," Dresden answered. "I heard every word you said. It's no wonder you kept banging on about the Grey Notice and how Captain

Kaine was such a dangerous man. You were priming me to kill him the whole time. You're a bloody disgrace."

"I-I …"

Wyndham lowered his hands but jerked them back up to shoulder height when Kaine jerked his SIG.

"Captain," Dresden said, "when the news broke about the plane, I read your service record. I never thought you were capable of shooting down a civilian aircraft … At least not intentionally. And when Wyndham told me about the Grey Notice, I knew something was off. This buffoon has all but confirmed that you were set up. Am I right?"

Kaine nodded, but he kept his SIG locked on its target —Wyndham's right eye.

"I was field testing a weapon for SAMS," Kaine said. "The target was supposed to be an unmanned drone."

Dresden puffed out his cheek. "I thought it must have been something like that. I was sure you couldn't be a terrorist. So, Wyndham, the PM, and God knows how many others in the cabinet want you dead."

"Yes," Kaine said. "So, what happens next, Inspector?"

"Well now," Dresden said, easing away from Stefan and further into the open. "For a start, you won't shoot Wyndham, and I won't shoot your man … Stefan, is it? Are we agreed?"

"It is, and we are."

"Good."

"What do you want, Inspector?" Kaine asked.

"Justice."

"Who for?"

Dresden glanced at Wyndham before answering. "For the victims of that plane and their families."

"Me too. How do you plan to get it?"

"Originally, I was going to arrest you and make you stand trial."

"Originally?"

"Yes, but I don't think that's going to work. There are too many vested interests to prevent it. Wyndham and his cronies"—he dipped his head towards the grey-faced Minister Without Portfolio, the Minister Without a Future—"can't let you have your day in court. That's what the Grey Notice is all about."

Kaine grimaced.

"That's pretty much the way I've seen it for the past nine months. So, what next? By the way, that's an interesting way to grab my attention," Kaine said, nodding at the SIG grinding into the side of Stefan's head.

"Come on, Captain. What would have happened if I'd barged my way in here screaming, 'Armed police. You are surrounded. Give up your weapons and come out!'" He pinched his lips. "You, or young Stefan here, might have reacted badly. I couldn't risk a gun battle. Someone might have been hurt. For God's sake, *I* might have been hurt." He stopped talking but threw Kaine a disarming smile. "I thought this would be a much better way to break the ice."

Kaine tensed, uncertain of his next move.

"Take it easy, Captain," Dresden said.

Slowly, Dresden eased his SIG away from Stefan's temple and pointed it at the ceiling. At the same time, he peeled his arm from around Stefan's neck, nudged him further into the office, and stepped to the side, into full view.

Kaine swung his gun arm away from Wyndham and aimed his SIG at Dresden's granite-jawed face. The police inspector dropped his smile and shook his head.

"No, Captain. I promise that won't be necessary."

Cautiously, Dresden turned his SIG sideways to make

sure Kaine could see him work the decocking lever and make the gun safe. He lowered the gun to his side, but kept it in hand, unholstered.

Kaine released his pent-up breath, lowered his SIG, but left it primed with his trigger finger running along the guard.

"That's better," Dresden said. "Less chance of accidental discharge this way."

"I'm all for that," Kaine said, nodding.

The tension had eased a little, but he couldn't afford to relax completely.

Stefan, looking a little sorry for himself, rubbed his temple.

"What's going on?" he croaked.

Kaine looked at Dresden, posing an unspoken question.

"Do you have any proof of your innocence?" Dresden asked. "Proof you can use?"

"I have Malcolm Sampson's confession on video."

Dresden's eyes widened. "Why haven't you released it?"

Kaine grimaced. "It's a long story."

Dresden shrugged. "We have a minute or two."

"A policeman friend of mine sent the Home Secretary a copy a week after the ... incident, but the government chose to sit on it. I always suspected why, but it's taken me a while to find out who."

"You can end this now, Captain," Dresden said, his voice animated, almost excited. "You know you can."

"How?"

"Release the video to the press. If it's as good as you claim—"

"Nope. I can't do that," Kaine interrupted, shaking his head. "Not yet."

"Why not?"

"I have to deal with the Grey Notice first."

"How are you going to do that?"

Kaine smiled. "Watch and learn." He raised his free hand and tapped the left arm of his glasses.

"Alpha One to Control, are you receiving me? Over."

"*Corky's here, Mr K. That was a bit hairy for a minute. You okay?*"

"Yes, thanks, Control. Have you prepped the package? Over."

"*Yep. Corky's just finished editing it.*"

"Excellent. Please send it now. Over."

"*One second. ... Yep, there you go. It's on its way.*"

"Thank you, Control. Alpha One, out."

He tapped the glasses again and nodded to Dresden.

"That ought to do it."

"Wh-What did you do?" Wyndham stammered, finding his voice again.

"Good question," Dresden added. "I was going to ask that."

"You'll find out soon enough," Kaine said, smiling. "I doubt it'll take long."

Much more relaxed, Kaine decocked his SIG, holstered it, and pointed to the woman on the floor.

"Simpson, isn't it?" he asked.

She nodded.

"I imagine you're a little uncomfortable down there."

Her answering scowl said plenty.

"Stefan," Kaine said, "would you mind doing the honours?"

Stefan jumped into action, no doubt relieved to have something constructive to do.

"The glasses," Dresden said, as Stefan closed on his colleague, "they're a comms unit?"

Kaine nodded. "With a built-in camera."

Dresden hiked his eyebrows.

"And you recorded everything?"

Again, Kaine nodded. This time, he added a happy grin.

"And the package you talked about," Dresden continued, "it shows what happened here tonight?"

"An edited version. We didn't want Stefan in shot, and we didn't think you'd like your part in the proceedings announced to the world."

Dresden returned Kaine's grin.

"How very perceptive of you, Captain. Where did you send the package? The BBC? ITV News? The broadsheets?"

"Not yet," Kaine answered. "The first recipients are much more selective." He stared at Wyndham, who had lowered his arms and slumped against the back of his chair. "I want to see the reaction it generates."

"Oh dear," Dresden said, "Wyndham's looking a bit green, eh?"

Stefan's honed dagger severed Simpson's bindings easily. He offered his hand to help her up. She slapped it away and climbed stiffly to her feet. A chastened Stefan backed away under her angry glare. Simpson stepped alongside Dresden and transferred the focus of her glare onto the sorry-looking man sitting behind the desk.

"Thank you, Stefan," Dresden said. "You okay, Lauren?"

"I am now, boss," she said, rubbing her chafed wrists, but keeping her eyes fixed on Wyndham. "That carpet isn't made for sitting on."

Dresden looked at Kaine. "Mind if I call my man up? I

imagine he'll be getting a little antsy down there on his own."

"Good idea."

"Hobbs!" Dresden called. "You can come up here now. Slowly does it."

Heavy footsteps clumped up the stairs again, accompanied by more ragged breathing. Hobbs strode through the open door, gagged, and pointed his Glock first at Stefan and then at Kaine.

Dresden reached out and forced Hobbs' gun arm down.

"Put it away, Ron," he said. "You won't be needing it."

"What's going on, boss?" Hobbs asked, his voice coarse.

Dresden opened his mouth, but the desk phone's strident warble interrupted his response. Judging by Wyndham's strangled gasp, the shock nearly gave him a seizure.

"Answer it," Kaine said, without seeking Dresden's permission.

"I-I … Really?"

The phone kept warbling. Silence fell around it. All eyes turned to the ringing handset.

"Do it, Jay," Kaine said, nodding at the landline, "but put it on speaker. We'll all want to hear this."

Slowly, his hand trembling, Wyndham reached out. He jabbed a finger at a button on the base unit and the ringtone stopped.

"W-Wyndham here," he said.

"Jay," a man said, urgency in his voice. "For God's sake what have you done?"

"What? Who is this?"

"Richard Farnsworth!" the deputy prime minister barked, sounding more than a little miffed.

Kaine stepped closer to the desk, allowing another smile to form.

"Richard? What's—"

"You're being broadcast on Downing Street's internal comms network. Half the cabinet's just watched you throw the PM under the fucking bus. What the fucking hell are you doing, you absolute shit-for-brains?"

Wyndham closed his eyes.

"Oh God!"

He groaned, punched the button again, and the phone fell silent halfway through another of Farnsworth's expletive-laden rants. He planted his elbows on the desk and dropped his head into his hands.

"That was interesting," Dresden said, flanked by his teammates. Simpson stood to Dresden's right with Hobbs to his left.

Stefan had taken up a position alongside Simpson, close to the door. His right hand hovered close to his holster, prepped for action.

"I thought so," Kaine answered, nodding.

"Your man sent the package to Number 10?"

"To begin with."

"What are you hoping for?" Dresden asked, raising his eyebrows.

"To see what would happen and maybe flush out a few honourable members of the cabinet."

"You're kidding, right?"

Kaine shook his head. "Let's see if any of the tax-payer-funded parasites are prepared to do the right thing."

Dresden snorted. "I wouldn't hold my breath on that front."

Kaine smiled and glanced at Stefan.

"Stefan, no!" he shouted.

Stefan jerked back and drew his Glock.

Dresden, Hobbs, and Simpson looked towards him.

In one seamless movement, Kaine drew his SIG, cocked it, and levelled it at Dresden's forehead.

"Sorry about this, Inspector," Kaine said, still smiling, "but it's time for us to leave. Please hand Stefan your weapon. And do it carefully. You too, Hobbs."

Dresden closed his eyes for a moment and drew out a sigh.

"Nicely done, Captain," he said, shaking his head, "but we're not handing over our weapons. You won't shoot us."

Kaine lowered his SIG and aimed it in the middle of Dresden's chest.

"You're wearing body armour, Inspector. A bullet in the chest at this range won't kill you, but I don't imagine it'll be a particularly pleasant experience. Hand your weapons to Stefan. I'll leave them downstairs in the garage on our way out. Do it. Please."

Dresden tensed his jaw and nodded to Hobbs. Using slow, deliberate movements, they passed their guns, butts first, to an eager Stefan. The unarmed Simpson looked on, helpless.

Kaine sidestepped around to his left and drew close to Dresden.

"Thanks, Alasdair," he whispered and snatched the radio from the clip on his webbing strap. "You could have made this much more difficult. I'll leave this downstairs with the guns."

He moved around and behind the police officers and signalled for Stefan to join him.

"Cheerio, Alasdair," Kaine said. "Please don't follow us. I'll shoot the first person to stick their head through the doorway. I won't hit anything vital, though. I promise."

He smiled, slammed the door closed behind him, and raced Stefan down the stairs, taking the treads two at a time.

"Kaine," Dresden yelled. "Wait!"

At the landing to the first floor, Kaine stopped and spun. Looked up.

Dresden's head and shoulder poked out around the corner of the stairwell.

"Wait!" he yelled again.

Kaine raised his SIG, squeezed the trigger. The bullet nicked the shoulder strap of Dresden's ballistic vest and drilled a hole in the wall above and behind him.

Dresden jerked backwards, and the gunshot boomed through the narrow stairwell.

Close, too damn close.

The glasses had thrown off Kaine's aim.

Ears ringing, Kaine called out, "Sorry, mate," turned, and carried on running.

Dresden shouted something else, but Kaine couldn't make it out for the ringing in his ears.

Chapter 45

Wednesday 9th June - Richard Hallam

Hayton Mews, Mayfair, London, England

Red blinked the scratchy dryness from his eyes. Staring at a target for minutes on end reduced the blink rate and resulted in dry-eye—an age-old problem for sharpshooters. A rapid drop in temperature and an increase in the wind from "dead calm" to "light breeze" didn't help either, but the conditions hadn't deteriorated enough to affect the shot.

"C'mon, c'mon," he muttered. "What the fuck's going on in there?"

The radio had remained resolutely silent in the minutes since China's recall of Paulson, and since he'd told Red to keep his eyes peeled—again. Anything might be happening. The wait was killing him.

He'd have done anything to find out what was going on inside homebase, but he couldn't risk breaking radio silence.

Slow seconds stretched out into three minutes.

Four minutes.

Still, nothing happened.

One hundred metres away to his left, a white saloon poked its nose out from the junction with Chesterfield Hill. It indicated left, but stopped at the broken lines, its driver giving way to oncoming traffic. It edged further out, paused again.

A bright flash caught Red's eye.

Inside homebase.

A single gunshot!

Fuck!

Second floor. First window on the left. The window on the stairwell. A gunfight? No. A single shot.

"What the fuck?"

Red's heartrate lurched. His mouth dried.

He reached for his radio mic, hit the PTT.

"Hallam to Dresden, come in. Over."

No response.

He repeated the call, waited.

Sill nothing.

Red hit the panic button on his radio, and called it in. "Shots fired, officers need assistance." He added his badge number, gave the location, and turned the radio's volume down. He needed to concentrate.

Breathing hard, Red tilted the PSG and confirmed he'd set the selector to single shot. He slid his finger through the guard and hooked it around the trigger. Prepped and ready.

He stared at the frontage of homebase. No more flashes. No more gunshots.

What the fuck's happening?

Keeping both eyes open, he peered through the sights and lined up his shot on the top panel of the front door. Slowly, he emptied his lungs to lower his heartrate and waited.

The front door remained closed.

Below and to the left, a dark van rolled past the front of the pub, on its way to Berkley Square. Behind it the white car, a Volvo, edged out of Chesterfield Hill and turned left, driving slowly towards homebase. The driver lowered his side window and the gap between Volvo and van grew. Another car, a cherry-red SUV, passed the van, moving in the opposite direction, heading away and closing on Waverton Row.

"Homebase, you idiot," Red muttered. "Concentrate on homebase."

Below him, the black door remained closed. To its right, the personnel door opened inwards a crack. Red swung the rifle, changed position.

Shit. This is happening. It's happening.

The personnel door's shiny, gloss panels caught the streetlight, highlighting the movement. It opened wider. Half a man's outline jutted through the opening.

Red adjusted his aim until the cross on the scope's reticles lined up with the centre of a round, youngish face. Not Dresden. Not Hobbs either. An intruder! Red added pressure to the trigger, feeling for the bite.

Christ. It's not Kaine!

Red didn't have the authority to shoot an unknown target, not without just cause. Slowly, reluctantly, he eased the pressure on the trigger.

The young man popped his head through the opening, eyes on the swivel, checking his surroundings before committing to leave. He edged further out. Behind him, a shadow moved. A shorter man. His head level with the younger one's shoulder.

Kaine!

Ryan-fucking-Kaine!

Bearded and with longer hair than shown on his mugshot, but definitely Kaine.

How had they got past Dresden? What about Lauren …

No. Don't think about that.

Red couldn't let what *might* have happened inside the house affect his decision-making. He needed to keep his head clear.

He adjusted his aim. The image in the sights rolled from right to left. The reticles swung and centred on Kaine's forehead.

I've got you, you fucking—

Kaine moved to his right, slipping behind the younger one, out of shot. In tandem, Kaine and his oppo stepped out of the house. Red followed their progress through the scope. The side of Kaine's head appeared. Not enough of a target.

"Wait," Red muttered, adding more pressure to the trigger. "Wait for the shot. Wait."

Dresden, Hobbs, Simpson.

What had happened. Where the hell were they?

Wait.

Bastards. They'd killed his team.

Anger boiled. The hot flame of rage.

Focus. Wait. Wait for the shot.

The Volvo drew closer, slowing even more. The front seat passenger searched the street to his left.

Kaine stepped out from behind his young oppo and glanced to his right.

The Volvo's driver screamed something. His arm pushed out through the open window.

Kaine looked up and stared straight into the eye of the scope.

Now!

Red squeezed the trigger.

Chapter 46

Wednesday 9th June - Will Stacy

South Street, Mayfair, London, England

Stacy slowed the Volvo, indicated right, and gave way to a black cab before making the turn into Chesterfield Hill. A continuous row of three-storey, Victorian red-bricks ran along the left side. Baskets filled with pink blooms dangled from hooks on either side of each doorway. Window boxes with similar pink flowers hung from every second window. Whoever said London wasn't pretty? A modern, six-storey apartment block loomed up on the right, its clean, straight lines standing out in contrast to the terrace opposite. The new facing the old. Stacy quite liked the contrast.

He threaded his way past two cars illegally parked on a single yellow line and another double-parked on the right.

"Not long now," he said nodding to the satnav screen. "Hill Street's just up ahead. Ready?"

Keeping his Glock low and pointed into the footwell, Cough nodded.

"Ready," he said, his voice grim. "What's the plan?"

"A slow drive-by ought to do it. Check for anything out of place. The captain won't want us to interfere, but more eyes outside won't hurt."

"Roger that."

They reached the junction with Hill Street and gave way again. Stacy lowered his window to give him an unobstructed view, drew and primed his Glock, and rested it on his right thigh. Prepped for action.

He indicated left and waited for a dark blue Renault Kangoo to trundle past from his right. Pulsing music thumped out through the part-open passenger window, and the driver's head bobbed in time with the beat. Lost in his own, little world of noise.

Stacy nudged the Volvo out behind the Kangoo, and let the van pull slowly away. The road behind was clear of traffic, but a bright red Porsche Cayenne growled towards them on the other side of the road, driven by a blond youngster who barely looked old enough to hold a driving licence. The Porsche rolled past and took the next left turn. The schoolchild behind the wheel didn't bother indicating.

You're getting old, Stacy.

Cops had been looking like kids for a decade. The first sign of the passage of time. He allowed his eyes to search the road ahead. Cars parked on either side presented a restricted view of the street. Stacy glanced in the rear-view. Still no traffic. He reduced speed even further.

Cough twisted to stare through his window.

"What house are we looking for?" he asked.

"Number 20."

"You mean that monstrosity up ahead?"

Cough pointed to a building with a jet-black frontage on his side of the road.

Stacy nodded.

"Yep. That's the one."

Wyndham's house wasn't exactly tough to spot. It hardly blended in with its neighbours. Stacy rolled the Volvo slowly forwards, acting as though they were locals, searching for a place to park. In front of Number 20, red box-hatching kept the road clear of parked cars, giving unrestricted access to its double garage.

"The front door's opening," Cough said. "That's Stefan. The captain's behind him."

"We'll pick them—shit!"

On the roof of a building at the far end of the street, movement caught his eye. A metallic glint.

"Look out!" Stacy screamed.

Glock in hand, he jabbed his arm through the open window, aimed, and fired.

Chapter 47

Hill Street, Mayfair, London, England

At full pelt, breathing hard, his right shoulder scraping against the wall on the way down to help his balance, Kaine hit the ground-floor entrance hall and darted left into the garage. He dropped Dresden's radio on a bench beside the discarded weapons and stopped before careening into Stefan who'd closed on the personnel door.

Stefan stretched out his left arm, twisted the handle, and tugged at the door.

"Careful!" Kaine called, his ears still ringing from his earlier shot.

Stefan nodded, opened the door a crack, and peeked outside, head on a slow pivot.

Standing close behind, Kaine tugged off the heavy glasses, collapsed the arms against his chest, and slid them into his jacket pocket. Relieved by the loss of weight, and the improved vision he blinked rapidly to refocus his eyes.

"Clear," Stefan said, pulling the door wider and stepping into the evening air.

Kaine followed close behind, eager to leave.

To his right, out on the road, a Volvo slowed as it approached the house. Kaine braced, but relaxed. In the front passenger seat, Cough smiled in recognition. Will sat behind the wheel, staring up at the pub on the opposite side of the street.

"Look out!" he yelled.

Will's right arm jerked up and out in a blur.

Kaine glanced up. Found the rooftop, a dark shape above a red-brick wall, and a white line of coping stones. Curved shoulders. Round helmet. Two circles, one above the other. The lower black, the upper orange glass.

Sniper!

Kaine punched Stefan in the back, jagged to his left, aimed deliberately low, and fired in one movement. Stefan tumbled forwards onto the pavement.

Three separate blasts shook the night, so instantaneous they merged into a single loud explosion.

A bullet slammed into the personnel door behind Kaine, the metallic clunk merging with the aftershock of three simultaneous gunshots. Again, Kaine's ears rang.

An engine roared, a white shape pulled into the red hatched markings in front of the garage door and stopped. A rear door flew open. Kaine raced forwards, picked up a scrambling Stefan, and bundled him into the back seat. He dived on top of him and screamed, "Go!"

Chapter 48

Hayton Mews, Mayfair, London, England

Red snatched at the trigger. The rifle coughed, and its butt jammed into his shoulder.

Two bullets slammed into the front edge of the coping stone below the bipod's feet. The rifle jerked in Red's hands. Dust and stones exploded into his face. One fragment dug into his upper lip and chipped a tooth, but his marksman glasses saved his eyes. Kept them free of dust and grit.

Shit!

He'd shot high. Missed.

Red knew it without looking.

Again. Fire again!

He stared through the scope. A dent marked the

door where his shot had struck. Below the dent, Kaine scrambled on the pavement, gun raised, but not shooting. The Volvo darted forwards and into the firing line, blocking Red's second shot. The nearside, rear passenger door flew open. Kaine picked up his mate and shoved him into the back of the car. Exposing himself to the shot.

Red took aim at the top of Kaine's head. His trigger finger tensed.

Movement. Homebase. Second floor, centre window. The top pane slid upwards. Wyndham's office. A figure filled the opening.

"Red! Stand down!" it howled. "Red, stand down! Do not shoot!"

What?

Red tore his eye away from the scope and looked up.

China Dresden stood at the open window, leaning out, waving both arms.

"Stand down!" he repeated.

Red released the pressure on the trigger and stared at China. Red pointed to his earpiece and mouthed, "What the fuck?"

What about the comms?

China shook his head and waved his hands in front of his face.

"Come across," he bellowed. "Now!"

Red ground his teeth and watched as Kaine dived into the back of the Volvo and it raced into the distance, out of sight. Out of range. Kaine was on his toes. The terrorist was getting away. For fuck's sake. What the pigging hell was going on?

Red winced and the chipped tooth grazed the inside of his damaged mouth. His upper lip stung like a bitch. Warm liquid dripped into his mouth, and he tasted the coppery tang of blood.

Fuck.

Red stood, pulled the PSG away from the wall, and lowered it to the roof. Cautiously, he pressed a finger to the cut on his lip which had already started to swell. The finger came away bloody. God knew what his face looked like. He'd be scarred for life. Have to grow a moustache.

Fuck's sake.

Up and down the street, curtains drew back in downstairs windows and lights illuminated the pavements. Upstairs windows slid open, allowing a few brave and inquisitive souls to peer outside, trying to identify what had happened near their expensive homes.

Red lugged the rifle to its case. He removed the mag, emptied the chamber, and folded the stock into the side. After confirming the rifle as safe, he stowed it and the mag inside the carry case, and locked it tight.

Way off in the distance, sirens wailed. Reinforcements arriving too late for the party.

By the time he'd clambered down the fire escape and marched out onto Hill Street, China Dresden and Lauren Simpson were standing in homebase's open doorway, waiting.

The sirens grew louder. Blue lights flickered, lighting the sky, drawing closer.

Red crossed the street, the strap of the heavy carry case digging into his shoulder, and stopped on the pavement in front of them.

"That looks painful," China said, nodding to his lip.

"Stings a bit, boss. But I'll survive."

Simpson winced at him.

"Better get the medics to take a look when they get here. It might need a stitch or two."

"Will do, boss." Red shrugged the carry case's strap higher on his shoulder. "What the fuck happened in there?" He glanced up at homebase.

"Nothing much."

"I saw a shot. On the staircase."

"That was Kaine warning me off."

"He shot at you?"

China nodded.

"He missed?"

China's eyes widened. "Clearly."

"He missed me, too," Red said, jerking a thumb over his shoulder towards his obbo point.

Again, China nodded. "He meant to."

"Really?"

"I saw it all while wrestling with the window catch. Two shots. Both low. Intentional."

"You sure?"

China nodded.

He'd have to take China's word for it.

"What happened in there, boss?" Red asked again.

"Later, Red. With shots fired, there'll be an investigation."

"Why did you order me to stand down?" Red asked. "I had Kaine in my sights. The bugger should be in a body bag right now. The Grey Notice—"

"Is defunct."

Red frowned. "Defunct?"

"Redundant," China said. "Obsolete. Non-operational. Invalid."

Red canted his head to one side and huffed out a sigh. "I know what 'defunct' means, boss, but how come?"

"That, Red," China said, arching an eyebrow, "is classified."

"Classified?"

"That's right, Red. Secret. Confidential. Hush-hush." China smiled as he spoke.

"Leave it out, boss. What the bloody hell's going on? And where's Hobbs?"

"Hobbs is watching Wyndham. Making sure he doesn't swallow a bullet."

"What?"

"In the old days, men like Wyndham would have taken the easy way out, but I want to make sure he and his cronies face the music."

Red dropped his shoulders in a sigh. "What are you talking about, boss?"

"Corruption, Red. Greed. State-sponsored murder. Ask Lauren," China muttered, turning to face the brightest set of blue lights. "She heard it all."

At that moment, a pair of Trojan units—two-tones wailing and blue lights flashing—screeched to a stop at the far end of Hill Street, blocking the road leading to Berkley Square. Two more squealed out of Chesterfield Hill and sealed off the other end of the road, forming a tight containment zone. ARU officers, armed and dressed for battle, piled out of the BMWs, and took up defensive positions behind their vehicles.

Behind them, patrol cars and transit vans filled the roads, lighting the whole street in flickering blue. Sirens fell silent, allowing voices to ring out. Voices of police officers taking control, issuing orders.

"I need to deal with this. We'll talk back at HQ," China said, marching out into the street, arms held out from his sides, showing empty hands. "And don't forget to have that injury treated and logged."

Red turned towards Lauren, totally confused.

She stepped closer, pulled a hankie from her pocket, and held it up to him.

"For your lip," she said. "Don't worry, it's clean."

He took the white cloth and pressed it against the wound. It stung even worse.

"Thanks. How bad does it look?" he asked, mumbling into the hankie.

She made a face that looked like someone who'd bitten into a lemon.

"Ever thought of growing a moustache?"

"Be serious, will you?"

"I am," she said, smiling.

Jesus. Everyone's a pigging joker.

In front of the first set of Trojans, China stood, talking to an officer who wore the reflective, yellow-and-black-chequered tabard of an incident commander. Running through an onsite debrief.

Good luck with that, boss.

"So," he said to Lauren, "what happened up there?" He jerked a thumb over his shoulder, towards the window to the second-floor office. "What did China mean about the Grey Notice?"

She pulled in a deep breath. "It's a long story, but it looks as though Kaine was set up. He's no more a terrorist than you are."

"What!" Red gasped. "You're kidding."

"No," Lauren said, shaking her head. "You could have shot an innocent man."

"Christ. I had him in my sights."

"Yes. I know. Lucky."

Red paused for a moment, thinking.

457

"But the bugger shot me," he said, holding out the bloody hankie. "How innocent can he be?"

"Shot *at* you," she said, shaking her head. "There's a difference."

"They could have killed me, for fuck—"

"Think about it, Red. Two men shot at you, and both hit the wall *below* you. The way I see it, they both hit what they aimed at, man."

Realisation landed with the force of a physical blow.

"They wanted to put you off your aim without hitting you," Lauren continued. "Damn fine shooting if you ask me."

Red gulped.

"Bloody hell. I had him in my sights."

"Yes. I know. You already said that."

"But I could have killed him."

Red's stomach churned. He struggled to hold onto his dinner.

Chapter 49

Mike's Farm, Long Buckby, Northants, England

Kaine tucked into his bowl of muesli and watched Will, Cough, Stefan, and Hunter demolish their Full English breakfasts, with hardly a pause for small talk. In Hunter they'd found a willing kitchen volunteer and a decent hand with a frying pan. Cough handled the coffees and teas. Every now and again, Stefan arched his back and winced, staring furtively at Kaine as he did so.

"Everything okay, Stefan?" Kaine asked after working a ball of muesli to the side of his mouth. "Didn't think I punched you that hard."

"Felt like a sledgehammer, boss," Stefan answered, his mouth full of half-munched bacon and eggs. "I nearly headbutted the pavement on the way down. You could have given me some warning."

Kaine smiled.

"Next time, I'll let the sniper shoot you."

"He was probably aiming at you, boss," Hunter said, grinning and adding an eyebrow hitch.

"Suck it up, Stefan," Cough said, elbowing him in the ribs. "And don't you have something to say?"

Stefan's face glowed a bright crimson.

"Yes," he mumbled, lowering his head. "I, er ... screwed up, boss. Left my post. Sorry."

Kaine swallowed the muesli and canted his head to one side.

"We all make mistakes, lad." He relented. "To be honest, it was as much my fault as yours. We went in undermanned. In a perfect world, I would have stationed someone in the garage, and someone else on the road outside. We were lucky Dresden was a decent, honest cop. Lesson learned, though."

Will pushed his empty plate away and reached for his cup.

"It's not a good idea to rely on luck," he said with an air of finality.

"Amen to that," Hunter said, mopping up a smear of his egg yolk with a corner of toast and popping it into his mouth.

Cough grunted, and Stefan kept his head lowered.

The door to the inner hallway opened, and Lara entered the kitchen, carrying a tray filled with Mike's uneaten breakfast. Kaine jumped up, took it from her, and carried it to the sink. Lara followed him and poured herself a coffee from the carafe warming on the hot plate. She offered Kaine a refill.

"No, thanks, I'm good. How is he?" he asked, glancing in the direction of Mike's ground-floor sickroom.

She shook her head.

"Not good," she said quietly. "No appetite. I'm making him as comfortable as I can, but …" She allowed her words to trail away.

Kaine reached out to squeeze her arm and smiled.

"I'll pop in and say hello. Let him know what's happening."

"He'll appreciate that," she said, returning his smile and covering his hand with hers.

She added a dash of milk to her coffee and carried the cup to the table. Kaine followed her. As he reached for his cup, his mobile vibrated. He snatched it up from the table, read the caller ID, and accepted the video call. Corky's round and smiling face filled the small screen.

"Hi, Corky."

The others paused in their munching and looked up. Lara dropped into Kaine's chair, and he took the spare seat beside her.

"Whatcha, Mr K. How you diddling?"

"Fine, thanks. Nice work with the global email, by the way. It reads just like Enderby. Pompous and full of his own self-importance. When will it arrive?"

"Corky sent it through Enderby's desktop and delayed the transmission for another ninety minutes. It'll ping everyone's screens just before elevenses. Should give all the agency's staff something to talk about over their morning coffee, eh?" A wide grin bunched up his round cheeks. "It'll answer a few questions, too. The reason he 'topped' himself, for example."

Kaine nodded. "I imagine it will. Do you have anything else?"

461

"Yep. Corky and Frodo have been trawling through Enderby's files."

"Find anything interesting?"

"Buckets. Corky can see the doc there ... Hi, Doc." He raised a hand and waved. "Who else is with you?"

Kaine held up the mobile, face out, and panned it around the table.

"Whatcha peeps," Corky said, fielding a chorus of greetings.

Kaine pushed his breakfast bowl to the far edge of the table and propped the mobile against it so that everyone could see the screen.

"Okay, Corky, what do you have for us?" Kaine asked.

"Enough evidence to convict the PM, the Home Secretary, *and* the Foreign Secretary. Not to mention the creep, Wyndham."

"What did you find on them?" Will asked, easing himself closer to the table.

"Well now," Corky answered. "Let's see. There's a bunch of recorded phone conversations. Photos. Bank statements. Copies of contract documents. All sorts of goodies. Mr K, do you want Corky and Frodo to package up the evidence into handy, bite-sized chunks easy enough for the NCA to sink their teeth into?"

Kaine glanced at Will, who nodded.

"That sounds like a plan," Kaine said.

"Corky thought that sending it to the NCA would be a good idea, seeing as how the cabinet might be considered an Organised Crime Group," Corky announced through one of his trademark chuckles. "And given that the Met is so ... *stretched* right now, what with one thing and another, Corky didn't think it would be a good idea to give them any more issues to deal with."

"You've got a point there, Corky," Cough said, grinning.

Beside him, Stefan's delayed smile showed he didn't quite catch Corky's drift.

Lara and Will nodded. They both understood Corky's meaning. The Metropolitan Police's performance over recent years didn't exactly inspire confidence—as shown by Kaine's recent dealings with a certain Inspector "Amazing" Grace Taylor and her team of corrupt officers.

Stefan raised a hand as though he were in school.

"Can I ask a question, boss?"

"Of course," Kaine said. "Fire away."

Stefan shot a quick glance at Cough as though looking for support. Cough rolled his hand forward in encouragement.

"Well, boss," Stefan said, "it's like this. You know we've dug up all this dirt on the prime minister and her cronies?" He paused, clearly unsure of himself.

"Yes, Stefan?" Kaine encouraged.

"And we're gonna send that dirt to the National Crime Agency?"

"Yes."

"Keep going, Stefan," Cough urged.

Stefan scratched the top of his head.

"Er, what's likely to happen?"

Kaine glanced at Lara.

"Do you want to try answering that, Doc?"

"Well," she said, looking at Stefan, "the government will be desperate to stay in power. The people behind the throne, the men in the grey suits, will try to cover things up, but the NCA won't let them. More to the point, *we* won't let them."

"If necessary," Kaine said, "we'll send the evidence to the media. They love a good political scandal."

"But in all likelihood," Lara continued, "the government will be forced to call a snap general election."

"Yeah," Stefan said, nodding, "I get that. I do. But what about the Grey Notice? Is it gonna stay in place?"

Kaine puffed out his cheeks.

"That's a good question. Will, any thoughts?"

"No idea. That'll be up to the newly elected government. My guess is they'll act as though it never existed."

Kaine nodded.

"Makes sense."

"And what about you, boss," Stefan asked. "Are you going to clear your name? After all, we've got that video—"

"Yes, boss," Hunter chimed in. "Wouldn't now be a good time to release it to the press?"

"I'm not so sure about that," Kaine said, again glancing at Lara. "It might be better to hang fire on that until after all the fuss dies down."

Hunter opened his mouth to comment, but Kaine raised a hand to cut him off.

"Think about it for a minute. Half the senior cabinet will be under arrest, including the PM. No stop-gap Home Secretary will have the stones to authorise my bail. If I hand myself in, I'll be charged and placed on remand. In most people's eyes, I'm still a terrorist. My case won't be heard for months. Years maybe. To be honest, I really don't fancy spending that long behind bars, mingling with all those old lags. No, thanks. It would be even worse than spending time with you guys!"

His comment raised the intended raucous responses.

After they'd settled down, Lara spoke.

"Reluctantly," she said. "I agree. Now isn't the time to go public. We need a stable government in place. An honest, credible government with—"

"Are you kidding?" Hunter said, sneering. "An honest, credible politician? There's no such animal."

Cough snorted. Stefan shrugged.

"Another good point," Kaine said, "but as the doc suggested, only a stable, credible government will be strong enough to do right by me. They need to be seen as squeaky clean. No. We're holding onto the video for a while longer. Okay?"

Kaine looked at each one in turn and, to signal an end to the discussion, he drained the last of his coffee and set the mug down on its coaster.

Decision made.

"Er, Mr K?"

Kaine turned to the mobile.

"Yes, Corky?"

"For what it's worth," Corky said, "Corky agrees with you, too. There ain't no point in releasing the video right now. Best to leave it for when it has more impact. For it to do any good, you need public opinion onboard, and that ain't happening when the media is banging on about a general election. Anyhow, that's only Corky's opinion."

"Thanks, Corky," Kaine said. "So, are we done for now?"

"Not likely," Corky answered, opening his eyes wide. "There's plenty more to chat about, if you've got the time."

More?

"I have if you have."

Kaine could hardly refuse to lend an ear to a man who gave up his time so freely, and whose value couldn't be measured.

"Okay," Corky said, taking a deep breath, "so here's what's happening. So far, Corky and Frodo have worked through a good portion of the data on Enderby's hard drive.

Along with all the other stuff, it looks like there's going to be plenty of dirt on private government contractors. Contractors the likes of T5S and GG Cleaning Systems. The whole system stinks. Loads of opportunities for people with sticky fingers to earn a dishonest penny or two." Corky ticked the list off on his fingers. "We've got bribery, false accounting, over-billing, charging more than once for the same work. You name it, Corky and Frodo's found it. Gonna take weeks to sift through all the data and prep it for the NCA. Oh yes, there's plenty of fun and games for Frodo and ol' Corky coming up." His chubby face stretched into another infectious grin.

"Okay, Corky," Kaine said. "That's brilliant. Thanks for every—"

"But"—Corky raised an index finger to interrupt Kaine's goodbye—"on top of all that, Enderby kept a diary."

"He did?" Lara asked.

"Yes indeedie," Corky said, grinning in Lara's general direction. "Most nights, the geezer dictated his thoughts into a voice-activated word processor. Hours and hours of it, there is. Mostly twaddle, you know? Stream of consciousness stuff. Trouble is, he never edited nothing. Didn't bother with punctuation, neither. The entries are a total dog's dinner. It *was* going to take ages to make sense of them."

"Why bother? Is it worth your time?" Will asked, as pragmatic as ever.

"Well," Corky said, looking directly at Will, "it's funny you should say that, Mr S. Corky *was* going to knock trying to decipher the entries on the head, but Frodo up and built this AI translation app. You guys should see it. Neat as a button, it is. Elegant. Makes sense of all the guff he spouted. Sort of sense, anyway."

Will lowered his hands to the table and curled his fingers into fists. His knuckles cracked under the pressure.

"Did it explain why he murdered Abdul Hosseini? What the hell was he thinking?"

"Nah," Corky said, grimacing, "'fraid not. His last diary entry was on the night *before* he became a guest in your cellar."

"Did we push him over the edge?" Hunter asked, a worried frown creasing his forehead.

"Oh God," Lara gasped. "You don't think—"

"We can't go there, Lara," Kaine said, dropping a hand over hers. "We'll never know what drives a sociopath like Enderby. I thought we had him under our control, but … damn."

Kaine raked his fingers through his hair, pulling at the tangles. If he thought for one moment their actions had resulted in Abdul Hosseini's death …

The kitchen fell quiet, the only sounds coming from the ticking pendulum clock in the hall, the water dripping into the kitchen sink from a leaky tap, and the birds singing in the trees surrounding the farmhouse.

Will's cough broke through the gloom.

"This AI translation app," he said, speaking louder than necessary, "has it turned up anything of value?"

Corky's expression turned from thoughtful to serious.

"As well as being a murderer, a blackmailer, and a thief, Enderby were also a sexual predator and a bully."

"What was that?" Kaine asked, sitting up straighter, thankful to have something else to focus on than his potential role in the death of another innocent.

"Corky thought you might find that interesting, Mr K," he said, dipping his head in a sage-like nod. "It's all there in his diary. He talks about how he gets his jollies by targeting female members of staff. Especially young ones. Been doing it for years, he has. Gets his targets alone someplace. In the lifts, in his private office. Always alone. That way, it's his word against theirs. He gets a kick out of scaring them. Bullying them. Then, when he's had enough, he works out a way to get rid. His latest victim—"

"Survivor," Lara shot out. "They're survivors, not victims."

Corky raised a hand in apology.

"Yeah, good point. You're right. Sorry, Doc. Corky's mistake," he said. "Anyway, his latest survivor still works at the agency. Claire Harper's her name."

Harper?

Kaine had come across the name recently, but where?

"A few weeks ago," Corky continued, "Enderby wrote her a suspect performance review. Not a real hatchet job, though. He was a bit more subtle than that. It called into doubt her suitability for promotion. He's done the same thing a couple of times before to other survivors, hoping to 'encourage' them to resign. Only it didn't work on Claire. Tough, she is. Clever too. She weren't going quietly. Enderby started getting worried that she'd find a way to expose him. And get this." Corky leaned so close to his camera, his face completely filled the screen. "He were going to take out a hit on her."

"A hit?" Stefan said. "You're kidding."

Corky frowned.

"Stefan," he said, sighing, "Corky don't kid about stuff like this. Enderby were paranoid. He reckoned Claire had started following him, listening at keyholes, searching for proof of what he were up to. The other stuff, Corky means. The corruption. He were so worried about her, he planned to have his pet hitman, Guy Gordon, arrange an accident for her. If we hadn't interfered in his plans, Claire Harper would have fallen down a set of stairs or been knocked over by a hit-and-run driver. Not only paranoid, Enderby were a total sociopath. His death couldn't have come too soon for Claire Harper. Guy Gordon's death, too. She's well rid of the both of them. So is the rest of humanity, by the way."

"What does she look like," Cough asked, frowning in concentration. "Do you have a photo?"

Corky nodded.

"Here's the pic from her driver's licence."

A monochrome photo of a woman with long, dark hair and a slim face with prominent cheekbones replaced Corky on the screen.

Kaine jabbed a finger towards the mobile.

"That's the woman we saw outside Body-Ring on Monday night," he said. "I thought I recognised the surname." He nodded. "Enderby may have been a sociopath, but he wasn't delusional. She *was* following him."

"Yep," Corky said. "Seems like it. So, is there anything you want Corky to do about the Harper situation?"

Kaine thought for a moment before answering.

"No, thanks. Nothing."

Corky arched a bushy eyebrow. "Is you sure, Mr K?"

"I'm certain, thanks. You and Frodo have got plenty to be getting on with for the moment."

Lara turned to Kaine.

"So, you're going to leave it like that?" she asked. "Just because Enderby's dead, it doesn't mean Claire Harper's life hasn't been impacted."

"Leave it?" Kaine said, eyes wide. "What on earth gave you that idea?"

"What are you thinking, Ryan?"

He scratched at his beard.

"If you remember, we have an inside man at the top of the NCTA," he said. "I can't see any reason we can't give him a call and let him know about this. Can you?"

Smiling, Lara shook her head.

"No, Ryan. I can't think of a single one."

Chapter 50

Sandbrook Tower, Soho, London, England

Breathlessly, Claire Harper checked her reflection in the rest room mirror. For the first time in months, she didn't totally hate what it showed her. Although the harsh fringe still remained—it would take weeks for her hair to grow out properly—to complement her dark skin tone, she'd chosen a light, low cut, knee-length, summer dress in pale lemon. Her gold cross dangled freely from its chain, and she'd added gold earrings to complete the look. She even wore a touch of makeup. Not much, but more than she would ever wear to work when Worm still prowled Sandbrook Tower.

But Worm wouldn't be prowling the office anymore. Dead men didn't prowl. Only in horror films.

The news had come as such a … relief. Despite her religious upbringing, Claire didn't have it in her to grieve for a man who'd caused her so much distress. So much anger.

Worm is dead.

Claire had read Worm's global email over and over, unable to believe the words on her screen, although it certainly *sounded* like Worm. The email used the kind of flowery and clichéd prose he often resorted to, but the sentiments didn't feel right.

Worm claimed to have been so "overcome with remorse" after killing Abdul Hosseini, that he "couldn't live with himself any longer". Trouble was, Worm didn't have a remorseful bone in his body. As far as Claire was concerned, he would no more commit suicide than give away all his worldly possessions and join a monastery. The conspiracy theorist in her landed on the idea that someone had killed Worm and set it up to *look* like suicide.

But who, she'd asked herself.

Who would want Worm dead?

The answer had hit her like a bolt of lightning.

A&W Associates!

As the thought coalesced, the blood had pounded in her ears.

But why?

What would A&W Associates gain from Worm's death? What would *anyone* gain from Worm's death?

Apart from anyone who'd ever met the man, she could only think of one person with a real motive to end Worm's miserable existence—Claire Harper.

Oh dear. Now that was a conspiracy theory too far. She'd be convincing herself to confess next.

"Stop being so ridiculous," she'd told herself. "Any more

of that nonsense and the men in white coats will be lining up to drag you into a padded room."

In any event, what could she do about it? If Worm's death did prove suspicious, the police would find out and investigate. It wasn't down to her to kick up a fuss. Her time for kicking up a fuss had passed with Worm's death.

In the days since she'd read Worm's global email, the world had seemed like a different place. A brighter, breezier place. A place full of hope and opportunity.

So why did the woman staring back at Claire in the mirror look so worried?

That woman had other things on her mind.

That woman had no idea what was about to happen. The call had come as a total shock.

Nancy Goodview, Sir Ernest's PA, had simply called and summoned her to his office. She'd given Claire half an hour's notice and hung up the call.

Why?

What did Sir Ernest want?

Claire had no idea. Couldn't even guess.

With the summons, a dark cloud had slid in front of the sun, and the gentle breeze had turned downright chilly.

How long to go?

Claire read the time from her wristwatch.

Four minutes.

The deep breath she sucked in did nothing to quell the butterflies swirling around her belly. What did Sir Ernest want?

"Come on, woman," she said. "Time to go. It will be alright. It *will* be alright."

Claire turned away from the worried-looking woman in the mirror, exited the Ladies toilet, and trudged up the stairs.

She'd never been to the rarefied environs of the top floor before. She expected plush carpets, but the floors were tiled just like in the rest of the tower. Somewhat disappointing, but this was the civil service, after all. Every expense spared.

The view through the top floor windows didn't seem any more impressive than those on her floor. They revealed the same buildings, but from a slightly elevated perspective, looking down on the world.

Her high-heeled shoes clicked on the tiles and the sound bounced off the walls as she strode down the long corridor —external windows to the left, directors' offices to the right. She stopped at an oak door at the end of the corridor, an oak door bearing the title, "Permanent Secretary, Sir Ernest Hartington, OBE". She raised her hand to knock, but the door opened inwards before her knuckles could strike the woodwork.

Nancy Goodview, a grey-haired woman in her late fifties, smiled and stepped back to allow Claire access to the inner sanctum.

"Ms Harper," Nancy said. "Do come in. Sir Ernest is ready for you."

She led Claire through the outer office and towards an inner panelled door identical to the first. A deep-pile, plum-red carpet absorbed their footsteps.

That's more like it.

Nancy knocked once and opened the door without waiting for a summons.

Sir Ernest sat behind a large, leather-topped desk. At his back, a wide, full-length window let in the bright, morning sunlight and bathed the large room in a golden glow.

He rose.

"Ms Harper," he said, "thank you for coming at such short notice."

You're my boss and you summoned me. What else could I do?

Claire tried to offer a warm smile, but nerves made her lips feel tight.

Nancy nodded to Claire and backed out of the room. She left the door open and took her seat in full view of the inner office. Acting as chaperone. Claire relaxed a little.

"Please sit," Sir Ernest said, waving her towards two upholstered chairs across the desk from him.

Claire lowered herself in the nearer chair and sat straight backed, waiting.

Sir Ernest took his seat again, leaned forwards, and rested his elbows on the desk. Steepling his hands, he studied her carefully. Were it not for the open door and Nancy Goodview sitting within earshot, Claire would have felt decidedly uncomfortable. As it was, she still found it difficult not to squirm.

Eventually, after what seemed like minutes, Sir Ernest cleared his throat.

"I imagine, you're wondering why I invited you here this morning?" he said.

She frowned. "Am I in any trouble, Sir Ernest?"

He jerked up straighter.

"Trouble?" he said. "But of course not. Why on earth would you think that?"

"After what happened to Mr Hosseini—"

"Good Lord, no." He shook his head almost violently. "Did you not receive Commander Enderby's global email? I was under the impression it was sent to everyone in the building."

"Yes, sir. I did, but—"

"Terrible business," Sir Ernest said, still shaking his head. Terrible, terrible business."

"You mean, Wor—the commander's suicide, sir?"

"No, I don't," he said, his concentrated stare drilling into her again. "I meant Mr Hosseini's death, Ms Harper. A terrible thing. As to the commander's early demise"—he sniffed—"suffice to say, I imagine his family might miss him."

Only his family?

"I dare say," he continued, "the agency will arrange some form of memorial service, for appearances' sake, but no one will be required to attend unless they feel inclined to do so."

I certainly won't.

"I see, sir," she said, feeling the need to say something.

Sir Ernest rested his forearms on the desktop, interlaced his fingers, and cleared his throat once again.

"Now, as to the reason for this meeting. I would have spoken to you earlier, but I've been … somewhat busy, as you may have heard."

Office rumours had been doing the rounds about Sir Ernest, a prostitute, and a death, but Claire had dismissed them as spurious nonsense.

"No, sir," she said, straight faced.

"No?"

"No, sir," she repeated, adding a slight shake of her head.

He nodded. "I see. The rumour mill clearly isn't what it used to be." He shifted uncomfortably. "Okay, Ms Harper, cards on the table. What I am about to tell you is highly confidential. It must stay within these walls. Am I making myself perfectly clear?"

No, you're not.

Claire tensed, unable to hide her surprise. She had no idea what was going on.

"This information falls under the purview of the Official Secrets Act," he said, emphasising his point by placing his right hand flat on the desk between them. "Apart from myself and Ms Goodview, you are the only other person in this building who will be privy to what we are about to discuss. Is that understood?"

Bloody hell.

"Yes, Sir Ernest," she said, swallowing hard. "I understand."

"Good. Are you familiar with the name Guy Gordon?"

"Yes, sir," she answered quickly. "He owns GG Cleaning Systems. Amongst other things, the agency uses them to vet asylum seekers. They specifically check for potential terrorist threats. In fact, they were the company that conducted the background review into Abdul Hosseini."

Again Sir Ernest nodded.

"Yes, indeed. Last Wednesday evening, Guy Gordon broke into my London home with the intention of killing me."

Good God.

"Excuse me, sir?"

Claire's heart started racing.

"You heard me correctly."

"Last Wednesday, sir?" Claire said, unable to move.

"Yes, Ms Harper. The same day Commander Enderby killed Mr Hosseini."

"Guy Gordon attacked you, sir?"

"He did. And I overpowered him," he said, staring her straight in the eye.

"You did?" she said, struggling to keep the disbelief from her voice.

He straightened in his chair and pulled back his shoulders.

"Don't let my advanced age fool you, Ms Harper. I am not as decrepit as I look."

Really?

Sir Ernest sat back. Grey-haired and gaunt enough to be called wizened, he looked as though the slightest breeze would bowl him over.

"No, sir," she said, unable to think of anything else to say. "Of course not, sir. Might I ask a question?"

"Please do."

"Why are you telling me this?"

"As you can probably surmise, the death of Mr Hosseini and Mr Gordon's attack on me were no coincidence. They were part of a coordinated attack on me, initiated by ... Commander Enderby."

Claire allowed her jaw to drop.

Talk about conspiracy theories. This one was way, way out there.

"The intention was to kill me and make it look like a terrorist plot to eliminate the head and the deputy head of the agency simultaneously. Enderby would have survived to take my place. Complete insanity, of course, but that seems to have been how the commander's mind worked."

"So, why did he really kill himself, sir?"

Sir Ernest's bony shoulders jerked up in a shrug.

"Who knows? He might have learned that Gordon's attack had failed and was afraid the game was up. We may never learn the truth."

"I still don't know why you're telling me this, sir."

"I'm coming to that, Ms Harper," he said, a tight smile stretching his thin lips. "Yesterday, I received a confidential report from a company I commissioned—at my own personal expense—to investigate Commander Enderby. A company by the name of A&W Associates."

"A&W Associates?" she gasped. "Peter Wingard?"

She knew it! She just knew they were involved in something.

"Just so, Ms Harper," he said, nodding. "I am aware that you and Ms Winters came into contact with Mr Wingard at Body-Ring Gym last week. I have spoken with Ms Winters about this issue, but not in as much detail as I'm giving you. You must *not* discuss this matter with her. Do I make myself perfectly clear?" He paused, waiting for her response.

"Yes, sir," she said. "Perfectly."

"Good. Now then, where was I?" He studied his fingernails for a moment before continuing. "Ah yes, A&W Associates. To be quite frank, I've been worried about Commander Enderby's dealings with our external contractors for quite some time. I commissioned A&W Associates because they are completely unknown on this side of the Atlantic."

Again, he smiled.

Claire's heart continued to thump hard inside a tight chest.

A&W Associates! They were involved up to their eyeballs. Could they have killed Worm? And Guy Gordon, too? Could they?

God above.

If they did kill them, so what? Good for them.

Claire certainly wasn't going to kick up a fuss. Good riddance to both the murdering arseholes.

She surprised herself with her forcefulness.

"During their investigation," Sir Ernest continued, "A&W Associates discovered a great deal about Commander Enderby's reprehensible activities. Not only was he accepting bribes from GG Cleaning Systems and others, and instigating murder, but he was also guilty of a string of other offences, including those of an abusive and … intimate nature." He lowered his eyes. "One of the people named in the report was you, Ms Harper."

Heat bathed Claire's face. Sweat formed in her armpits and ran down the middle of her back. She struggled to breathe, to swallow.

"I won't go into detail, Ms Harper," he carried on, "but I know what you suffered, and it disgusts me. Please accept my sincerest apologies."

"I-I …"

Sir Ernest held up a hand to forestall her stuttered response.

"There really is no need to say anything, Ms Harper. I fully understand that this must be difficult for you to talk about, especially to a man. … Forgive me, but I have taken the liberty to broach this matter—in the strictest confidence—with Veronica Hoare-Robinson, our head of HR."

"But—"

"Veronica has cleared her calendar for the rest of the day," Sir Ernest interrupted, his tone gentle, sympathetic. "She would like to speak to you as soon as we've finished here." After a breath, he carried on. "If you choose to leave the agency—and no one could blame you for doing so— Veronica will prepare a generous compensation package and provide a glowing review. However, if you—"

"But I don't want to leave, sir," Claire said, shaking her head. "I love my job."

And I'll love it even more without Worm to worry about.

Sir Ernest smiled and relaxed his skinny shoulders. The idea that he could have defended himself against a man as heavily built as Guy Gordon could not have been more preposterous. She almost giggled at the thought.

"That is excellent news," he gushed. "Truly excellent. I can't tell you how pleased I am to hear it. By the way, did I tell you how impressed I was by your support in the House the other day?"

What?

With so much happening and so much going on in her head, Claire found it difficult to follow the man's unexpected changes of direction.

"I-I … Yes, sir. You did. And thank you again, sir."

"Credit where it's due, Ms Harper. Those sub-committee interrogations can turn into bloodbaths, but your command of the topic and the statistics was quite remarkable. In fact, you acquitted yourself so well, it only made my decision easier to make."

What decision?

"And since I now know you want to stay with us, I have something for you." He tugged open the middle drawer of his desk and removed a manila envelope. "I delayed giving this to you earlier, because I didn't want it to appear like a bribe." He smiled and offered her the envelope.

Hand shaking, Claire took it.

Was she expected to open it there and then?

"In there," Sir Ernest said, nodding to the envelope, "you will find a letter from the agency, signed by me. It contains an abject apology for the dreadful way you have been mistreated. It also contains a formal offer of promotion to Higher Executive Officer with immediate effect. I hope you can bring yourself to accept both."

Claire glanced at Sir Ernest and then stared at the sealed envelope. Once again, she couldn't think of a single thing to say except, "Yes, sir."

Chapter 51

June

UK Media Releases

BBC Early Evening News, Monday, 14th June.

"...*following the stunning arrests of the Prime Minister, the Home Secretary, and Government Minister, Jason Wyndham, we are expecting the leader of the opposition to call for a vote of no confidence in the government on Wednesday—his earliest opportunity to do so. And, since the government's majority is wafer thin, the confidence vote is likely to be carried. In which case, the deputy PM, Richard Farnsworth, OBE, in his position as interim leader of the party, will be forced to call a snap general election.*

"*We have contacted the government and asked for a comment, but they have yet to respond. The leader of the opposition, however, was more forthcoming ...*"

. . .

SKY NEWS, Tuesday 15th June.

"...*Metropolitan Police has yet to make an official statement, but an inside source, who wishes to remain off the record, has told this reporter that possible charges against the ministers include, corruption in a public office, tax avoidance, and inchoate offences.*

"*Inchoate offences include incitement or conspiracy to commit criminal offences. These are serious charges which, if proven, will inevitably lead to long prison sentences.*"

CHANNEL FOUR EVENING NEWS, Tuesday 15th June.

"*Next, we turn to the National Crime Agency's ongoing investigation into the sudden death last week of Commander Gregory Enderby, Deputy Head of the UK's National Counter Terrorism Agency. It is understood that Commander Enderby's suicide note was instrumental in the stunning arrests of the PM and two members of her cabinet on charges of ...*"

BBC BREAKFAST NEWS, Thursday, 17th June.

"*Following yesterday's vote of no confidence, which was carried by a massive majority after more than half of the government's backbenchers abstained, the Deputy Prime Minister, Richard Farnsworth, will address the House of Commons at eleven o'clock this morning. He is widely expected to call a snap ...*"

The DCI JONES series

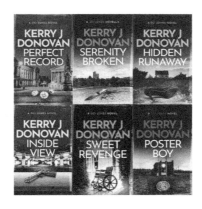

If you enjoyed Ryan Kaine, you may enjoy Kerry J. Donovan's
fast paced detective series, DCI Jones.

vinci-books.com/dcijones

About Kerry J Donovan

#1 International Best-seller with *Ryan Kaine: On the Run*, Kerry was born in Dublin. He currently lives with Margaret in a bungalow in Nottinghamshire. He has three children and four grandchildren.

Kerry earned a first-class honours degree in Human Biology and has a PhD in Sport and Exercise Sciences. A former scientific advisor to The Office of the Deputy Prime Minister, he helped UK emergency first-responders prepare for chemical attacks in the wake of 9/11. He is also a former furniture designer/maker.

http://kerryjdonovan.com/

Made in the USA
Middletown, DE
08 September 2024